PRAISE FOR *DREADNOUGHT*

"I didn't know how much I needed this brave, thrilling book until it rocked my world. *Dreadnought* is the superhero adventure we all need right now."

—Charlie Jane Anders, author of *All the Birds in the Sky*

"A thoroughly enjoyable, emotionally rich, action-packed story with the most exciting new superheroes in decades. Unmissable."

—*Kirkus* Starred Review

"…A fascinating exploration of gender identity in a fantastical setting."

—*Publishers Weekly*

"This first title in the series offers a rich, unusual mix of subjects and themes for fantasy fans."

—*School Library Journal*

"I'm not normally a fan of superhero narratives, and then I find an exception that grabs me by the throat and makes me love it. *Dreadnought* is one of those exceptions."

—Liz Bourke, Tor.com

"*Dreadnought* is a coming-of-age story: it's all about Danny coming to terms with her own power and her own agency, not just as a superhero, but as a person (and as a person who chooses to be a superhero), and it's one that doesn't shy away from consequences, either. People get hurt, sometimes badly—sometimes killed, and it's this willingness to highlight the fact that standing up doesn't come without real cost that gives *Dreadnought* its real heart."

—Locus Magazine

SOVEREIGN

A P R I L   D A N I E L S

DIVERSIONBOOKS

Diversion Books
A Division of Diversion Publishing Corp.
443 Park Avenue South, Suite 1008
New York, New York 10016
www.DiversionBooks.com

For more information, email info@diversionbooks.com

First Diversion Books edition July 2017.
Print ISBN: 978-1-68230-824-0
eBook ISBN: 978-1-68230-823-3

For the girls who are free.

CHAPTER ONE

"Don't let your wife hear you say that," he says. A late-night talk show host is joking with someone offscreen. A smattering of laughter leaks out of the crowd. "Yeah, we're gonna hear all about it at Thanksgiving. Anyway, moving on. I'm really excited about this next guest. Tonight is her first television appearance since the Battle of New Port. She's mightier than a battleship and faster than a jet—ladies and gentlemen, please give a big welcome to Dreadnought!"

Cut to the curtains opening and Dreadnought steps out. Her blue bodyglove is snug and high-necked, with a white mantle and cape that brushes the back of her knees. Her blond hair has grown out, cut in a more feminine style than the butchy haircut she made her debut with, but still short enough not to be a problem in a fight. She waves at the audience and skims across the stage, toes inches from the ground, to land gently on the couch next to the host's desk. The applause is thunderous.

My lawyer and publicist, a dark-haired woman named Cecilia who's wearing a skirt suit and tie, pauses the video. "Good. That was good. They like that sort of thing."

"That's why I did it," I say, trying to keep the boredom out of my voice. Outside the window, the Southern Ocean foams against the first rocks of Antarctica. We're almost there, finally. Since I learned to fly, riding in airplanes—even hypertech jets like this one—only slows me down. When I *really* want to move fast, I just go up into orbit and come back down wherever I please.

"Pay attention, Danny, this is important," says Cecilia. It's been important the last three times we did it too. After that disastrous interview with *Rolling Stone*, we've had to get serious about my media strategy.

God, I have a *media strategy*.

This is not what I thought being a superhero would be like.

Cecilia hits play and the video continues. Onscreen, Dreadnought and the host—it's easier to do this when I think of the Dreadnought onscreen as different than the Dreadnought I am right now—trade some banter. Like she planned, Dreadnought lets the host do most of the heavy lifting for making the interview funny. The other Dreadnoughts weren't funny, and she's got a serious gravitas deficit as it is, so she only smiles and chuckles appropriately, doesn't try to make anyone laugh.

"So how have things been since that all happened?" he asks in a caring voice, the signal that the interview has moved into the Serious Topics phase. He's referring to the Third Battle of New Port, nine months ago. The day Dreadnought made her debut. The day the Legion Pacifica was destroyed and a fifteen-year-old girl shouldered the responsibility of protecting an area of four hundred thousand square miles with seventeen million people. Alone.

"They've been all right, they've been all right," says Dreadnought.

"Are you still in school?"

"No. I was for a while, though. The ROTC guys wouldn't leave me the hell alone." The audience laughs. Dreadnought looks like she's going to say something more, but then realizes this was the line of conversation that spiraled so horribly out of control when she was talking to *Rolling Stone*. She was quoted saying some pretty venomous things about the Pentagon's hypocrisy—how they were dragging their feet about accommodating transgender soldiers in the military, but were willing to cut her an exception so they could get her while she was young and put Dreadnought back under Uncle Sam's thumb, the way no Dreadnought had been since the early '60s.

When the story ran, the thrust of the article was "Dreadnought hates the army!" rather than the basic biographical piece she thought she was being interviewed for.

For a moment it looked like the controversy would derail my federal caping license, which would mean I'd never be able to work outside of my home district in the Pacific Northwest. One particularly noxious anti-transgender member of the House of Representatives even suggested stripping my parents of their federally-provided witness protection detail if I kept making such "anti-American" statements.

"You left because the army was hounding you?"

"No," says Dreadnought, sitting up straighter. "Not at all; the sergeant in charge was very professional. The school district gave me special permission to test out early, and I decided to do it so I could go caping full time, is all." She leaves unsaid the context of the matter, how she hadn't really asked for that permission, and how if she'd turned it down she would have been expelled. Superheroes are disruptive to a school environment, they had said.

"Right, okay," the host says. "So you're still not a member of the Legion, right?"

A flash of something passes across Dreadnought's face, there and gone. Cecilia pauses the video. "You slipped."

"It's a sore topic," I say.

"That makes it more important to be able to hide your feelings."

She's right, of course. But it still sucks.

The video starts rolling again. "Well, the Legion is basically defunct," Dreadnought is saying. "And anyway, I wouldn't have been able to join until I was eighteen anyhow."

"How's it gone, protecting New Port without them?"

Dreadnought pauses before answering. What does one say to that? That she's fought twelve major battles in nine months, and as a result she gets tense whenever her phone rings? That the night-mares wake her at least once a week? That she's had to learn basic lessons the hard way every time, and other people have paid with their lives? That she's done it all alone? That she's been without her family, without anyone to talk to, because Calamity changed after she was wounded, and because Doc Impossible was always drunk? That even though she's got a place to stay, she hasn't decorated, and it still feels like she's homeless? That sometimes when she's alone she starts sobbing, and she doesn't know why?

Or should she talk about the other side of it? About how much she loves the power, about the intoxicating thrill of her own strength? Can she explain how much better food tastes when she buys it with money earned in blood, *her* blood? Should she tell them about the feral joy of living at the edge of death? About how battle makes her feel dangerous and savage and complete? Should she let them know that sometimes she's disappointed when a fight ends too quickly? Can she explain how the lattice gets more beautiful every time she looks at it? Would any of them understand if she told them that sometimes she flies for hours, in any direction, just watching all the little people with their little lives, and how she can't tell if what she feels for them is envy or pity? How can she explain that for the first time in her life, she is free, free, FREE, and she's never going back, and she'll kill anyone who tries to take it away from her?

Is she brave enough to say that for the first time since puberty started, she doesn't daydream about being dead? That she's wonderfully, terribly, gloriously alive? That the world is so beautiful it hurts?

What she says is, "I think I'm getting the hang of it." And smiles.

The conversation goes off on a tangent about what it's like to run face-first into a bug at four hundred miles an hour, and then circles back around to weightier topics. The Biannual World Conference is happening this year, the closest thing to a meeting of all the world's capes as possible. Not every cape attends. Not every team sends representatives. But officially, everyone is invited. Dreadnought has been getting emails and phone calls from other capes ahead of the conference, welcoming her to the fold—as if she hasn't been slugging it out with blackcapes on an almost weekly basis—and despite her occasional annoyance at the tone of some of the welcomes, her enthusiasm for attending the conference is palpable. Which is why, of course, Cecilia made sure that it came up in the conversation. Dreadnought's eyes light up, and her shoulders loosen.

"I'm really looking forward to meeting everyone," she says.

There's a little more, but that's the meat of it. A speaker in the ceiling of the cabin clicks on. "Buckle up, we're on final approach," says Doc Impossible.

"Finally!" I say. Cecilia kills the video, and I climb out of my chair to head up front.

"You know, most kids would be really excited to fly in a supersonic jet," Doc Impossible says.

"Most kids don't get up into orbit every week," I say. The cockpit door slides open at my approach, and Doc Impossible looks over her shoulder from the pilot's seat.

Doc cut her thick black braid off earlier this year. Her hair frames her face now. Sharp bangs, longer at the side, higher in the back. Her round glasses flicker and glow with telemetry readouts scrolling past her eyes. "How'd it go?" she asks.

"I need to practice in the mirror more," I say as I slip into the chair next to her and buckle myself down. (Force of habit.) "It's too easy to see what I'm thinking."

Doc presses a button to snap the door shut. "Don't worry so much. Cecilia's paid to obsess over that so you don't have to. Trust me, people love you."

"Yeah, well." A familiar unease settles in me. People like me because they don't know me. Because I'm young, and pretty, and powerful. Everyone wants Dreadnought. I'm not so sure they want Danielle.

"Don't grow up so fast, Danny." Without taking her eyes off the controls, she reaches over to punch me in the shoulder.

"Says the seven-year-old," I say.

Doctor Impossible smiles. "*And* eight months, don't forget the months." She taps a few buttons on a touchscreen built into

11

her armrest. "Okay, we're ready for final approach, I'm gonna need to concentrate." Manual flight is an eccentricity for her. Doc Impossible is an android. She could link up to the jet's computer and fly it with her mind if she wanted to. Same with a lot of other hypertech. She never does. Manual controls all the way.

We come over a ridge of stony hills, and there in the distance are the convention grounds. The world's only luxury hotel south of the Antarctic Circle. It's used once every two years. My knees are bouncing. My seat is suddenly uncomfortable. I want to head over to the jet's door, get out, and fly there myself, because holy crap, I'm going to the world convention! All the people I'm going to meet, all the things I'm going to see—the next two days are going to be amazing.

"Can't this thing go faster?" I ask Doc Impossible.

"Yes, but we need to slow down for the final approach."

It takes *forever* to come around for a landing, slow, tilt the jets to the vertical landing configuration, and touch down just outside the hangar. Then it takes another forever to taxi inside and up to the heated boarding tunnel that extends out to greet us like an expanding caterpillar. I'm the first through when the hatch opens, and Cecilia is close behind. I take to the air and do a slow pirouette as we head down the tube. On my second time around, I notice Doc hanging back at the jet's door.

"Come on, Doc, hurry up!"

"Uh, maybe you two ought to go on ahead without me," she says, not meeting my eyes.

"Why?"

"I don't think I'm going to be really popular this year. It'll go better for you if we don't show up together."

Nine months ago, Doc's mother, Mistress Malice—now working under the name Utopia—hacked her brain and used her body to ambush the Legion Pacifica. Valkyrja and Carapace died. Magma was forced into retirement because of his injuries. Chlorophyll suffered brain damage, and when he was stable, his sister showed up to take custody of him. Nobody's heard from them since. The thing is, everyone thought Malice had been dead for fifty years. Doc Impossible was scared that if anyone found out she was an android built by a supervillain, they'd throw her in prison, or worse. So she kept her mouth shut, and the Legion died.

I float back to her and take her by the arm. "It wasn't your fault, Doc. It was hers."

Doc Impossible sighs. "Let's say I believe that; other people won't, or won't care."

"She's right," says Cecilia. "It would be better if you two weren't seen arriving together."

"No," I say, with more force than I intended. "I mean, no, I don't care. Let them talk."

"Danny, what did you hire me for?" says Cecilia.

"I needed a lawyer."

"Okay, but I'm also your publicist, and *as* your publicist, I have to tell you the Doctor is right," says Cecilia with calm, measured words. "She's not really popular right now. Doc, if you want to talk to me about rehabilitating your image, we might be able to work something out in time for the next convention, but right now—"

"Yes, agreed," says Doc.

"No, not agreed," I say, and immediately hate how much like a whine it sounds. "I mean, look, what is it going to say about me if I won't even be caught showing up with the woman who lets me crash in her condo?"

"That you're not an idiot?" says Doc.

"Oh no, I am totally an idiot, if that's what it takes to get you off this friggin' jet," I say as I get behind Doc and start pushing. She laughs and lets herself be carried along.

"This might complicate our bid to take over the Legion," says Cecilia.

"Don't worry about it. I'm a superhero."

CHAPTER TWO

And so is *everyone else*. Even the walk through the hotel to our room has me so excited my feet barely touch the ground. My head is constantly on a swivel. There's Gravestone, with his high-collared cape of shadows! And there's the Crimson Rose with her enchanted rapier! And they're just like, chilling out, waiting around for more jets to come in. Okay, sure, there's a lot of people out of costume too—hangers-on, con volunteers, capes wearing civvies—but I see more superheroes just in the ten-minute walk to the rooms than I have in the nine months since I started this gig. It takes a concerted effort not to dig into my bags for my little notebook and start demanding autographs right here and now.

You'd think that after almost a year of being Dreadnought, I wouldn't still be such a superhero fangirl.

You'd think that.

But what happened is my fangirldom got *worse*.

"Down, girl," says Doc, tugging at my cape until my boots touch the floor. I'd started to float without realizing it.

"This is so cool!" And the convention site is pretty amazing too. Everything here is elegant, restrained. Polished stone floors and subtle design touches on the walls. It feels like we're wasting money just walking through the place.

"Wait until we get to the meet and greet," Doc says. An elevator opens with a pleasant chime and we step in. "You'll squee so hard they'll hear you in New Port."

"Yeah, it's gonna—well, I mean, I'll try to keep it in check," I say, with a guilty glance over at Cecilia. Image control is important, because without people's trust, I can't do my job.

But no, Cecilia only smiles. "Just be yourself, Danny. This isn't an interview; these are your peers. Let them get to know you."

My stomach flips over. Let them get to know *me*. I'm better than I used to be. A lot better. I don't reflexively assume people won't like me anymore, for example. But, well…sometimes it's hard to tell if they like me, or if they like Dreadnought.

The elevator's walls are glass, and we slide up the side of the building, the concourse roof falling away from us. The sparse beauty of the summer Antarctic falls away from us on all sides. You think of Antarctica, and you think of ice, and in a lot of places that's always true, but at this time of year, the land around the hotel is scrub grass and tumbled rocks reaching out to distant, snowy mountains.

Finally, I say, "Are you sure that's a good idea?"

"If I thought it wasn't, we wouldn't be here," says Cecilia, putting a hand on my shoulder. "Some of my clients are…difficult in person, and for them, an event like this would be an invitation to disaster. You're not that kind of client."

"Are you sure?"

Cecilia nods. "Just put your best foot forward and go meet a lot of people. You'll be a hit, trust me."

• • •

The first World Conference happened in 1969. Eight years before, Mistress Malice's campaign for world domination had ushered in a new era. Now capes were more than colorful criminals and the heroes who fought them or obedient instruments of existing state power. In the new age, superheroes were—or could be, at least—major powers on the international stage in their own right. As this new understanding took hold, some in the cape community called for greater cooperation and coordination across national lines.

The first World Conference was attended by only twenty-three capes. The political tensions of the Cold War meant they had to meet on neutral ground, and since none of the non-aligned countries wanted to host, that meant they had to meet in Antarctica. Almost a half-century of growth and development later, the World Conference has become one of the most important trade shows on the planet. So that's the history of it, the why, the what, and the how. But knowing that doesn't prepare me for what it actually *is*.

We step onto the convention floor and get slammed by an almost palpable wall of noise. A thousand conversations burbled through with video playback and all sorts of distant music clashing in the background. It's difficult to get a sense of the size of the place at first. Right away, colorful tech demos and flashy ads grab at my eyes. The convention space is cavernous, the ceiling vaulted way up high. A few people sail through the air rather than making their way through the maze of booths, so I pop up about twenty feet to get the lay of the land.

Everything a superhero could possibly want to buy is spread out beneath me. Rows and rows of booths and pavilions stretch across the floor, draped with glowing holograms and shifting signs beckoning capes to try their wares.

Bystander insurance. Hypertech components. Mystical ingredients. Training DVDs and seminar packages. An entire row dedicated to earbud radios. A row of government booths offering liaison contracts and operating licenses for capes who want to take their work to the international scene. Weapons, handcuffs, and a dozen kinds of grappling hooks.

There's an entire block of costume fitters, tailors, and designers. Some have fancy hypertech fitting booths, with lasers to take a person's exact dimensions for a truly skintight fit. There's a booth wreathed in shadows and fog, where a gnarled old witch sits behind trays of enchanted jewelry to accent and supplement a mystically inclined superhero's arsenal. And there are plain old tailors with pins crimped between their teeth, holding measuring tapes up to capes who stand on stools in front of mirrors.

It's the goddamn promised land.

I shoot back down to land next to Doc as she steps into the light and noise, and I'm practically shaking with excitement.

"Why don't they have this every year?" I ask. The thought that I'll have go two years without seeing this again is suddenly loathsome.

"There's not enough of a market to support an annual event," says Doc, popping a small lollipop into her mouth. She's trying to quit smoking, which she could do with a few seconds of concentration if she were willing to edit her own configuration files, but she's not. She says it doesn't count unless she does it the human way. "What do you want to see first?"

We do a whirlwind tour of the convention floor, trying to get a feel for where we want to return for some serious shopping. One of the vendors is selling a set of matched revolvers with built-in laser sights that would be perfect for Calamity, and a pang goes through me. I invited her to come, but she brushed me off. This is nothing but a whitecape circle jerk, she said, and waved me away with her prosthetic hand. Ever since she lost her arm, she's been different. Distant. Harder. Less willing to trust. Being wounded meant more than becoming one-handed for her, but she's vague about the specifics. When I asked, all she would say is that even hypertech can't fix everything.

I buy the guns and have them sent to my room.

All throughout this, people are calling out to me, shaking my hand, introducing themselves. Even capes think it's cool to meet Dreadnought, I guess. It feels sort of weird, like I haven't earned this, but I smile and try to remember everyone's name. Nobody seems to mind that I'm hanging out with Doc Impossible.

We're at an intersection, looking at the schedule of panels to see if there are any talks we want to attend. The panels here have titles like *Whitecapes Who Aren't White: Modern Challenges for Superheroes of Color* and *Passing The Torch: When Capes Get Old*. I'm trying to decide between *#CapesLikeUs: Do Superheroes Belong on Social Media?* and *Are Graycapes a Menace, an Asset, or Both?*

when Doc tugs at my cape and points. The crowd is parting, and a living legend steps up to us.

Red Steel is about six-and-a-half feet tall. His black hair has been shot through with silver, and he's got wrinkles like oak bark, but he still carries himself with the confidence of a man a quarter of his age. He's wearing the classic Cossack pants and silk shirt he made his debut in, but the red in his shirt isn't the scarlet of socialism triumphant. It's the dark rust of a dream denied. Since the fall of Communism, he's made his way as a high-end mercenary, living off the worst parts of the capitalism he spent his life fighting.

"Holy shit," I mutter.

"So you are the new Dreadnought," he says. His voice is deep and carries just a touch of his Russian accent.

"Uh, yeah, that's me." People are stopping to watch. I suppose I shouldn't be surprised he'd seek me out, but I still feel very small all of the sudden. This guy is the real deal, way more than I am. Red Steel has fought every Dreadnought since the first. We keep dying. He's still standing. Often enemies, sometimes allies, the story of Dreadnought can't be told without talking about Red Steel. I hold out my hand. "Pleased to meet you."

Red Steel chuckles and shakes my hand. He's got a grip like a power vice. His gaze is sharp, and I realize I'm being tested. I squeeze back, hard. Hard enough that if he wasn't who he was, I'd turn his hand to mush. He nods.

"I wonder what we shall fight about, you and I?"

My stomach flops over. "I'm sorry?"

"I fight Dreadnoughts, little girl," he says. "All of them. Or did you think you were somehow different?"

"Oh, uh, well, just don't do anything bad in New Port, then."

Red smiles. "We shall see, yes?" He nods at Doc Impossible. "Doctor."

"Red," she says, voice clipped.

Red Steel turns and walks away, the crowd parting before him like waves before a ship's prow.

"Well that was cool," I say.

"Danny, he *threatened* you."

"So? I can take him."

"Maybe," says Doc. "He's more experienced than you. I'll send you his dossier."

"Already read it." I'm a superhero fangirl. Of *course* I read all the intelligence reports about other capes that Uncle Sam is willing to give me.

We poke around the convention floor a bit longer and then wander over to the food court in the next hall over. I'm staking out a table while Doc grabs the food when a familiar voice booms out at me across the crowded floor.

"Danielle! Over here!" He's enormous, easily seven feet tall and nearly half as broad. He waves over the heads of the crowd.

"Hi, Magma!" I call as I pop up into the air and fly over. Magma is leaning on a cane, and his cheeks seem sunken under his wiry brush of a beard. The nerve gas Malice hit him with last year didn't do him any good, and he's had to retire. He went off on a soul-searching trip after he finally got out of the hospital, and from what I've heard, it's kind of amazing he made it down here. "How have you been?"

"I'm getting along, I'm getting along," he says. "How's caping suiting you?"

"It's amazing. I feel good."

"Excellent," says Magma, smiling. "I figured you'd do well. Here, let me introduce you to—" He turns and beckons to someone over the crowd. He starts forward, cane and step, cane and step. "Aloe, Aloe come over here. I want to introduce you to Dreadnought."

Magma brings me to a table, and as we get close a devastatingly beautiful woman stands and makes her way over to us. She's green. Every part of her—skin, hair, lips, eyes, everything but her clothes and her teeth. All shades of green. I know who she is immediately, and it takes effort not to tense up. I've read her dossier too. She's a nasty piece of work.

"Aloe, I'd like you to meet Dreadnought."

"Wait, aren't you a—?" I start.

"Supervillain?" she says with an arched eyebrow. "Yes. I'm reformed." We shake hands. Her palm is cool and dry.

"Aloe and I met when I went to look in on Chlorophyll," says Magma. "She was already on parole and going straight, so we decided to give it a shot."

Aloe purses her lips, and I get the feeling she doesn't agree with that interpretation of events. But then she leans against him and goes up on her tiptoes so he can bend down and kiss her. When they part, I look closely at Magma's eyes. The reports say you can tell who she has mind-controlled because their pupils often don't match, one dilated more than the other. She notices me staring and starts to giggle.

Magma frowns. "Danny, she's gone straight. She wouldn't do that kind of thing anymore."

"Just being safe, big guy." I glance at Aloe. "No offense."

"None taken," says Aloe. "You saved my brother. That counts for a lot."

"How is Chlorophyll?"

"Oh, he's here with us," she says, turning to look at the table she came from. "Hey, honey, come over here, I want to introduce you to someone."

Through a brief gap in the crowd, I glimpse a man as green as his sister get up from a table and come over to us. Chlorophyll looks much the same as the last time I saw him. The scar on his forehead and the bald spot in his hair don't even stand out that much. But his body language is all wrong. The Chlorophyll I knew was all languid grace and open gazes. This man has his shoulders drawn in tight, and he clutches a coloring book in one hand, a box of crayons in the other.

"Scott, hon, this is Dreadnought."

"Hi," says Chlorophyll. "Have we met?"

It feels like I'm listening to someone else answer with my voice. "Yes, briefly."

"Oh." Sorrow, frustration, rage. It all flits across his face between one moment and the next, there and gone. "Sorry, I don't remember you. I don't remember lots of things from before. Before I got hurt, I mean."

Aloe puts her hand on his shoulder. "It's okay." He looks over at her, his expression grateful and relieved.

Utopia shot Chlorophyll in the head while she wore Doc Impossible's body like a puppet. To be honest, I didn't like him when we first met. I thought he was too keen to use me and not interested enough in standing up for me. But right here, right now, I wish Utopia was on the loose again, just so I'd have an excuse to beat the shit out of her one more time.

"Do you want to see my coloring?" he asks me.

"Sure," I say.

He opens the coloring book and shows me his work. "The doctors say this is good for me."

"It's very nice." It looks like a five-year-old did it.

"Thanks."

"Danny, where the hell are you?" Doc's voice asks from inside my ear. I've got an earbud radio I wear all the time now. It's actually superglued in there, only comes out once a week for cleaning, and is all but invisible from the outside.

I put a finger to my ear. "I'm about three tables closer to the door from where you left me. Come on over."

Doc makes her way through the crowd, and it all goes straight to Hell.

Chlorophyll looks up, and the crayons slip out of his hand and spill across the ground.

"It's her." He starts to shake. "She's the one who hurt me."

"Oh shit," says Doc, going pale.

Magma's face darkens. "What the hell are you doing here?"

"*Don't let her hurt me again!*" says Chlorophyll.

Aloe steps between them, her back to her brother, arms spread to defend him. "Get *away* from us!"

I am *such* an idiot.

Doc spins on her heel and starts to push back through the crowd.

"What the hell do you think you're doing?" asks Magma as he hobbles after Doc Impossible.

She glances back over her shoulder, seems torn between waiting for him and leaving as fast as she can. "I'm sorry, I didn't know he was over—"

"You shouldn't even be here!" Magma says.

"Hey, wait, Doc has every right to be here," I say, catching up.

"Danny, *don't*," says Doc with a warning look. "Magma, I'm sorry. Really."

"Apologies don't mean much for things like this," says Magma. "He wakes up screaming half the nights, did you know that?"

Doc mutters something else and disappears through the ring of curious onlookers. Magma watches her go with an expression like looming thunderclouds.

I hit him in the shoulder, hard enough to stagger him a little. "What the hell was that about? She didn't do anything wrong!"

"She lied, Danny," says Magma. "She lied to us about who she was, about *what* she was, and she didn't tell us Malice was still alive. If she had, maybe—things might have worked out differently."

My chest feels all clenched up. This is all wrong. It's not supposed to go this way. "She was scared."

"We trusted her!" he snaps. "All that time we trusted her, all that time we let her be one of us. She stopped wanting to do fieldwork, and we let her stay on. She stopped wanting to leave the tower, and we let her stay on. We never asked why. We never told her she wasn't pulling her weight, because we *trusted* her. Because we thought we understood what she was going through, we thought we understood why. She *lied* to us, Danny! For years. To our faces."

The hard, hot nugget of defiance in my chest that tells me I can never back down again flares up. I square my shoulders and look Magma dead in the eye. "Dreadnought knew."

"What?" Magma seems caught off guard.

"Dreadnought, the last one. He knew."

He shakes his head. "How do you know that?"

"I can see things, like the underside of reality, all the strings holding it together," I say. "When I look at you in the lattice, I see your bones, and where your nerves are all clotted up with damage. When I look at her, it's obvious she's an android. I only met her a few times before she told me, and I never had a reason to check her out in the lattice, but Dreadnought lived in the same building as she did for, what, five years? There's no way he didn't realize what she was. He kept her secret because he knew it wasn't his secret to tell."

Magma is quiet for a long moment. When he speaks again, his voice is calmer, but no less firm. "Then he made a mistake, and Carapace and Valkyrja paid with their lives."

"That's not—"

"You're right. It isn't. Death *isn't* fair. I'm not going to tell you who to work with, Danielle. And if you still want to talk, I am always here to listen. But me and her? We're finished, and I need you to respect that." Magma turns to head back to Aloe and Chlorophyll. She's hugging her brother tight as he shakes, whispering into his ear as he presses his face into the crook of her neck.

We've drawn quite the crowd. I feel the weight of eyes on me.

"What the hell are you all looking at?" I snap at the onlookers. Most decide to find something else to pay attention to. I pop up into the air and scan for Doc Impossible. She's over at the exit to the rest of the hotel, sucking on a cigarette like her life depends on it.

I set down next to her. "Doc, look, maybe we can go over there and—"

"Danny, let it be, okay?"

"But I only wanted—"

Doc explodes. "We're not all friends anymore, Danny! It doesn't work that way!" She seems to sag, goes to take another drag on her cigarette and discovers she's broken it between her fingers. "I wish it did, but you aren't going to fix this. Let it die." She drops the broken cigarette on the floor and grinds it out with the toe of her boot. "I'm going back to my room. Do whatever you want."

"Doc, wait—"

"Go...go have fun, Danny," Doc calls over her shoulder. "I shouldn't have come here."

She leaves me there feeling very young and very alone.

CHAPTER THREE

I try to have fun. I really, genuinely try. Wandering up and down the aisles, looking at everything for sale, I hope to get back in the mood. I'm paid a ridiculous amount by the city government of New Port, and I had about fifty thousand dollars burning a hole in my pocket on the way down here. But now it's difficult to care. Everything is sour now. I end up back in the eating area, sitting at a table with a stack of catalogs for superhero gear, resting my chin on my palm and flipping pages.

Someone sits down across from me.

"I kind of want to be alone right now," I say without looking up.

"Oh man, I am *so* disappointed about that," says a voice I know, and I look up and wilt. Crap. I totally forgot. "I was *really* looking forward to meeting the first transgender superhero."

Kinetiq sits with their arms crossed on the table in front of them and their lips pressed tight. Kinetiq is genderqueer, a non-binary person who is neither male nor female. They've got their long black hair shaved like a horse's mane, and their Kevlar vest is strapped down tight over a chest binder. Their arms are bare except for a pair of fingerless gloves.

"Oh shit."

"Hell yeah, '*oh shit*,'" they say.

"I forgot, I'm sorry." I'd promised them that when I went on *The Late Show* that I'd mention that I *wasn't* the first transgender superhero, as a lot of cis people seem to think I am. I'm just the most famous. In fact, trans people who get superpowers are way more likely to become superheroes than cis people who get powers, because we tend to already be alienated from mainstream society, so the sacrifices of being a hero mean less to us. But my nerves had paralyzed me, and it completely slipped my mind until I was leaving the set.

"Oh, well then, I guess that's all okay," says Kinetiq. "Or, wait. No, it's not. At all."

"I'm sorry. Really."

"I don't care about your apology, Dreadnought. I care about the oxygen you keep sucking out of the room. We were finally getting somewhere, and then you come in and bigfoot the whole movement!"

"It's not my fault that the press is interested in me," I mutter.

"No, but it is your fault that you don't use your platform to increase visibility for the rest of us!"

"Look, I know I screwed up, but I am really not in the mood for this right now."

"That's a real tragedy." They hold a hand up to their ear. "You hear that? My heart is breaking."

I close the catalog. "Last year one of my best friends was possessed by her supervillain mother and forced to murder half the Legion. Now the survivors all hate each other and the fallout from this just got plopped in my lap. So, if you're done, kindly piss off for now."

Kinetiq sits back, seems suddenly unsure what to do with their hands, and settles for folding them. "Oh. Sorry."

"Don't worry about it." I think for a moment. "I can have my publicist set up an interview with *Autostraddle* or something."

"Oooh, your *publicist*. Ooh-la-la."

I snort, and throw a catalog at them. They bat it away, laughing.

I met Kinetiq in combat. They're a stringer operating out of California's Bay Area, a freelance superhero without a steady municipal contract like the one I have with New Port. They were only thirteen when their parents drove them to run away from home. Six years later, they flit from job to job as needed, and barely make enough to cover their bystander insurance premiums. We met when I went down to California to help put down a rampage by Mr. Armageddon, a three-hundred-foot-tall nuclear psychopath who breathes fire. The fight covered a twisting loop of destruction about two hundred miles long and lasted for thirty-nine hours. It was an interesting day.

When it was over, the press mobbed me as usual and acted like Kinetiq hadn't even been there, even though they'd been fighting Mr. Armageddon for longer than I had. I was too tired to realize what was happening, just started answering questions the way I always do, and in the process made it look like I agreed that it was all my fight. Kinetiq has been trying to get trans capes to go mainstream for years, and to make nonbinary trans people in the cape community visible to the outside world. I basically stomped on that effort by accident.

Being genderqueer is hard. Being Iranian-American is hard. Being a superhero without a steady paying gig is also hard. Kinetiq had been swimming upstream for years to be all of those at the same time, and the credit for what should have been their big breakthrough, their first headlining victory, ended up getting handed to me by default. Why? Because I'm a pretty white girl with an easy-to-understand narrative.

Given how hard I accidentally screwed them, they're remarkably friendly.

"I really am sorry," I say. "I don't think I can get another TV interview so soon after the last one, but I mean it, I'll do something about this."

"Good, good," says Kinetiq, bending down to pick the catalog back up off the floor. "So what have—"

A speaker in the ceiling crackles to life. "The first assembly for business is starting in the Kirby Room in five minutes. Once again, the first assembly for business is starting in the Kirby Room in five minutes."

"Oh, damn!" I say. I'd totally lost track of time. "I've got something I need to do there. Wanna come?"

"Sure," says Kinetiq. I arrange the catalogs in a neat stack for someone else before taking to the air. Kinetiq is right behind me, and we zip across the show floor to the main hotel area.

"What's up with the business meeting?" says Kinetiq, pulling up next to me in the air. Their hands are pointed backwards, palms splayed open and light bursting forth from their fingers. "Those things are so boring!"

We pass out of the show floor and take a hard left through the hallways. The ceilings around here are all extra high to accommodate people who can fly. "If this goes the way I want it to, I might be able to get you a municipal contract."

That sure gets their attention. They look over sharply and then say, "Maybe I don't want your handout."

"It's not a handout. I'm going to need you more than you'll need me."

"Oh come on, D, we both know that's true already."

"Smart-ass."

We get to the Kirby Room, a large conference room with a raised stage at the front. Capes are still trickling in, but the place is mostly packed. We touch down outside the main door, and Cecilia looks up from her phone when we approach.

"I was just about to call you," she said. "They're almost starting."

"Sorry. Uh, Cecilia, this is Kinetiq. Kinetiq, this is my lawyer, Cecilia."

"Pleased to meet you," says Cecilia. Kinetiq nods hello but keeps their mouth shut. Cecilia turns to me. "Are you ready?"

"Yes," I say.

"Good," says Cecilia, all business. "Graywytch is in there. Be on point."

"What? She's the on-call this week, she's not supposed to leave New Port!"

"Well, she did. I'll be sure to mention it next time we can screw her at a hearing, but right now I think she's going to try and steal our thunder. Be ready for it."

"Right. Sure thing." My guts knot up. Graywytch is the last member standing of the Legion Pacifica, the only one not killed or wounded or forced to quit in shame. Since most of the Legion was destroyed, she's been living alone in their tower, not helping me protect New Port at all. I only see her at the monthly City Council meetings where I make my reports about everything I do for the city. She justifies her continued paycheck by making all sorts of freighted allusions to supernatural threats that she has protected us from. I know a few magic users, and none of them have seen any evidence of her actually doing anything, but tell that to her friends on the Council. They think the sun rises because she tells it to.

"Remember what we talked about."

"She won't get to me."

"I know." Cecilia puts her hand on my shoulder. "Remember who you are and what it means."

I nod. Sometimes when it's hard to be Danielle, I try to become Dreadnought instead. Dreadnought doesn't get ruffled. Dreadnought isn't petty. Dreadnought is bigger than me, and stronger. This doesn't always work, but it's always worth a try. I take a deep breath and step into the conference room.

It's packed. Business meetings are the real heart of this convention. Capes from all over the world can swap information, have face-to-face discussions, air grievances, and make offers. By tradition there are no chairs, and everyone stands for the entire meeting. I think it's to keep us from feeling like dorks at a trade show.

The crowd in here is one of the strangest ever assembled. There's a woman whose head is a purple flaming skull. There's a man made of ice, his body moving in creaking jerks. A minotaur is having a quiet argument with a glob of protoplasm holding itself in the rough shape of a person. And then, of course, there are the costumes: capes and masks, bodygloves and trench coats, and other, more exotic garments. A woman with fiber-optic hair turns when someone calls her name and accidentally pokes the man next to her in the eye with the pommel of the katana strapped to her back. There's a man who appears to be made entirely out of muscle, and he's wearing a vest that seems to be exclusively made of pouches, a look I thought had gone out of style all the way back in the '90s.

The moderators sit behind a table facing the crowd. Thunderbolt, the Californian heavyweight, is one judge. Maybe I can get him to sign a print of that team photo of Northern Union's last mission, the one where he debuted his new pressure suit for missions in outer space. The other judge is the Patriot, who fronts Empire City's Algonquin Guard. In deference to being indoors, he has taken off his enchanted steel helmet—supposedly a genuine World War II paratrooper helmet that is possessed by the spirit of Liberty Herself—and placed it in front of him. As international as these things are, Americans tend to dominate in administrative positions, which is a joyous source of ongoing drama that never fails to provide the superhero community with enormous headaches.

We're stuck at the back of the crowd, so Kinetiq and I take to the air again, just a few feet up so we can get a good view.

"This is the first open business meeting for the Twenty-Fourth World Conference," says Thunderbolt. His costume is dark blue, with raised filigree designs curling around and over his chest. "First, let's take a moment to review old business…"

Someone with neon feathers for hair steps up to the podium facing the moderators on the dais and begins a long, droning report on the state of superhero affairs in the past two years. Three geological eras and a short ice age later, he finally shuts up and the floor is thrown open to discussion.

It's a catchall session, full of announcements, comments, unrelated trivia. Those of us who signed up to speak line up on one side of the room and inch forward a cape at a time as everyone gets a chance to say their piece.

"The floor recognizes Graywytch," says the Patriot. Somebody in the back of the room loudly boos, and her lawyer elbows her in the side.

Graywytch steps up on stage. She's basically all the worst parts of '90s goth thrown in a blender. Billowing black robes, a raven sitting on her shoulder, pale face, and dark eyes. And, oh yeah, she's a trans-hating bigot who outed me as a superhero to my parents, which caused them to kick me out of the house with nothing but my cape and a cell phone. At one point she wanted to strip me of my powers and give them to someone she decided was more deserving—someone who wasn't transgender.

When Utopia killed or wounded most of the Legion, Graywytch took it as an opportunity to try to remake the Legion in her own image. Doc is still technically a reserve member and managed to halt that plan through some bylaw shenanigans that gave her a veto on any new members, but Graywytch hasn't stopped trying to convince the City Council to revoke my contract every chance she gets. She's basically the worst person I know who isn't a supervillain. (And to be honest, I'd rather hang out with Utopia, who, I remind you, is a genocidal psychopath.)

"Thank you, Patriot," says Graywytch. "As you know, the Legion Pacifica remains inoperable due to a lack of members to establish a quorum. Without a quorum, no decisions can be made, and thus the Legion and its assets have been placed into receivership. Due to concerns about the qualities of some of the prospective recruits—" Here, she looks directly at me over the heads of the crowd. I flip her off. "I have exercised my member's veto to prevent any new members from joining. However, given the ongoing threats to New Port and the Pacific Northwest of the United States in general, I find that I must bow to inevitability and lift my veto. I will be accepting applications for new members starting at the end of the month. Thank you."

Without another word, she turns and walks away from the podium. With a dagger pulled from her robes, she cuts a hole in the air, and through it I can see Victory Park in New Port. Graywytch steps through the portal and it seals behind her with a shimmer like a heat mirage. The crowd erupts in chatter, instant speculation on what the new Legion lineup will be. A seat in the Legion is a career-maker. Almost any unaffiliated whitecape would want the job.

My heart clenches with anxiety. I turn to Cecilia. "She can't do that, right? Doc's put a block in." Doc is a reserve member, along with Magma. She told me that this kind of thing wouldn't be possible. If Graywytch has her way, she'll stock the Legion with flunkies who are just as bad as she is.

"My understanding is that no, she can't. But she may think she'll get away with it, or more likely, she's got a lawyer of her own who thinks he can win if it goes to arbitration." Cecilia's lips are pressed thin.

"What are we going to do?"

"We're going ahead with the plan. Make your announcement, but be sure to let people know that Doctor Impossible is still pressing her veto against new members as well. We've got contracts in hand; Graywytch can only offer a messy fight. I think most capes will find that what we're offering is the better deal."

Somewhat reassured, I nod and turn back to watch the next speaker. Cecilia puts a hand on my shoulder and squeezes it. Razor has just finished inviting people to her sparring retreat in South Korea next month when a man in a long, red coat steps up to the speaker podium. He's bald, with deep lines around his mouth. *Finally*. Just this last guy out of the way, and then I'll get my turn. A little flutter of nerves dances around in my chest. This announcement I have to make is going to knock people's socks off.

"The floor recognizes Professor Gothic," says the Patriot.

"Thank you," says Gothic in a German-inflected baritone. "I have completed the latest round of the metahuman population survey, and the results are…concerning. The metahuman population growth continues to accelerate, but this is not news. What is news is that the growth curve has recently left a linear curve and has become, to early appearances at least, exponential." There's a ripple of murmuring through the crowd. Gothic waits for it to subside before proceeding.

"Should this growth continue its current pattern, as much as 7% of the human population could have superpowers by the end of the decade. By the middle of this century, that number could be as high as 41%." The murmuring is open discussion now, voices calling out in denial or excitement. Arguments are cracking open all over the room. Gothic raises his voice to be heard above the noise.

"Unless this trend reverses itself, I project that the entire human species will have superpowers by the year 2100 at the latest."

CHAPTER FOUR

Conversation explodes across the room. Thunderbolt whacks down the rising pandemonium with his gavel, again and again, calling for order. At last, he batters the noise down low enough to ask Professor Gothic to continue. "What's causing this?"

Professor Gothic flicks his tongue over his lips, looks down at his note cards. "I don't know. We still have not identified the common cause of superpowers."

"There *is* no common cause," says Thunderbolt. "Everybody knows that."

Gothic inclines his head. "That is what we have believed since the explosion in the metahuman population began in the twentieth century, to be sure. And, taken individually, everyone's path to power seems unique. A lab accident here, an ancient curse there. However, given the preponderance of evidence before us, there is now very little doubt that somehow these incidents are all linked. The fact that magic and hypertech have become more potent and more common as the years go on would seem to lend support to this hypothesis as well. Simple statistics rules out coincidence. But why is this happening now? Why not a hundred years ago? Or a hundred years hence? There can be no doubt left: the common cause is real, and it is getting stronger."

Someone in the crowd shouts out a question. "You said *if* this trend reverses itself; do you know if that will happen?"

"Order! Order!" Thunderbolt cracks his gavel again. "Recognized speakers only!"

Professor Gothic turns to address the crowd. "With the

common cause yet to be identified, we have no way of knowing if or when this trend will reverse itself. It is imperative that we make a concerted effort to identify and understand this cause. Until we can determine what is behind this and if it will ever stop, we should prepare to deal with ever-increasing numbers of metahumans. In the long term, we may have to consider a world without superheroes."

"What? Why?" someone shouts.

"Think about it: if everyone has superpowers, then what use would police and fire departments have for us?"

That's about the last anyone is able to make out over the sheer noise of a room full of superheroes losing their goddamn minds. I don't really notice the details, because the bottom has dropped out of my stomach, and I'm trying to keep myself from screaming.

It's all coming back to me in terrifying detail. The world seems far away, and I am back in that private Hell. The roaring of the flames, the smoke hot and sharp in my chest. The factory was coming down all around us. Utopia amidst the wreckage, calling me by name.

The Nemesis is coming, she had said. *Nobody is safe,* she said.

She was telling the truth. About one thing, at least, she was telling the truth. The Nemesis is coming. First, there will be more of us, but then worse things will follow. The scars on my chest and my stomach are perfectly circular. I have two in front, and two in back. The wounds had gone all the way through. The scars begin to itch. Nothing good can come from the Nemesis. *Nothing.* I'm not worried about the end of superheroes; I'm worried about the end of *everything.*

Professor Gothic looks at the chaos he unleashed with his lips pressed tight. I grab him by the arm, a little harder than I mean to, and pull him to face me.

"It's the Nemesis, isn't it?" I say, leaning in close to be heard.

"What did you say?" says Gothic, startled.

"That's what Utopia called it. Thirty million tons of exotic matter passing through the solar system and causing quantum observer effects—"

"Not here!" Gothic hisses at me.

"You have to tell them!" I shout.

"*Nein*. We must not speak of this here." Gothic tries to peel my fingers off his arm. They're like steel bands around his bicep.

"Nobody believed me when I told them what Utopia said. You have to tell them, you have to tell them what's happening!"

His face grows dark. "Dreadnought, if you value your life, you will not speak of such things in public. Not yet." He seems to consider for a moment. "You have enemies you won't recognize until they strike. We all do. More than that, I cannot say for now. Let go of me."

"Come to New Port," I say, letting go of his arm. "I can protect you."

He smiles, but there is something grim and forlorn in his eyes. "I somewhat doubt it. Even this was a risk, but the seed needed planting."

"What's going on?" I ask. I'd almost started to hope it had been just another one of Utopia's lies, a ghost story to frighten me away from beating her.

Gothic scans the crowd for a moment. "I will conclude my work in Germany and come find you. There are things we must discuss in a more secure setting. I will call you in a week, *ja*?"

"Fine." I give him my private number. "Stay safe."

"Be discreet, Dreadnought. Be safe." He turns and begins pushing his way through the crowd towards the exit.

The business meeting has basically fallen apart now. Thunderbolt has left his seat and is nowhere to be seen. The Patriot is still up there, just kind of looking around; he doesn't seem in any real hurry to call us back to order. I push through the crowd toward where I thought I saw Cecilia.

"Danny!" she calls out from somewhere off to my right. "Over here!" I slip between several heated conversations and make my way over to her.

"This is bad," she says.

"Yeah, I know. I don't think we're in danger right now, though." Her brow crinkles in confusion. "What are you talking about?"

"The—" I stop myself before I say *Nemesis*. "The…metahuman population?"

"No, I mean he just squashed our announcement."

"What announce—oh. Right." That Big News we had planned for so carefully? It's nothing now. Tiny. I came down here to tell people that the New Port City Council is willing to sign three new municipal hero contracts as a stopgap measure to protect the city and its surrounding suburbs until we can figure out what the hell's going to happen with the Legion now that it's basically a hollow shell under Graywytch's control.

Today was going to be the beginning of my backdoor coup. With three other heroes at my back, we would form an ad-hoc superteam to replace the Legion, and by the time I was old enough to be a member we'd have a track record strong enough to contest ownership of the Legion and all its assets on behalf of Doctor Impossible and…well, it seemed really interesting and exciting when we were scheming behind the scenes to set it up, but now it's all just so much inside baseball.

"Look, that doesn't really matter right now," I say. "I think something very bad is going to happen soon."

Cecilia frowns. "What is it?" One of the things I like about her is that she doesn't pretend the paperwork half of caping is the important one.

"I'm not sure. I need to talk to Doc about this. Can you stay here and call me if it looks like they're going to get the meeting back in order?"

"Sure," she says. As I turn to leave, she puts a hand on my shoulder. "Danny, how big is this?"

"I don't know yet. Big."

• • •

It takes just a few minutes to zip through the hotel to the suites we rented. The rooms are great: deep, plush carpet, dark wood everywhere, the works. Doc Impossible is sprawled out on the couch, flipping through the on-demand options on the plasma screen and swirling the ice cube around in her lowball glass of whiskey. The track lighting in the room is set to a soft dim glow.

"Hey, kiddo," she says, without looking up when I shut the door behind me. Her voice is very careful, overly precise. "You make your big play?"

"Doc, sober up, we've got a problem."

"Eh? Something go wrong?" Doc raises the remote and kills the picture on the screen. The lights begin to rise automatically.

"Sort of. What can you tell me about Professor Gothic?"

"He's a crank of the highest order," she says approvingly. Doc Impossible sits up and sets her drink aside. "He does excellent, idiosyncratic work."

"He knows about the Nemesis." I take a seat in one of the plush armchairs near the coffee table.

She looks at me sharply. "He said that?"

"No, not exactly, but he said everything up to that." I tell her about his announcement, and about our little conversation during the chaos afterward. "He was only giving them half the truth. He said he didn't know what the common cause to superpowers is, but it has to be the Nemesis."

"Well, hold on, does it?" she asks. Doc crosses the room to the minibar and slides her half-finished whiskey into a tiny refrigerator. She pulls a bottle of water out and twists it open. I'm glad I caught her before she'd gone too far, or she might have been soggy for the rest of the convention. She might be an android, but she's a *really human* android, and I've come to learn that that means really human problems too. "Utopia said there was a large mass of exotic matter coming our way, that it did something with quantum observer effects, and that it would be dangerous. That's *all* she said about it. It doesn't mean it's been the cause of metahumans and magic and hypertech and all the rest."

"No, Doc, I mean I *called it* the Nemesis, and he knew what I was talking about. If that was just her pet name for it—"

"How would he know?" Doc finishes for me, suddenly thoughtful. She takes a swig of water. "Mom was always…weirdly social. Maybe she had some aliases online, talked this over with other hypertech developers?"

I shrug. "Maybe. When I tried to ask Gothic about it, he didn't want to talk here. He said it was too dangerous."

"Dangerous, why?"

"I don't know. He acted like there were blackcapes in the crowd just waiting to hear him say the wrong thing. He's coming to New Port in a few days so we can talk in private."

Doc looks thoughtful. "He might be paranoid. It's a known job risk in the super science racket."

"You don't believe me."

"I didn't say that." She holds up a hand. "If Gothic thinks there's something to this, then it's worth hearing him out. I'll ping him online and ask him to send me some files."

A weird sense of disappointment washes over me, and I lean back in the chair. For nine months I've been worrying about the Nemesis, trying to learn anything I can about it. All I've been able to find were some references to a hypothetical planet, an undiscovered member of the solar system on a super long elliptical orbit, passing through the inner system only once every few thousand years. I'd started to let myself believe it was nothing, and now suddenly it's back and it's real and other people see it too, but all I get to do about it is just…wait and see. Wait and see if Gothic is a crank. Wait and see if the Nemesis is real. Wait and see if Utopia was right about the doom that's coming for all of us.

"Thanks," I say. "I guess that's it for now."

"Cheer up, kiddo," says Doc Impossible, smiling brightly. "You never know, it might still be the apocalypse after all."

"That makes me feel so much better."

"Always happy to help. You wanna grab something to eat?"

"No, I should probably head back down there," I say, standing up. "They might be getting the meeting back in order soon. I just wanted…well, I thought you should know about this."

Doc nods, and then after a moment she asks, "Are you going to be okay?"

"Yeah," I say, with a weird sense that I'd rather not be answering that question. "Why wouldn't I be?"

"Danny, every time Utopia comes up in conversation, there's a change in you. You get tense." Doc's voice is gentle. "It's not okay, what she did to you. That kind of thing leaves a mark. It's normal for it to leave a mark."

And I really don't know what to say to that. I feel uncomfortably exposed, like that trick I do with everyone else where I stop being Danny and start being Dreadnought won't work on her. She knows me too well.

"Well, this isn't really about her, so I don't think it's going to be a problem," I say carefully.

"It doesn't have to be directly about her. It could still dig up a lot of things for you. I just want to know you're going to be okay."

"I'll be fine," I say.

"Okay." Doc nods. She looks like she's going to say something else when the part of the suit over my forearm vibrates and my earbud sounds a ringtone.

The hidden screen on my forearm blooms to life, a glossy color display showing the photo of my police liaison officer, Detective Phạm. I tap the answer button, and the suit dims and fades back to its normal matte blue.

"Hi, Detective. Something up?"

"Sorry to call you on your week off, but Graywytch isn't answering her phone. We need you back here right away. Somebody is tearing up downtown with his superpowers and he's taken hostages."

CHAPTER FIVE

I'm moving before Detective Phạm is done talking. "On my way." I cut the signal. "Doc, are you good to plot an orbital hop back to New Port?" I ask as I cross to the suite's door.

"Yeah, I'm okay, get going." She's moving to her tablet and flicking open the orbital calculator. "Should have it ready in two minutes."

"Tell NORAD I'm on my way; I don't want them trying to shoot me down."

"Will do. Go get 'em, kid," she says. That last part I hear through my earbud because I'm already in the hall and blasting down to the emergency stairs.

"Oh, and tell Cecilia I won't be able to make it back to the meeting, and she should make the announcement herself." I'm zipping down the emergency stairs in a tight spiral, flight after flight flashing past. "See if you can get her to talk to Kinetiq about getting one of those contracts, would you?"

"You need me to drop off your dry cleaning too?"

I almost snap the doors off their hinges as I come out into the lobby and boost for speed. A few other fliers juke out of my way and shout angrily at my back, but by that time I'm in the hangar, and a few moments later I'm under open sky and pushing hard for altitude. Earth falls away from me like somebody dropped it, and soon the moisture in my eyebrows freezes. I take a last deep breath and hold it. It's the last air I'm going to get for the next twenty minutes or so.

The wind roars in my ears, a rumbling pressure builds at

my forehead, pushes, and then I snap through the sound barrier. Higher and faster, the clouds falling away below me like a cotton ball carpet. My sleeve vibrates at me again, and I tap it to open the telemetry Doc sent me. I push my arms through the wind up in front of me and make a diamond with my fingers. Between them a hologram flickers to life. Glowing emerald squares are projected in front of me, hollow and strung out in a line. They're gates marking the optimal flight path for an orbital injection. I correct my angle a little bit to start passing through the gates, and as I zip through each one, my suit squeezes me gently to let me know I'm on the right course. I drop my arms beside me and push like hell.

I really don't know how fast my top speed is. I've never gotten there. What I do know is that within about fifteen thousand feet of sea level, I can only get up to Mach 3 or so. Past that, the wind resistance is too much, and I'm simply not strong enough to batter my way through. If I want to go faster I need to get higher. The thinner the air, the faster I go. And to go *really* fast, I need to get up to where there is no air at all.

The pressure on my arms and face seems to drop gradually, and then all of a sudden I'm up in sub-orbit. The silence is perfect. The world vast below me, stretching out almost unimaginably far all around me. It's fuzzy blue at the edges, and way off near the horizon, the sun is distant and searingly bright. Below me, the world curves away.

Earth is almost heartbreakingly beautiful from up here. It's home. It's everything. I wish everyone had a chance to see it like this.

I give myself a few moments to enjoy the view, and then I put on a fresh burst of speed and pass through ten thousand miles per hour like it was nothing at all.

I bring the gate diagram up again to make sure I'm on course. The trouble with orbital jumps is that they're not nearly as simple as they seem. It isn't just go up and come down. The Coriolis effect means coming down where I want to isn't as trivial as pointing myself in the right direction. I could just try to follow the coastline up South America, past Mexico and into the United States, but it would be tricky, and if I made a mistake it would cost so much time to correct it that it might almost defeat the point of coming up here in the first place. I don't know how the other Dreadnoughts got along without orbital calculators and satellite navigation.

For a good fifteen minutes I glide silently over Earth, splitting my time between checking my telemetry and scanning ahead in the lattice. In the past nine months I've gotten a lot better at reading the lattice, the tangled net of light that hangs behind reality. I'm better at seeing through walls now, and I can scan almost fifty miles ahead of me if there's no atmosphere in the way to clutter up the view. That's important, because even for me it would be a little uncomfortable to slam into a low-flying satellite at twenty-six thousand miles an hour.

The navigation gates are turning amber now, and in the distance they fade toward red, my signal to begin slowing down for reentry. A feral grin stretches across my face, and I can feel my body begin to come alive with anticipation.

Being a superhero means a lot of things. It means I'm a public figure. It means that most of the people around me don't consider me one of them. It means learning to keep my head together when everything is falling apart. It means living life at the edge of death. These are things that everyone knows about, things everyone thinks they understand. But there's another truth to it, one I've learned not to speak about too loudly. People don't want to hear it, not from Dreadnought, at least. Because here's the truth of the matter, here's what my job really means:

I beat people up for money.

And I love it. God help me, but I love it more than breathing. To be honest, I'd do it for free. Hell, I'd *pay* to do this. When I get into a serious fight, it is almost always the high point of my week. There's no bullshit in combat, no convenient fictions and easy lies. Open battle is the most honest relationship you can have with somebody. They want to do something bad. I want to stop them. Whoever is stronger gets what they want. So far, I'm always the one who wins. The bad guys keep getting surprised by that. They know I'm Dreadnought, of course, and they know I'm strong. But I don't think any of them ever expected that I could reach down into me and pull out the kind of rage that I hit them with. They see this cute little blond girl and think I don't have it in me to hurt them. Very quickly, they learn better. When I'm in a really good fight, the anger explodes out of me. The battle joy takes me, and it's the best feeling in the world. It is *right*. It is *necessary*. When I'm fighting, everything is perfect.

It's time to make my descent. I nose down and adjust my path to follow the gates into New Port, still hundreds of miles ahead of me. It's just a matter of ballistics now, so I'm not putting any effort into accelerating. The first wisps of atmosphere begin to whisper past me, almost imperceptibly gentle. It's time to get into position. There are two ways I can reenter the atmosphere: under power, where I use my flight powers to slow me down so I don't burn up, and free falling, where I slam into the atmosphere at full speed and bear the brunt of its fury. The second way is faster, but dangerous. Even I can't be exposed to those kinds of temperatures for long before I start to get seriously burned.

I flip onto my back, my legs stretched out in front of me. Crossing one boot over the other helps me keep them together during the turbulence that's going to start here in a few moments. That's important because I've got to stay stable; if I begin to tumble, then things will get very bad, very fast. I reach behind me and pull my cape up around the back of my head and neck. As the first glowing streams of plasma begin to gather at my heels and slide up the back of my legs, I tuck my chin down against my chest and cross my arms. My cape is fluttering up behind me, cupped against the back of my head by the atmosphere, which is just now finding its voice. The sky roars at me, dragon's breath hot and bright all around me. In a matter of seconds, I'm uncomfortably hot. My suit is spreading the heat out evenly, dissipating it as much as it can. I've got to keep my arms crossed in front of me and my fingers out of the plasma, or I might lose them.

I think of the fight waiting for me on the other end of this Hell, and my smile grows. The pressure pummels my legs and back. Falling to Earth at Mach 25 in a bathtub of fire, I begin to laugh. Other girls my age worry about midterms and prom dates. Those poor, ignorant children. They will never get to feel this amazing. Some people get superpowers and pretend they don't have them. They hide from their power. They throw it all away just so they can be *normal*. Idiots. Cowards. Who the fuck wants to be normal when you can be *this* instead?

The plasma rips away from me, and now I'm falling through the night sky, wind howling at my back. I flip over and point my head down. Down in Antarctica it looked like late afternoon, but up here it's been dark for hours.

Something's wrong. I can't see the I-5 corridor. The West Coast of the US is a pretty simple place—almost all the major cities are on Interstate 5. Most of the minor ones too. That's extra true in the Northwest, which doesn't have the big coastal cities of California. What that means is there should be a big ribbon of light right below me, millions of white and amber lights marking out civilization. But there's nothing; it's only flat, black nothing. After a brief moment of confusion I realize I'm over Pacific Ocean. Looking over to my right, way off the in the distance, I spot the lights of the coast. I bank hard against the stiff wind and start pushing for new acceleration to change my course.

Goddamnit, Doc. The Coriolis effect is a *thing*. I should have calculated the plot myself, even if it did take me ten minutes. I'm bound to lose more on this correction than I would have if I'd stopped to make sure my navigator wasn't drunk. She'd *looked* sober. Sober enough. Shit.

My turn is a wide, looping thing as I try to husband the remaining fragments of velocity from my orbital insertion. Coming down from space gives me way more momentum than I can normally get, and I'm going to need every spare joule of it to get to New Port on time. My forearm starts buzzing and my suit sounds a warning tone in my earpiece, telling me I'm off course. I silence the alarms and push for more speed. It's all going to be over by the time I get there. People might be getting hurt. Come on, come on…

The Pacific Coast slides toward me, the horizon an abrupt end to the vast, black ocean below me. My chest unwinds a bit, a few portions of my anxiety torn away by the wind. I can do this, bad course or not. I can do this. My nerves are singing with anticipation as I tap out a text message to Detective Phạm on my wrist screen. I'm a few minutes out. Where are the hostages being kept?

Almost instantly, she replies Galatea Tower, top floor. Command post is in the parking garage opposite.

The clouds over New Port glow with the light of the city beneath. They are cold and moist when I tear through them. I'm approaching downtown now, and slow down to only a few hundred miles per hour. Huge towers of glass and steel soar past me on either side as I slip into the canyons at speed. There's Galatea Tower, and there's the parking structure across the road. I bank in and cut a steep turn down to the circus of police vehicles spread out across the garage's top floor.

I whistle sharply as I'm about to land; cops *hate* it when I land near them without warning, but they're too lazy to look up. Nobody ever really looks up. A couple of patrol officers glance my way as I come in for a landing and tap down next to them. "Where's Detective Phạm?" I ask.

One of them gestures with a Styrofoam cup of coffee. "In there."

"Thanks." I hop the police tape and head into the center of their little encampment. One of the cops behind me radios ahead that I'm coming. Every time something big happens, the cops set up shop like they're planning to stay there for weeks, and then a few dozen of them just stand around doing nothing until the crisis is over. Your tax dollars at work, ladies and gentlemen.

A light drizzle has made everything wet and gleaming. There's a few cruisers parked crookedly across the lines, washing everything in flickering blue and red. Command trucks and SWAT vans are circled around the central gathering. Under a big folding pavilion, they've set up a table with laptops and floodlights hooked up to a generator. As I approach, a plainclothes officer comes over to greet me.

"Hi, Danny." Detective Phạm is my liaison officer with the New Port cops. She's in her late twenties or early thirties and is wearing a beige overcoat and a solid blue sweater. Her badge hangs off a chain like a pendant around her neck.

"Hi, Detective. What's up?"

"It's hard to tell. One of the hostages escaped and said there was a guy up there who got insulted by a waiter and went *Carrie* on the whole room. Now he doesn't seem to know what to do and is sitting there, threatening to kill the hostages if we try to come in."

I wince. "Yikes. Any description of his powerset?"

Detective Phạm looks back over at the senior officers. One of them nods at her. When she turns back, I don't like the look on her face. "Look Danny, I'm sorry I called you all the way up here for nothing, but you arrived too late. The MRU is going to take this one."

My heart plummets. The MRU is the Metahuman Response Unit. They're a glorified SWAT team that specializes in taking down people with superpowers. I've fought beside them a couple times, and I was not impressed.

"Oh come on! I ditched the convention for this! Have they even breached yet?"

She shakes her head. "No, but they're just about to."

"So there's time to call them off, then!"

"The decision to go has already been made. You can watch on the monitors with us, if you'd like. If things go sideways, they might need you to back them up."

"I don't want to *watch*," I say, and hate how much like a whine it sounds. "I want to fight!"

Phạm shrugs. "I'm sorry. That's the best I can do."

My shoulders slump. "All right."

God*dammit*, Doc!

"You want some coffee?"

No, I don't want any freaking coffee. I want to be doing my job. But it's not her fault Doc's a drunk, so I suck it up and say, "Sure."

"It's over there." She indicates a table that is fairly crowded with uniforms jostling for caffeine. "Catch up with us in the command tent."

The coffee is watery, but hot enough.

"So you're Dreadnought, huh?" asks one of the uniforms as I'm trying to decide which of the creamers I want to use. Is Hazelnut Bliss enough to make this disaster worthwhile, or am I more of a Nutmeg Joy kind of girl?

"Yep. Hey, is there any raw sugar around here?"

"It's over there," he says. "What's that like?"

"What's what like?" I say absently, hoping he'll take a hint. Cops are fun to talk to sometimes. Not always. Not tonight, when I'm already in a bad mood. They have a strong us-and-them mentality that can be uncomfortable to navigate. Then there's the weird hero worship some of them have toward us—toward capes, I mean—and the equally weird resentment that some of them harbor instead. Put that all together, and I've learned to take my time warming up to cops I don't know.

"Being Dreadnought," he says.

Okay, so we're not going to take the hint after all. Time for a bland reply and then I'll go hang out in the command tent where people don't shove awkward small talk at me. "Oh. It's cool. I get to—"

The distant crackle of gunfire drifts down from the top of the tower across the street. Everyone stops and looks up.

Detective Phạm breaks away from the group of senior officers in the command tent.

"Dreadnought!" she shouts. "Get up there!"

CHAPTER SIX

"Hold this," I say to the uniform next to me, and push my coffee cup into his hands. The next instant I'm in the air and approaching the sound barrier.

The top floor of Galatea Tower is a swanky restaurant with floor-to-ceiling windows that shatter nice and dramatically when I punch through them. This used to be a nice place for overpriced dinners. Dim lighting, white tablecloths, real silver in the silverware. Now it features scorch marks on the carpet, dozens of screaming hostages, and a SWAT team having a firefight with a supervillain. Not really a place I'd recommend for the ambiance.

The main entrance to the dining room has been frozen over completely. A quick peek in the lattice tells me that the cops are trapped on the other side, several of them partially frozen into the wall, and they are frantically trying to chip their way out with utility knives. More cops in black tactical gear have burst in from a kitchen entrance, but are pinned down behind a pair of heavy, overturned tables. Their rifles bark and snap across the room, and everywhere hostages are pinning themselves to the ground, screaming.

And there in the center of the room is the bad guy, a man in his thirties who's dressed like he was one of the guests. His tie is undone and his jacket hangs loose. His sleeves are charred and fraying near the cuffs, and there are scorch marks all around him. He's got his hands spread out in front of him, blasting winds filled with ice and sleet to rebuild a crumbling ice bullet shield in front of him.

Almost immediately I start taking hits from an assault rifle, cracking pops of pain across my chest and neck. Irritating, but not damaging.

"Check your fire, dumbass!" I shout, getting up into the air to draw any further fire up away from the hostages. This is what I don't like about fighting near cops; even their "elite" officers probably haven't been in a real battle before, and that means that some of them tend to ride the edge of panic every time things get really serious. The officer shooting at me finally lets up on the trigger, adjusts his aim, and starts blasting away at the ice wall the bad guy is putting up.

The vil looks at me, eyes wide, swings one arm over, and his hand glows hot yellow just before—

The SWAT team all run out of ammo at the same time.

There's a moment of silence, and then the cops are all scrambling for pistols or spare magazines.

The vil throws a bolt of fire at some hostages, splashes a puddle of liquid flame all around them. They shriek and try to back away, but the flames have them penned in. The fire is closing in on them, and they reach out for me with pleading hands. I snap across the room, catch hold of two people's wrists, and hoist them up out of the noose of fire, then shout to the others, "Grab my ankles!"

Their landing isn't very pretty or comfortable, but I don't have time to worry about the little things. Once this group of hostages is safe, I whirl on the bad guy, ready to fight.

In the time it's taken me to rescue the hostages, he's hit the cops' position with heavy ice. I can hear one of them shouting into his radio for backup, and a few more are trying to chip away at the ice around them with knives. Some of them are entirely encased, and have maybe a few minutes to live.

"Wait!" says the vil as I close in on him. His eyes are wild and desperate. "Look, my name is John Crenshaw; I have a lot of really important friends. We don't need to fight. You can understand, right? We're better than these people! Just let me go. Nobody important has been hurt, right?"

He says this while standing a few yards from the charred remains of the waiter he killed.

"What the hell are you talking about?" I demand, pointing at the corpse.

His face twists with frustration. "I'm too *important* to go down for this! I was trying to get them to understand, but they're too far gone. The cathedral has infected us. Even these people, who are supposed to be the cream—"

"Shut up."

Between one heartbeat and the next I cross the space between us, grab him by his collar and his belt, and throw him a good thirty feet out the broken window. He leaves the building like he's been shot out of a cannon, and I'm already over by the frozen cops, smashing the ice to wet chunks with a few quick punches. The cops who'd been completely frozen in take deep, convulsive breaths and begin coughing and vomiting. Then I'm out the window after the bad guy to try to keep him from becoming street pizza.

The city spreads out beneath us as we fall, canyons of black glass and distant yellow lights. The cold wind tugs at my hair, and I am *alive*. The only thing I don't like about being a superhero is that this kind of thing doesn't happen every day.

There he is, jacket snapping in the wind as he falls. I power down to catch up to him, but he twists in the air and starts throwing lances of fire at me. I loop out of the way and shout down to him. "Stop shooting, you idiot! I'm trying to save you!"

Maybe Crenshaw shouts something back. I can't hear it over the wind. A bolt of ice slams into my chest, cold and heavy, but I shatter it off me with a ripple of my shoulders. We've sailed completely over the road and are coming down in a major construction site just next to the parking structure all the cops are camped out on. We're running out of space before he hits the ground, and the closer I get, the harder it is to dodge his attacks. I might just need to take it on the chin here in a few moments...

But then he just twists in midair again, points his hands down, and starts shooting fire and wind from his palms like a pair of jet engines. He lands in an enormous white cloud of dust and steam, and I frown, disappointed. I like catching people while they fall. It's fun.

The construction yard is bathed in harsh floodlights. Half-poured columns of rebar and concrete reach up like fingers from the foundation pit. Where the ground isn't fresh cement, it's a gritty, yellow-brown mud that's been packed down hard by hundreds of workers and dozens of vehicles.

I slam down a dozen yards from him, look into the lattice to see through the clouds to check if he made it in one piece. He has, and a few moments later I'm dodging streams of fire and ice. I dart in and hit him in the solar plexus with an open-palm strike. He goes skidding across the ground as he hacks and wheezes and tries to reinflate his collapsed lungs. In the past year, I've gotten pretty good at pulling my punches. That one was pretty gentle, somewhere between a heavyweight boxer and a mule's hind leg. Most people will decide it's time to give up when I hit them with something like that. But not Crenshaw. No, he's too *important* to give up, I guess, and he comes out of the cloud throwing fire and ice with both hands.

Excellent.

His aim is better when he's on the ground, and I find out that his fire is hot enough to sting and the ice hits hard. But the way his ribs crack when I send him sprawling out in the mud makes me think this will be a quick fight. That's kind of disappointing, to be honest.

During my first real battle, I was hesitant. I was reluctant to go full power on the bad guys. The idea of hurting people was repulsive to me. That is not a problem I have anymore. Sometime in the last half-year or so I became the kind of person who can snap bones and rip tendons and feel nothing but satisfaction. But people don't like to think about that kind of thing, about how the person they depend on to fight their battles for them might actually *like* it, so I don't talk about it too much. Which is fine. After being in the closet for seven years, keeping my mouth shut about how much I like fighting is easy.

"You're just like *them*, you…you *peasant!*" says Crenshaw as he rolls over and gets his arms under him.

"Give up, dude. This isn't going to end well for you." I wish he had a durability power. He's so fragile; this will be over before I really get to cut loose.

He comes to his feet with a lot of wincing and straining, and then out of the goddamn blue throws a freaking lightning bolt at me. It hits like Zeus' backhand. My whole nervous system lights up with agony, my muscles locked and straining. I'd be screaming but my lungs aren't working, and my heart is trying to turn itself inside out. The pain passes, and I'm falling to my knees, then my stomach. Shit. Nobody told me he had electricity powers. Stupid, Danny. Real stupid.

Crenshaw laughs, relief mixed with triumph. "You don't like that, do you, bitch?" he calls, and then he hits me with another bolt.

This time I do scream, long and loud as my back arches and my arms clench up. I'm not actually invincible, just really tough, and I'm not equally tough to all things. Electricity hits me almost as hard as a baseline human. My suit is doing its best to insulate me from the worst, but I still feel little electric knives sawing at all my nerves. The electricity passes, and my eyes aren't synced anymore, a pair of worlds dancing a wobbly waltz as I try to bring things into focus.

This is an embarrassing way to die, I think, just as the flash grenade lands between us.

A flutter of cloth, a whine of spooling cable. Someone grabs me by the cape and hauls me up and away just as the grenade goes off with a flat bang. We swing to the lip of a half-finished second floor. I land on the naked cement in a heap, and a pair of boots clops down next to me. The girl they belong to wears cargo pants crimped in at the knees with pads, and her torso is encased in black tactical gear under a long, brown riding coat. And, of course, she's wearing a gray cowboy hat.

"All right, partner," says Calamity. The cable she swung us up here on finishes rewinding back up into her left hand. There's a hypertech rocket/grapnel at the end that disappears into her palm with a metallic click. "Tap out. I've got it from here."

"The hell you do," I say, pushing myself to my feet. "I'm going to kick this guy's ass."

Calamity rounds on me, eyes narrow over her bandanna. "You ain't got no business squaring off with someone packing lightning powers! Not when I'm around to do it instead."

"This isn't your job, Calamity."

"Then I must wonder whose it is, 'cause you sure as hell weren't doing it!" she snaps. "This should be over by now."

Frustration knots up inside me. It's been like this between us for months. I don't know why. Calamity took some time off for physical therapy after the big battle last year, and then when she came back it was like we were strangers again. Now I only see her when we run into each other on a job.

"Look, would you just—"

"Get down!" shouts Calamity, and she tackles me to the cement as another bolt of lightning fries the night over our heads.

There's a lip of concrete where a wall rises up a few feet to meet a future window, and we take cover behind it. Fire blooms and roars around us, and lightning splits the sky with a cracking bang.

"We'll fight later!" shouts Calamity over the noise. "You go right, I go left!"

"Got it!" I say, more relieved for her to be giving orders again than I want her to know. The way things used to be. The way I wish they still were.

She pulls another flash grenade out of her jacket and tosses it over the concrete. "Go on the bang!"

The grenade bangs, and we go.

CHAPTER SEVEN

Calamity's revolvers bark loud and low as she sprints along one side of the unfinished second floor. Even she's not good enough to score hits while running flat out, but she kicks up dust around Crenshaw and keeps him busy. I'm moving the other way to try to circle around and pin him between us. Fireballs bloom, and lightning cracks and thunders. I'm varying my speed, zigging and zagging, and between the two of us, Calamity and I manage to keep him distracted and frantic enough not to land any more hits. But we can't go on like this forever; we've got to take him down. And the first cape dumb enough to try to finish the deal is going to eat shit in a big way.

Stupid, Danny, really stupid. I should have finished him off when I had the chance. A couple quick hits to his upper arms to break the bones, and he wouldn't be able to even lift his hands, much less throw lightning at me. Maybe take out his legs too, just to be sure. I mean, yeah, sure, that all sounds really brutal...

And it is, I guess. But that's how these things work. You can't just handcuff a supervillain and expect him to go quietly. Unless I put him down hard, the moment my back is turned he'll be barbecuing cops and making a break for freedom. Of course, now we've lost our easy chance to end this quick because I like to play with my food. Hey, it seemed like a fun idea at the time. It always seems like a fun idea at the time.

"All right, we've pincered him," says Calamity through my earbud radio. "Any ideas?"

I skid to a stop behind a cement column and tuck in behind it. "Yes! Switch up to hollow points and blow his goddamn knees off!"

"Not happening. Too much bacon around here. Can you find something to throw at him?"

"Uh, stand by—" My eyes land on some stacked bags of cement lying under a tarp. "Get ready to rush him. He's going to be down in a moment."

I heft a fifty-pound bag of cement, step out of cover, and fling it at him like the world's heaviest Frisbee. As it goes, I reach out into the lattice for the strings of its momentum, catch and tweak them to guide the bag in for an accurate hit. Crenshaw sees it coming and hits it with a bolt of lighting. The bag bursts open just in time for him to get hit with fifty pounds of loose, powdered cement. Not the Mack truck knockout I was hoping for, but still enough to send him ass-over-end.

Calamity raises her left arm and shoots a grapnel that trails cable out of her prosthetic hand. The cable finds purchase across the open yard, and she flies out of cover as the cable whizzes back into her arm. She lands next to him in a roll, and as the limp cable whips back into her arm across the mud, she snatches it up and wraps it twice around Crenshaw's throat.

"Best be tapping out soon, partner!" she shouts as she jerks the cable tight.

Crenshaw struggles a little more, so she bangs his head against the ground once, twice, and finally he goes limp. Before he can come to, Calamity reaches into her tactical vest and pulls out a syringe. She jerks the safety cap off with her teeth, then plunges the thick needle through his jacket into the meat of his shoulder. That's what she does instead of beating the bad guys into a hospital bed. If I could manage to get through a fight without shattering everything fragile I was carrying, I'd probably use those little tranquilizers too.

"That ought to keep you," she says as she lets the cable go slack. Crenshaw inhales deeply, but doesn't stir from the deep sleep he's fallen into.

"Good work," I say, setting down next to her.

"What the hell is wrong with you?" says Calamity as she gets to her feet and brushes off her hands.

"Oh great! We're doing this again." All that earlier relief from when she took charge has vanished. It seems like nothing is ever right between us these days. For a while there after the battle with Utopia, it seemed like we were going to be close. *Very* close. But then…I don't know, then it kind of fell apart. I was off making my first rounds as Dreadnought, getting to know my new life, and she was trapped in Legion Tower or at home, going through a series of surgeries to get ready for her prosthetic arm. That's when we started to lose contact and drift apart. She stopped answering my calls, and then I stopped calling. It wasn't until a few months later when we ran into each other on a midnight roof that I even knew she was still caping.

What makes it worse is that sometime in the nine months since we fought Utopia, Calamity hit a growth spurt and is now a good two or three inches taller than me, and that's flipped a switch in my brain for how I see her. She has gone from being kind of cute to urgently, *painfully* hot. The way she holds her shoulders, straight and high. The way her eyes are the color of liquid chocolate. Sometimes she catches me staring, and I think sometimes I catch her staring, but maybe that's just wishful thinking.

"You almost got yourself killed," says Calamity.

"I almost die on a monthly basis, what makes tonight so special?"

"Dammit, Dreadnought; this ain't funny!" Whoa, wait a minute, that's real fear in her eyes. It doesn't work this way.

"I'm sorry," I say, trying not to sound insincere.

"I thought once you'd had a chance to grow into your powers you'd get over doing shit like this," she says, which is the exact wrong thing to say.

"Oh, piss off!" I snap. "I don't need you tell me what to do with my powers!"

We're saved from the fight getting worse by the arrival of

Detective Phạm, who charges into the construction site at the head of a SWAT team. They all point guns at Calamity.

"Calamity, freeze! You're under arrest!" shouts Detective Phạm.

"Funny. I don't feel arrested."

"Dreadnought, step away from the vigilante!"

"Why?" I ask. "Are you afraid your bullets might mess up my hair?"

Calamity drops a few black pellets out of her jacket, and an instant later they're all hissing thick white smoke. Visibility drops like a curtain, and Calamity's grapnel fires.

"See you around, partner," she says, and then there's the sound of cable whizzing and her jacket flapping as she flits away into the night.

Well, I'll give the cops some credit: they don't fire after her. We're in one of the most densely packed cities in the country, and those bullets would have to come down somewhere. Phạm speaks rapidly into her radio, and in the distance sirens answer her. They're going to try to chase her with cars, and will probably call in some helicopter support. It won't work. It never does.

It takes some time for the smoke to clear, and while that's happening the cops are rushing around setting up a new perimeter and calling in some paramedics to get Crenshaw laid out on a stretcher.

"What'd she do to him?" asks Phạm as she slides her gun back into her shoulder holster. Crenshaw is completely out of it, flopping limply and drooling as the medics load his stretcher into the back of their truck.

"It's a hypertech sedative," I say. "Puts him down for eight hours with no side effects."

Phạm nods, then seems to remember something. "Danny, you shouldn't be working with her."

"Why not? I need all the help I can get."

"She's unlicensed and working off-contract. That makes her a criminal."

"So what?"

"So? So that's kind of a *problem* for us. You may have noticed that we're cops?" She taps the golden shield on a chain around her neck. "See the badge?"

"Oh yeah, speaking of which, one of your boys *shot* me about six times tonight. The MRU really needs to get their shit together…"

Phạm and I head back to the main command post. She's lodged her formal protest about my continued association with Calamity, but we both know that's all it is: something done for form's sake so everyone can say they were doing their job. Calamity isn't the only vigilante in New Port, and if the cops seriously tried to crack down on unlicensed superheroes the crime rate would jump overnight. *They* say that's because it would divert manpower away from regular police work; *we* say it's because there are lots of crimes they just can't handle. It's no different than how things work in other big cities, except maybe a little more intense. New Port has always had more than its share of weirdos in tights and super-powered narcissists with god complexes.

There's some paperwork the police want me to do, and I sit down to do it without grumbling, because that's a fight I've lost enough times to not bother anymore. After it's done, I briefly consider asking for permission to fly back down to Antarctica to catch the rest of the convention, but decide against it. The answer will be no. Every time I work with the cops, I have to stick around for the next forty-eight hours in case their investigators decide to ask me any questions. Even though I specifically arranged for this week off, and even though it was Graywytch who wasn't answering her phone, I'm the one who threw the punches, so I've got to stick around.

Frustration knots in my chest. Two years until the next World Convention. Goddamnit, Graywytch. You're going to pay for this.

With nothing better to do, I decide to go back to the condo I share with Doc Impossible.

I take to the air and head towards the condo towers in outer New Port. Below me, tiny cars wait at tiny stoplights, and minuscule people pass through yellow circles of streetlamps. I tap my forearm to activate the screen and bring Doc up on speed dial. She answers a few moments later, still drunk. Maybe more so than when I left her.

"Hello…Danny? Danny?"

"Hi, Doc."

"How was the fight?"

"It's fine. I'm fine. I'm going to stay in New Port tonight. I've got to be available to the detectives."

"Oookay. You're going to miss the after-party."

I laugh. "That's fine. Cecilia would kill me if pictures of something like that got on to the web."

"You're probably right."

Something in her tone makes me worried. Doc was in a really bad way after the battle with Utopia. She held it together just long enough for us to move into a condo on the outskirts of downtown, and then fell into a bottle for six months. A human woman would have died from all the alcohol she put into herself. The low point was probably the day I came home and found out she'd cut the word *machine* into her face with a razor. After what happened today with Magma and Chlorophyll, I'm becoming concerned about a relapse. "Doc, are you going to be okay?"

"I'm not a drunk. I'm just drunk at the moment. It's fine."

"Just promise me you'll be sober when you fly up again. I don't want to have to look for a new lawyer." Making it a joke works sometimes, but not always.

"Of course!" blurts Doc, her voice frightened. "Of course. I would…you know I never want to hurt you, right?"

"I know, Doc," I say, suddenly embarrassed. "It's fine. Have fun."

"Okay, Danny. I just want you to know, you know, right? That I wouldn't betray you?"

"I know, Doc." Shit, she's *really* fallen down the hole. Magma, you asshole. You didn't have to yell at her like that. And just when she'd started to get better too. Now there's nothing I can do but wait to see if she stays down there this time. I hope not.

"I care about you," she says, like she's not sure I know it already.

"I care about you too. Get some sleep."

"Sure, sure. G'night."

"Night." I cut the line, and feel mingled shame and relief at getting out of the conversation before it got any worse. She's not a bad person, exactly, it's just that sometimes she'll be drunk for weeks on end and forget to pay the electricity bill, or something like that. It can be difficult to live with her, but if I didn't, I'd be completely alone. I'm not sure I could deal with that right now.

Doc's condo is one of four on the top floor of a middle-quality condo tower. It seems like kind of a down-rent place for a pair of professional superheroes to live until you realize that she owns the other three units on the top floor and all the condos on the floor below us too. Buying up a whole lot of units is the only way to ensure the kind of security and privacy that a superhero, or even a former hero for that matter, needs.

As I approach the tower, my stomach flips over when I notice the lights in Doc's condo are on. When we were leaving for Antarctica, I *know* we turned everything off. I look into the lattice, to see if anything jumps out at me, any cloaked bad guys or hidden power sources. Nothing on the outside. The walls are thick enough and I'm far enough away that I can't see too clearly inside.

When I tap down on the patio outside the sliding glass door, I find a girl sitting in our living room, reading a book. She's sitting forward on the couch, and is wearing a strange, almost poofy white backpack. She looks up when I slide the glass door open.

"Oh good, you're here." The girl stands up to meet me. She's Asian, and fairly tall. Her clothes are all wrinkled and dirty, and her hair is lank and messy.

"You have ten seconds to convince me not to call the police," I say with all the ice I can muster. Most people flinch a little when I hit them with something like that, but this girl doesn't even seem to notice. Cecilia warned me I might have to deal with stalkers, but until this moment I never really took her seriously.

"I'm sorry I broke in. My name is Karen," she says. What I took to be a strange backpack unfurls a little. It's not a backpack at all. She has wings. "Valkyrja was my mother, and I really need your help."

CHAPTER EIGHT

A long few seconds pass.

"Okay," I say. "What do you need?"

Karen sags with relief. "Really?"

"Sure. Valkyrja was nice to me." I gesture at her wings. "And you're obviously not lying about being family."

Her eyes flick away from me for a moment. "…Yeah. Well. Thank you anyhow."

"Don't worry about it. So what do you need my help for?"

Karen fidgets with her fingers, doesn't meet my gaze. "Um… do you have anything to eat?"

I nod. "Yeah, I'll put a pizza in the oven." I walk past her and into the kitchen. The stove is of course one of those ultramodern pieces with more buttons on it than Apollo 11, but it's not hyper-tech, just overly fancy. I don't know what half of them do, but after weeks of trial and error I have figured out preheating.

"Thank you," she says quietly. "I know it's a lot to ask, especially when I just showed up here and—"

"Don't worry about it. I've been where you are." It feels weird to say I was homeless. That only lasted for one night. Technically I still meet the definition since Doc is just letting me crash with her, but it seems dramatic to try and say I'm full-on homeless. But Karen obviously has nowhere else to go; her cheeks are slightly hollow and she's having trouble focusing her gaze.

"I kind of doubt that," she says.

I look up. "Well, maybe not as long as you, but I got kicked out—"

"Uh, not that," she says, blushing. "Never mind. Thank you. Really."

"All right. So. Uh, I don't mean to be rude, but when was the last time you had a shower?"

"Two weeks. I think. It's getting hard to keep track of time."

"This will take some time to bake. Why don't you go get washed up? The bathroom is down that hall and to the left. Guest towels are in the cupboard to the lower right of the sink."

"Thanks," she says quietly. Karen picks up her book and heads into the bathroom. A few moments later, the shower turns on.

Valkyrja never mentioned a daughter. Not that we talked very many times before she was killed, but it surprises me she had a daughter around my age walking around and never mentioned it. Or that someone living her lifestyle wouldn't have a life insurance policy or something set up to take care of her kid when she was gone. Well, I'm sure Karen will explain. Valkyrja wasn't the kind of person to hurt her own child.

While Karen is in the shower, I go into my room, shut the door, and strip out of my dirty uniform.

My supersuit is a surprisingly thin, surprisingly heavy gel computer matrix sandwiched between an underlayer with all sorts of comfort and health functions and an outer layer that changes color, insulates against heat and electricity, and serves as armor. Not armor for me; I don't need it. Armor for the rest of the suit. Gel computers are tough, but not invincible, and I lose a lot of my best support functions if the computer goes down. For example, the fight against Mr. Armageddon got about twice as hard once my satellite phone was knocked out of commission.

Over where the suit covers my chest there are a few black scorch marks where the lightning and fire hit me. I drop the suit on its charging pad in the corner of my room and open my closet to pull out the spare. It can take up to 48 hours for the self-repair functions to fix everything, so I've started keeping more than one around, just in case. I hang the fresh suit on the hook near my door and then strip off my underwear, which is all specialized microfiber stuff designed especially for wearing under my suit to make sure there's no rubbing or chafing or anything. Believe it or not, that's the one thing my skin is still all too human about.

I throw on some normal panties and a bra, and a gray t-shirt and blue shorts over that, then head back out into the apartment. I take a seat in the living room, click some music on from the hidden speakers, and wait for Karen to finish her shower.

• • •

Karen attacks her food like it kicked her dog. My own appetite is stronger than normal after the flight up from Antarctica, and between us we murder the pizza in record time. Then we're sitting in the living room, plates set aside, and she's obviously working herself up to saying something.

"Are you feeling better?" I ask.

"Yes, thank you." She twists her fingers through her hair, which lies damp and heavy down the front of her shoulder. "Um, yeah, so, anyway. I kinda need your help with something."

"What is it?"

"Uh, shit, this is hard to explain. So. Crap. So, uh, this spring my wings grew in overnight."

"That must have been an interesting morning."

"Yeeeah. 'Interesting.' We didn't know what was happening. The doctors couldn't find anything wrong with me. We thought it was just a random mutation or something. Before I learned how to fly with them, we were considering amputating them. Then the dreams started, these really vivid dreams about places I've never been to and people I've never met. But then I'd see something on the news or in a book about them, and I'd realize they were true."

Karen stops. Opens her mouth again, closes it. Finally, she says in a shaking voice, "Do you have any liquor?"

"Ah, that seems like a bad idea."

"But do you?"

"I mean, well, Doc does. But—"

"Please." Her fingers gnarl into fists. "She's loudest when I'm sober. This is Hell."

It's probably a bad idea, but I'm not stern enough to say no. Karen is desperate in a way I haven't felt since I transitioned. Before I can think of a good reason to say no, I'm standing up to get her a drink. Doc doesn't bother to hide her liquor or lock it up.

I set the bottle and a glass down in front of Karen, and she unscrews the cap and pours herself a brimming glass of rum. She drinks half the glass like Kool-Aid, grimaces, almost chokes.

"So the dreams got worse," she says, voice rough. "And then I started having them when I was awake too. I started remembering what New Port looked like in the '60s, or what New England was like before the Revolution. I can remember the smell of a log fort at the head of a fjord from eight hundred years ago. Eventually I figured out that these were coming from Valkyrja. My wings grew in the night she died. It didn't make any sense." She takes another long drink. Karen looks at me with hollow eyes and says, "And then I remembered giving myself up for adoption. Like, it was *my* memory. But it isn't. I can recognize the baby. I can recognize myself in the memory. That's how I found out who my birth mother was."

"Oh. Oh shit," I say.

"My parents never hid from me that I was adopted," she says quietly. "But they said they got me from an agency. I can remember now that it didn't really go down that way. Valkyrja hand-picked my parents, and tried to warn them this might happen, but they didn't listen. They said I was normal. That lots of kids were adopted and it doesn't matter." Karen's face twists with sudden fury and she leaps to her feet, throws the half-full glass straight out the patio door, over the balcony, into the night sky. The way it was flying, it looks like it won't hit the ground for miles. "*Well you were wrong about that, weren't you!*" she shouts after it.

I rise and put my hand on her shoulder. "Hey, hey. It's all right, okay? I'll help you," I say. "Getting powers is…it's weird. I'll walk you through it."

"You don't understand!" says Karen, shrugging away from me. "I've got her memories. And her mother's memories, and *her* mother's memories. All of them. All the way back to the beginning. More of them every day."

"And that's…that's bad?"

"Yes, it's fucking bad!" shouts Karen. "Memory isn't what we remember, it's who we *are*. The way we think, what we want, our opinions. Everything. I'm sixteen. She was *twelve hundred*. I don't—I can't compete with that!" She begins to pace, hugging herself tight. "Her memories are changing me, making me think thoughts that aren't mine. It's getting harder and harder to remember what's me and what's her. Keeping track of myself is like squirting an eyedropper full of dye into a swimming pool. I see a dog and I remember a German Shepard I once had, but it's not me, it's my fucking *great-grandmother* who had a dog."

Karen sinks back down onto the couch. Her wings fold protectively around her shoulders. "Valkyrja wants to come back from the dead, and she'll kill me to do it."

"She…" I have to fight not to stammer. "Valkyrja wouldn't…" Karen sets her jaw, eyes daring me to finish that sentence. "Okay. Okay, that sucks. What can I do to help?"

Karen's wings relax. "You're stronger than the other Dreadnoughts. You can do things they couldn't. You told me—" she flinches "—told *her*, I mean, that you could see…what did you call it, the lattice? And tug on it?"

"Yeah, the lattice. It's sort of the backside of reality."

Karen nods. "I want you to see if you can reach into my head and pull this…*thing* out."

I sit down across from her. "Karen, I can try, but—"

She nods sharply. "Good. Try."

"I've never done anything like this and—"

"I've got nothing to lose," says Karen.

"Yes, you do, is what I'm trying to say. I've healed my body with the lattice, but only at the cost of creating other injuries. If I pull something out of your head, it might give you brain damage."

Karen's wings flare, her fists clench. "This *is* brain damage! She's eating me!"

"Calm down," I say, trying to sound placating. "I'll help you. I just…we're going to do this slow, okay? We might not get it all on the first try. I'm not going to be responsible for turning you into a vegetable."

She takes a deep breath. "Okay. Please. Please, can we do it now? I'm not sure how much longer I can keep hold of myself."

"Yeah, come here." I scoot forward on my seat, pull the chair a little closer to her. She leans forward on the couch. I roll my shoulders, take deep breaths. There are tricks I've learned to make the lattice "cleaner," more precise in my head. I rub my hands together and blow out a long breath. When I shut my eyes and hold my hands out to either side of her head, the hard white net of light and heat leaps into focus. Everything in the Universe—*everything*—shows up in the lattice, represented in my mind's eye as an infinitely complex grid of glowing white strings, endlessly dense with more detail unfolding the closer I look. Her blood squirts through the arteries and back down through the veins. She swallows, and I watch every muscle and fold of tissue flex and release. Her eyes are shut, and her retinas quiet down, cones and rods no longer firing information at the optic nerves.

And behind and above her eyes, her brain.

There are two things I never get tired of looking at. The stars from low orbit and human brains. Once you're above the atmosphere, the stars are a brilliant spray of millions and millions of points of light. It's hard to believe how many of them there are until you get up there and *see* them. You can sort of get a feel for this if you head into the deep woods on a cold, still night, but that's nothing compared to the view you get from orbit.

Brains, viewed through the lattice, give me that same kick of awe. The squishy stuff inside your skull is a densely complicated biological computer. Millions of cells, billions of connections. Nerve endings fire in waves, each thought traced in swirling wet fractals. Every one of us has a miracle wrapped up inside our heads.

Sometimes I don't even sleep at night, I just lie down, close my eyes, and look at my own brain for hours until it's time to get back up.

Karen's brain is beautiful. A compact, folded-up galaxy swirling with energy and light, a bundle of heat and potential. But there's something else here too. It's almost like there's a second pattern, laid over and alongside the first. It definitely feels like a different entity. Denser. Colder. As I watch, two of the strings from the second pattern get tangled with a string from the first. There's a flash of light and heat, and then I can't tell where one pattern is and another begins.

"I can see it," I say. "It's uh, it's tangled up in there."

"Get it out, get it out!"

"Hold on, this might be painful…"

I've been practicing with the lattice for months. The first time I directly grabbed the strings of reality and pulled them in a new direction, I hurt myself badly. Since then, I've started small, worked on delicacy and control. Now I can be very subtle when I have time to put effort into it. But this…this is something way beyond anything I've ever tried. Slowly, I extend my senses until I can feel one of the strings of her pattern. It seems to slide through my fingers, vibrate in my chest. When I have a good grip, I reach for a string from the other pattern, the interloper. Gently, I begin to pull them apart, let them relax, pull again, let them relax. One by one, the patterns begin to pull away from each other, threads parting with bursts of light.

Karen hisses, clenches.

"Are you okay?"

"Keep going," she says.

"I want you to tell me if it gets too painful."

She grunts out a yes, which turns into a whimper.

Little by little I separate the two patterns until I come to a big tangle of these strings, wrapped in and around Karen's mind. I search and I search, but there's no easy way to undo these knots.

"Can you tell if it is working?" I ask.

"I…I don't know. I think so. There are…I can't…yes. Keep going."

"All right. I think this next part is really going to suck; are you sure you want me to—"

"Yes!" she practically screams. "Just do it!"

With another deep breath to steady myself, I try to work the bundle loose, separate it out into its individual strands. The patterns start to peel away from each other with pops of heat. Karen hisses and clenches and then begins to scream.

I slam out of her head as fast as I can. "Okay, that's enough, no more tonight."

"No, wait…" Karen reaches out for me and almost falls on her face before I catch her. "We have…we have to keep going." Her left wing spasms.

"And we will, but not right now. You need to rest."

"Please," she mutters into my chest.

"I think I got some of it," I say as I set her back on the couch. "Why don't you see if you're missing any of Valkyrja's memories?"

Karen closes her bloodshot eyes and wraps her wings around herself. After a moment, a quiet smile softens her face. "Yes, I can't remember what Sveldholt's main hall looked like anymore. I know that I did have that memory, but it's gone now." She opens her eyes, and it's like she's a different person, happy and free. "Thank you. I feel…more like myself."

A memory comes back to me. Valkyrja approaching me on the roof of Legion Tower. She knew my father was—and this has taken me months to be able to say, even to myself—she knew he was abusing me. She offered to help me, but I was too scared to take her up on it. And now here's her ghost trying to murder her own daughter. Her daughter who she abandoned. We didn't know each other very long. Looks like I didn't really know her at all. I stand up, suddenly uncomfortable.

"Do you want some aspirin?" I ask, trying to keep the disquiet off my face.

Karen chuckles. "Yeah, that'd be pretty cool. Thanks."

When I return from the bathroom with the medicine, Karen is swigging rum straight from the bottle.

"Hey, uh, look I just flew up from Antarctica and got my ass kicked by a blackcape tonight," I say. "I sorta want to conk out. Do you want me to show you the guest room?"

"Sure, sure," says Karen.

She screws the cap back onto the rum. A good third of the bottle has disappeared. Doc is going to kill me. I take Karen into the hallway outside Doc's main condo, show her to the one we've got set up as guest rooms.

"The interior doors are all unlocked, except for that one over there. Doctor Impossible's sealed it with some pretty nasty hyper-tech. Don't try to go in there. Seriously. The elevator is keyed to our thumbprints, and the fire doors all lock behind you, so if you leave you'll need to fly up to get back in."

Karen nods. "Right. Hey, Danielle, thank you. I mean it." She wraps me in a sloppy hug. "I thought I was going to die."

"I'm not going to let her hurt you, Karen. I promise."

The next morning, I'm yanked out of a nightmare by the pounding at my door. For a brief, horrible moment I forget I don't live with my parents anymore, and I think my father has come to scream at me. But no, that part of my life is done. He can't get to me anymore. My hair is soaked through with night sweat again.

I float out of bed and open my door to find Karen standing there, barely holding back the panic.

"They're back," she says with a trembling voice. "All of the memories we killed, they're back, and I think they're even stronger now."

CHAPTER NINE

"I'm going to die."

"You're not going to die."

"I'm so fucking dead."

"No, you're not. Pass the syrup."

Karen hands me the warm plastic jug of syrup. "This is taking too long. You said you had a plan."

"Mhmm, I do," I mumble around a big bite of waffle. We're sitting at the breakfast table, demolishing a stack of waffles. Doc's pug Guts is camped under my seat, waiting to dart in and claim any fallen morsels. "We're gonna go see a friend of mine who does magic. If he can't help us, I think he'll know where to look. But it might take some time, so I need you to be as much yourself as we can get you to be, and I don't know about you, but I have a hard time focusing when I'm starving."

"I guess," Karen says quietly. Then she takes an enormous bite. "Tell me about you. What were you like before, you know, *this*?"

"Uh," she says. Chews for a moment, swallows. "I play saxophone. I'm leader of the school's jazz band. Or was, anyhow."

"Cool. What else?"

"Um. I'm a big math nerd."

"Really? I hate math."

"It's not so bad," she says between bites. The edge of panic that's been behind her voice all morning starts to fade. "The way they teach it is stupid and pointless."

"I'll take your word for it. So the maid-bot should have done laundry overnight. Are your clothes clean?"

"Yes. Thank you." Karen pulls the last waffle onto her plate. Her clothes may be clean, but they're still worn after what I'm guessing must have been a few months on the street. Her polo shirt is one of those corporate shirts you can find in a thrift store, with a big crown over her breast pocket—even after being washed, there's a dark stain on one of the cuffs, and the collar is frayed at one end.

"Sure thing. Are you going to want more, or is that going to be enough?" I ask.

"This will be fine, thank you," she says quietly.

"It's going to be okay," I tell her.

Her smile is drawn. "All right, sure. Thank you. I feel a little better now. More like myself."

We finish breakfast and push the plates aside. The maid-bots will take care of everything. (Living with a mad scientist: it doesn't suck.)

"I called Charlie, and he said he'll be waiting for us. Do you want to try and do this incognito, or should I bring my suit?"

She shrugs. "Whichever way is faster."

"Okay, wait here a moment, I've got to get dressed."

A couple minutes later, I'm in full Dreadnought regalia, my white and blue bodyglove snug all the way up to the top of my neck. Karen is waiting for me on the balcony, her back turned, looking out at the city. Her wings are folded, but for the first time this morning they don't look like they're clamped down with tension.

The clouds blew away overnight, and it's one of those hard winter skies that lets you see for miles. The downtown towers glitter in the sun. A blimp is circling the stadium.

"Charlie likes to hang out at a used bookstore at the edge of town," I say. "We can get there in a few minutes, if you're okay with flying."

"Yes, I can fly," she says. She turns to me. "You've grown into your role, Danielle. I'm glad."

The bottom falls out of my stomach; I can *see* Valkyrja behind her face. The twinkle in the eyes. The quiet, understanding smile. "Uh—"

Karen goes pale, claps her hands to her mouth. After a moment, she hisses, "Do you see what it's like? She's *eating* me!"

"Let's go. Right now."

I step onto a stool, then push off of the handrail and shoot up into the sky. A moment later, Karen spreads her wings, pumps once, twice, and then they snap taut, surrounded in a pale nimbus of power.

"This way!" I shout over the wind, banking hard toward the edge of town. Karen catches up to me, and a moment later pulls ahead. In a matter of seconds we're at the threshold of the sound barrier. The city whips by beneath us, just a few hundred feet distant. As we near the bookstore, I reach out to tap her shoulder, and point. We spiral out of the air and skid to a stop on the roof.

Karen pulls her wings in tight and hugs herself. "So he should be here, right?"

"Yeah." The roof access door doesn't budge when I try it. "Shit, they locked it again. Hold on, I have to find the key. They said they'd leave one around here somewhere..."

"It's on top of the door frame, near the left," she says. She's right. I look at her, confused. "I can sense where things that open the way are," she explains, voice tight, face blank. "It's...one of those things she did."

"Oh."

"Also people who are about to die, and any serious violence within a hundred miles. Plus ravens, swans, horses, and alcohol. Technically, it's not a hundred miles, it's twenty-seven leagues."

I point at the door. "Let's go get Charlie."

"Yes. Let's."

The stairwell is dark inside. It was only used by the occasional maintenance guy coming up to take a look at the air conditioner until I started dropping in a lot. The owners don't mind me traipsing through the store in my uniform, since it's a bit of that distinctive New Port local flavor that's so important for an independent bookstore trying to stay afloat. We step out of the stairwell and pass through a small office area blocked off by bookshelves, and then on to the main sales floor itself. The shelves here reach all the way to the ceiling, with wheeled ladders in each aisle to access the top shelves. A shelf-stocker looks up as we pass through her aisle.

"Hi, Dreadnought."

"Hi, Lucy. Is Charlie here?"

She nods. "Yeah, he's in the rare books room." And then, with dexterity and a command of throwing objects that is too smooth to be natural, she tosses four books in a row up onto the top shelf. They land neatly one after the other, spines out, perfectly placed. Lucy turns, grabs another armful, and flicks them up one by one with a careless snapping of her wrist.

That's the other reason they don't mind me coming through here: Raven's Used Books is staffed almost entirely by metahumans. They don't advertise it, but they understand what it's like to have powers and be gawked at because of it. Here, at least, I'm almost normal, and sometimes I need that more than I'd like to admit. Most people with superpowers don't want to be superheroes or supervillains. Most of them just want normal lives, and while it's hard to understand why anyone would trade what I do for stocking shelves, I am grateful that there's a place where it's not a big deal that I enter through the rooftop door. Karen is not so blasé. Being superhuman is still new to her, I remind myself, and she tightens up, begins to stare.

The rare books room is a walled-off section of the top floor with chest-high dividers of glossy old wood looking in on a spread of polished oak tables and an eclectic collection of chairs. Charlie is in his usual spot near a window, hunched down behind a tower of ratty old leather books. He's Calamity's ex-boyfriend, a skinny black kid who tried out the superhero gig for a few months and decided he wasn't overly fond of running around on rain-slick rooftops hoping not to get shot by drug dealers. He's much happier skulking about what he ominously refers to as his sanctum, occasionally emerging into the light of day to do research or test his new projects. He looks up as we enter.

"Hey, Dreadnought." Charlie and I met before I became

Dreadnought, but he's hung out with enough capes that he knows to use my supranym in front of someone he doesn't know. Yes, even though my identity is not a secret. It's a subculture thing. "I was just getting settled. What's up?"

"Charlie, this is Karen. Karen, this is Charlie. Karen is Valkyrja's daughter."

Charlie's eyebrows jump up. "I wasn't aware she had kids."

"Yes. It turns out I'm half-Korean, half-Scandinavian death goddess. Honestly, I'm as surprised as you," says Karen with an edge in her voice. And then a moment later, with sinking shoulders, "I'm sorry, I'm being a bitch right now."

Charlie stands and holds out his hand. "Don't worry about it. I'm pleased to meet you." After a moment, Karen shakes it. "I'm sorry that your mom died," says Charlie.

Karen snorts. "I'm not. Fuck that bitch. I just wish she'd leave me out of it."

Charlie glances at me like, *who is this crazy chick and why did you drag me out to meet her?*

"That's sort of the problem we're hoping you can help us with. When Valkyrja died, all her powers and memories got passed on to her daughter." I explain what's happening so Karen won't have to go over it all again.

"That sucks," says Charlie when I'm done.

Karen smiles thinly. "Yes. Yes it does."

"So like...*all* of her memories? There are some questions I'd have loved to ask her, but she wasn't in a really great mood the last time we spoke." Apparently Charlie once almost accidentally summoned a demon into Victory Park downtown. Valkyrja and Graywytch stopped things before they got out of hand, and he doesn't like to talk about the incident much.

"I'd really rather not, if it's all the same to you," says Karen.

"Ah. Right. Sorry." Charlie goes back over to his seat and closes the book he was reading. "Well, I am not super versed in mind-altering magic. That stuff is hard to find texts about since most of it gets into really forbidden territory. The Council of Avalon—that's the international body governing magic and—"

"I know what the Council of Avalon is," says Karen. Her arms are crossed over her chest, and her fingers tighten where they are squeezing her biceps. "My birth mother was—never mind. Can you help me or not?"

Charlie nods. "I think so. I mean, I can give it a shot, at least. The charms against intrusion, those at least are easy to come by." He goes over to a shelf in the corner of the room. It has a glass door with a lock, and I'm not surprised when he pulls out a key and unlocks it. Charlie spends so much money here, they'd probably give him a key to the building if he asked them to. "If a basic charm doesn't help, we could probably explode it into a full thaumaturgical grid and recompile the spell into something more customized for you." He pulls a few leather books off the shelf. "Do you have anything precious with you?"

Karen nods and reaches into her shirt to pull out a round locket. "This is a thumb drive. It's got a video on it of the first time I led my jazz band in concert." Karen blushes deeply. "I, uh, I keep it around for when I'm scared I can't do anything right."

Charlie smiles. "That's perfect. We can start with the basic charm right away. Dreadnought, do you want to stick around? This might take some time."

I shrug. The convention was important to me. It sits hot and sour in my gut that I can't go back, but that choice was taken out of my hands the moment Graywytch refused to pick up the phone. It helps to remind myself that we had only planned on attending the first two days before we returned home for some family business. At least, I tell myself it helps. "I've got nowhere to be."

So we dig in and research. After about an hour, Charlie says he's ready to try the charm on Karen, but it doesn't seem to do anything one way or the other. If anything, this only makes Charlie more excited about the project, because it means he gets to put in a request to the Secret Archive, which I gather is something of an invite-only library he's got a membership with. At one point he mentions offhand that there's a copy of a book he could use in the occult section of Powell's in Bridgeton, so I pop down to Oregon at Mach 1 and buy it for him. (It's nice being able to drop a thousand dollars on a book without blinking. Being a superhero with a municipal contract is great work if you can get it.) As the sun goes down, the manager at Raven's tells us they're closing, so we gather up our things and move over to Charlie's house. He makes some awkward introductions to his parents and we set up camp in his attic bedroom.

Charlie is as happy as a pig in shit to be tackling a new problem. Karen is less enthusiastic. I want to help, but there's not really much I can do. As much as Karen hates to access Valkyrja's memories, she knows more about magic than I ever will. She probably knows more about it than Charlie, to be honest, and that's half the reason he's so excited. He seems to think that if he can figure out a way to keep Karen's mind intact, she'll be able to access her birth mother's memories on demand and be his personal encyclopedia of the occult.

Wizards tend to be hopeless optimists. It's the only reason they do such a dangerous job.

Charlie's mom comes up to ask if we'll be staying the night, and I guess we are since we all say yes, and I offer to pay for the pizza. About six liters of soda later, the sky starts turning pale, and I sit up with a jolt from the pillow nest I've constructed against the side of Charlie's bed.

"What time is it?"

"Like six in the morning, why?"

"Shit!" I haul myself to my feet and go to open Charlie's window. "I've got a court date in less than an hour. Sorry, guys, I gotta bail."

"What are you going to court for?" asks Karen. She looks a little dim around the edges, but seems to be weathering the all-nighter better than Charlie, whose eyes are open out of pure stubbornness.

I open the window and get ready to take off. "Nothing important, I'm just finalizing my divorce with my parents."

CHAPTER TEN

So there's this thing called an emancipated minor, and I really want to be one. It's not *technically* a divorce, but it's basically a divorce. My parents go one way. I go the other (at Mach 3). You see, my father is a world-class shithead. He thinks that because he never laid a hand on me, what he was doing wasn't abuse. Like it's normal for a kid to invent reasons to stay away from home. Or to be scared to speak up for herself and to think she's a failure before she's even really started life. Like it's okay to be surprised to learn that other families don't treat lies and denial like currency. Like it's not a problem that his daughter used to have daydreams about him dying suddenly, peacefully in his sleep.

He was a looming ogre who never found a topic he wasn't willing to scream at me about, and until this past year I didn't even know how bad it was because I didn't know what it was like to live in a house without shouting, without the fear that at any moment he could explode into the room, red-faced and flinging spittle.

And Mom just let it happen. For fifteen years, she betrayed me to him over and over again. I've never bought that bullshit about a mother's love being stronger than anything, not for an instant. It's not a delusion I could afford.

When you get right down to it, this family *needs* a divorce. We've needed one for years, and if she won't do it, then I will. They want to stay together, they're welcome to try, but I'm done being an accessory for her martyrdom act, both the justification for and the instrument of her poisonous denial about the man that she married.

New Port Superior Courthouse is a deco-brutalist monstrosity squatting like a calcified turd downtown. You've got City Hall— soaring Greek columns in white limestone—on one side of the block. On the other side, you've got the stern gothic lines of the police station, Atlas straining with the globe on his shoulders above the main entrance. Then between them, you've got the courthouse, which looks like a Soviet machine gun bunker tried to dress up for company. Naked brown cement with holes in it every two yards and parallel seams of overflow from where the molds were set up. Every window is tall and narrow, with iron shutters like they're expecting a riot at any moment.

• • •

I take a cab to my court appointment. The case is being handled as Jane Doe v. Jane and John Doe so it doesn't get in all the papers, and it would kind of give things away if I showed up in my cape and bodyglove. Instead, I'm wearing a baggy sweatshirt with my hood up and a brunette wig. I've got sunglasses too, but honestly at that point I might as well get Kinetiq to follow me around projecting a neon sign above my head that says DO NOT PAY ATTENTION TO THIS OSTENTATIOUSLY ANONYMOUS YOUNG WOMAN, so they stay folded up in my pocket.

There's a bit of a media scrum on the front steps when I get there, but I don't think anything of it at first. Every time a meta-human gets arraigned, the media is there to cover it. Not because people with superpowers getting arrested is super rare or anything, but more because there's always the chance he'll turn out to be a really nasty supervillain later, and none of the news stations want to be left out on having B-roll footage of his First! Public! Appearance! when it's time to interrupt *The Simpsons* with breaking news or whatever.

I'm about halfway up the stairs when someone shouts out a sentence that turns my blood to icy slush. "There she is!" and here comes the stampede. Between one flight of stairs and the next, I am mobbed by pretty much every news outfit in town. Shit. My hearing starts in like ten minutes; I really do not have time to play twenty questions with the field correspondents. And there is no fucking way I want any of them to figure out that I'm here for family court, not a criminal hearing. Maybe the sunglasses would have been worth a shot after all.

Okay, okay, I've trained for this. I can handle this. I reach into my memory and pull out the basic brushoff line: "I'm not going to comment on any ongoing case." Let them jump to the obvious conclusion—that I'm here to testify against Crenshaw. I'm in and out of this place like once a week due to my work with the cops, so they'll figure—

"Dreadnought, do you have anything to say about your father's allegations that Doctor Impossible is manipulating you to gain access to your municipal hero funding?"

The gears in my head seize up. My mouth sort of flaps up and down while I try to deal with the world crumbling beneath my feet.

"*What?*"

Diane from *Action News Team Five* shoves her mic in front of my mouth and says, "Your father is alleging that you are not psychologically competent to be living without your family and that Doctor Impossible is taking advantage of you to further fund her own operations. How do you respond to these allegations?"

Hairs up and down my spine stand up. "I—I don't—no comment! Okay? No comment!"

I try to push my way up the steps, but I'm capped in by a tight phalanx of cameras and boom mics. "Get out of my way," I tell them, but the reporters keep shouting questions at me, pressing in, mics in my face, squeezing me tight, pushing me down. *Why is your family broken, Danny?* My chest is tight. "Let me through." I can't breathe. *What's wrong with you, Danny?* "I need to get through here." *Are you still a freak, Danny?* I can't breathe; there's something wrong with my chest. Need to leave. Need to get out of there. *Is he right about you, Danny?* "Move." *Are you saying you're not crazy?*

Aren't you a freak, though? They're shouting, they're shouting and they're close and I need to leave—

"I SAID GET OUT OF MY WAY!" As the echo off the front of the courthouse slaps the air, the press scrum seems to remember that I can pulp them anytime I please. The ones in front of me take a shaken step back, and that's all the opening I need to power up the steps. I'm ten steps up and twenty feet inside the building before the first camera hits the ground.

My heart is slamming in my temples as I skid to a stop. Instant regret stabs me. You can *fly*, idiot! My cheeks are scalding as I watch the two or three news crews who didn't go tumbling immediately start narrating back to the station what's happened. Shit, I hope none of them are hurt. Cecilia is going to kill—

Wait, why am I learning this from them and not her? I fumble my phone out of my pocket and dial Cecilia. It goes straight to voicemail. Fine. Whatever. Turning away from the doors, I wave at the bailiffs with a tight-lipped smile to reassure them that the brief display of superpowers in the front lobby is no reason to break out the assault rifles quite yet. There are a few other people here on court business waiting at the security line, and they stare at me with wide eyes. I step into the back of the line. The inside of the courthouse is just as dreary and depressing as the outside, stopping just shy of dripping pipes and flickering bulbs territory.

After a moment, the bailiffs start processing people through the checkpoint again. When it's my turn, the bailiff working the metal detector smirks and says, "Reporters, huh?"

It's not funny, but I'm so grateful to him that I laugh way harder than is cool. Danielle Tozer, Queen of Social Catastrophes, that's me. Once they're sure I'm not carrying anything as harmless as a handgun or a pipe bomb, they let me through, and I jog to get to my assigned courtroom in time.

Where, wonder of wonder, miracle of miracles, I find more reporters gathered outside. It looks as if every newspaper and every stringer in the country has someone waiting for me, and when I show up, it's like I went diving in a shark tank while wearing a meat bikini.

"No comment!" I bellow at them as I march on the doors to the courtroom. Print reporters, at least, have some semblance of manners and don't mob me quite so badly. I mean, they still shoot lots of questions at me even though I just said no comment, but there isn't the jostling, the shoving, the sense that they're going to pin me down and pull answers out with heated tongs. I get into the courtroom, and shut the door firmly. This is one of those dingy basement cubbies with a low ceiling and not much audience seating. The audience's chairs sit empty and silent. Family court is closed to the public, which is a blessing I am thankful for every day.

Cecilia is already at the plaintiff's table, and she rises when she sees me. The long flight up from Antarctica last night would probably require a day of rest for anyone else, but like so many other people who keep it quiet, Cecilia is metahuman. She doesn't get tired. Ever.

"Sorry I'm late, but what the hell is going on?" I whisper when I get close. "Why are there reporters everywhere?"

"I don't know," says Cecilia. "I've been trying to reach you for an hour, but my phone is dead."

"You couldn't borrow someone else's?" I ask, more waspish than I really mean to be.

"Your number kept kicking back as disconnected," says Cecilia. "When I tried texting you my phone bricked, so I thought it was a software issue, but the payphone kept dropping the call. I take it Doctor Impossible wasn't able to get through to you?" Doc hadn't been there when I went home to change into my civvies. I shake my head. "Well, that's unfortunate. She said she'd be looking into what was causing the problem. I'm sorry you walked into this blind. Are you okay?"

My cheeks go warm again. "I guess I'm all right."

"Good."

"We, uh, we might have a media problem to deal with after this is over," I mumble.

Cecilia pinches the bridge of her nose. "Can you at least promise me there are no broken bones in play?"

"Uh, well there *might* not be," I say, trying to sound like that's totally within acceptable parameters.

"All right. One crisis at a time." She gestures for me to sit, and we put our heads together. "If what I'm hearing from the reporters is right," says Cecilia, "your parents are about-facing and contesting the petition after all. We're in for a fight now, and this is going to get messy. My guess is they want to put your paychecks into a trust that they can access. It's asset stripping, as naked as can be, but the law may support their claim."

"Shit." I glance over at the respondents' table. Nobody is there yet.

"Quite," says Cecilia softly. "Now, I need you to be ready to hear some fairly awful stuff. These things can be brutal, far worse than any criminal trial you've been to. And the galling part is that the things they'll say will all be prefaced with the excuse that it's in your best interest. Remember what I taught you: no reactions, none. If you need to leave, just step out and head directly to the bathroom. Stay there as long as you need to, but don't speak to anyone. Can you do that for me?"

"Yes, I think I can."

"You *think* you can, or you can?" asks Cecilia.

"I can."

"Good. Remember that you're Dreadnought. They can never take that from you, but you can give it away if you're careless."

I nod. That's what we've said from day one. It helps to hear. "I'll remember."

"Now, tell me about what happened out there."

My shoulders sink. "The cameras mobbed me. I wasn't ready. They knew more about the case than I did, and...I panicked. I'm sorry."

"What did you do?"

"I...I ran. Some people got knocked down. I mean, it's not like I punched any—"

"Okay, good. That would be very bad. If people fell over, we can work that. Don't worry."

"Good. Good."

"Who are you?"

"I'm Dreadnought," I say again, and even start to feel it.

"We're ready."

I nod. We're ready. We can do this.

Shit. I'm not ready. I can't do this.

I've fought the worst of the worst. Heavyweights like Utopia, Acid Andy, and Mr. Armageddon. I've fought metahumans, hyper-tech, wizards, and kaiju. I've been shot with cannons and stabbed with vibroblades. I've been scalded, crushed, torched, and frozen. I've had broken bones and chemical burns, and I've spit out so many shattered teeth I know exactly how long it takes each one to grow back.

I'm not saying this to puff myself up, but let's be clear: I don't back down from fights. Ever. I don't care who you are or what you can do. I don't care how much I'm outnumbered or how badly I'm hurt. You bring the fight to me, and I'll bring it right back to you twice as hard, and I will make you *regret* the day you thought you were hard enough to take on Dreadnought. I'm not just unde-feated in personal combat; I am *undefeatable*. Nobody wins against me. Nobody.

And right now, all of that matters about as much as a dog's wet fart.

I have never been this freaked out in battle before. On a reg-ular basis, people try to murder me, and I laugh it off. But now, I'm that scared little girl again, and there's nothing I can do. This hearing was hard enough when it was secret. With the circus wait-ing outside, I might last half an hour before I need to go to the bathroom and lock myself in a stall. The next few hours are going to be miserable. My shoulders pull themselves in tight. I take the wig off my head and shove it under the table. I don't feel much like Dreadnought right now.

The door opens, and I jump. My parents enter the courtroom.

As with all the other hearings, I only see them out of the corner of my eye, my gaze locked forward. Cecilia straightens up next to me, and I glance over at her.

"They've got a lawyer," she says, and now I do look. Shit, they've got a lawyer. He's middle-aged, sort of a ridiculously handsome dude with silver temples and a thousand-dollar suit. They wouldn't cast this guy as a lawyer on TV because he looks too much like what he is. And then, by accident, I look at my parents.

I almost don't recognize them. In the last nine months, my mother has gained all the weight my father has lost. Their eyes fasten onto me. My father's eyes have the familiar cold anger that only people who've lived with him can recognize. My mother has an expression I can't—or won't—read clearly. She opens her mouth, and I tear my eyes away, very deliberately show them the side of my face and nothing more. Under the table, the wig has already been torn to ratty pieces as I wind the hairs around my fingers.

The judge comes in and the bailiff calls the court to order. The preliminaries hum along, lots of arcane introductions and curiously stilted language.

Then the judge turns to my parents' lawyer and says, "Mr. Trauth, I'm surprised to see you in here. It is rare that a firm takes a pro bono case on behalf of the respondents in this sort of situation."

Trauth even sounds too much like a lawyer when he says, "My firm believes in taking the side of the case that, in our estimation, most benefits the child, even if that is at the respondents' table."

Go fuck yourself is on the tip of my tongue, but Cecilia lays a hand on my wrist and I let the moment pass.

The judge nods and laces his fingers in front of him. "And tell me, did you have anything to do with our little media powwow this morning?"

"Of course not, Your Honor," says Trauth. "We were just as surprised to learn that Ms. Tozer had been identified in the press as you are."

Cecilia stands. "If I may, Your Honor?"

"You may."

She looks at Trauth. "Do you really expect us to believe that you swooped in to represent her parents, reversed their decision not to appeal the prior motion, submitted a new petition on their behalf earlier this morning, and this all just *happened* to take place around the time every news outfit in the city learned who Jane Doe was?"

"My clients are in the Federal Witness Protection Program, and have only flown into town from their safehouse for this hearing; of course I wouldn't compromise their safety by publicizing the event." Trauth says. He doesn't seem flapped. "If you wish to allege misconduct on the part of my office, I hope you've got more than vague implications to back it up."

"That's enough," says the judge. "Mr. Trauth, since you've submitted the latest documents, let's start with you…"

And the hearing has finally begun. I immediately start trying to tune out. God, it used to be so easy. I could just flip a switch and go blank inside. There's got to be something else I can think about. Something I can hide behind.

Cecilia's phone is still on the table. It's still bricked. My eyes are stuck on it. How'd it die? Why didn't I get anyone's calls? Shit, at the very least I should have gotten a notification that Doc's tilt-engine had landed at her aerodrome on the outskirts of town—I usually get automatic text alerts whenever her jet arrives or departs, and only now do I realize that I never received them. Professor Gothic's words come back to me: *You've got enemies you won't recognize until they attack.*

One missed call is unfortunate. Two is a coincidence. Three is enemy action.

The more I think about it, the more I'm sure that this is asymmetric warfare. The enemy—whoever they are—knows it's a fast trip to the hospital to bring the fight to me in person, so they're trying to hit me here. But who would want to, and how would they do it? More to the point, how would they even know about—

Graywytch.

She knows who my parents are. She knew I hadn't told them

about being Dreadnought's successor—it wouldn't be too much of a leap for her to guess we weren't a happy home. Hell, after she outed me, she might have gone invisible and stayed to watch the fireworks for all I know. She could know I was petitioning to get emancipated and set this up—and I mean all of it, the reporters, Trauth, everything—to screw with me. But why?

The answer comes to me immediately: she's a TERF—a Trans-Exclusionary Radical Feminist, though I hesitate to use the word feminist in there. The difference between an *actual* feminist and a TERF is sort of like the difference between your average white dude and the KKK. She thinks I'm some sort of monster just because I'm trans, and in her mind, spite is its own reward.

I grab one of the pads of yellow lined paper on the table and scribble *bathroom* on it, slide it in front of Cecilia. Trauth is having some back-and-forth with the judge. Cecilia looks at the paper and nods. Out in the hallway, a gaggle of reporters look up hopefully from their laptops. A few start shadowing me down the hall.

I turn back to look at them. "You need to watch me shit now?"

At least they've got the good graces to look embarrassed and stop acting like I'm in a zoo. The women's bathroom is around the corner and down the hall a ways. A little past it, a side exit to the building. I push open the door and glance around. Nobody is looking down the side of the building, so I shoot up into the air. The courthouse falls away beneath me, and now I'm all but invisible because most people almost never look up. Wind batters my sweatshirt, flapping and snapping as I push for speed. In a handful of seconds I'm across downtown—

—and punch through the windows of Legion Tower like a cannonball.

The briefing room is not as I remember it. The giant holographic globe is gone, the projector cold and dark. Plastic sheeting has been thrown over all the furniture. Almost nothing on this level is powered on, that much is obvious in the lattice. The lines are live, but nothing is drawing any juice. I didn't get overly familiar with the layout inside the Tower, but I know the residential levels are below the briefing room and lounge. A few moments later I've yanked open the elevator doors and am falling down the shaft. As each floor whips past, I check it for heat and electricity, and catch myself in midair as I pass the fortieth floor. The elevator door goes in with a squealing crunch and then I'm zipping through the hallway, vectoring in on the greatest source of heat.

Graywytch is eating a late breakfast when her front door explodes inward. She jerks back in her chair in surprise when I kick the table against the wall. When I dart in to catch her by the front of her shirt—and God, it is so *weird* to see her in a baggy t-shirt and sweats instead of that charcoal robe she always wears—she snaps into shadows and slips through my fingers. She reforms a few yards away, a glinting silver athame in her hand. She points it at me and snarls, "Get out of my house."

"You're going after my *family* now?" I shout at her.

Graywytch shakes her head. "I don't know what you're talking about," she says, and for half an instant I falter. But you know, she sure doesn't *seem* surprised.

"Bullshit! You're paying for their lawyer, aren't you?"

"No." She smirks. "Maybe you're not as popular as you think you are."

"It's none of your business, Myra!" I stalk across the room, and she backs up just as quickly. "My family is *off-limits*. You're butting out of this fight, do you hear me?" I've got her backed up against a wall, but she drops into a pool of shadow at her feet—just sinks right down into the ground and disappears.

"You're trespassing, young man." Graywytch's voice comes from everywhere and nowhere. "And I tire of you. Leave, before you get hurt."

"Fucking try it, bitch." My eyes are unfocused. The lattice gleams in the dark. She's not here. No heartbeat, no heat.

"Did you really think you could do as you please and nobody would speak up? Nobody would do anything?" Graywytch asks. Not even the vibrations of her voice show up in the lattice. "You don't deserve the mantle. You don't deserve to be Dreadnought.

Your parents know it, and so do I. Give up this farce. You will never be a woman, no matter how many lies you tell."

Shit, what was the plan here? Stupid, Danny. My fists tighten. If she'd just show herself—but of course she won't. I should have taken her out straight away. Come through the door and punched her through the goddamn wall. Shoulda, coulda, woulda.

"You're a coward," I say.

"No. Only a woman," says Graywytch. I swear, there's *got* to be something in the lattice when she speaks. For an instant I think I see it, some shimmering…then it's gone. "A woman who has been surviving in a world of violent men since long before you were born. I use the tools that are available to me. Now leave, before we both become embarrassed for you."

Graywytch's condo is luxurious. All that work she refuses to do pays pretty well, even if she doesn't pick up the phone. Dark wood furniture, soft track lighting, and a million-dollar view over downtown New Port. Above her fireplace—and it's a real fireplace, somehow, even though we're in the middle of a skyscraper—there is a cracked stone tablet. Circular, with worn grooves in the pattern of a Celtic knot. I cross her main room and pull the disk down off the mantle.

"Put that back," says Graywytch.

The stone snaps in my fingers like a stale cookie. There is a hiss of outrage, so I smash the two halves together into gravel.

"This is me asking nicely. Next time, I'll be angry," I say. "You're going to pull that lawyer off the case, and you're going to do it today. I promise, you don't want me to come back here."

Graywytch doesn't have an answer for that. I walk over to the floor-to-ceiling windows overlooking downtown and kick a hole in one. The entire pane shatters and slumps outward, held fast to the building by the tough safety film. Graywytch's condo is still empty when I turn to take one last look at it before stepping into the air, but I think she's gotten the message.

CHAPTER ELEVEN

When I get back to the courtroom, the lawyers are still in the early phase of their argument. My little field trip took less than ten minutes, even including the two or three minutes I spent hovering above the alley waiting for a clear moment to drop.

I start doodling on a spare legal pad and do my best to tune out the conversation. A few phrases sneak in. *Her own best interest.* *Financially unstable.* And so on. We break for lunch, and Cecilia disappears for a few minutes to call her assistants back at the office. Her lips are pressed tight, and she's got a look in her eye like we're going to have to go to war. I want to tell her that it's all right, I took care of it, but I'm not sure it's something she'd want to hear. She likes to do things by the book, so it's best if this stays between me and Graywytch. After lunch, Cecilia immediately asks the judge for a week to consider the new claims my parents' lawyer has made.

On the way out of the courtroom, I make the mistake of eye contact with my father. His eyes are depthless pits of rage. His lips are pressed tight under his brushy mustache, and every part of his body language gives off the warning signs I spent my childhood learning to avoid. The soft, vulnerable parts inside of me shrivel up and go cold. Cecilia's hand on my shoulder brings me back to the present, and I manage to keep my face blank as our eyes meet.

My mother pushes past him as we leave. Her face pleads as much as her voice. "Danny, please, won't you even talk to us?"

Like magic, Cecilia is there between us, gently but firmly pushing her back. "Ma'am, the conditions of your restraining order enjoin you from speaking to my client."

"Who are you to keep me from my child?" My mother's voice shakes; her fists are like claws.

"You picked your side, Janet!" I shout as I try to get my feet to move toward the door.

"Don't talk to your mother that way," says my father, his voice dangerously controlled.

"Danielle, we are leaving," says Cecilia, taking me by the arm and shoving any reporter too enthralled with the family drama out of the way. A gaggle of reporters follows us down the hall until we duck into the ladies' room and Cecilia shuts the door with emphasis. "Are you okay?"

"I'm fine," I say, rubbing my arms.

"That was worse than I expected it to be. It's an asset stripping, just like I thought," she says. "Most of your income is sheltered by the trust I set up for you, but they're contesting control of it. There're some things I need to do to shore up our defenses. Are you going to be okay if I leave you now?"

"Sure." I'm coming down from the anxiety spike. "I'll be fine. But give me a moment."

"Good. Now, there are going to be some nasty stories in the paper over this. Don't read them, don't watch the news, and no comment to the press. Okay?"

"What if this blows up?" I ask.

"It will, but no comment. I'll have my assistant put something out this afternoon." Beyond the doors we can hear the muted rumble of a gathering press gaggle, waiting to pounce on us when we leave. "You did well today, Danielle. I'm glad you could keep your head."

My cheeks get warm. "Well, uh, thanks."

We step out of the bathroom together. The press swarms up to greet us, and Cecilia moves in front of me to start no-commenting. I duck away toward the side door and take off at a forty-five degree angle up into the sky. Little wisps of fog dance around my nose, and I edge back from the sound barrier. I'm not supposed to go supersonic over the city unless it's an emergency. At a hair under

760 miles per hour, the New Port skyline rips past me, here and gone between one moment and the next. As Doc's condo tower comes up, I start dumping speed and come down at a skid across the porch.

Karen and Charlie are probably still doing research. I've got four hours of patrol scheduled for later today, and I might as well drop in to chat with them for a few minutes after I've suited up. But one look at Doc's face when I slide the glass door open blows that plan right out of the water. She's sitting in an armchair, facing the patio door, like she was just waiting here for me to get home.

"Um, hi, Doc. How was your flight?"

"Danielle, I still have access to Legion Tower's security net," she says.

"Oh?" I try to sound light and unconcerned as I shut the glass door behind me.

"What do you mean, 'oh'? Don't you have anything to say for yourself?"

I turn back to face her. My toes are clenching inside my shoes, but I won't back down. Never again. "She brought the media into my emancipation hearing, and she's paying for a lawyer for my parents. She crossed a line."

"So did you! You can't do this, Danny." The TV blinks on, showing footage of me smashing my way into the Legion briefing room. A few moments later, I'm kicking in Graywytch's door. "I've wiped the footage remotely, but if something like this got out, you'd be done. The government would drop you faster than a rabid weasel."

"I could find another job," I say, trying to keep my voice level. "This isn't even any of your business."

"It is, actually," says Doc. "We're in this together. Why do you think I built all that fancy gear for you? You don't think I drop a quarter million dollars in hypertech on *all* my roommates, do you? We were *supposed* to be partners."

"Well, not about this, we aren't!" I snap.

"Did you hurt her?"

That brings me up short. "Wha—no! How can you ask me that?"

She softens her voice. "Because people who make you angry keep winding up in the hospital."

"Blackcapes who are hurting people, yeah!"

"What about Acid Andy?" asks Doc.

I roll my eyes and walk past her through the living room. "This again?"

"He was surrendering, Danny." She rises from her chair and begins following me.

"Acid Andy is a psychopath," I say, heading down the hall to my room. "He's done fake surrenders before; I had to be sure." As I try to shut my door behind me, she catches it, pushes it back open.

"Yes, and now he's a quadriplegic," she says. "This isn't the first time you've gotten close to the line, but it's the worst, and you have to *stop*."

"I'm getting dressed," I say tightly, and push the door closed. Sweater, shirt, and pants come off. Fancy underwear, bodyglove, and cape go on.

When I come out, Doc is pacing in the main room, arms wrapped around her sides. "I owe you an apology. I should have seen this coming, and I didn't. If I hadn't—" Her voice cuts off. She tries again. "I'm sorry. But I'm really scared right now. For you, for me, for all of us."

"What the hell are you talking about?"

"Do you know how to make someone become a dangerously violent person?" Doc stops pacing. "It's basically a recipe. You hold them down and treat them like shit. Destroy their self-esteem, strip away all their pride, all their self-respect. Then you give them a chance to solve a problem with violence, and when they do, you immediately reward them." Doc takes a breath. "Does that sound like anyone you know?"

My gut turns to lead. I bite the words out by syllables: "I am not a blackcape."

"Not today. But if you don't take what I'm saying seriously, you'll be one sooner than you think. What happened in court must have been terrible, and you're right that this is exactly Graywytch's style. But it's no excuse. What you did today can never happen again. You need to learn to handle your shit, kiddo."

The hard ball of resentment in my gut explodes. "I *have* been handling myself, and I've been doing it without you!"

Doc's jaw clenches, but not like she's angry. "I'm sorry for how I've been, but—"

"I don't need you to take care of me. If I need help finding the bottom of a bottle, I'll give you a call."

Doc rocks back on her heels like she's been slapped. Her mouth hangs open, but nothing comes out. For an instant I feel bad, but I grind that down and turn to leave. I slam into the sound barrier just a few seconds after leaving the balcony. To Hell with the city's noise ordinance.

In a few moments I'm over the Pacific and climbing hard. This kind of airspeed is a frozen wall being pressed against my face, and I tell myself that the ice forming at the corners of my eyes is just wind getting to me.

CHAPTER TWELVE

Mach 3.3. That's how fast my suit's nav computer says I'm going before my grip on the lattice fails and I'm punted into the wind like a leaf on a freeway. Flying that fast at sea level is *hard*. It's tiring, and it wears on my focus. Once I get past my limit, my mind tends to butterfinger the lattice, and *whoops*, there goes my controlled flight. I become a ballistic body, tumbling through the air. Today I manage to catch myself before I smack into the ocean at two thousand miles an hour. I flip onto my back and do lazy backstroke arms at a mere eighty miles an hour or so. I needed this. A good fly over the ocean sets me right every time. I nose up for some altitude and head back to New Port.

When I'm entering the city airspace I text the police that I'm starting my patrol early and drop down among the towers downtown. Patrol is easy. I fly low and slow through New Port, focusing especially on downtown where there are more people to see me. The whole point is to let people know I'm around. Civilians feel safer, and bad guys think maybe that daylight diamond store robbery wasn't such a hot idea after all. If I stumble across something happening, I can get involved, but mainly I wait around for a call from Detective Phạm or the chief of the fire department. Because I'm a minor, I can only do this for twenty hours a week, but in a few years my contract will be renegotiated, and I'll be out here full time.

The hard flying has burned the hottest part of the rage out of me. The ashes are a low, warm throb behind my heart.

I spend a few hours gliding around downtown, taking pictures with tourists, that sort of thing. For a hopeful moment I think I'll have a little bit of excitement with an armed robbery, but they surrender immediately so all I get to do is sign autographs for the perps while we wait for the cops to come arrest them. We take a group selfie as the police are rolling up, and then I'm back on patrol.

But, you know, it's nice. Patrol is nice. People wave at me, and I wave back, and I don't think about anything else. About Graywytch being horrible or about how much it hurts that Doc took her side. Especially not about my parents making a grab at my money, like they even wanted me to keep the powers that make my paychecks possible. The more times I drop in on people and have little conversations with them—give directions, answer questions, do quick favors—the better I feel. The warmth behind my heart fades down to the very edge of feeling. My smile isn't tacked on anymore.

My suit buzzes with a call from Detective Pham. I put a finger to my earbud radio and answer the call. "Hey, Detective, what's up?"

"Danny, I need you to come down to police headquarters." The bottom drops out of my stomach. Graywytch didn't call the cops on me, did she? That would be—I don't want to think about how bad it would be if they reacted the way Doc did. But then she continues, "That perp you collared a couple nights ago was found dead in his cell two hours ago."

Can I be relieved by that? Is that okay to feel? Immediately on the heels of that relief, concern begins to pool in my chest. People aren't supposed to die when I hand them over to the cops. "Yeah, sure, I'm on my way."

I open the phone app in my suit and bring up Sarah's phone number. My finger hovers over the call button for a moment. I shut the app without calling anyone. After this morning, it was hard work to get back into a good mood. Calamity mixes me up and gets me flustered every time. Not worth it. Not today.

It only takes me a few moments to cross downtown and come

into a shallow spiral, landing on the roof. The statue of Atlas over the main entrance is lit up, his face stern and the shadows hard in the white spotlighting that's come up as the sun goes down. Above us, the first stars begin to peak through the blue velvet of the evening sky.

Detective Phạm is waiting for me there, her face drawn and serious. The roof lights throw an X of shadows out from her legs.

"Thank you for coming, Dreadnought," she says. "I need to ask you some questions about the night you captured Crenshaw."

"I put everything in my report," I say.

"I know, but he was killed in the M-double-C—"

"*What?*" The MCC is the Metahuman Containment Cell. It's the world's most expensive drunk tank. Built like a bank vault, with magnetically active shackles for the wrists and ankles that even I would have difficultly pulling out of, it's designed to be airtight with the ability to administer a variety of sedatives, either as a gas or through an IV drip, and is the only place the cops can safely store someone with superpowers. Whenever it is occupied, there is a fully armed MRU team on guard twenty-four hours a day, as much to protect the (still legally innocent) prisoner as to keep them locked up. It's a big deal, is what I'm driving at. Someone getting killed in there is...bad. Really bad.

"That's why I need to ask you questions. The homicide division is going nuts over this, and the MRU is looking for someone to point a finger at," says Phạm. She pulls a notebook out of her jacket, clicks open a pen.

One of the things I've learned in the last nine months is that seeing how city governments really work is super depressing. "That doesn't sound good."

"Oh, don't worry, because it gets worse: we rent out the M-double-C to departments all over the Northwest; just having the *option* to send someone here costs ten thousand a year. If we can't guarantee the safety of the inmates other departments stash with us, we stand to lose almost a half-million dollars out of the department's annual budget in lost rental fees alone. *And* there's a city council election coming up too, so this is going to be the worst pissing match I've ever seen. You and I need to be ready for it."

A creeping anxiety takes hold of me. "Wait, how could we possibly be to blame for this?" I ask.

Phạm shrugs. "Who *is* to blame and who *gets* blamed aren't always the same thing. So let's go over what happened from the beginning."

I suppress a sigh and begin the story from when I arrived in New Port. It's nothing I haven't told the cops already before, and in writing, but Phạm has a bunch of extra questions about everything. Every one of my answers gets scribbled down again.

We're almost done now, and she asks, "When you were apprehending him, did Crenshaw say anything about any enemies he might have?"

I close my eyes and try to think back to that night. We're in the restaurant at the top of the tower. There are flames crackling quietly somewhere nearby. Civilians whimpering.

…and Crenshaw sounds like the adults in a *Charlie Brown* cartoon.

To be honest, I don't really pay attention to what supervillains say very much anymore. It's always *misunderstood genius* this, *you'll regret the day* that. Supervillains are, as a rule, drama queens. It gets old. I shake my head. "I'm sorry, we didn't talk—no, wait, he said something about a cathedral?"

Phạm flips to a fresh page in her notebook. "Okay, which cathedral?"

"Hell if I know. He said it was brainwashing me, and everyone else too."

She raises her eyebrows at me. "Seriously?"

"I'm pretty sure, yeah."

With a grunt of annoyance Phạm closes her notebook and slips it back in her jacket pocket. "We already knew he was nuts."

"How did he die?" asks Calamity.

Phạm's hand jerks toward her gun, and I'm tensing for takeoff.

Calamity is crouched on top of the roof access hut, just a few yards off from us, and neither of us heard her arrive.

"I knew you were ballsy; I didn't think you were stupid," says Phạm, drawing her weapon. She doesn't point it at Calamity, just keeps it down by her leg. "You realize we've got like thirty warrants out for your arrest, don't you?"

"I'm known to be industrious," says Calamity. Her left hand—the mechanical one—flexes. "But you haven't told us how Crenshaw died."

Phạm turns to me. "Dreadnought, did you call her down here?"

"No," I say, glancing between Phạm and Calamity.

"How'd you know to come down here?" Phạm asks her. Calamity doesn't say anything. Detective Phạm gets tight with anger: "Have you been bugging my phone?"

Calamity keeps her silence. Tilts her head.

"Dreadnought, arrest Calamity," says Phạm.

"Um, no?" I say. "That's not going to happen, like, ever."

Her eyes stay locked on Calamity while she chews that over. "That's fine, I just had to ask," she finally says. "And I won't be able to lie about you refusing, if anyone puts the question to me."

Liaison officer, I am coming to realize, does not mean *advocate*, in much the same way that *mother* didn't mean it, either. She must be extra scared by this Crenshaw stuff if she's letting slip that she doesn't have my back when it comes down to it. Or maybe she thinks I won't notice what she just said because I'm a kid. Maybe she didn't grow up in the kind of house where people learn cynicism alongside how to tie their shoes.

"She's got a point, though," I say. Phạm breaks away from death-glaring at Calamity to look at me quizzically. "How *did* Crenshaw die?"

"His throat was slit," she says. "He was still in his manacles. CCTV shows nobody going in or out, but there's one frame with a blurry smudge of someone inside his cell with him. Our perp might be metahuman, so you'll need to be ready to serve an arrest warrant when we have one."

"Wouldn't the MRU want to do that?" I ask. They don't like me doing their jobs for them in the best of times. If they let a suspect get murdered under their noses, they're definitely not going to want me swooping in to make them look even worse.

Phạm glances at Calamity before she answers. "There might not be an MRU by the time we have an arrest warrant. That's the kind of shakeup that's coming, and that's why you really can't be associating with criminals right now."

"You're going to bruise my tender and vulnerable feelings, Detective," says Calamity.

"Get the fuck out of here before I drill you, kid," snaps Phạm. She doesn't point her gun at Calamity. Not quite. But her fingers get awfully tight around the handle.

Calamity rises from her crouch and leaps off the backside of the roof access hut. A tap of boots, the flutter-snap of her jacket, and she's over the edge of the building. She fires her grapnel and *vizzes* away on a cable.

"I hate you so much," mutters Phạm under her breath. She doesn't know how sharp my hearing is. After Calamity is well gone, she turns back to me. "If you think of anything else Crenshaw said to you when you were fighting, let me know. But other than that, stay out of this one until I call for you."

"Okay."

"I mean it. And don't let Calamity stick her oar in, either."

"Detective, she and I don't really—"

"Save the bullshit for someone who's buying, Dreadnought." Phạm slides her gun back into her shoulder holster. "I'm trying to protect you here. Those new caping contracts the City Council offered you haven't even been written down yet, and this is exactly the sort of thing that gets promises rescinded, do you understand?"

I straighten in surprise. If the City Council takes back their offer to sign three new cape contracts, I'll never be able to get Kinetiq a job up here. Hell, I might not even be able to get control of the Legion back. I could get *fired*. "They'd do that?"

"They'd do worse to win an election," says Phạm, "and there's a smell in the air that's got everyone with any sense ducking for cover. Go home and keep your nose clean. I'll call you if there's any news."

"Right." When I turn to leave, she calls my name.

"I saw what happened today at the courthouse on the news," she says. She looks concerned. "I'm really sorry you had to go through that."

"Thanks," I say. "I'll see you later, Detective."

And then I'm up. A few moments later, as I expected, someone is shining a laser in my eyes. I've been shot in the face with actual laser cannons without much more than a bad sunburn to show for it, so I'm not worried about going blind, but it's still pretty annoying. I angle down and come around the back of an office tower a couple blocks away from the police headquarters. Calamity is on the roof, tucking her laser away in one of the infinite pockets inside her long duster.

"You've got my phone number," I say as I land.

"Where's the skill in that?" says Calamity.

"You really shouldn't tease the cops like that."

"They're big kids, they'll get over it. Anyhow, we got bigger fish on the pan," she says, eyes bright with excitement. "To wit— who would want to murder Crenshaw?"

I shake my head. "I'm not getting involved; that's Homicide's job."

"You ain't a cop, Dreadnought," says Calamity.

"Politics matter, Calamity," I say, holding onto my calm with both hands. Why does she have to be so difficult about everything? Why can't she just let something go for once in her life? Why does it always, *always* have to be the hard way? Just as I feared, even being near her is knotting my guts back up. It drives me mad, the way she's so arrogant, self-righteous, stubborn, and *way too hot!* "If I want to take over the Legion, I can't get mixed up in this."

Calamity rocks back on her heels, hands in her jacket pockets. "Do you even listen to the song they've got you singing?"

Between the fiasco at the courthouse, and Graywytch's insufferable smugness, *and* Doc's weird freakout, I'm at my limit. "I've had enough shit for today, Sarah," I spit, low and hot. "Go have fun committing more felonies, but I swear to God if you fuck this up for me I will never talk to you again!"

Her eyes widen, her hands come out of her pockets. "Danny—"

But I'm rolling now, and I can't stop. "The Legion *matters*. What I'm trying to do *matters*. And all goddamn week people have been stomping over everything I've tried to do. The convention, my emancipation, and now even the new cape contracts I'm trying to open up—they're all getting burned down as I watch, and I am sick of it!"

Calamity goes blank. Turns and starts walking to the edge of the roof. Ten thousand tons of cold regret smash down on me. Maybe I'm a horrible person after all. I reach out like I can grab the words and yank them back.

"Calamity, wait. I'm sorry," I say. Stupid, I'm so stupid. "I've had a really bad day. I'm sorry."

She stops walking. "Is that what you think I'm trying to do here, Danielle? You think I want to stomp on you?"

"No. No, I'm sorry."

Sarah—and she is Sarah now—turns back, her arms folded against her stomach. "You're not—we're changing. I don't like it."

"I…I don't know what to say." I run my hand through my hair, frustration tugging at my insides. She stops taking my calls, and now she's, what, missing me? Upset that I've got responsibility now? Or something else? Maybe I am changing. Maybe I'm…no, Doc is wrong. I'm not a bad person. That was what my father wanted me to think, but it was a lie. I'm a good person. Aren't I? "Things have been weird."

"Is this how being a hero is?" asks Sarah, from that weird space where she's half-Calamity. "Steppin' aside. Letting the law act like it owns justice?"

"I screwed over a friend of mine by accident," I say. "And I need these contracts, at least one of them, to make it right. I can't risk that. Not over someone like Crenshaw. Please, just don't mess this up. I'm sorry I yelled. It's…being me is hard right now."

Sarah stares off to the side, at some middle distance where a decision is being made. She nods. "Okay. But I'm keeping my ear to the ground. If something falls in my lap—you can't ask me to ignore that. You can't ask me that."

"I won't. I don't," I say. Her shoulders relax. She nods and lets her arms drop back down to her sides. I feel like we've edged back from a precipice.

My suit buzzes with a text. I swipe a finger down my forearm and the screen swims to life out of the material of my bodyglove. It's from Charlie, asking if I'm coming over tonight.

"Got a line on something?" asks Calamity, perking up.

"Yes, actually. Valkyrja's daughter is in town, and she's got a problem I'm helping her out with. Do you want to come along?"

"Valkyrja had a daughter." Not quite a question. Not quite a statement. That damn bandanna over her face hides a lot of her expression, but her cheeks shift like her lips are twisting. She takes a step backward.

"Yeah, her name's Karen. She's pretty cool."

Calamity hunches her shoulders and turns away. She starts walking toward the edge of the building. "You go on ahead there, Dreadnought. I wouldn't want to get in the way."

"What are you talking about? You're not going to—"

"'Course I would," says Calamity. "I can't fly."

And then before I can stop her, she's off the building, hissing into the darkness on her cable.

CHAPTER THIRTEEN

For a few minutes I only stand there blinking, trying to figure out what went wrong. I could catch up and ask, of course, but—

You know what?

Fuck you too, Sarah. I am done with shit going wrong today. You can plant your little conversational land mines in someone else's evening.

About forty seconds later I'm ringing Charlie's doorbell. His mom, Louise, opens the door. Charlie's dad is a doctor, and his mom's a homemaker who wears a lot of knit sweaters and is always quiet and friendly. She's sort of got a black June Cleaver vibe going on. "Oh, hi, uh, Dreadnought." Louise vaguely knows that Charlie and I were in school together before I dropped out. I don't think she knows we met because he used to go caping with Sarah.

"Hi, Louise. Can I come in?"

"Sure." But as I'm passing her in the hall, she catches me by the cape. "Does…does Karen have a place to stay?"

Uh, crap. I'm not sure how much Karen wants me to say. I shake my head. "She's homeless. Charlie and I are trying to figure out how to help her with a metahuman problem." Louise's brow pulls in and she nods like this confirmed something for her. "If you don't want her around, she can come stay at—"

"No, I'm going to tell her she can stay as long as she likes," says Louise. "I'm glad you and Charlie are helping her." She says this super seriously, like this is really hard and important stuff. I mean, I'm a superhero. Of course I'm going to help her, that's what I'm *for*.

Karen is with Charlie in his room, about half a library spread out between them. Neither looks like they've taken a nap since I left them this morning, and between the books there is a forest of empty soda cans. Charlie's digging it, though. Focused, intense. He doesn't notice I'm in his room until Karen pings an empty can off his head. And that's kind of what does it, what makes it a little too perfect for me to buy that they've been laser-focused on a cure since I left this morning.

Or maybe it's the way Karen's cherry lip balm is smeared a little bit onto her cheek.

"Oh, hey Danny I didn't expect you so—that was fast," Charlie says.

I suppress a smirk. "It was only subsonic."

"Showoff," mutters Karen. She's lying on her stomach, wings relaxed against her back, chin in her palms. Her fingers seem to be trying to cover up the fact that she's blushing.

"Any luck?" I ask, closing the door behind me.

"Not yet," says Charlie, not quite meeting my eyes. "There's still thirteen days of Christmas break left, though."

I take a seat in midair, fold my legs up into a lotus position, and pick up a book. *Basics of Counter-Magic to Mental Intrusion*, says the spine. The first page jumps right into a discussion of the historical roots of psychoanalysis, and I am bored almost instantly.

"We already ruled that one out," says Charlie.

"Oh, thank God," I say, shutting the book and setting it aside.

There's a sort of Hanging Cloud of Awkwardness over the room until I offer to pay for more takeout. Chinese this time, and Charlie's mom insists we eat at the dinner table, so we all troop downstairs, and during the meal Karen explains to Louise that she's being possessed by a dead woman, but leaves out all the complicated parent stuff. The tone of Louise's questions suggest a woman who is only now realizing how much she doesn't know about her son.

When we get back up to Charlie's room to restart our research, the whole almost-walked-in-on-you-two thing isn't looming over the conversation anymore. We get about another twenty minutes into fruitlessly combing through Charlie's occult library when Karen closes her book and stands up. "Look, unless we've got something we can actually try tonight, I don't think I want to waste more time on this right now."

Charlie looks up, eyebrows drawn in. "I think we're making good progress."

"I—thanks, for everything, Charlie, but we've tried one spell. Unless you have another…"

"I told you, mental magic is hard to learn about—"

"And I get that, Council of Avalon and all that," says Karen, her voice a cross between placating and tense. "But it's really hard holding her back right now, and there's something else I'd like to try."

"What did you have in mind?" I ask.

"Um." Karen seems to psych herself up for something. The words come tumbling out on top of each other. "Actually, I was hoping you could come with me to retry one of the options I already checked out. There's this guy with a weird sort of powerset, and he couldn't really help me, but I was hoping that between him and you working together…" Her voice sort of trails off, and she's not meeting anyone's gaze.

Well, I've never tried mixing my powers with someone else's before, but I know it's theoretically possible. Some of the best cape teams of all times have figured out how to do it, so it's worth a shot. "Sure, that sounds doable. Who is he?"

"His name's Richard Garrison. He lives on—sort of an island thing off the coast."

"Sort of an island?"

"You'll see," says Karen.

"Wait, why do I know that name?" says Charlie.

"He's one of those people who's so rich he's famous just for being rich," says Karen.

Something clicks in my head. "Right! Right, he was big in the tech scene, wasn't he? I didn't know he was metahuman." It's not entirely surprising, though. More people have powers than like to admit it, even if they wimp out and call them "special abilities" instead of full-on powers. And like I said, most people with super-powers don't become superheroes. This is double-true of people who were already well-off before they got their powers, and tri-ple-true of people who were actually rich. When you've got more to lose, the whole make-enemies-of-superpowered-psychopaths part of the gig is way, way less appealing.

Karen shrugs, shoulders pulled in tight and nervous. "Neither did I, but he emailed me after he saw something I put online asking for help. Anyway, his power only temporarily fixed it, but if we combine it with what you tried—"

I start nodding. "Yeah! Yeah, that could totally work."

Charlie's looking back and forth between us. "Okay, so, when were you planning on leaving?"

"Um. Now," says Karen, looking at the floor. "Is now good?"

"You don't want to call him?" I ask.

"It won't be a problem," she says quickly. "I mean, I'll text him, but he said I could drop by anytime."

Charlie is putting books in order, trying to hold a poker face. "Well, I'm sorry I couldn't help you," he says stiffly.

"No!" says Karen, suddenly urgent. "It was a help. Thank you. If this works, do you...mind if I come back?"

Charlie smiles, and I suddenly decide I need to use the restroom.

A few minutes later, Karen meets me in the front yard. Her wings are tight against her back, and her face is set. "We're headed to a place about seven hundred miles southwest of here, but I don't have specific—"

Her phone buzzes. "He sent me GPS coordinates. Do you know how to plug these into a phone?"

"Hold on." I tap my forearm to bring the suit's interface up and start inputting the numbers to my navigation computer. The color on the back of my glove melts into a high-resolution map with a line pointing from my location to someplace off the California coast, a bit north of the Bay. "How fast can you fly?"

Karen shrugs, and with visible reluctance, opens her wings. "Pretty fast, I guess. I haven't spent a lot of time experimenting."

"Let's get moving."

We power into the sky. A carpet of amber lights falls away beneath us. In a few minutes we're over the ocean, nothing but a hard black void beneath us. The coast is a line of glowing jewels far off to our left. Bits of static spark off the magic bubble Karen's wings generate, a subtle corona in front of her and trailing behind.

We get out from under the high cloud cover, and without city lights to mute them, the stars are a brilliant spray of diamonds above us. The moon sits to the south like a fat, silver coin. It's a beautiful night for flying, but every time I start to get into it, I glance over at Karen and see the grim set of her jaw in the moonlight.

Valkyrja betrayed her. It's still hard to believe. We'll make it right. Somehow. If this doesn't work, maybe Charlie and I can get the Council of Avalon to take a closer interest.

My glove vibrates to let me know we've reached another way-point. We're maybe thirty miles out. I drift over and tap Karen on the shoulder. Where my hand intersects the flight bubble around her wings, I get a sensation of pins and needles that is gone almost as soon as I notice it.

We slow down enough to be able to speak. "We're close. I don't know what this place looks like, so you should take the lead."

"Trust me, you'll know it when you see it," she says.

"Not so fast," says a girl above and behind us. I flip over on my back to get a look, but spotlights clack on, obliterating the night in a wash of hard, white glare. "First, tell me who you are."

It's all but impossible to squint through the glare, but someone's up here with us, and she's somehow brought God's own flashlights with her. Questions about *how* and *who* and *why* crowd my mind, confusion and surprise gumming up my thoughts, making me nervous. I shut my eyes and look in the lattice, and nearly fall out of the air in surprise.

The girl confronting us can't be more than twelve or thirteen and is wearing a militarized pink princess dress with a gleaming silver chest plate and shoulder guards. She's surrounded by a halo of equipment floating on invisible pedestals of antigrav—powerful spotlights, autocannons, a laser projector, and enough high-density hypertech to start and win the third world war. There's some kind of signal I can't make out linking all the tech to the fat red gem set within the silver tiara on her forehead, and she's got an imperious sneer on her face that makes me think she's never been told "no" in her life.

"Kill the lights, Lilly," says Karen, hand up to her eyes against the glare.

"I told you, it's Princess Panzer!" snaps the girl. She'd probably stamp her foot too, but it's hard to do that while flying.

"Point those guns somewhere else, kid," I say. My first big fight was with mecha armed with similar weapons. She's got about as much firepower hanging around us as Utopia's entire goon squad was carrying at their peak. I wasn't strong enough to take them all on at once then, and I don't like the idea of facing down that much firepower now.

Panzer looks at me. "How did you see them through the glare?"

"I'm not going to ask twice, Panzer." No, I don't really relish the idea of beating down on a twelve-year-old, but the idea of getting shot to death by hypertech death machines clarifies my priorities.

She smiles, her delight palpable in the lattice, a cascade of twitching muscles and a brief spike in heart rate. It's a pretty weird reaction to being threatened by Dreadnought, but I get the feeling that nobody really takes her supranym seriously. The floating spotlights dim and die as the autocannons pull into themselves, fold up, and disappear into pops of fading light. Her light suite reconfigures itself in a twist and furl of metal and glass, becoming a soft cluster of track lighting, enough for us to all clearly see each other in the night sky.

"How'd you tell?" she asks again. Her boots are gleaming metal and hiss softly with antigrav jets.

"Sorry, trade secret," I reply. "Who are you?"

"This is Lilly—" Karen begins.

"Princess Panzer," says the girl.

"—and she's Richard Garrison's daughter." Karen's face is carefully blank, and Panzer seems oblivious enough not to notice.

"I'm the defender of virtue and champion of excellence!" says Panzer. "Pleased to meet you. Are you coming to sign a contract with my dad?"

"We're here to see if he can help me," says Karen evenly.

Panzer glances between us for a moment, and then a sly expression crosses her face. "Oh. All right. Well, I can guide you in. Follow me!"

She kicks her jetboots behind her and squirts between us, powering down into the night. The lights fold up into nowhere and disappear. Karen is muttering something just at the edge of hearing that's not very complimentary.

Panzer is already a half mile out in front and pulling away fast. Her voice echoes back to us, amplified a hundredfold by some kind of hypertech bullhorn she's pulled out of nowhere. "Are you guys coming or what?"

"I was hoping she'd be, I dunno, on vacation or something," grumbles Karen as we fall in and begin trailing the kid. Panzer deploys big, neon Look At Me beacons behind her that get ever more insistent until we fall in beside her, and we cover the last few miles at a relatively sedate hundred miles per hour.

At first I think it's an oil derrick. A cluster of lights in the black glass of the ocean at night. But as we get closer, I realize it's bigger than that. A lot bigger. What I took to be a modest workers' housing block turns out to be a glass and steel tower like I'd see downtown. Then we come close enough for the angle to shift and I see there are three of them, linked by bridges and studded with broad, hanging balconies. They sit at each point of a triangle of parkland the size of a pro soccer stadium, and then beyond that, there's a walking promenade of smaller buildings and plazas that surrounds the towers and goes down to three full-sized small-boat marinas. Most of the berths are empty, and most of the lights are off. But there, suspended between all three towers by sky bridges, is a circular patch of lawn about as big as the city block I grew up in, and it's lit up with powerful spotlights so the classically-styled mansion at the peak of this whole place is visible even from a mile or two out.

All of this sitting out there in the middle of the ocean, just a few dozen miles off the coast.

"This wasn't here the last time I was down in California," I say.

"Of course not," says Panzer. "It was being built in Bangladesh. We just arrived off the American coast last month." Panzer smiles at me. "I told Dad we're coming, so he should meet us at the balcony. He'll give you a tour if you want."

We soar in between the towers, down under the arches that meet at the mansion grounds. Beneath the broad, grassy platform the mansion sits on, there is a hanging cluster of glass-walled offices, a small tower inverted and suspended between the other three. About midway down, a balcony with thick blue walls of glass runs around the circumference of the tower. One segment is lit up with holographic landing lights that hang in midair, beckoning us in on an approach vector. There's a man waiting for us in front of a set of open double doors that each have a stylized crown logo printed on them.

As we come within a few yards, soft spotlights light us as we land. Panzer lands with an ostentatious hard stop, slamming from full speed to dead halt within about a half-yard to skid in between the open doors. Karen and I tap down a moment later, and she jerks her wings in tight as soon as her feet touch the floor.

"Daddy, Dreadnought's here!" says Panzer. "And, uh, Karen too, I guess."

The man she's speaking to is dressed in a lightweight suit of gray silk, the jacket and top two buttons of his shirt open, his tie hanging around his neck undone, like a long blue ribbon. He's got dark brown hair that's starting to frost over, skipping gray and jumping straight to white. He's got a strong face, tough and weathered with deep laugh lines and a pale raccoon tan line around his eyes. "And did you remember your manners?" he asks his daughter, gentle chiding in his voice as he reaches out to muss her hair.

Panzer goes still. "Uh…yes. I totally did."

He looks up and locks eyes with me. I get the strange sense that I'm being tested. "Greetings," he says after just a sliver too long. "My name is Richard Garrison. Welcome to Cynosure."

CHAPTER FOURTEEN

"Thanks," I say, unsure how to take that. Who the hell says *greetings?* "I'm Danny, and Karen says you've already met."

Garrison laughs and throws his arm out, beckoning us inside. "Yes, yes, Karen said you two were on the way. I've got some food ready if you're hungry from the flight."

Karen, Panzer, and I fall in behind him. The balcony enters into a lounge area, with low, gray leather seats everywhere, smoky glass and polished steel, a carpet so deep you could drown in it. From there we head into a hallway lit every ten yards with soft sconces of diffuse amber light that splash up the wall and across the pale ceilings. The whole place is like that, sort of a scientifically calibrated luxury, no concessions to tradition, no wood, just the latest and greatest in environmental ergonomics.

"This is a, a nice…boat?"

Panzer laughs. "It's not a boat!"

Garrison frowns at her. "Lilly, be polite to our guests. She's never seen something like this before. Almost nobody has."

Panzer hangs her head. "Sorry, Dreadnought," she mutters.

"Thank you," says Garrison. "Now, I can see you're tired after a big day. Why don't you go to bed?"

She looks up at him. "But, Daddy—"

"To bed, Lilly."

Panzer waves at me, and says, "Goodnight, Dreadnought. It was nice meeting you."

"Goodnight, Panzer," I say. The girl beams and damn near skips away down an intersecting hallway to an elevator. I notice she's basically ignored Karen the whole time, and for that matter, Karen has been silent and staring at the floor since we got here.

"She's not wrong, you know," Garrison says. "Cynosure is not a ship. She's a new form of vessel, a mobile seastead, the first of many. We have over forty acres of sovereign, privately owned territory here. We're totally self-sustaining. Every window you see here is a high-efficiency transparent solar cell. When we come to a resting posture, we're kept in place by two dozen suction anchors that hold us fast to the mud on the sea floor, and every one of those anchors is topped by a wave motion generator. With new efficiencies in design, we actually start running a surplus of electricity the moment we drop anchor, and that's projected to hold true even when we're at population capacity. We make our own fresh water, and we've got over fifty thousand square feet of high-density hydroponics bays. We can feed more people than you'd think, and let me tell you, soy is not what it used to be—we're going to have some turkey sandwiches in a moment, and I *defy* you to tell me you can taste that they're vegan."

He's really into it, ticking points off on his fingers as we go. We enter a large room that's part cafeteria, part presentation room. More of those low, leather chairs around teardrop-shaped tables set at knee height, floor-to-ceiling windows looking out into the black night at one end, and a full buffet area at the other.

"Come on, help yourself!" he says, leading us to the food at the back.

I'm about to speak up and say we're not really here to be wowed by how neat-o his big floating house is, but Karen brushes past me and grabs a plate. She begins piling food on it with grim, mechanical purpose. I follow suit. Then Garrison leads us to one of the clusters of chairs, and we sit down around the low glass table.

He bites into his own sandwich with gusto, and I've got to admit, the tofurkey is not bad. "This was all harvested last week, including the grain for the bread," he says. "We've got plans to expand production soon so we'll have something to export."

He says this with a look in his eye, like he's baiting a question.

Okay, fine, I'll humor him. If he can help Karen, he can try to sell me the moon for all I care. "What does a resort need with exports?" I ask obediently.

Garrison laughs. "Nothing! But this isn't a resort, it's a country!"

"A country?" Holy shit, I kept a straight face. Cecilia would be so proud.

"Yes, of course! We're not recognized at the UN yet, but that will come." He hunches forward at the edge of his seat. "Look, Dreadnought—may I call you Danielle?—Danielle, the nation-state is dying off. Small, privately owned communities in a global network are the future. Out here, we're free of territorial disputes, of the archaic and rotting Westphalian system—we've got a clean slate! There's no bureaucracy, no handouts, no petulant special interests; it's the urgent and inevitable path forward for human development, and we're taking the first big steps here."

"That's really cool," I say, and it even sounds like I mean it. The truth is, Garrison's personal crusade seems like another rich dude's fantasy of remaking the world so that it will kiss his ass just that much more, and I cannot scrounge up even half a shit to give about this. Not that you'd hear it from my voice or see it in my body language. Hooray for media training! "But, and I hope you won't mind, I actually came here because I was hoping that you and I could help Karen with her problem."

Garrison, like his daughter, seems for a moment to have forgotten Karen was in the room. "Oh! Oh, yes, of course. We can get right to that, but I was hoping I could show you a little presentation I've been working on."

"With all due respect, Mr. Garrison, I think it can wait until we've gotten rid of Karen's extra memories."

"Yes. Please," says Karen.

Garrison blinks. "I...well, if you'll agree to listen to it afterward—"

"Can we just do this the way we said?" asks Karen, just above a whisper.

"That was the arrangement," says Garrison. Karen sucks in a horrified gasp. "I give Karen her cure, and she brings you here to hear my pitch."

Wait, what? She said he'd had trouble making a cure stick. And she didn't mention anything about a deal. I look over at Karen, confused.

Her words jam into each other. "That wasn't—you said you wouldn't—!"

"Karen, I don't know what you're talking about," says Garrison. "If you've misrepresented yourself to Dreadnought—"

Karen's face has gone crimson. Her hands are clutched white against her knees. "Fine, whatever, just give me the necklace."

"What necklace?" I ask. She's not looking at me. Her jaw bunches and unbunches. "Karen, what necklace?"

Garrison has reached into his jacket and pulled out a small phone, not a smartphone, but an old-style digital-faced cell. He pushes a single button and speaks into it. "Jonathan, why don't you come take Ms. Kim to one of the other lounges, and bring her payment with her."

Even as the words leave his mouth, Karen is standing. Eyes locked to the ground, shoulders tight and high to her neck she marches away. A man in a dark suit, this one buttoned up, meets her near one of the halls away from the lounge and hands her something. I twist back around in my seat to look at Garrison.

"What the hell was that?"

"I really could not begin to say," says Garrison. He cracks a can of soda and takes a sip. I look down at my own food and suddenly lose my appetite. "Karen came to me in quite a state. We each had something the other wanted, and I offered to make a trade. If she decided to keep you in the dark about our arrangement, well, she'd been on the streets a long time. She might not be very stable anymore. God knows the poor girl has more pressure on her than anyone should have to bear."

"I see. Why are you so interested in me?"

"Aha, yes! To the heart of it!" He shakes his fists with that kind of Silicon Valley excitement that tastes stale everywhere else. "I've got a major project in the works, totally world-changing. Cynosure is part of it, but it goes so much further. And I need a spokesperson. Someone with name recognition, someone who's modern and polls well. What about the world's preeminent cape? What about the first transgender superhero?"

"I'm not," I say.

"What?"

"I'm not the first transgender superhero. The first was Masquerade in 1959, though she only came out in the '70s after her retirement."

Garrison processes that for a moment, then goes on: "Regardless, you're a very *in* person right now, and you've got a strong reputation. I'd like to show you what I have in store, and I hope that you'll agree to become part of this project."

Karen's gone; I can't see her anymore. What the hell was she thinking? And...crap, she spent *days* with us in New Port, pretending to be looking for a cure. Or was it even pretending? Maybe she was hoping to find an alternative. Or maybe she doesn't need a cure at all. And what's so special about a necklace? When I'm done here, she and I are going to have a long, long talk.

"So, Dreadnought, will you listen to my proposal?" At least he's not talking down to me for being young. That still happens sometimes, despite all the footage of me beating the crap out of supervillains two or three times my own age.

"I have a publicist," I say. "Why didn't you just call her up and arrange a meeting?"

"I like to do this sort of thing one-on-one, without the help. It builds investment."

The help, he says. Now there's an interesting way to describe a woman with degrees from Harvard, Yale, and Princeton. I hang an opaque smile on my face and nod. "Sure. If that's the condition of Karen getting the help she needs."

"Excellent!" says Garrison, truly excited now. He stands up and punches another button on his phone. A holographic screen pops to life at one end of the room, ten feet high and twenty wide. It's showing a picture of low orbit, the Earth a slightly curved, fuzzy blue line along the bottom of a star field, a crescent moon hanging high to the left. "Now I've got to start with a little bit of background. Since the '90s, private spaceflight has really taken off. One of my subsidiaries is a pure-science outfit, and they piggy-backed an orbital telescope up on one of my heavy-lifter contracts. That's how we spotted this."

The screen snap-zooms in on a segment of the sky to focus on a fuzzy blue dot. My blood freezes. It's the Nemesis. I know it is.

Garrison doesn't seem to notice that I've gone rigid with shock and prattles on: "At first we didn't know what it was, but after we consulted with NASA we realized what we had here. When Northern Union went out to stop that asteroid a couple years ago, they were heading off a fragment of this thing. It's exotic matter, of a sort we don't really have the science to describe yet. Every three-and-a-half-thousand years it makes a close pass through the inner solar system. It's also the cause of all superpowers."

He tosses this last bit off like it's nothing, but then waits a moment, hoping for a gasp or some sort of reaction.

"And you're sure about this?" I ask. I'm remembering Professor Gothic's words. *You have enemies you won't recognize until they strike.* Without taking my eyes off the screen, I turn my gaze inward toward the lattice. The steel skeleton of the building jumps out at me, pretty standard construction. I don't see any hidden weapons systems, and Garrison himself reads as thoroughly baseline. There's a couple of men with guns and one without hanging out in a room behind a discreet door just a few yards away, but they're probably just his security detail. The nearest exit is the windows directly to my front, but I could punch through the floor or ceiling if I had to.

Reassured that this isn't an ambush, I relax fractionally. But he sure has my attention.

"Quite certain," says Garrison. "We've matched up its trajectory with the historical record, and we're pretty sure this is where the myths about Greek Gods came from. And not just the Greeks, either. Every ancient culture has stories of people or entities with fantastic powers, and many tell of a twilight of the gods or an era when the magic began to fade. Now the hour of the gods has come again.

"And this time, we're ready. Mankind stands at the threshold of a new age. Because this photo? It's five months old. Here's what the anomaly looks like right now."

The screen whips back around to a shot of the Moon, silver-gray and mottled with craters. The view is close enough that the edges are razor sharp against the shadows. The camera pans down and I catch my breath. The Nemesis is floating above it, wreathed in swirling blue mists that bob and weave in the vacuum like the tendrils of some living thing. It is surrounded by white scaffolding, tiny strands of steel and fabric against the immense bulk of the asteroid. Boxy protrusions jut from the scaffolds where they meet, an encrusted pentagon miles wide and blinking with running lights.

"That's a live feed of L2, the Lagrange point on the far side of the Moon," says Garrison. "It is an island of stable gravity. You put something there—like this asteroid, for example—and it will stay there indefinitely, with no need to orbit. My company has ensured that humanity will never again watch its power slip away as it passes out of—"

"The Nemesis is already here?" I say. I didn't mean to say it. It just sort of slips out.

Garrison looks at me, surprised. "Yes, that's what some call it. But I like to think of it as a friend. It's not here to destroy us. It's here to disrupt the old world, to empower those who are strong enough to seize its opportunity."

The first time I saw what this thing could do, I nearly vomited. Utopia had used a fragment of it to create a weapon that undoes reality itself. Since then, I've lived with constant anxiety in the back of my head. The Nemesis was coming, and when it arrived, life as we knew it would change irrevocably. If we were lucky. "Utopia told me that the Nemesis would destroy the world."

"Obviously she was wrong. Look, I'm not saying there isn't any danger, but we've got it well contained. The quantum destabilization effect of the exotic matter relies on line of sight to operate, and by hiding it behind the Moon we're able to limit its effects on Earth. My company has satellites in polar orbit of the Moon, monitoring the anomaly and allowing us to precisely control the observer effects."

"How? Utopia could barely control her fragment."

Garrison smiles. "We're cheating. We use magic."

The screen shifts again, back to Earth this time. A series of orbital tracks are highlighted as throbbing gold lines. The image zooms in on one, and we see a satellite with a strange, almost bulbous projection at one end. "For the past six months, my company has been launching a new satellite every week under the guise of creating a new satellite Internet fleet. That's mostly true, and they do pass data packets, but each one of these is also a node for a powerful ritual that our Head of Thaumaturgical Operations has constructed. With tomorrow's launch, we'll have full global coverage. With this satellite fleet in place, we can bring Phase One to completion."

My head is whirling with so many fears and epiphanies that I barely note his cue to play along. I sort of vaguely nod for him to go on and hope Cecilia's training is keeping my friendly banter smile in place.

Garrison nods enthusiastically. "The satellite fleet is just a tool to cast spells on a global scale, and Phase One is perfecting a spell to boost the probability curve in certain sectors—in layman's terms, we're fudging the dice roll to pick who gets superpowers. Until recently, we thought it was just random chance. A lab accident here, an ancient curse there. Nothing seemed connected, and yet from the very beginning there's been a suspicion that something was causing all these people with strange talents to show up starting in the late nineteenth century. And for them to become more common and more powerful as time went on? There had to be something connecting them all, right? Now that we've definitively

SOVEREIGN

concluded that it's all just the expression of a lot of weird quantum math, we can—and have—systematized it."

The screen has switched to an animated infographic showing how the cameras near the Moon take observations of the Nemesis. How those observations cause quantum instabilities of a predictable nature. How, by taking advantage of those instabilities, a spell cast from a ritual chamber here on Cynosure gets beamed up to the satellites and then repeated all over the planet. How a single individual can be picked out, and their probability graph pulled way, *way* up, so that it's all but guaranteed that by the end of the week they'll encounter a mysterious woman selling special rings, or experience a non-fatal accident with exotic chemicals, or some other canned origin story. Despite myself, I'm up off my chair and drifting toward the hologram.

This is…huge. Bigger than I thought possible. Utopia's failed plan to turn everyone into software she could control suddenly seems like it lacks ambition.

"Our initial calculations were pessimistic by an order of magnitude," says Garrison. "We're not only able to pick who gets superpowers, we can even pick roughly what sort of powers they can get. Further refinements are on the way, but this is really just a means to an end. Ask yourself, what are the implications of being able to pick and choose—?"

One of the implications occurs to me immediately. "Is it limited?" I ask.

"I'm not sure what you're asking."

"Is it limited?" I ask again, pointing at the part of the infograph that represents the probability of what they're calling an Empowering Event occurring. "The probability of someone somewhere in the world getting superpowers on a given day—is that a fixed number, and you're just shifting who it happens to, or can you change the probability itself?"

And for the first time, something genuine breaks through Garrison's sales pitch. He's surprised. Impressed. Like, I guess he

121

expected because I look like a blond swimsuit model, I'd be an idiot or something.

"We can adjust the total curve, yes."

I look back at him, excitement blooming in my chest. My smile isn't media-ready armor anymore, it's real, and growing. "We could give everyone in the world superpowers, and we could do it in a safe and controlled way."

Garrison's smile falters a little bit. "But, well that would almost defeat the point, wouldn't it? I mean, what's the point of powers if they're common?"

"No!" I shake my head. "You're wrong. It's not like we'd all have the same powers, right? We'd all have something unique that we can do. We could let people pick what they want, be whatever they chose. We don't have to wait for the Nemesis to do it natu-rally; we can do it *right now!* Look, I absolutely do want to be your spokeswoman, okay? Of course I do, this is huge! But if we're going to do this, we need to do it for everybody."

Garrison purses his lips. "You're picking up on this quickly, so I think we can skip ahead to some of the more advanced material in the presentation."

"There's more?"

"Oh yes. You see, this is Phase One. It's the big one, but this is a holistic project—we're not stopping there. There's a lot of problems we're going to solve." He shrugs. "All of them, more or less. And like in any great undertaking, we're going to make ene-mies." Garrison pauses, seems to calculate some odds. He pulls out his phone again. "Peter, would you come in here? I think maybe Dreadnought could use your perspective."

A discreet door in the side of the room opens, and out steps Thunderbolt. Electric thrills go up my spine. He's one of California's premier heavyweight superheroes, and would likely be the head of his own team if the cape laws in California weren't so screwed up. He's smaller than he looked up on stage in Antarctica, wiry and tough. The blue on his bodyglove is dark almost to black, set in relief by the jagged yellow lightning designs wrapping around his chest. He was the first to use the half-cape off one shoulder, a banner of yellow silk that's become almost as iconic as my own blue-and-whites.

"Danielle, this is my friend Peter," says Garrison.

"Hi, Thunderbolt!" And then I clamp down before my fangirl reflex goes into overdrive and I embarrass us all to death. I'd seen him at the business meeting in Antarctica, but it's different talking to him one-on-one.

Thunderbolt crosses the room and offers me his hand. "It's a pleasure to meet you, Dreadnought. I was hoping to run into you at the convention."

"I had to go smack down a blackcape," I say, returning his (inhumanly powerful) grip.

Thunderbolt and Garrison trade a glance, and then Garrison says, "Well, I think I'm gonna turn this over to Peter here; he's really better at this part of the presentation than I am. And, well, my own powers aren't really much to write home about, so I think maybe you'll relate to his understanding a little better than mine."

Thunderbolt motions for us to sit again, and I take a seat across from him. My earlier disquiet is gone. Karen should have leveled with me, but shit, I'm sitting here talking to Thunderbolt! It's really hard to be mad at her right now.

"Can I call you Danny?" he asks, and I nod because of *course* I do. I wonder if it'd be too dorky to ask for an autograph. "Good. Danny, I think you've been in the game long enough to notice some of the problems with how superpowers currently work."

"Uh, I guess? I don't really know what you mean."

"Well, for one, most people with powers are in the closet about it," says Thunderbolt. "It's all *special ability* this, *peculiar talent* that. They might use it for a job—a job!—or just to dick around, but they don't really get the most out of it."

The fangirl blush fades a little. "I guess I don't really see the problem. My job is super dangerous; not everyone wants that kind of life."

"But *you* want it, don't you?"

"Well, yeah. New Port kinda needed me. Even if I didn't like it, I'd probably still do it."

"But you do like it, don't you? It's okay to say you do. I love it," says Thunderbolt, putting his hand to his chest. "And if someone wants to stay conventional and safe, they can do that. But isn't it kind of a waste for them to have their powers, if that's what they want?"

That sounds off somehow. But it's hard to put my finger on why. In fact, it sounds a lot like what I've asked myself when I saw people with powers who were obviously more interested in blending in than standing out. So maybe I've never called it a waste. But still. Why settle for normal when you can do the kinds of things that I can do? Hell, look at Calamity, she's *barely* superhuman, and she's still way cooler than basically anyone else in the city. "I...I guess. I mean, *waste* is a strong word—"

"—but you see what I mean, right?"

"I think I do."

"Well, what we're going to do is remove the random chance from who gets powers and who doesn't. Only people who want them—and who've *earned* them—will get them. The best people should have the best powers. No more supervillains, and no more slackers. That's what Phase One is all about, and everything else flows from there."

"What's Phase Two?" I ask. My trepidation grows.

"That's not ready to be revealed yet," says Garrison with an even look at Thunderbolt.

Thunderbolt dips his head and moves away from the topic. "Right now, there's no efficiency to how superpowers are allocated. A market-based system would be vastly superior, and Richard already showed you how we're going to bring some creative disruption to that problem. But more important is what it means for the wider world. There's a lot wrong with the world these days. We're at a—what'd you call it, Rich?"

"An inflection point of history," says Garrison. He sips his soda.

"Right. The old world is rotting. There are too many problems that are going unaddressed because of special interests and small-minded politicians. And it's not just in government; the West's culture is sick too. Flabby mediocrity is the order of the day. We're raising generation after generation to believe that the worst thing you can do to someone is offend them. We're told to pretend that everyone is equal, but excuse me, some of us can *fly!* Excellence isn't celebrated anymore, and it's suffocating humanity."

Garrison chimes in, "I started homeschooling my daughter because the other students were taught it was okay to shame her for using her powers. They get scared because she can do things they can't, and so they expect her to stifle herself simply because of their cowardice. And this was at a so-called elite academy in Zurich. It's like that all over now." The way he says this makes me think he's voiced this complaint before. A lot. "There's no escape. Someone does something outstanding and they get shouted down for not being fair to the people who can't."

"Right!" says Thunderbolt. "And that's who they care about. The people who can't. There's no concern anymore for the people who *can*, the people who *do*. They've murdered the meritocracy! No civilization can thrive if it insists on strangling its best members. We can take the best lessons of history, and abandon the failed ideologies that got us here."

My enthusiasm has completely drained away. This conversation has more red flags than the Chinese Embassy. Cecilia's media training is in full effect, and I crack a soda of my own to cover my unease. After a sip, I ask, "Which ideologies are those?"

Garrison and Thunderbolt trade a look. It seems to say *well, it's now or never.*

Thunderbolt looks at me and says, "Democracy."

That's the moment I realize that a supervillain has literally sat me down in his lair so he and his buddy can explain their Evil Plan over drinks. There is no amount of media training that can keep the incredulity off my face when I say, "I'm...sorry? Are—are you joking?"

"Not at all," say Garrison.

"Look, I know that's kind of a lot to take in, but you adjusted to having superpowers," says Thunderbolt. "I haven't had the pleasure of working with you, but the capes you've fought with who I talked to speak very highly of you. They say you get it, that you're understanding your role almost instinctively. Now take that shift of perspective to its logical conclusion. Democracy is the political form of equality. One man, one vote, that sort of thing."

"Uh-huh," is all I can muster up to say to that.

Thunderbolt rolls on like he's making perfect sense. "What's equality, really? It's make-believe. Not everyone is equally strong. We're not equally fast, or equally smart. Some of us are geniuses. Some of us are retards. There's no magic quality we all share equally, nothing that really makes us the same—I mean, come on, who are they kidding? But our obsession with pretending that everyone is equal—or worse, that everyone should be, no matter the cost—has bogged us down as a culture. We're *not* all the same. We're not all equal, and we never will be. That's why communism didn't work. And that's why democracy is falling apart too. Now, don't misunderstand, we're not against freedom. We're the most pro-freedom people around, including the most important freedom, the freedom to rise as far and as fast as you can, without worry about what the flabby mediocrity thinks is polite. And that's a pretty big thing to say, these days. I know, I know. It sounds crazy, but we've got to face the facts as they are."

Despite Garrison's plan of having another cape introduce this to me as a way to get me on board, he doesn't seem to be able to help himself from butting in. The words seem to erupt from him, like a bark of pain after a struck nerve. "We've got swarms of refugees in Europe. Recessions in America. Who's doing well? The Chinese. They don't give a shit about being PC; they just get things done. That's what radical inequality does—it lets the cream rise. The people at the top have the resources to set their own path in life, and the people at the bottom get some sort of structure and guidance, which, if the feckless corruption of the Western democracies is any guide, they sorely need."

"Right, right," says Thunderbolt, trying to keep things light and conversational.

"We're trying to create a new society here on Cynosure," says Garrison. "We'll be a model to the rest of the world, combining the best in modern thinking with the most timeless and enduring human wisdom."

"Like what?" I ask. I think Thunderbolt is twigging to the fact that they haven't made the sale, but Garrison is still so euphoric after coming out of the closet as a fascist lunatic that he answers without hesitation.

"Hereditary dictatorship. It's the oldest form of government, and when left alone, the most stable. We'll have the best and the brightest living in luxury, not just here, but in seasteads all over the planet. Hierarchy is natural. It's healthy. Why do you think people love stories about kings and queens so much? They're yearning for the past. They *want* to pay us tribute. Aristocracy means rule by excellence, and that's what we'll be—the excellent, trained from birth to excel, leading the mundane. Trust me, Dreadnought, when they see the benefits of going back to the old ways, they will *beg* us to save them from themselves, and we will be happy to oblige."

"No, you won't," I say. Garrison's train of thought derails and he stares at me, confused. I clarify for him: "Because I'm going to beat the shit out of you instead."

Without turning my head away from Garrison, I kick a leg out at full power and smash the low table into Thunderbolt's legs. It crashes against him in a wave of shattered glass, but I'm already closing the gap and driving him across the room into a man-sized divot in the wall, slamming punches into his face. Thunderbolt's fist crackles with power, curling snakes of lightning, and he cracks a good one across my jaw, another at my throat that I choose to take on the shoulder. My skin is alight with the burny-numbness I've learned to associate with electrical burns, and I am thankful all over again for the extra insulation Doc Impossible put in the soles of my boots. With a vicious combination of hooking punches,

Thunderbolt forces me back long enough to flit clear of the wall and take a fighting stance.

The door to the side room bangs open, but I barely pay attention to the pair of goons with pistols who charge out. In an eyeblink I've covered the space Thunderbolt opened between us, and we're locked in a flurry of attacks and counters. I get good shots in. So does he. We can both fly, but we're content to keep this one intimate, stay in close and wail away at each other. My nerves are singing with the first strains of battle joy, and my grin has gone feral.

Then my fist lands on Thunderbolt's kidney, and my wrist seems to explode. Hot, deep pain blasts up my arm to the elbow. Thunderbolt doesn't even seem to have felt a blow that should have doubled him over in agony. I duck back in surprise, try to check the lattice to see what the hell has happened.

I can't.

It's gone.

• • •

I try to fly and can't even leave the ground. I screw my eyes shut and try to force the lattice to appear, but there's nothing. The goons I've discounted tackle me and twist my arms behind my back to click handcuffs around my wrists. I try to pull away, but their arms are so much stronger than mine. The handcuffs should be like tissue to me, but they hold fast when I jerk on them. One of the goons hauls me into a kneeling position by my bound wrists, and my shoulder sockets scream. From there, I'm yanked to my feet and held fast between the bodyguards.

Garrison is crossing the room, pulling his rings off. "I told you my own power wasn't very impressive. And it's not. Power is about change, and mine are more the creation of absence. But I find that there are many places where a carefully considered disruption is more useful than anything else."

Garrison's first punch lands like the end of the world. It hurts *so* much. I've been shot, and it didn't hurt that much. My head swims. My lip stings.

"I'm disappointed in you, Danielle. Here I thought you could overcome your degeneracy. You *seemed* bright, at least. I could have made you rich. I mean true wealth, not that chicken feed the city is paying you. But more than that, you could have been in on the ground floor of the next evolution of humanity. For the sake of pragmatism, I was even willing to overlook your gender issue, since you seemed different from the rest of the filth." More punches. Thunderbolt is watching from the side, his face hard.

"You said you wouldn't hurt her!" It's Karen. She's standing at the hallway, aghast, terrified.

"Get the fuck out of here!" shouts Thunderbolt. "You got what you came for, now go!"

Karen turns and runs, and Thunderbolt goes after her.

Garrison grabs my chin and forces my attention back on him. "We're going to rule this planet like gods. The peasants will know their place, and we will have the worship that is our due. Governments will tremble to defy us, and all the world will be ours, as is right. You could have been one of us, and you spit in my eye." He spits in mine. "She was right. You're just another degenerate, after all."

An absurd thought jags through my mind: *This really hasn't been my day.* After that, there's no more room to think. Only rage, struggling to be heard over the fear.

And the blows continue to fall.

CHAPTER FIFTEEN

They throw me in a hole. No light in this cell, just a hard cot and a combination toilet and sink I've got to find by touch. No light until there's nothing *but* light, searing white from the ceiling, and a squawking buzzer to jerk me awake. My hair is soaked through with cold sweat. The echoes of one nightmare resolve into the shape of another I can't wake up from.

My suit and cape are gone. Instead I've got rough cotton clothes on, a plain green top and bottom, and a thick steel collar around my neck. My ear is painful and irritated where they tore the glued-in earbud out with some pliers. I grope for the lattice, but it's not really there. I can feel…something. More at least than I did last night during those awful seconds when it was sinking in that Garrison had muted my powers. But not enough to do anything with. Vague hints of the strands underlying everything, ephemeral and flimsy to the point where I can't decide if I actually see them, or if that's simply what hope looks like.

A slot in the door clacks open and a tray of food slides in. It's like a microwave dinner, but with breakfast food. Mushy, lukewarm waffles and syrup that tastes of industrial chemicals. Orange juice that's mainly yellow water with some pulp in it.

How could this get any worse is a question I am scared to find an answer for. But then the door opens, and there's Graywytch, and oh, *that's how.* Armed goons in green polo shirts slip into my cell and seize me by the arms. No speaking, no orders, they simply rush in, grab me, and haul me up on my feet. Graywytch watches me with pinched lips, like I'm a rabid dog being carried away by animal control.

We're somewhere deep in Cynosure. There are no windows, and the halls are austere nautical architecture all the way—steel, raised lips at every hatch, naked fluorescents shining down on blue linoleum. No portholes. I bet we're under the waterline.

About halfway down the hall, I make my first break for it.

I feint one way and dive hard the other, slamming one guard into the lip of a hatch and spinning to try and kick the other in the—

My head is pounding when I wake up. The blue linoleum has little silver swirl patterns in it, which I notice because my cheek is pressed hard against it. My stomach and sides sing with new bruises. Another kick comes in, and all my breath whooshes out of me.

"That's enough," says Graywytch. "I need him healthy." She steps into my line of view, looms over me with a disgusted sneer. Little flits of shadow dance around her fingers, and as I watch they suck back up into one of her rings and disappear. "No more of that, boy."

I suppose I'd like to say I have something witty to say, but I don't. The fear is so tightly packed into my chest I can barely breathe, barely think. I don't nod or shake my head or even glare. At this point, I'm proud that I haven't shit myself.

The guards haul me to my feet and click handcuffs tight around my wrists. We start walking down the hall again, and we come to an operating theater. Well, that's what it looks like at first. A crane with lights coming down from the ceiling, a reclining dentist's chair beneath it. Every wall crammed with glass-doored cupboards, and a few rolling surgical carts with locks on the wheels. But then I start noticing the other stuff. Like how each wall has a carved stone sitting in something that looks like a torch sconce. How the dentist's chair has manacles built into it. The large brass spell circle built into the deck, inlaid with silver and copper.

"Strap him in," says Graywytch. She disappears into a room

just through another hatch, and the moment she's out of sight I'm trying to make another break—

Wow, getting punched in the kidney *really* hurts when you don't have superpowers. My legs buckle underneath me, and the guards heave me onto the chair while I'm still trying to figure out how to control my body below the waist again. The handcuffs come off, and they strap my wrists down to the arms of the chair. My legs are strapped in as well.

Graywytch returns with a bowl of water and begins splashing my forehead, my chest, my stomach, my groin. She sets the bowl aside and retrieves a needle from somewhere behind me. It pinches into my elbow, but she misses the vein. That's okay, though, since she's not at all shy about digging around inside my arm until she finds it. After she's got her blood sample, she pulls the needle out and lets the wound trickle until the bleeding stops on its own. She's moved on to cutting my shirt off with a pair of surgical scissors and snipping my bra away as well. With my own blood she begins painting squiggle figures on my chest and down my stomach. She's muttering under her breath, some kind of chant.

Through it all, I am silent. I'm holding myself in tight, because if I don't I will start screaming, and I'm not sure I'll stop. I am *not* giving this bitch the satisfaction.

Then Graywytch turns on the lights, and there's some quality in them, some ineffable weirdness in the pale blue light that the blood responds to. It starts to bubble and hiss and *BURN oh God I'm burning it hurts IT HURTS so—*

So despite all my best intentions, I'm screaming.

And I was right.

I don't stop.

Back in my cell, the door clunks shut behind me, a fusillade of locking thumps as the bolts engage. A few moments later, the slot clacks open and another terrible meal is shoved through the hole. I'm barely finished with it before the lights die, plunging me into pitch darkness. And that's the day.

I curl up on the cot, twitching and exhausted. My mind is

empty. My body aches, and my chest stings. The bruises on my face, so painful last night, seem like distant afterthoughts now. After what might have been minutes or might have been hours, I manage to find the will to pull myself out of bed and begin exploring the cell. It's slow work, feeling over every inch in the dark. I find the door. No handle on the inside, hinges on the outside. The food slot is fixed firmly in place. The toilet-and-sink is riveted to the floor. The cot is a metal protrusion from the wall with a hard pad on top. I can move the pad, but it only weighs a few pounds and I can't find any way to rip it open. It's useless as a weapon or armor. The food tray is made of very light plastic, and the flimsy spork that came with it flexes in my hand when I hold it, never mind if I tried to attack someone with it. After a few hours of testing and experimenting, I reluctantly admit that nothing in this cell will help me escape or fight them off tomorrow.

With nothing else to distract it, my mind begins circling back to the…

Shit, was that torture? Can I call that torture?

Okay, fine. To the torture.

Graywytch seemed like she was trying to figure something out. Not that she was asking me anything. It isn't an interrogation. It's an experiment, and I'm the lab rat. Whatever question she was investigating, she didn't find the answer today. But that doesn't seem to have surprised her—at the very least, she showed no signs of frustration.

It's obvious who rigged up Garrison's magic for him. Now that I know she's linked up with him, I recognize that together they form that most ancient and venerable of all Silicon Valley pacts—the Hacker and the Backer. One puts up the money, the other puts up the talent. Sooner or later, one stabs the other in the back, but until then it's a game of screwed-you chicken to see how long the partnership can last.

Doc explained the relationship to me once during one of our long, aimless conversations as we sat on the balcony and watched the sun slide red and wet behind the horizon. She was talking about software development, particularly the version of the Internet that she was first instantiated on. The way Doc tells it, in those days the Internet was a cyberpunk playground through which she, as an infant AI, first came to know and love humans. That was several versions of her core code ago, a time and place she still harbors a longing nostalgia for. When she says she's only seven years old, she's talking about when she first started walking around as a physical entity. In other ways, she's a bit over thirty.

I might never see her again. It bothers me more than I'd have expected it to.

My chest stings and throbs when I run my fingers over the rough spots where the burns crinkled my skin up. One of the security guys, who I gathered was some sort of medic, smeared a chemical-smelling goop on them. It helped a bit. Then he stood by and she hit me with the lights again. When I get out of here, I'm gonna punch him in the mouth. Hell, I'll be generous—mouth punchings for everyone! So I start laughing, and then I start shivering and clenching, and eventually I fall asleep.

The screaming buzzer wakes me up again. My heart is sprinting, my hair is damp. Another awful, awful breakfast, and then they drag me into the experimentation chamber again. I don't fight this time. No point. Until I have a plan, I need to play along and minimize the damage. If I could get my hands on one of their guns, maybe.

Shit, I wish Calamity was here. She'd know what to do. Or, better yet, wouldn't have gotten captured in the first place.

I'm strapped into place again. Off goes the shirt, again. More blood samples, more Finger Painting of the Damned, and then more pain. Lots more pain.

For an instant, I sense the lattice.

With every ounce of will I leap at it, try to catch and pull on it, tear myself loose and blast out of this room at speed. But it slips through the fingers of my mind and fades. The collar at my neck gets hot. This happens a few times. Sometimes the lattice is clear and bright. Sometimes fuzzy and indistinct. She keeps making adjustments to her equipment or the cadence of her chanting, trying again and marking down the results in a ledger.

Graywytch purses her lips after one round of experiments. I sag and gasp in the restraints. The medic comes by to swab my wounds with a soaked cotton ball held in some forceps. The red haze of pain fades, and for a moment I can think again. My temples are wet from where the tears have streaked back from my eyes into my hair.

Someone back in New Port must have noticed I'm missing by now. Right? Doc will be looking for me, and there are GPS beacons sewn into my suit. But Graywytch or Garrison might have destroyed it by now. Maybe Charlie will—no, damn. We barely told him where we were going. Goddamnit, Karen. You towering asshole. I trusted you. I was trying to help you.

No, stop it, that's not useful. What would Calamity do? She'd focus on the here and now. Wait for them to make a mistake. Be ready to explode into violence, or quietly slip a tool down her pants, whatever the situation calls for.

A guard pokes his head into the chamber. "Sovereign would like to speak to you."

"I'm busy," says Graywytch, not looking up from her notebook.

"Now," says the guard.

Graywytch straightens and I can only see the back of her head, but whatever is on her face makes the guard go pale and duck out. She closes her notebook and follows him. The hatch stays open behind her.

"We agreed that you would not interrupt my work," says Graywytch by way of greeting. I can just see a slice of her back through the hatch, but whoever she's talking to is out of sight.

"Unless absolutely necessary," says Garrison, as if he were concurring with what she was saying. I guess Sovereign is his supervillain name. That's a bit on the nose, dude. No class at all. "Where are we on Phase Two?"

After a silence just long enough to be uncomfortable, Graywytch says, "He's resisting me. That makes it harder."

"They're *all* going to be resisting you. We've got to get this right. The market for proven powersets is predicted to be our best-seller. Have you made any progress, at least?"

"Yes," she says. "I've eliminated some of the more obvious solutions. I can also clearly identify the mantle and separate it from the rest of his pattern—"

"You can separate it!" Garrison says. "That's good!"

"Conceptually. I can separate it *conceptually*, and tell where he starts and his power ends." After another pause, Graywytch adds, "This would go much faster if you would allow me to work without these onerous restrictions—"

"No," says Garrison immediately. "If he dies, the mantle might be lost entirely. I'm not willing to take that step yet."

"Yet?" she says. Oh man, Graywytch, don't sound too hopeful, now.

"We've already had to plug one leak. I think we've got maybe two weeks before we're forced to go public. I need to be able to fly for the camera when we make the announcement, or the optics will be all wrong. That's the classic superpower; nobody will take me seriously if I can't do it." Garrison sounds almost anxious. "You've got to make it work. One way, or the other."

"Well, in that case—"

"You know what? Hold on," says Garrison.

Footsteps, and then Graywytch is saying "Wait, that's not—"

Garrison steps through the hatch. He's not wearing a super-villain outfit or anything, just a polo shirt and khakis, and he still has his people call him Sovereign. That's not how that works. The name goes with the suit, even for blackcapes. Shit, everyone knows that. Fucking rich boy tourist. If I had more guts, I'd be working up a loogie just for him. Right now I'm satisfied to be able to keep my face blank. Then his eyes catch on my bare chest, and his cheeks go pink as he looks away.

You unbelievable dickhead! Oh, sure, he can order me imprisoned and tortured, but the sight of my breasts is just too much for his pure soul. And somehow the sheer hypocritical bullshit of it all cracks through the fear and gives me enough courage to sneer at him.

"Your concern for my modesty is touching." I say.

Graywytch pours in after him. "You said you'd stay out of my laboratory."

Garrison ignores her. "Danielle, I'm willing to cut you a deal. Give up your powers and I'll let you go. All will be forgiven." He says this to the back wall, carefully avoiding looking at me, like somehow that makes any of this even remotely okay.

Now, I despise Graywytch. I mean I loathe her with a purity of hate that almost scares me. But there's something in my feelings about her—not quite respect, but almost. She's consistent. In her own screwed up way, she's even honest. When she cuts my shirt off, there's no emotion, no suggestion of intimacy or transgression. It's only a job she's doing. It's mortifying, at least until the soul-scalding pain blasts all thoughts of modesty out of my head, and I hate her more than ever…

But at least she's not hiding from everything she's done to me. She needed my shirt off to do her experiments, so she cut it off. She's not pretending she gives a shit about my dignity. In a weird way, that almost seems respectful. Like we're not kidding ourselves that this isn't messed up and gross beyond all reasoning. Like we've agreed that we will never be anything but enemies. It's a strange sort of understanding. Tacit, and sour. But also real.

There's none of that almost-respect for Garrison. If I was ever going to feel anything but disgust for him, it went out the porthole the moment he decided he was okay with strapping me in a chair and torturing me for days on end, but not with seeing me half-naked.

I don't respond fast enough for his liking. "Danielle? Are you willing to cooperate? This can go on for as long as it needs to."

"I've been thinking about your offer," I say slowly. "After long consideration, I've decided that you should go fuck yourself."

"Give me your powers," he says, just at the edge of stammering.

"Eat shit!" I shout, jerking against my restraints. "You don't get to do this to me and then ask nicely, understand? You get *nothing!* Not a goddamn thing!"

"I said, give me your powers!"

"Look at me, coward!" He does. He's gone pale with rage, but it doesn't scare me. What can he do? Torture me? Kill me? "You don't deserve my powers, and I will die screaming before I let you have them."

Garrison turns and begins to walk stiffly out of the room. I lean over the side of the chair and spit on the deck. He hears me, turns, and crosses the room in three quick strides to backhand me across the mouth. I spit again, blood this time.

And smile.

I win, motherfucker.

But better than that, I see my way out. All this was just instinct, some urgent need to prove they didn't control me. But now I have a plan. Doc was right. The Hacker and the Backer always end up turning on each other, and these two aren't going to be any different. I've got to find the sore spot between them and push on it.

Garrison would be easier, since I know how weak he is now, but I don't have access to him. I'll have to go through Graywytch. She's tougher, but it doesn't matter. She's not tough enough. I'll find her tender spot. I've got two weeks. Plenty of time.

She closes the hatch behind Garrison and pulls a lever to crank the array of watertight latches shut. For a moment she stays there, face to the door, quiet and still.

"You really don't like him, do you?" I ask.

She slowly turns. Under the glare of the fluorescents, she looks pale and old. "Shut up."

"Why are you helping him?" I ask. "I mean, I get why you hate me in particular, but why help him with this plan of his?"

Graywytch ignores me and returns to the lectern where she's got her notebook set up. She begins writing notes. This is one of the precious few breaks in the session that I'll get. I need to make the most of it.

After a few moments, I think I know what to say. "You don't strike me as being on board with his politics."

"You know nothing about me."

"So, what, you're a fascist now too?"

"Your strategy is transparent, young man. Be quiet. I must concentrate."

"Did you murder Crenshaw? Or was it someone else on Garrison's payroll?"

Graywytch looks up at me, surprised. People always think I'm stupid. (To be fair, until a few months ago, so did I.) "I don't know what you're talking about," she says without even trying to sound sincere.

"Garrison killed Crenshaw to keep him quiet," I say. "Do you think he'll be any more forgiving when he decides you're a danger to him too?"

Graywytch steps away from her lectern to flip the switch for the torture lights again. Searing pain erupts through my chest, and I can't speak anymore after that.

Maybe this isn't such a hot plan after all.

Back in my cell. The new shirt they've given me is cheap and scratchy and I end up taking it off because it's only making my burns hurt worse. After the lights go out, I lay on my bunk, trying to organize my thoughts. The plan isn't going well. She's too stubborn. But until something else comes along, I don't know what else to do.

The conversation between Garrison and Graywytch, that's important. Phase Two isn't just about my powers—he said that "they'll all be resisting." So I'm the guinea pig. They're trying to figure out how to steal powers. What's Phase Three?

A few possibilities suggest themselves, but after a while of picking over what little I know, I find that I've run out of things to think about, and my mind spirals back down to my predicament.

What a clean word. Predicament. Like I've locked myself out of the house or something.

Maybe I'm not getting out of this one. Maybe these are the

last few days of my life. I wish Calamity was here. Not just because she'd have them all broken and groaning by now. I just…I wish I could see her again. I wish we could stop fighting and go back to the way it was before.

Sleep creeps up on me, and I dream of Sarah.

Graywytch starts the torture up again. She's narrowed the beam of light this time, and passes it back and forth across my chest according to some unknowable pattern. It kind of hurts, in the same way that the sun is kind of bright.

When she shuts the light off, I lie sagging, gasping, sweating in the chair, trying to unkink my brain enough to speak.

"What are you getting out of this?" I ask when I'm able to get my mouth to work. "Money? Power?"

She reaches over and flicks the switch for the lights. One long, scalding second, and then off again.

"Shut up."

"How long have you been working with him?"

But she only ignores me. Stands at her lectern and scribbles her notes. Then she pulls the light fixture down and replaces the lens with another one, darker in color. A few moments later the lights start up again, and so does the burning.

The lattice shimmers into being. It's hard and clear, so close I swear I can grip it. But I can't. My mind won't tangle with it properly. There's a buzzing in my gut, just behind my navel.

The light dies, and I collapse with relief. Think. I've got to think. I've got to try something new. I flop my head over to the side to look at her, grope for something useful to say. Nothing. Can't think. The fear smothers me. My mouth goes on ahead by itself.

"Myra," I call. She looks up at me. "When I get out of here, I'm going to kill you."

She snorts, and looks back down at her work. "No, Daniel. I don't think you will."

She makes more adjustments. Now, when she shines the light on me, the lattice is clearer in my mind now than at any time since my powers got muted. But I can't touch it. I can sense it, but I can't touch it, can't grip it, can't do anything but watch it. All the while, the buzzing behind my navel continues, rising into a hot, crunchy sting that hurts almost as badly as the boiling blood.

When I'm not terrified, I'm twisted into hard little knots with frustration. Oh, the things I would do if I had my powers back. But it's just a daydream at this point. Tears of pain and rage trace cool lines down my temples as I try to hold it together between sessions. My plan is a shambles, my throat raw from screaming.

Then it happens.

During the last session of the day, my chest begins to glow. A bubble of fizzing white light starts to rise from my skin. Horror locks me stiff as I watch the mantle nearly pull itself out of my chest. Worse, I can feel my bones begin to shift and flex. Not just my ribs, but all of them.

No.

Please, no.

I can't go back.

I'll die. Please don't do this.

Don't take it from me.

Graywytch grunts with satisfaction. The light fades, and the mantle snaps back inside of me. The skin over my sternum stops glowing, but I don't feel better.

"The crystal needs to cool," says Graywytch. "But tomorrow? Tomorrow, I think, is the day."

No more bravado. No more courage. She's beaten me. "Myra, please don't do this." It's contemptible begging. Weak. Not worthy of Dreadnought. "I'm sorry. Whatever I did to make you hate me, I'm sorry. Please don't do this."

"It's not about you, young man. You were only the catalyst. Push women far enough, and we push back. And we win. You'll see."

The guards drag me back to my cell. It's over. I've lost. I can't get to her, and tomorrow she'll take the mantle from me.

When it really comes down to it, I don't give a shit about my powers. I lived my whole life without them, and I could go back to

APRIL DANIELS

that. But what will happen to my body? Will it go back to the way it was? I can't survive that. I can't go back. I can't face the world with those shoulders and that voice. Maybe they'll kill me when they're done. Maybe they'll roll me off the side of the deck and into the deep, and I won't have to live through that nightmare. It seems almost too much to hope for.

They say that your real identity is who you are in the dark. The lights shut off, and I figure out that I'm really a trembly little girl who is too weak to protect herself. Down, down I spiral into the depths. For hours.

Curled tight in a ball, sobbing until my chest hurts, I miss the sound of gunfire through the thick metal walls until it's just outside my cell. A flurry of shots, and then silence.

The hatch opens.

"Get up, partner," says Calamity. "We're leaving."

CHAPTER SIXTEEN

Oh God, no. Not now. She can't see me like this, half-naked, covered in wounds, my face still wet with tears. But as much as my heart wants to be a wailing drama queen, my feet are much more sensible. I'm up and throwing on the cheap shirt they left me with before I really have time to think about it.

As I come into the light and Calamity sees me clearly, she goes rigid. "Jesus, Danny…"

"That bad, huh?" I ask.

"We're gettin' you out of here," snarls Calamity. Footsteps from up the hall. She whirls and fires in a single smooth motion, the blast of her six-shooter like God's dynamite in the metal confines of the hallway. A guard in a green polo shirt goes down coughing blood, his larynx shattered by a high velocity jelly round. A submachine gun tumbles out of his hands and he makes a hissing animal noise as he writhes and thrashes on the deck.

"I can't fight," I say. My cheeks are red. Fighting is what I'm *for*. "My powers are gone."

"Thought as much," Calamity beckons for me to follow as she strides down the hallway. "Didn't figure you were sticking around out of the joy of their company."

I follow close behind her. "We need to get out of here before Thunderbolt gets involved."

"Kinetiq's tanglin' with him outside," says Calamity. "Don't know how long they can hold 'em."

"Graywytch is here too."

"I see," is all Calamity says. I catch up, and she turns, puts a hand on my shoulder. "No, stay behind me. I'll take the hit."

Reluctantly, I hang a step back. We turn a corner and begin walking down a long hallway lined with broken, groaning bodies. What looks like every guard I've seen down here in the past few days is curled up and bleeding. One of them tries to grab Calamity by the ankle and she casually shoots him in the wrist. More jelly rounds, it looks like. No penetration, but they land like sledge-hammers. The guy who grabbed at her has a new bulging fracture for his trouble. "Don't step in the blood, or they'll track us by our footprints."

We get to an intersection and begin climbing a flight of stairs. At the landing, she scoots around the corner with both guns out and high, clearing it before waving me up with a jerk of her chin. A few more flights of stairs, and we're above sea level. The austere steel tunnels give way to polished glass and smoky gray carpet.

A voice blares out over an unseen PA system. "The intruders are under Moldbug Tower and climbing out to the promenade. All tactical teams converge on their location. Continue trying new radio frequencies. If you find a clear channel, let your teammates know immediately."

"Tactical teams, *plural*," says Calamity as we jog up the stairs. "You don't expect to hear something like that on a resort island, that's for damn sure."

"This place is amazingly screwed up," I say, trying to keep up with the banter. Trying not to let on that, without my powers, I am absolutely terrified of the men with guns coming to kill us. We emerge from the stairwell into another corridor, this one lined with low, leather benches over dark blue carpet. Through three or four layers of glass, I can see the tile-lined plaza and promenade, and beyond that, the ocean. Calamity immediately pushes me down behind one of the benches and hits the deck next to me.

She squeezes the throat mic around her neck. "Doc, Dreadnought's out of gas, we're gonna need to get picked up the hard way." Almost as an afterthought, she reaches into her jacket and clicks a switch near her shoulder. Doctor Impossible's voice filters out, thin and tinny from Calamity's radio.

"—py that. Can she walk?"

"Yes'm, but it's gonna be a bit of a hike to high ground. Keep your distance and we'll call ya when we need ya."

"We're not really going to climb thirty more flights of stairs, are we?" I ask.

"I was thinking we'd take the elevator," says Calamity. Her eyes are gleaming over her red bandanna mask. "But if you've got your heart set on it—"

"I see them!" I hiss, and try to smoosh myself down harder into the carpet. We're lying in the inner walkway of what appears to be the skeleton of a high-end strip mall. Every room here has lots of doors at the front and the back leading to the promenade or the inner corridor, but not so much side to side. Around the curve of the promenade, I spot a goon squad in dark blue tactical gear marching in loose order up the hallway. They're maybe fifty or sixty yards distant and don't seem to have seen us yet.

Calamity sees them as I point them out, then cranes her neck to look the other way. "From behind too. Looks like they're further away." I can't make out what she's indicating, but I'll take her word for it. "Stay here."

Calamity rolls away and slips down a cross-corridor, then around a corner toward the team coming in from the front, and out of sight. A moment later, I lose sight of the goons as they get to the part of the curve where the shop walls block my view. I scrunch down behind the bench as much as I can and watch the curving corridor ahead. It's going to be okay. She's coming back.

An hour passes. Then a week. The team comes around the bend and immediately spots me. The one in front points and shouts. They all aim their submachine guns at me and start double-timing it toward me. I keen with terror and start scrabbling backwards on hands and knees. They enter a corridor intersection—

A flashbang skids and tumbles across the carpet just before—

Calamity's grapnel fires, whizzes past a hand's breadth above head level and—

—and then she's among them. A whirl of fists, boots, and point-blank gunfire engulfs the team. Wherever they're shooting, she has just left. Wherever she shoots, her rounds land hits. Calamity's cable wraps twice around a goon's neck and hauls him in close to her just in time to be her human shield, a burst of friendly fire shattering his armor and leaving him a groaning heap. Her toe catches another behind the knee and puts him down kneeling where she shoots him in the back of the helmet. Bullets tear up the back of Calamity's jacket, digging deep into the armor beneath. She stumbles into a roll, comes up firing as another flash grenade whites out my vision.

Thumping, crunching, the slap of fist on flesh. More gunfire.

The green fog fades in time for me to see her shoot her grapnel directly into the face of one trooper, then whip it around like a flail and break another's jaw. A third climbs back to his feet and draws a knife. Half a second later he finds its planted hilt-deep under his own kneecap. As she's spinning away to shoot his partner, Calamity kicks backwards and lands a solid boot on the handle, and he goes down screaming. Only two remain on their feet now. She grabs one in her hand and choke-slams him through a bench. The other is hobbling away as fast as he can, shouting for backup into his radio and drawing his pistol for one last, desperate stand. A jelly round shatters his ankle, and another punches the handgun from his grip.

Just like that, five hard men are on the ground bleeding and stifling their cries of pain.

"Dreadnought, let's go!" Calamity shouts, and I'm so stunned she has to shout again before I get up and dash after her. Behind us, I can hear pounding feet and jostling gear as the other team sprints toward the sound of gunfire. We run past the team she tore up, and it's hard not to slow down and stare. One part horror, one part awe, three parts insecurity.

Calamity doesn't need real powers. She's perched at the very upper bound of human ability.

Right now, so am I. My body is still the way it became in the moments after Dreadnought gave me the mantle. Still as fit and strong and flexible as the entire US Olympic team put together. As bendy as a gymnast, as enduring as a runner, as strong as a heavyweight lifter. There are not enough hours in the day to train a normal body up to the level she and I are at.

The difference is, she's a badass on top of it.

But me? I can only lean into my powers. Take those away, and basic rent-a-goons can smoke me every time. No wonder she barely talks to me anymore.

I grimace and try to shake the bullshit out of my head. Falling apart can come later, when people aren't shooting at me. Head down, my bare feet are slapping the hard carpet as we sprint along the corridor.

Spiderweb cracks smash across a window to my left. The team behind us sees us around the bend and is firing through an open door.

"Keep going!" shouts Calamity over her shoulder. I get an arm up to the side of my head to protect my face, and we push through the storm of glass splinters. Stinging little cuts sprout all over me.

We get far enough around the bend to disappear behind another empty building, one that looks like it will be a restaurant when it is complete. We reach the end of the corridor and explode into the open area between two of the towers. The PA is shouting our location, bringing more goons down on us. It's just after dawn, the sun only now starting its climb up the watery blue sky. Cold ocean air pulls and snaps at us.

Calamity squeezes her throat mic again. "Doc, we're out of the building, can you come get us at the northern marina?"

A window-shaking detonation erupts in the air above us. I can just make out Kinetiq and Thunderbolt flitting around each other, the air a boil of energy blasts. Thunderbolt throws more

147

lightning; Kinetiq bounces it off their shields and lashes back with an emerald laser.

"No can do." Doc's voice crackles tinny over the radio. "Getting that low is suicide right now. I've got MANPADS painting me from the tower roofs and—shit!"

Like it sometimes does during a crisis, my brain fixates on a piece of semi-relevant trivia: MANPAD is an acronym that stands for Man-Portable Air Defense—shoulder-mounted missiles, basically. Usually I can snap out of it, but right now my mind feels like it's made of glue. I start to wonder where they got these, how much they must have cost. A lot, I'm sure.

Doc's tilt-engine comes screaming across the sky, a stub-nosed aircraft with pivoting wings and howling jet engines. It twists and weaves in midair as fingers of white smoke leap from the towers to chase her. Double-handfuls of crimson flares leap from the jet's tail, and the wings pivot with the engines so the whole thing back-flips over the missiles.

"Get up to a roof right now!" shouts Doc over the radio. "We can't last long up here!"

I grab Calamity by the shoulder, a sudden fear crashing through my stupor and bringing me back to the present. "Tell her to watch out for Panzer!"

Calamity's eyes bug. "They've got a *tank*?"

"No, Princess Panzer, she's Garrison's daughter and she's super dangerous." In my mind, I can see her summoning a dozen or more heavy gun emplacements and tearing Doc's jet into shredded aluminum litter.

"Oh, then I think we'd have seen her by now," says Calamity, turning to run again. I'm right behind her. "She's probably on the mainland with her father."

"How'd you know he would be gone?"

"Simple! I burned his biggest house down so he'd go inspect the damage." She cranes her neck to look up at the towers looming above us. "Well. Second biggest, anyhow."

Bullets start to snap past us. Calamity reaches into her coat and tosses a grenade high in the air; it bursts into a cloud of purple smoke that covers us until we get into the base of the next tower over.

Something is confusing me. After a few dozen yards it hits me. If Garrison isn't here, how come I don't have my powers back? My fingers start playing over the steel collar around my neck, not for the first time. Maybe there's something in this that's still muting me.

We come to a skidding halt in front of the lobby elevators and wait a tense few moments for a car to arrive. Bullets start slamming into the wall around us as we scramble inside. Calamity hits the door close button while I cower in the corner and try not to piss myself with terror when a bullet hole appears in the floor a hand's breadth from me. As the door shuts, Calamity's left ring finger, the one on her prosthetic hand, clacks open. There's a key in there that fits the firefighter's keyhole in the control panel. She cranks the lock over to manual operation and sets us to rise to the top floor.

"That should keep them from overriding it remotely," she says. "But I want to be ready in case these things ain't running normal software." She laces her fingers together to make a step. "Up you go. Get the hatch open."

I put a foot—torn and bloody from running through broken glass—in her hand, and Calamity boosts me to the ceiling panels. The panel comes undone easily and slides out of the way. There's an access hatch that I crank open and then pull myself out of. The elevator shaft is surprisingly warm, a dark vertical tunnel of creaking, quarking cables and gusting breezes. Calamity grabs my hand when I reach back down for her, and this at least I can do without issue, because even I can't screw up lifting someone straight up out of a hole.

"Almost there, partner," says Calamity as we sit back from the hatch. She squeezes her mic. "Doc, can you hear me?"

"I'm a little busy," Doc replies.

"We're coming up the northernmost tower. See you on the roof in a minute or two."

"I'll be—Kinetiq, get him off me!"

And then Kinetiq's reply, "Break hard right!"

Listening to them fight and helpless to get out there myself, I clench up and begin to shiver. If any of them die because I was stupid enough to get captured, I don't think I'll be able to live with myself.

The elevator slows and comes to a halt. Calamity and I both look up; we're at least fifteen floors short of the top.

"I guess they had an override after all," she says as she reaches into her jacket. "See if you can get that door open," she says, nodding at the shaft doors a couple yards above us.

I scramble up the access ladder and lean out to try and catch the seam with my fingers.

The elevator doors beneath us open with a ding, and a burst of automatic fire rakes the back wall of the empty car. Calamity pulls the pin on a silver canister with a white stripe painted around the base.

"Heads up for Willy Pete!" she calls before she tosses it through the hatch. The canister bounces off the back wall and rolls out of the car and into the hallway. There's a flat bang, and then some white smoke pours up out of the hatch.

"You—you didn't just drop white phosphorous on those guys, did you?" I ask, aghast. White phosphorus is evil, evil stuff. Sticks to flesh, burns down to the bone, and dousing it with water only makes it worse. I knew she was hardcore, but *damn.*

Calamity is stepping away from the hatch and laughing. "Hell no, it's just a glue grenade. Betcha they shit their pants, though." From the amount of dejected profanity wafting up with the last of the detonation fumes, that's probably a good guess. Calamity pulls another canister out from inside her jacket. This one is marked with a big red 'CS' on the side. "Last party favor. Hold your breath."

We get the doors open and scramble out of the shaft as the first burning hints of tear gas waft out of the elevator to taint the air. We let the doors shut behind us as the first round of coughing and choking really gets going.

Through the windows, we can see a glass and steel sky bridge linking this tower to the next one. Calamity points, and we start jogging toward it.

"Doc, change of plan," she says. "We're coming up on the eastern tower instead."

"Just make it fast," says Doc.

"But the scenic route is so pretty this time of year," says Calamity absently. As we're running she's digging deep into a pocket and pulling out handfuls of what look like cybernetic cockroaches. She scatters them behind us, and they disperse into corners, climb through ventilation grates, and disappear.

"This is all my fault." I say.

"What? No." Calamity scowls. "Any bad guy who gets hurt today has only himself to blame. It's just tear gas; they'll be fine."

We reach the bridge and start sprinting across it. Halfway across, another group of tactical goons comes around a corner and spots us across twenty yards of open hallway. No cover, nowhere to run.

My heart seems to stop as the world turns to glassy silence.

Something kicks me in the back of the ankle. I go down.

A bullet snaps through where my head would have been.

The rustle of cloth, the jitter of holsters clearing to my right.

More bullets bite holes in the air. Muzzles flicking pale orange.

The window next to me cracks, a streak of white in the corner of my eye.

My scalp goes numb, and then hot.

The report of Calamity's six shooters isn't something I hear, it's something I feel.

Impacts tear into the men down the hall. Visors shatter, weapons spin out of hands. They break and scramble, patting themselves down for wounds as they get out of the line of fire.

Calamity's pistols click dry, and the world snaps back into motion with a rush. She is breathing very quickly, her face pale, eyes wide.

"They'll figure out I'm shootin' jelly in a moment," mutters Calamity. "Can't hurt them right at this range."

Behind us, faint but clear nonetheless, we both hear an elevator ding open.

Calamity holsters one of her pistols and squeezes her throat mic. She shakes the other pistol's cylinder open and lets the brass tinkle to the ground. "Doc. We're pinned down in the sky bridge."

"Understood. Can you open a window?"

Calamity slaps the cylinder of her pistol shut on a fresh load of bullets. "Sure thing."

"Right. I'm coming to you, low and slow. Be ready."

Doc's tilt-engine banks hard into a looping dive towards us. Calamity steps back from the wall and unloads her gun into the window. It cracks into a square of white spiderwebs. With a solid kick, the whole panel, at least ten feet wide, peels off and falls down to the plaza below. Goons to the front and rear of us are starting to peek around the corner, getting ready to rush us from both sides.

One of the side doors on the tilt engine slides open and the jet tips up on one wing.

"Oh no," leaks out of me as I realize what she and Doc are planning. "No, no, no!"

"Hells yeah!" shouts Calamity. She wraps an arm around me and charges the hole. We leave the sky bridge.

For a frozen moment of terror we hang in space.

The tilt-engine roars beneath us, and we're falling through the door, deck and ceiling rotating about us even as we drop through the cabin to the other side. The door slams shut, and we both tumble against the back wall as Doc jerks back on the control yoke and pulls us into a spinning vertical climb.

"Strap in," she shouts as the world spins outside the small windows. Calamity and I claw our way into the jump seats and pull the harnesses around our shoulders. The very instant I get mine latched shut Doc kicks in the afterburners, and we are *leaving*.

"Kinetiq, break off and get out of there. We've got her," Doc is saying through the radio. Everything is suddenly calm. The jet judders and vibrates with the muted roar of engines, but we're level and stable. Doc twists in her seat to look back through the cockpit door. "Are you okay?"

"I…" I'm suddenly dizzy. "I think so."

Doc nods, concern and anger mixing on her face. I am so worthless. This was so stupid. Nobody's ever going to trust me again.

And I *still* don't have my powers.

CHAPTER SEVENTEEN

At Mach 2, it only takes about thirty minutes to get back to New Port. Thirty minutes is a long, long time when you're so mortified you wish you could pull your head down into your chest like a turtle. I'm blushing so hard it feels like if any more blood goes into my cheeks, they're going to pop. Eyes fixed rigidly at the floor. Jaw clamped shut.

People ask me questions, and I barely hear them, barely want to hear them. Shake my head no to everything, hunch down into my arms crossed over my stomach. At some point, Calamity takes her jacket off and lays it across me, and I almost start weeping. With my forehead against the bulkhead, I bury my face in my hands and try to forget I exist.

Please, Sarah, just ignore me. Just pretend I'm not here. You're better than me and you always have been and you don't need to pretend I'm not pathetic because I'm pretty sure we all just proved that I couldn't pull my weight when it really counted.

I begged her. I looked Graywytch in the eyes and I *begged* her.

This isn't who I wanted to be. I thought I had changed, that I was strong now. But I'm a coward. And now I know I always will be.

I hang my head and screw my eyes shut and wait for this to all be over. One way or the other.

My scalp stings, and a nasty headache finds me as the horizon outside the window dips and we come in for a sharp landing. The ground comes up, up, up and then past as we're touching down inside a deep pit. Above us, the roof winches close, and when the massive doors meet, a hologram will flicker to life and make this all seem like an empty gravel field in one of the disused industrial parks at the outskirts of the New Port metropolitan area.

This used to be a facility owned and operated by a hypertech merchant called The Artificer. Since he's dead and nobody was using the place, Doc moved in and set it up as a safehouse/airfield. When Utopia killed The Artificer, she used her inversion beam, which mangles the underlying structure of reality. I had to spend weeks tying up the frayed strings of the lattice one by one before any of the equipment in here would work properly for any length of time. Once I was so proud of it, but now I couldn't care less. My fingers won't stay away from my collar for long. I need to get this thing off, and then hope my powers come back.

What if they don't?

My fingers move away from the collar.

We touch down, and the engines die. For a moment there's only silence as Doc shuts down the flight systems and starts the automated ground crew into action.

"We're home," says Calamity, subdued in the aftermath of an adrenaline high.

My voice is barely a whisper. "Yeah."

Doc pops her hatch and hops out of the jet. Calamity and I are still unlatching our harnesses when Doc wrenches open the side door and drags me from the jet and into a tight, trembling hug that knocks her glasses askew. After a moment, I hug her back.

"Danny, I'm so sorry."

"It was my fault," I mumble into her shoulder.

Doc takes me by the shoulders and looks me dead in the eye. "Don't you *ever* start thinking that way. What they did is not your fault. In any way."

I can't maintain eye contact.

"Danielle, I mean it. They chose to hurt you. That's on them." Her voice gets hard. "And we're going to make them pay. Come on, I need to get you cleaned up."

She puts an arm around my shoulder and helps me limp to

the section of cots and dressers we have set up for overnight stays. Every step twists pebbles of broken glass in my feet. When Doc sees my bloody footprints, she cries out, "Why didn't you tell me your feet were cut?"

"I didn't want to be any more trouble," I mumble, mortified. Footsteps behind me, and then another Doc Impossible is there, identical in every way to the first, and they each get an arm under my shoulder and a hand under my thigh and carry me the rest of the way. I can't stop looking between them, surprised. Doc never uses more than one body at a time. It's against her android rules, the self-imposed rules she follows to act more human. Calamity falls in behind us, curiously silent. She probably wants her jacket back.

The Doctors Impossible set me on a cot and click a lamp on. One of them pulls a crash cart up and starts running leads to my arms and chest. The other fusses with the stinging place in my hair that's matted with blood. Electric clippers are produced from somewhere and she starts mowing a row in my hair.

"Do you have a headache?"

"Yes."

"Where?" They've gone clinical, and it's more of a relief than I can describe.

"Sort of all over. Well, the sides."

"Are you dizzy?"

"No."

"Nauseous?"

"Nope."

"Okay. Don't freak out, but you've been shot in the head. Just a graze, but there's the chance of a concussion." She holds up her hand, and the skin on her palm slides open, a lens peeking out. It lights up and she shines bright light into both my eyes, asks me to track it up and down and side to side. "I want to do some tests with you, okay?"

"Sure," I say, a little stunned. A third Doc Impossible has arrived now, this one forgoing her traditional lab coat for a full-body ensemble of carapace armor and an automatic shotgun. She paces restlessly around the perimeter of the living area.

Calamity stands off to one side. She's got her arms crossed, then in her pockets, then crossed again. She's looking anywhere but at me. I watch her trying to figure out the polite way to ask for her jacket back so she can finally get out of here, and feel sick.

One of the Docs tending to me notices, and stands up to pull a privacy screen on wheels from against the wall and make a little cubicle around my bed. "Sorry, Calamity, I've got to examine her."

The Doc next to me gently takes the jacket from me and hands it off to her counterpart who passes it to Calamity behind the screen. One of them hands me a blanket to wrap around my shoulders in its place.

"Uh, do you need me to stick around?" Calamity says.

I shake my head. *Please, just go.*

The Doc with me sees this, and the one who has her back to me says, "I think Danielle needs to be alone for a little bit. We'll call if there's anything else."

"I…okay. Sure. Yeah. Sure," says Calamity. I hear her boots clicking and hang my head. She'll never talk to me again, obviously.

"Sarah," calls out one of the Docs. "Thank you. Really."

After a long moment, Calamity replies, "Anytime."

The door to the stairs open and then shut again.

"She thinks I'm a total loser," I say.

"I can pretty much guarantee you you're wrong about that, kiddo," mutters the Doc picking broken glass out of my feet.

"I *am* a loser. I don't even have my powers anymore."

The Doc doing the scalp wound leans down, tilts my chin toward her with a finger. "Danny, nobody who matters only cared about your powers."

My shoulders curl in. "I can't be Dreadnought anymore."

"We don't know that," she says firmly. "Do you know how he took them away?"

"No. It was…one moment they were there. Then they weren't."

One of them is writing this down on a clipboard. "He didn't touch you or shoot you with anything?"

"No, nothing like that."

"Okay, so he's not a drainer. This collar they put on you, could that have something to do with it?" The one with the clipboard is asking the question, but it's the one dealing with my scalp wound who runs her finger over the collar. It's weird, seeing Doc in full android mode. With the staples finished, the Doc at my head sets the stapler aside and begins running a neurological scanner that looks like a flashlight across the surface of my scalp.

"Maybe. I'm…I'm kind of scared to find out." Graywytch's torture brought the lattice into sharp relief in my head, but I couldn't touch it, couldn't engage with it. What if I'm broken? Part of me wants this collar off yesterday. But a bigger part was hoping I could avoid the issue for a while. Luckily, I grew up in a house full of shouting, so if there's anything I know how to do right, it's avoid the issue. "Um, if you don't mind me asking, why are there three of you?"

They don't answer for a while. The one next to me sprays my scalp with something cold, and the pain in my scalp recedes into a chilly numbness. As the silence curdles, the one with the clipboard says, "I got tired of people I care about getting hurt because I was too scared to stop pretending I'm human. I'm not. It's time to stop playing."

"Oh." I reach out and take one of her hands. "Thank you."

Their faces get troubled. "Danielle, I am so sorry."

"For what?"

The tactical Doc has her back turned, but she's gone very still. The one running the scanner across my scalp stops working. "They had you for *days*," says clipboard Doc. "It should never have taken me so long to realize something had happened. I…" Doc's face cracks into tears. "I'm sorry. I was drunk. Even after Charlie came to tell me something was wrong, it took me *hours* to sober up. And…and look what they did to you." She's not working on my wound anymore. Doc sets the scanner aside, folds her arms around my shoulders, hugs me. "I'm so sorry. I'm so, so sorry."

"It's okay," I say softly.

"It's *not!*" snaps Doc. "You deserved a better friend than me."

"You got me out. That's what matters. It's not like I've never dropped the ball before."

Doc's mouth twists up in a bittersweet smile. "You're really something else, kid."

"Yeah, well. Nobody's perfect. I'm sorry for that crack about you helping me find something at the bottom of a bottle."

Doc wipes her eyes. "I'm sorry for being a drunk."

We sit there together, staring at the wall. Staple Doc picks up the scanner and finishes up—I don't have a concussion after all, which is one bit of luck in an otherwise *terrible* week—before she wanders off to work on getting the tilt-engine ready to fly again. Tactical Doc sets off with a purpose, says something about false positives on the motion sensors. The remaining Doc sits down in front of the medical computer I'm hooked up to and starts running tests on my heart and nervous system.

Whenever I look at her in the lattice, it's obvious she's not human. Her bones are basically fancy plastic. Her brain is synthetic gel. She's got a power cell next to her heart, which is itself made of a weird mix of hypertech materials I can't identify. Doctor Impossible is emphatically *not* human. There's a contradiction here. One I've mulled over sullenly a few times in the past months as her addictions got the better of her and made life difficult time and again. Finally, I work up the courage to ask.

"Doc, do you mind if I ask *why* you're an alcoholic?"

She shrugs. "It's bad form for a psychologist to self-diagnose, but I'd have to say that it's a coping mechanism for my inability to process the guilt from having murdered some of my friends. And from—" She stops for a moment. "From other frustrations."

That video of her—or maybe Utopia, since we never did figure out if Doc was conscious of what she was doing or if she was possessed—shooting Chlorophyll in the head plays through my mind again and I flinch. "No, I mean…why can't you just edit that out of you?"

"Oh." Doc looks at her toes. "Yeah, I guess I owe you that much."

"I mean, if it's private—"

"Danny, would you think less of me if I told you I was scared?"

"No, no of course not."

"Good, because I'm fucking terrified," she says. "At least once a week, I sit down with my configuration files to write a patch, and every time, I say today's the day. I'm gonna get better. And then I see that they go *all* the way down, and I freeze up again. I could make myself an entirely different person. Mom had a backdoor into me once before. My neural net is modeled after hers—it's not just a metaphor when I say I'm her daughter. I think like her, and sometimes the things I think scare me. How do I know that I can trust myself to make more changes? How do I know that in editing my code, I won't make myself more like her, and say I'm doing it to become better?"

"I'll make you a deal," I say.

Doc pushes back from the computer to swivel on her chair and face me. "Yeah?"

"We get my powers back, and when you're ready to patch yourself, I'll sit with you, and if it looks like you're turning evil, I'll totally kick your ass for you."

We start to laugh, and right now, despite it all, I feel okay.

"Can we cut this collar off of me now? I think I'm ready."

The tactical riot party version of Doc appears around the privacy divider with a power tool that looks like the unholy child of a pipe grinder and a surgical saw. "Sure thing. No time like the present, kiddo."

One of the Docs holds my hand while the other tilts my head over and then very carefully cuts through one side of the collar. I tilt my head the other way, and she slices through the other side as well. The two sides come off cleanly, and she sets them aside.

"Well?"

I close my eyes. For a moment I'm scared to reach for the lattice, but—

It's there. Oh thank God, it's there. With a flex of my will I engage with it and float a few inches up off the bed. I open my eyes and Doc is smiling. But not the pure, sweet joy I'd expect. Her smile is hard. It's mean. I like it.

"Good," she says. "You can still fight."

"That's nice to hear," says Kinetiq as they enter the living area. They've got a sheen of sweat on their face from the long flight. A few shining burns on their bare arms have gone an angry red, but they don't seem to notice or care.

I flit over to them and give them a hug. "Thank you," I say.

Kinetiq smiles and runs a thumb across the staples in my scalp. "Nice train tracks. You want to shave the rest off and get a mane like mine? You'd look super badass with these in."

I laugh, and now I'm not sure why I was scared that everyone would suddenly hate me. Fast rebounds are something I'm good at. Something I've needed to practice a lot. As much as I hate my parents for what they did to me, I don't mind knowing how to compartmentalize and move on. "Maybe later."

"We can talk about that once we've figured out how we're going to take down Garrison and Graywytch," says Doc.

My insecurities make one last valiant stand against the relentless forces of optimism: "What if he mutes my powers again?"

Doc shakes her head. "Everything has a countermeasure. You'll be ready for him next time. And there *will* be a next time—they didn't just hurt you, Danny, they made you look weak. We can't tolerate that."

"She's right," says Kinetiq. "You look like a target now. Gotta make an example out of him; it's the only way."

"Fine," I say. "So we take him out. How? He can turn off our powers if we get close enough to do anything."

One of the Docs comes over from the freestanding dresser with a spare set of clean clothes. "Well, first, you get dressed. I've spotted Charlie on the CCTV perimeter about a half-mile out, so when you're ready, we're going to have to go over everything that happened while you were their prisoner. That will help us figure out what our next step will be."

So I get dressed. The Docs smear antiseptic on the burns around my neck and bandage them, wrap my feet up too. By the time I'm all cleaned up, Charlie is staggering across the hangar, bent under the weight of a backpack crammed tight with books and magical equipment, a bike helmet dangling from his fingers.

The backpack goes down with a thud, and he arches up on his toes to stretch out his back. "You couldn't have built this place closer to the bus stop?"

"Get a car," I tell him.

Kinetiq picks up Charlie's bag and hauls it over to a workbench Doc has set up for him. She ran some scans on the collar and found that there wasn't any technological mechanism that she could identify suppressing my powers. There was, however, a glass slide, like something you'd use in a microscope but much thicker, inset on one of the inner edges. It was thickly etched on both sides with symbols we didn't understand. Charlie's here to see if he can figure out what this thing is and how it works.

"Sure, because gas money and insurance are exactly what I want to blow my allowance on," he says, one arm across his chest, the other pulling it tight to his shoulder to stretch. "Are you okay?"

"I am now."

Charlie looks abashed. "Danny, I had no idea—"

"It's not your fault," I say quickly.

"I should have known there was something up with her. She was barely paying attention."

"It's fine, really," I say, eager to move away from the topic. Karen is the last person I want to talk about right now.

"All right. So what's this text I got about a talisman?"

We head over to the worktable, and I show him the collar. Kinetiq looks at it and sniffs. "This is what muted your powers?"

"Yeah. It heated up a lot when Graywytch was torturing me too."

Charlie's already into it, eyes intent with focus. He picks up one half of the collar and looks at the cut. "It's a composite. This is steel, right?"

I examine it in the lattice. "And aluminum too."

"Right. Uh, Danny, this might suck, but I'm gonna need you to tell me everything that happened out there. Everything."

One of the Docs has wandered over as well, and I feel everyone's eyes land on me.

"Fine," I say. "Everyone grab a chair."

Story time! As I talk, I try to detach, the way I used to at home. The trick is to get safely dead inside and pretend I'm talking about someone else, some*thing* else, something that doesn't matter. I tell them how Karen pitched the idea to me, how we flew down south. About Princess Panzer, and how Garrison gave me his Sales Pitch of Evil.

At this, Kinetiq speaks up. "Did he say anything about will to power, or anything related to an ethnic or cultural purity?"

"Uh, no, I don't think so."

"Anything about the leader principle, or a great rebirth of some bygone era? Maybe a golden age, either in the past or promised in the future?"

"No. They were pretty down on equality, and said they wanted to create a hereditary dictatorship—"

"One dictatorship? Worldwide? Or multiple smaller dictatorships, with Cynosure acting as the model?"

"Uh, they weren't clear on that." I sift through my memories, try to squeeze out more detail. "Maybe the multiple dictatorships? They said they were going to build more islands. And it didn't sound like they wanted to rule the world directly, just that they wanted all the world governments to be obedient and give them special rights and pay them extortion money."

"What about a cathedral?"

I blink, surprised. "Well, *he* didn't, but a rich guy with powers I busted a few days ago wouldn't shut up about it, and I'm pretty sure Garrison had Graywytch kill him in his cell so he couldn't talk."

"Likely not a true fascist, then. Probably a neoreactionary." They shrug. "It's a different flavor of shit, is all. They're both authoritarian ideologies, but their emphasis is different. Fascists are a populist movement, deeply wrapped up in racism and misogyny and other forms of bigotry—essentially, it's about hating anyone who's different and enforcing a right-wing style of conformity on everyone. Neoreactionaries, on the other hand, are elitists who are all about bringing back the age of kings, and think that 'common people' should know their place and let themselves be ruled. They'll use fascists as foot soldiers, but they don't really care about things like ethnic purity among the labor classes, except as a bargaining chip to keep their toadies happy. They're still super racist, though.

"Naturally, the neoreactionaries see themselves as the ruling class that everyone should kiss up to. 'The Cathedral' is the weak-sauce conspiracy theory they use to explain why their incredibly stupid ideas aren't more popular."

Doc looks sideways at them. "You spend a lot of time parsing their buzzwords, do you?"

"Gotta know the enemy," says Kinetiq. They tap the circle-A button pinned to the shoulder strap of their body armor. "It ain't just the gentrification of the Bay that makes me hate Silicon Valley, you know. Lots of neoreactionaries and fascists are mixed up with the big money boys."

"I don't think Graywytch is one of them," I say. "Not politically, anyhow."

Doc nods. "Yeah, Myra's basically a communist. I can't imagine how much they had to offer to get her to agree to work for a bunch of right-wing STEMlords."

"Maybe she's getting something else out of it," says Charlie.

"Like what?" I ask.

"I dunno. But payment in kind or through favors is a common way to do business among practitioners. Can you tell me more about how they're trying to lock down who gets superpowers?" I give him details, and describe what I can remember of the satellite constellation. His eyebrows go up, and then go up further. "You're serious? She's mixing magic with hypertech?"

"Yeah. Is that unusual?"

"It's illegal," he says emphatically. "If Graywytch is seriously doing this she's...well, the term 'death wish' comes to mind."

"You mentioned Phase One?" prompts Doc.

"Yeah. That's what they've already got in place. It lets them pick and choose who gets superpowers, or decide if anyone gets them at all. From what they showed me, it sounded like with more time to develop their techniques, they could start mass producing supervillains."

"What's Phase Two, then?" asks Kinetiq.

"That's what Graywytch was testing out on me," I say with a suppressed shiver. I explain the details of the experiments, and how she'd almost managed to pull the mantle out of my chest before I was rescued. "I think Phase Two is being able to depower people who stand up to them, and then turn around and sell the stolen powersets to their cronies. Or hell, they might just start kidnapping metahumans and draining them for profit."

"That seems like an awful lot of trouble to go to," says Doc Impossible. "Capturing a superhero is hard. Unless Garrison wants to be personally involved in every op, that doesn't seem like a viable plan."

"There's still Phase Three," I say quietly. "They didn't explain it, but I've been thinking about it. They've already got satellites that can project a spell across the whole planet. And that collar let Garrison's power keep my abilities suppressed even when he wasn't there."

Doc and Charlie get there at the same time. "He's going to turn off everyone's powers," says Charlie.

"Maybe magic and hypertech too," I say. "He seems like the meticulous type, I don't think he'd leave any way to fight back unaccounted for."

"Welp," says Doc, reaching into a lab coat pocket for a crumpled pack of cigarettes and a lighter.

"How long do you think we have?" asks Kinetiq.

"They were going to make an announcement in a week or two. That's probably just Phase One, though."

"Can't be much longer than that," say Charlie. "Once the Council hears about this, they'll look into it, and it won't be long before they figure out Graywytch is breaking their laws. They'll come after her and Garrison hard. I mean spinning hurricanes out of the clear blue sky hard. She has *really* screwed herself."

"If Garrison's powers work on magic, she won't have to worry about the Council," says Doc.

"Oh." Charlie's a smart guy. The fact that he needed this pointed out to him before we see the light go on over his head says more about how scary the Council of Avalon is to him than anything he could have said out loud. He finishes scribbling a last note in his notebook. "All right, I think that's enough for now. I might have more questions—actually, here's one, where's Calamity?"

My stomach flops over. Right. "Uh, she stepped out," I say.

"Let's get her back here; she needs to hear this."

Doc and Kinetiq trade a look I only see out of the corner of my eye. Without saying anything, they both stand and leave. "I, uh, don't think she'd be interested. She wasn't impressed that I got captured, and team jobs aren't really her thing."

"You're sure? We could really use her help."

"Look, Charlie, she was embarrassed for me," I say, blushing. "I was pretty pathetic back there, and she probably thinks I'm a loser now."

"I can pretty much guarantee you you're wrong about that," he says. He closes his notebook and sets it aside. "Danny, you realize how incredibly weird Sarah is, right?"

"She's not—"

"To you. She's not weird, *to you*. Because you can fly and go on talk shows. But to the rest of us, yeah, it's a little strange that her hobby is beating up drug dealers."

"So she's…different. So what?"

"So she's not really good at normal people things."

"Yeah, well, that's no crime," I mutter at my chest. "Neither am I."

"I noticed," says Charlie, making a heroic effort not to roll his eyes that nonetheless falls short. "Danny, when she and I were together, we never went out on a date. She doesn't do dates."

Blood is thundering in my ears. My heart rate has gone from 60 to 100 in a second and a half. "So?" I hear myself ask.

"So when she likes someone, she asks them to go caping with her."

"...oh."

About thirty seconds later, I'm hitting the sound barrier.

CHAPTER EIGHTEEN

I am a towering moron. A champion of idiocy. They're going to build a monument to the great clueless minds of history, and my face is going to be on it. My guts are so tight with anxiety that I overshoot Sarah's house by three or four miles and have to circle back. Coming in low and slow over her neighborhood, I scan the streets to try and remember where exactly her house is. There! The ranch set back from the road, with the oversized backyard. As I'm coming around for a landing, I see her.

Sarah's backyard is huge. It takes up the entire lot behind their house, clear over to the next road. It's surrounded with tall hedges and trees for privacy, and one significant corner of it is riddled with bare wooden posts of various heights. If you've ever seen a kung fu movie where they train to fight by jumping from one post to the next without slipping, you get the idea. Sarah does a handspring off one. At the top of her arc, she twists in midair and throws a knife. It thunks into a wooden target a half-instant before she alights softly on another post with one foot.

She's amazing. Her brown hair is pulled back tight in a pony-tail, her tank top is dark with sweat, and she's beautiful. While balancing on one foot—rock still, as stable as most of us are with both—she rolls her shoulder where the prosthetic interfaces with her body. From the shoulder down her left arm is a charcoal gray machine. Electric muscles bunch and flex under a metarubber coating. The arm was enough for her to drop out of school, just to avoid the questions that might compromise her identity. In only a few months, it's become so much a part of her that sometimes I forget she didn't always have to wear a prosthetic.

I'm careless. My shadow flits across her, and she looks up sharply. We lock eyes and her face darkens. No. Oh, please no, don't let me have fucked this up. Sarah hops down from the post she's on, a twelve-foot drop straight down, and lands like she's only skipped a stair. A moment later I touch down a little ways off from her, and I'm dimly aware of the grass between my toes and against my bandages. Her good arm crosses her stomach, grabs onto her prosthetic. Shoulders in, turned away from me. But there's something on her face, and I want it to be hope. My heart is charging in my chest, blood roaring in my ears. There's probably some suave, charming way to defuse this, but I can't find it.

What comes out is, "Are you straight?"

Sarah tightens a little. Her mouth gropes for a reply. "…I don't know."

"Do you want to kiss me?"

She nods. "Uh-huh."

And then we're stumbling towards each other, and we collide, actually knock heads, but we're kissing, and I'm laughing and that makes it harder to kiss, which makes it funnier until she gets a hand around my back and snugs me up against her and *yes*.

Yes.

I've never kissed anyone before. It's not what I expected. But it happens so easily. It's nice. Calming. Far too soon Sarah pulls away and looks up the yard to her house. "My mom is home. Let's go to the park."

I cup a hand to her cheek and pull her gaze back to me. "Sarah, thank you. I'm sorry I didn't—I was embarrassed. Thank you for coming to get me."

Some distant confusion comes over her, but she leans in and kisses me again. "Anytime. Come on, I need to get changed, and then we'll go."

Hand in hand we trot up her sloping backyard to the rear of the house, entering through the kitchen. Sarah's mom, Anita, a fit woman in her forties with short black hair, is slicing vegetables for a stew when we come in.

"Hi, Mrs. Castillo," I say with a nervous thrill when she sees me holding hands with her daughter.

"It's nice to see you, Danielle," she says. "I hear you got in some trouble recently."

"Uh, yeah. Sarah really helped me out."

Mrs. Castillo smiles and says, "I'm glad."

"We're going to the park," says Sarah as she edges past her mother and deeper into the house. "I'll get my things," she says to me, and then disappears into her room. I take a seat on one of the stools on the living room side of the counter, trying to look cool, like it's totally normal, like my head isn't spinning. Less than four hours ago I was in a cell waiting for my final torture and probable execution. Now I'm sitting in Sarah's (can I call her my girlfriend?) house, waiting for her to get ready to go (can I call this a date?) to the park.

This is only the second time I've been here. The first time was shortly after the battle with Utopia, when Sarah lost her arm. It was so uncomfortable, with a thick fog of regret and sorrow hanging over everything, that I never came back.

As far as houses go, it's just slightly off normal. Like, the kitchen is pretty standard, very neat and well squared away, but instead of drawings or report cards tagged to the refrigerator, there are old paper targets. One of them has a tight grouping of five shots in the ten ring and a blue crayon scrawl that says SARAH, AGE 7. The lattice tells me there are at least five hidden guns in this room alone.

"So, Danielle, I couldn't help but notice that you arrived from the backyard," says Mrs. Castillo, and I wince. Crap.

"Uh, yeah, sorry," I say. "I forgot."

"I understand. It sounds like you've had a hard week. But I need you to be sure to remember our rules here. No powers that can be seen from the street." And, I belatedly realize, descending from the heavens certainly counts.

"Right. Right, I'm sorry," I say quickly, twisting on my stool to look down the hall and see if Sarah is coming back.

Mrs. Castillo sets down her knife. I hear her footsteps as she crosses the kitchen, and I turn back in time to get a front-row seat to Sarah's mom plunging her hand deep into my chest. There's no pain, no tearing of skin, only a buzzing cold fullness as her hand phases straight through my flesh, all the way up to her wrist. Her fingers clasp around my heart, every beat a new moment of pressure.

"Danielle. Please pay attention," she says. "I take my family's safety very seriously. Do you understand?"

My jaw jumps a few times before I can engage my vocal cords and choke out a breathy, "Y-yes!"

"Good. So what aren't you going to do anymore?"

"No flying."

Mrs. Castillo shakes her head. "No, the rule is no powers. None that can be seen from the street, right?"

I nod frantically. "Right, right, no powers."

"So how are you going to come back here next time?"

"Uh, uh, taxi! I'll take a taxi."

Mrs. Castillo smiles. "Good. That's good." Her hand unclenches from around my heart and emerges from my chest coated in a wet scarlet glove of blood. She takes a paper towel and cups it under her hand to catch the blood while she crosses back to the sink to wash up. "I'm glad to have you over anytime, Danielle. Sarah has been so lonely lately. I'm happy you two are growing close."

"R-right."

"Jesus, Mom," mutters Sarah as she comes around the corner. She's wearing her motorcycle riding gear—the civilian, non-capey version—and has a spare bike jacket thrown over her shoulder. With stiff, robotic movements I rise from the stool and start walking toward the garage door. Sarah catches the look on my face and glances back at her mother.

"Have a good time!" says Mrs. Castillo.

When the garage door closes behind us, Sarah holds out the jacket for me with a twinkle in her eye. "She did the heart trick, didn't she?"

"If that's what you call it," I say.

"Did I forget to mention that my mother is a reformed super-villain?" asks Sarah, perched at the edge of laughter.

With trembling slowness, I turn to meet her eyes. Not even a drop of pity from her. "That might have slipped your mind, yeah."

"I'll make it up to you." Sarah steps around me and sets the jacket on my shoulders. "This is my old riding jacket. It's too small on me, but I think it'll fit you perfectly."

It doesn't. But it's close, and it faintly smells of her, so I slip my arms through the sleeves and pull the zipper all the way up. Sarah hands me a spare helmet—more to avoid getting pulled over than because something as minor as a traffic accident could hurt me—sets her own visored helmet down on her head.

The bike we're riding isn't the Calamity bike, with the fat, sticky racing tires and riding posture that's practically horizontal. It's a little blue Honda upright, with a modest engine, wire spokes, and a narrow leather saddle. It's exactly the sort of thing a young woman might get for her first bike, and for once, I connect the dots ahead of time and realize that this is probably the bike that Sarah rides to wherever she stashes the Calamity gear so that her mom doesn't give her trouble about bringing vigilante heat back to the house.

The garage door goes up as I'm gingerly swinging one leg over the back of the bike.

"You comfortable back there?" Sarah asks over her shoulder.

I wrap my arms around her waist and lay the side of my head on her shoulder. "Yeah."

With a throaty roar, the bike wakes, and we leap out of the garage and onto the street. We tip way over when we take a corner, and for a moment I'm sure we'll crash, some fragmentary instinct from my pre-Dreadnought days causing me to bunch up with anxiety. Sarah laughs and guns it.

She weaves us through side streets until we hit the highway and climb the onramp with a grumbling roar. Wind whips at my bare legs. The engine is warm between our thighs, and vibrating with power. Cars tear by us in the other direction just a few arm-spans away, and to the left and right of us, the last of the morning rush hour streams into downtown New Port.

Sarah is firm and unwavering in my arms. She takes a hand off the bars to stroke my hand, and I close my eyes and enjoy the strength of her against my chest and stomach.

I let myself forget I'm Dreadnought. It doesn't matter that I'm more used to seeing this road from the sky. When I shove all of that out of my mind and see the city from her eyes, it's like a whole new world opens up to me. To us. Here we are, the road hissing beneath our tires, wind tugging at our shoulders, the engine running flat out and barely making sixty-five. I've never flown faster.

We peel off the highway exit to downtown, duck and bob through morning traffic, and pull into the northern parking lot at Victory Park. Sarah kills the engine and makes to get off the bike, but I've decided I like it here so I anchor myself in the lattice and sigh contentedly. Sarah pushes against me with as much effect as she'd get from leaning on a cement wall, and I sigh again, squeeze her a little bit.

"All right, you brat, release me," she says around her chuckle. With great and dramatic magnanimity, I peel myself off Sarah and allow her to dismount. Sarah locks the helmets to her bike with a cable, and then we head into the park. I wrap my arm around hers and lean into her, head on her shoulder.

Victory Park is a broad strip of green in the heart of down-town. It goes right up to the water of Puget Sound and is lumpy with rolling hills. Ancient oak trees splash the ground in shade during summer, but today their knobbly fingers scrape a white sky. Sarah and I head toward one of the hills that is most densely wooded. We find a soft depression between two ridges, carpeted in dead grass and fallen leaves under the shifting, clicking branches of a tree older than the city.

We sit down together, backs to the broad oak trunk. Her fingers find mine and lace through them. Down the hills a ways we can barely see the Sound, glinting in the morning sun beyond the trees. I lay my head against her and close my eyes.

After a moment, Sarah says, "Uh, do you mind if I take my prosthetic off?"

"No," I say, sitting up. "Do you need help?"

"I got it," she says, releasing my hand and reaching over to her left shoulder. She reaches up inside her t-shirt and finds a catch. Two more thick clicking noises, and her dark gray prosthetic slides cleanly away from her body. The attachment point at the socket is already being covered up by the automatic contraction of the synthetic shoulder muscle bundles. Sarah carefully places her prosthetic off to the side and leans back into me. Her smile is a little crinkled, a little unsure.

"You're beautiful, you know that, right?" I tell her. And she is. There's something about her hard, athletic lines that makes things spin inside my chest.

Sarah blushes. We scoot closer together, and I pull her remaining arm around my shoulder, sit halfway in her lap.

"So you're not angry at me?" she asks in a small voice.

"No! Of course not. I'm sorry I freaked out when we got back to the hangar. I'm…I was ashamed of getting captured. And you're so great at this stuff, and—"

"But I'm not! I nearly got you killed again." She stares at the shaved part of my head and the zipper row of staples I'm sporting.

"Wait, *again*? I mean, you didn't, not today. But what are you talking about?"

Sarah shakes her head, like she can't believe I'm so dumb. "You were right. We never should have gone into that warehouse. Going after Utopia on our own was stupid. But I—I didn't want to back down in front of you. And I didn't want to admit you were right about the Legion." She looks away. "And I keep screwing up. That's why—I thought you didn't want me around anymore."

"Whoa, hey, no," I say. I reach around to hug her with both arms, but she leans away. "I would never—I *always* want you out there with me."

"Why?"

It doesn't compute. My mouth makes noises in the general direction of an explanation, but struggles to put together a coherent sentence. Finally, I manage: "Sarah, you're a better superhero than me." She blinks with surprise. "When I'm in a really bad spot, when things are falling apart and I'm about to lose it, I think *what would Calamity do*? And that gets me through it."

Sarah smiles like the sun after a storm. "Really?"

"Absolu—"

She tackles me with her mouth, lays me out against the ground. We go rolling over a few times and come to rest with me on top of her, lips and tongues grasping at each other.

We finally come up for air. I'm laying across her chest, her breast under my hand. I blush, but she smiles. Staring down into brown eyes that draw me in, set me right. Sarah runs her hand down my back.

"I'm sorry about Mom doing the heart thing," she says.

"It's all right. She's just protective."

"That's a generous word for it," says Sarah, rolling her eyes.

"Is it?" I ask, lying down across her, head cupped in the hollow of her neck. "She's concerned. I wish my mom had been that hardcore about looking after me."

Sarah doesn't say anything for a moment. Her arm tightens around my waist. "Yeah. Mom's all right."

"This is nice," I say after a while.

Sarah murmurs agreement, deep and rumbly against my cheek. "It's not every day beautiful girls fall out of the sky and ask me to kiss them."

"Would you like that to be an everyday thing?" I ask. "Because I can arrange that."

Sarah laughs, and it's glorious, and I will never get tired of that sound. My eyes slide closed. Her shampoo smells like coconuts. For the first time in what seems like years, I feel safe. Sarah is warm and solid beneath me, and her arm strokes up my back, down my back. My body is heavy. I put up a languid smile, and then I'm…

CHAPTER NINETEEN

My room is barren. Something is coming. I'm hiding on my bed. Not under or behind, just on top. It feels like that's the only place to hide, even though I know it's not any good.

The door bangs like gunshots. Once, twice, an ogre bellowing on the other side. I don't want to open the door, but I know I have to. From my spot on the bed I reach out, and the door is opening, and then my father has me by the shirt collar and is dragging me away. The noise is indescribable. My ears are bleeding.

Into the cage I go. The walls are solid iron, or maybe rusty old bars, or maybe both, or maybe something else, and I'm up against the bars, up against the window, and I'm screaming, screaming for help.

Pricklepins on my legs, and there are the beetles I was expecting. I know they're Graywytch. I know they're going to eat me from the inside out. Up against the door again, screaming through the window.

My mother and Doctor Impossible stand with their backs to me. "I told you he wasn't worth it," says my mother.

"Mom!" I'm screaming. "Mom, please! Let me out of here!"

They start walking away.

"Mom! Come back! Mom, please!" They don't care. They don't listen.

The beetles are chewing now, have gotten into me. My lips squeeze tight to keep them out, but they chew their way through. It burns. It stings. They swarm up my legs and over my body, and they're prickly and sharp on my tongue as they go down, down inside me.

When I reach for the lattice, I find beetles crawling across it. Twitching antennas, chewing mandibles. They center in my chest, and they grab hold of my power, and they start eating, eating it all up. My chest—my male chest that I thought I was rid of forever—starts to warp and bend and bubble up like a blister, glowing with the light of my stolen power, and it begins to burst and—

CHAPTER TWENTY

Sarah's hand fastens around my ankle. My body is wire-tight with terror. I take another breath and I realize I'm screaming, floating, my body curled up protectively around my chest in midair.

"Danielle! Wake up!" Sarah is hanging from my ankle, her toes just barely scraping the ground. When I go to tell her I'm awake, all that comes out is a messy cry of fear. My body is slick with icy sweat. "It's just a dream; you're okay," she says.

My voice is steadier this time. I can almost get the word *okay* out in one piece. My heart is going flat out, tripping over itself, skidding around the corners, a headlong mad dash scramble away, away, gotta get *away*.

"Come back down here," says Sarah. "Please, come back down."

Getting out of the air is hard. It's like peeling my fingers off a bar I've been hanging onto for dear life, but slowly, with dips and jerks, I bring us back down to the ground.

Sarah sweeps me into a one-armed hug and squeezes me tight with her shoulder and chin. "You're okay. It's okay."

"No, I'm not," I say, and I start crying, and I can't stop. I put my face into her shoulder and let go, sob and weep until there's nothing left in me. I'm dimly aware of Sarah telling someone else that I'm okay, that I had a nightmare while we were napping, and I keep my face hidden. The last thing I need is this popping up on YouTube, and right now I resent that more than anything else in the world. But whoever came to check on my screaming leaves without a hassle, and Sarah turns her attention back to me. With kisses and stroking rubs down my back she helps me put myself back together.

I go limp, my cheek resting on her shoulder. "I'm sorry, I should have known that would happen," I say quietly.

Sarah shakes her head, hums a negative sound that vibrates in my chest. "Does this happen often?"

"Not that bad, usually," I say. "But, yeah."

Sarah makes sympathetic noises deep in her throat, and I am almost pathetically grateful. God, what did I do to deserve someone like her? She doesn't push me away. She doesn't politely tolerate me. She hugs me close, and with her helping me along I feel better faster than I expect. The hard knot of terror and sorrow fades, in its place I have an airy joy that makes me feel weightless. I'm not alone. Not anymore. I've got Sarah.

"Let's get something to eat," she says after I'm calmed down. "I think we both skipped breakfast."

"It'll have to be takeout," I say. "I don't want to deal with being famous in downtown right now."

Before Sarah can reply, her phone rings. "Sure thing," she says, digging the phone out of her jacket one-handed. "Hello? Yeah, she's—shit, sorry. Yeah, she's fine. We're at Victory Park. No, I don't—okay, we're on our way back. Yes. Yes. It's a .38 Detective. No, JHPs. Not when I'm in civvies, I don't. Okay."

"Who was that?" I ask as I slip the riding jacket on.

"Doc Impossible."

I wince. "Oh shit. I forgot to tell her where I was going."

Normally that wouldn't be a problem. This isn't a normal week.

"I gathered," says Sarah, slipping her phone away. "Help me put my arm back on, and we can brainstorm how you're going to make it up to her."

Sarah's arm slips back into its socket with a shunk-and-click-ing noise. We wind our way back out of the park, hand in hand, and peel out of the parking lot with my arms around her waist. We snag a couple bags of gyros from a drive-through place she likes

APRIL DANIELS

and tuck them in the cargo pod on the back of the bike before shooting back down the highway to the industrial park at the outskirts of town.

The topside of what's now our hangar used to be an abandoned factory. Now it's the melted-down, slagged-out *remains* of a factory, and Doc is standing near the main door, sucking on a cigarette like it's her job.

Sarah pulls into the parking spot we've got set up a ways from the main ruins. It's between two hillocks of gravel with a desert-pattern camouflage net strung between them, all but invisible from the sky. She pops the cargo pod and we each grab a bag of takeout before starting the long walk to the hangar entrance. Doc drops the cigarette and twists it out beneath her toe. As we get close, Doc's eyes track down to my hand clasped in Sarah's.

"Oh, fucking *finally*."

She turns to head back down into the hangar, and we follow her, our cheeks a matching shade of red.

The chewing out I'm expecting doesn't start until halfway down the stairs. And it's way, way lighter than what I anticipated. "You need to tell me where you're going. At least until this whole thing is over with."

Her voice is heavy with relief, tinted with anger. And almost shaking with fear.

"I'm sorry," I say quietly. She nods.

"I need to replace your earbud radio too," she says as we exit the stairs into the main hangar space.

A new wave of mortification falls over me. I'm so used to always being in contact now, I completely forgot she couldn't reach me unless I took my phone.

We cross the hangar, and the cement is cold under my bare feet. Her other two bodies are mounting a particle cannon under the nose of her tilt-engine. At the collection of cots and divider screens that passes for the living area in here, Doc hands me my backup suit and stands on the other side of the screen while I slip

180

it on. Then she grabs my chin and tilts my head over to look at my ear where the radio was torn out.

"This side is too irritated to risk gluing it back in. We're going to have to put it in your right ear instead."

"Okay," I barely have time to say before Doc is squirting antiseptic glue down my ear, then wiping the excess away and shoving a tiny earbud radio as deep into the canal as it will go. After a few seconds of holding it, she lets go and starts snapping her fingers next to my ear.

"Yeah, it's working," I say.

And with that, Doctor Impossible lets go of a visible load of stress. Man, I am such an asshole sometimes. Of course she would freak out if I left without saying where I was going. "I'm sorry," I say.

She shakes her head, puts the back of her hand up to her mouth. "I don't mean to overreact. It's important, is all."

"We're going to get them, Doc. Don't worry."

That comforting core of determination returns to her expression. "You're damn right we are."

We gather around a beat-up old coffee table set between two flea market couches. Kinetiq scoots right up to the coffee table and sits cross-legged. Charlie wanders over from the workbench he's claimed as his own, and Sarah and I pass out food before sitting practically in each other's laps. Over the first few bites I bring Sarah up to speed on what happened. Her face gets dark, and she's got one hand clamped on my knee like she's scared someone's going to pick me up and put me in their pocket.

To be honest, it's a little surreal how angry everyone is on my behalf. I'm not used to people giving a shit, and I sort of wish they'd knock it off. The grand shows of concern are new and uncomfortable. Can we please pretend all this never happened?

Doc comes over and pockets her cell phone before grabbing a gyro and digging in. "Cecilia is on her way. We're going to explore legal strategies for the counterattack."

Sarah snorts. "You need a lawyer to do capework?"

Oh boy, here it comes. The law and order debate. Get more than three capes in a room together for the first time, and sooner or later we've got to hash out this hoary old argument. It looks like today's the day. Joy.

Doc looks at me. "Hey, Danny, how many warrants are there out for your arrest?" she asks around a mouthful of chicken and lettuce.

"None," I say between dainty little bites.

"Funny how that works out," says Doc. She takes another bite, and is obviously not of the defiantly-femme school of table manners. She's wearing a napkin like a bib and it's getting a workout.

"Don't get too cocky," says Kinetiq. They take a sip of a soda from out of Doc's fridge. "The cops are not your friends. Sooner or later, you'll see."

"So we should give them reasons to come after us?" asks Charlie with a raised eyebrow. "That's…um, insane? Yeah, that's the word I want."

"Ain't about givin' them reasons," mutters Calamity, who has suddenly displaced Sarah. "They ain't never had trouble findin' their own. Way I see it, you can set your mind to doin' the right thing, or the legal thing. Sooner or later, you gotta choose."

"Right on," says Kinetiq with vehemence.

"What about rules of evidence?" asks Doc. "What about making sure the perps get convicted?"

Kinetiq shrugs. "I don't really care about that. The American prison system excels at a lot of things, but justice isn't one of them."

"So when a serial killer gets out because you fouled up the crime scene, what then?" I ask.

"If I was a Sherlock—" Cape slang. Go ahead and guess what it means. "—that might be an issue," Kinetiq says. "But I'm not. I do crisis containment."

All eyes land on Calamity. She's suddenly really interested in her food. After a moment, she mutters, "Sometimes you can only mail a wiretap recording to the detective in charge and hope for the best."

"Oh, so suddenly the police serve a purpose!" says Doc brightly.

"Ain't never said they didn't—look, do we gotta talk about this over lunch?"

"No, we don't," I say with a pointed glance at Doc. She looks up and away like the picture of innocence. "Charlie, have you had a chance to figure anything out about how that collar worked?"

Charlie swallows a big bite, nodding. "Yeah, actually. I was really surprised by how simple it was. It's—well, I think I know what Phase Three is." That perks up ears all around the circle. Charlie goes on: "So the collar had a pendant built into the inner side of it. Quartz and blood, right? It's a basic—and I mean *really* basic—sympathy charm running off of Garrison's powers. Whoever wears a pendant like that is subject to his power-disruption field, even if he isn't around."

"Step back a moment," says Kinetiq. "What?"

Charlie grins sheepishly. "Sorry, I got excited. I'll start from the beginning. The two big laws in magical theory are the Law of Similarity and the Law of Contagion. Similarity means symbolism, more or less, and Contagion doesn't mean disease in this context, it means something more like mixing. I mean, technically it's about cross-contamination, but that's really way more pejorative than it needs to be so—"

"Getting off track," says Kinetiq.

"Right. So. A sympathy charm combines both, with symbolism that has some element of contamination as well. The classic example is how to brew a potion with moonlight in it—the textbook answer being that you place a bar of silver at the bottom of a cauldron and reflect the light of the full moon off it. Silver is the moon metal, so that's Similarity, and a reflection inside the cauldron is literally putting moonlight inside where the potion is being brewed. With me so far?"

"Well enough," says Kinetiq.

"Right, so what we've got in these charms is basically the same thing. The sample of his blood is used for contagion and quartz is one of the most basic and direct symbols for power, clarity, and energy around. Put them together with some other markings I found inside the collar once I got it disassembled, and you've got a very robust magic charm that mirrors Garrison's powers. When someone is wearing one of these collars it's like he's right in their face, cutting them completely off from their own powers."

"I kind of figured that out for myself," I say.

"Right, but I don't think you have the full implications yet. First of all, this charm is really straightforward, dangerously so."

"Dangerous how?" asks Calamity.

"Well, she didn't do *anything* to prevent a backtrace attack up the sympathetic connection. With this pendant, I can cast spells on him as easily as if he was in the same room with me. That's insane. Nobody runs sympathy like that; it's too dangerous. It would be like remembering your passwords and social security number by posting them on your Facebook wall—yeah, you'll never lose it, but the first person who thinks to look there is going to have you by the balls."

"So she's getting ready to double-cross him," I say.

Charlie shrugs. "Maybe. It sure does seem like she's willing to take huge risks with her boss' safety. But I think there might be something else in play. The charm is reversible too. It didn't have to be designed that way, but it was."

"Reversible how?"

"Well, right now what it does is shut down the powers of whoever is wearing it. But if you reversed the charm, it would make whoever is wearing it *immune* to Garrison's suppression field. So you've got to ask why? There are other, easier ways to run the charm. Why make it reversible, if doing it that way nerfs her team's big advantage? So I got to thinking—what if it wasn't a nerf? What if it made their advantage stronger to be the only ones who were immune to the field?"

I shake my head. "They're already immune when he wants them to be. When they kidnapped me I was fighting Thunderbolt, and his powers didn't disappear. Garrison just chose not to mute them."

"But what if Garrison wasn't around?" says Charlie. "What if they wanted to be able to ensure their people wouldn't have their powers muted when he wasn't there to pick and choose?"

"How would they even mute people if he wasn't—" I stop, the answer arriving like a smack upside the head.

"The satellites," says Doc.

Charlie nods. "The satellites. I think Phase Three is shutting down everyone's powers. If they can magically project Garrison's power-muting field with these amulets, there's no reason they couldn't use a similar spell to broadcast his field from the satellites as well. The amulets could then have their charms reversed, so that they would let their own people keep using their powers while everyone else was stripped of theirs. And if this stuff shuts down magic too, then it wouldn't matter how simple and vulnerable she made the charms. Nobody else would be able to exploit the loophole. That's Phase Three. I'd bet you anything, that's Phase Three."

"Shit," says Kinetiq, speaking for all of us.

"That ain't happening," says Calamity. "I ain't lettin' it. *We* ain't lettin' it."

"So where do we start?" I ask.

"First step," says Doc, "we should call up Detective Phạm and tell her that one of the superheroes she's responsible for tried to kidnap and murder the other."

"What will that accomplish?" asks Kinetiq incredulously.

"Phạm needs to know that Graywytch can't be relied on." Doc shrugs. "Also, it's vindictive and bitchy and will ruin Myra's day."

"I like that plan!" I say. "I am all for that plan!"

"Then we knock down his satellites," says Doc, flicking her phone to life. "With a little data mining I can get you the orbital track of everything Garrison's company has put into space. We take those down, and we stop him before he gets started."

"That might be dangerous," says Charlie. "Magically speaking, I mean."

"How sure are you?" asks Calamity.

Charlie shrugs. "Zero percent; I really have no idea, but it's a risk we need to consider before you send Dreadnought up there."

"Doc, get to working on those orbital tracks," says Calamity. "Charlie, what would you need to be absolutely sure?"

"I'd have to read Graywytch's notes, at the very least. The satellites might be magically booby-trapped. If they are, the spells she put on them would need to accommodate for the traps so that the traps don't interfere with the magic they are supposed to be guarding. Her notes should tell me if it's safe to approach the satellites or not."

"We'll work on getting those for you," says Calamity. "Meanwhile, you learn whatever else you can about these mirror charms they're making, and see if you can make more of them. If we can make our heavyweights immune to Garrison's power suppression field, then that's our highest priority right now." She *almost* manages to say this without her eyes flicking over to me, worried and possessive.

"There's something else to consider," says Doc. "As a permanent reserve member, I only have a tie-breaking vote, but since Graywytch hopped the aisle—" More superhero slang. It means a whitecape going evil or a blackcape trying to reform. "—then as far as the bylaws go, she's forfeited her seat in the Legion. Which makes me and Magma the only two voting members left. Bylaws say I've got to inform him that I'm lifting the membership veto, but I doubt he'll object under the circumstances."

"Meaning what, Doctor?"

"Congratulations, we just refounded the Legion Pacifica."

CHAPTER TWENTY-ONE

"*WHAT?*" That's Detective Phạm, learning that one of the heroes she's supposed to be riding herd on is moonlighting as a supervillain. I start explaining again, from the beginning, but she interrupts me, "Are you sure?"

"Yes, I'm pretty sure she's the one who strapped me down and tortured me with magic." Doc, Cecilia, and I are sitting around a speakerphone set out on the coffee table in the safehouse. So far, I'm the one doing all the talking. Cecilia is spilling out the top of out of an ankle-length scarlet dress with a corset, petticoats, and matching parasol. I gather she was interrupted at a convention to come here, but she's as sharp as ever and has been scribbling on a legal pad throughout the entire conversation.

"Could she have been mind controlled?" Phạm asks, grasping at one last straw.

"I can't prove a negative, Detective," I say calmly. "I can say that if mind control was in play, wouldn't they use it on me to get me to cooperate rather than escape and snitch on them?"

After a long moment, she speaks again, her voice weary with acceptance. "I'm going to need you to come down to the station and fill out a statement. And I need you to understand that my jurisdiction doesn't cover international waters, so there's a limit on what I can do. This will probably have to go to the City Council."

"I'm faxing over a statement to your office right now. I'm not coming—"

"Cut the bullshit, Danny. If you're telling me a city contractor is a violent felon, then you're gonna tell me that in person, in front of a camera, and you're going to answer as many questions as I care to ask."

Cecilia slides a note across the table to me: *no way.*

"These people kidnapped me once, Detective," I say into the phone. "I'm staying in hiding until I can figure out a way to keep that from happening again."

"We can protect you—" she starts reflexively.

"Against *supervillains*? Isn't that what you guys pay me and Graywytch to do? If she's the perp and I'm the victim, where does that leave the police room to come in? You can't ask me to sign a suicide note."

"Danny, I know you're scared, but with things as unsettled as they are, we really need to cooperate with each other on this."

Cecilia clears her throat. "Hi, Detective Phạm? My name is Cecilia Rhodes, and I'm Dreadnought's attorney." Phạm's groan of dismay is plainly audible over the line. "My client has real concerns about her physical safety that the police, with all due respect, cannot plausibly address, especially not with the current political stresses being placed on the Metahuman Response Unit. More immediately, Dreadnought could risk being found in breach of her contract if she continued to cooperate with the New Port Police Department, so long as Graywytch has not been arrested and/or released from her duties. Section Two specifically prohibits her from cooperating with felons or organizations affiliated with felons. Since we know Graywytch is willing to commit kidnapping, assault, and possibly even murder, and that she has established ties with your department, that makes the NPPD a group we cannot do business with until you clean house. Bluntly put, it's her or us, and you've got to choose your side very quickly."

"…you've got to be kidding me."

"Not at all!" says Cecilia, opening up a binder. "If you'll open your copy of the Enhanced Samaritan Services contract, current revision, I can show you where—"

And that is all I care to hear of this conversation. I signal Cecilia asking if I can leave, and she gives me the thumbs up. I float toward the ceiling far above and pull up another number on my suit's phone. With everything that's happened, I completely forgot Professor Gothic was coming to town. I only remembered when Cecilia sat me down with a checklist to ensure we weren't missing anything obvious.

From below, Kinetiq hangs out the side door of the tilt-engine. "Yo, Dreadnought, if you're finished with the paperwork…"

"Almost!" I call down, as I hit *call* on my suit's phone interface. The phone signal is bounced through my earbud receiver, and it's so weird to be hearing it through my right ear instead of my left.

Not many people have my number, so Professor Gothic's answer is hesitant. "Yes?"

"Professor Gothic, it's Dreadnought."

"Oh! Hello, Dreadnought! I am leaving for the airport now. My flight plan is a bit random, with a few buttonhooks to throw off any tails, but I should be arriving in New Port in three to four days."

"Okay. If you encounter anyone associated with Richard Garrison, Sovereign Industries, Thunderbolt, or Graywytch, turn around and run the other way."

His voice is guarded. "Why?"

"They're moving on a plan that's going to get a lot of people killed. It's about that thing we discussed at the convention. Doc Impossible will be sending you some encrypted files with what we learned."

There is an interval of what I take to be German profanity. "They are further along than I had feared. Are you quite certain of this?"

"They kidnapped and tortured me over it. So yes, I'm pretty certain. Some friends and I are getting ready for the counterattack, but I'm not sure I can provide the kind of protection for you that I thought I could. If you know other people who can take you in—"

"*Ja, ja*, I will do that. Thank you for the warning, Danielle."

"Stay safe. When we're done with this, we're going to need a Nemesis expert who isn't a supervillain."

"I have no intention of going quietly, I assure you of that, young lady."

• • •

It's a short trip to Legion Tower. The Doc who's piloting the tilt-engine knocks the engines into silent running mode, trading speed for whisper-quiet running, and pushes away from the airfield. I take up position off the left wing and shadow the jet into town. At only a hundred feet off the ground, we still get far fewer people looking up in confusion than I would have expected before I started this job. People don't look up, they just don't. Even if a shadow flits over them, most ignore it. (Unless you're overflying the astronomy or meteorology departments at the University. Then you'll always get spotted.)

Weaving between buildings, we come up on Legion Tower sneaky-like right up to the final pop up, when the engines whine for altitude and Doc slips the whole craft over the edge of the landing balcony. Calamity is already hauling the doors open as they breach. She, Charlie, and Kinetiq scurry away from the tilt-engine even as Doc is peeling back away from the landing point to go squat on a helipad on the roof of a tower across the street. Is there a name for the crime of using someone's helipad without telling them? Aggravated super-loitering, maybe? Eh, what the owners of Century Tower don't know won't hurt them, and keeping the jet in one piece is more important than good manners right at the moment. Better we get a ticket for trespassing than the tilt-engine gets blown up by Legion Tower's defenses the moment Graywytch realizes something is happening. Doc'll stay out here for external surveillance, the invisible fingers of every active sensor she has flicking up and down Legion Tower, with the engines kept warm for a fast exit if we need it.

This is, I realize with a thrill, my first real team op. *Badass.* As the other three reach the glass roof access doors, I touch down next to them. The hidden machine gun nests stay quiet, which suggests that, at the very least, Doc's security codes still work. There are no obvious traps or signs of sabotage on the elevators.

As the elevator sinks down to the residential levels, Calamity turns to Charlie. He's wearing a black balaclava, ski-goggles, and thin non-latex gloves. His shoulders are narrow enough that with the baggy hoody over the bulky Kevlar vest Sarah made him wear, Charlie could be anyone. Black, white, boy, girl. Charlie isn't like the rest of us. He doesn't like capework, but he'll do it in a pinch. His identity needs to be protected, or he'll be trapped in this life forever.

"We need something to call you," says Calamity.

"Codex," he says.

"I like it," says Kinetiq.

"Thanks."

When the doors to the elevators open, I go in front, and everyone makes sure to walk behind me. There probably aren't any landmines or booby traps in here—after all, Graywytch lives in this place, and who puts a minefield in their own house?—but it doesn't cost anything to put the chick with the bulletproof skin up front. Calamity and Codex are behind me, and Kinetiq brings up the rear.

Graywytch hasn't repaired her door yet. The splintered halves have been neatly stacked in the hall outside her condo. Calamity gives me an even look when she sees them.

"You feel the need to mention anything, Dreadnought?"

I shrug. "She paid for a lawyer to help my parents try to screw up my emancipation petition. I told her to knock it off."

"If you hurt her, I need to know now."

My lips twist. "No, I didn't hurt her."

I really should have, though.

That satisfies Calamity, and we push into Graywytch's condo. The mission is simple: Codex needs to see Graywytch's notes to know if it's safe to knock Garrison's satellites out of the sky. So we're stealing them.

As we pour into her condo, I become aware of a distinct stillness, that strange sense of *stop* that occurs when you're in someone's home without them. The smashed-out window I exited through last time has been taped over with cardboard. When I look for her in the lattice, peering through the mesh of walls to take in every room at a glance, I can't see her.

"I don't think she's here," I say.

"She can go invisible, though, right?" says Kinetiq.

"You see her library?" asks Calamity. Her guns are both out, down at her sides, fingers carefully off the triggers.

"Yeah, through there." I point down a hallway.

"Codex, go check it out. Dreadnought, you go with him," says Calamity. She and Kinetiq have arranged themselves in the living room to give total coverage of the door without getting in each other's line of fire.

Graywytch's library is clearly the main event in this house. It's just across the hall from her bedroom, and it's part of a cutout between the floor above us and the floor below—it's three stories tall, with the level we're on as the middle layer. Below us is a maze of bookcases packed tight together with narrow, slate-floored aisles between them. The middle level is made up of a walkway around the outer edge of the room and crisscrossing bridges meeting in a broad platform in the center of the room, with short bookshelves and a reading area set up in the middle and a good view of the maze of taller bookshelves on the floor below.

The walls are all solid bookcases that stretch all the way up to the—oh, no, bullshit, *bullshit!*—up to the skylight. The skylight on the thirty-second floor. Of a fifty-seven floor building. There's a moment of unease as I'm processing all that, and even in the lattice it looks like a skylight—I can't see anything beyond it but open sky.

Codex throws his hand out and catches me by the shoulder before I enter the library.

"There could be traps."

"Claymores don't really bother me."

"Would having all your blood instantly turn to pus bother you? Because it'd really suck for me."

With great care, I set my foot back down.

Codex whips off his backpack and rummages through it. He comes back up with a magnifying glass that he's gone at with a home engraving set. Spidery runes and looping whorls trace the outer side of the lens. He looks through the lens, and with his free hand he throws a handful of sand through the doorway.

"The walkway is clear, I think," he says.

"You think?"

"It's magic, Dreadnought," Codex says tightly. "There's no one way to do things, and she's better at this than me."

He nerves up to take a step through the doorway. He doesn't die, which I take as a good sign. Codex and I cross the bridge to the reading nook set up in the center of the library, a long, low wooden table in front of an old leather couch. There's also a lectern with quill and ink nearby.

"How do we know which books are the important ones?" I ask. There's got to be tens of thousands in her collection. This could take all year.

Codex shrugs. "Look for the ones that seem like they've been referred to recently—but don't touch them!" He goes over to the shelf nearest the couch. "I think they'll be in here—these volumes aren't organized in any order I recognize, and the shelf is only half-full. These are probably what she's currently reading. If it's not one of these, we might need to find her laboratory and see if she keeps the notes there." Codex gets another handful of sand out of his pack and rolls up the bottom of his balaclava. With a hard blow he puffs sand across the books. When he looks at them with his magnifying glass, one volume in particular prompts him to hiss with a sharp intake of breath.

"Found something?"

"You ever disarmed a bomb?" he says, just barely turning his head.

"No."

"Neither have I, so shut up." He rolls the balaclava back down and squats on his haunches for a long moment. After some determined thinking, he reaches into his pack again and comes back up with a glass mason jar and a straw. When he unscrews it, I smell vinegar. With a finger stopping up the top end of the straw, Codex takes a few drops worth of vinegar out of the jar and flicks it at the book. The vinegar hisses and bubbles away into steam. "Shit."

"Do we need to back off?"

"I don't think so. But I might need your help here in a moment." He screws the lid back on the jar and makes it disappear. Out comes a bowl and a candle that, even from here, reeks of blood. "Come over here."

He lights the candle and sets it in the bowl, and then backs quickly away. The flame turns crimson and begins leaking a thick, white smoke.

"When I tell you to, I need you to very gently blow that smoke onto the book."

He's still backing up. Still backing up. He's outside of the room and ducking out of sight.

"Codex, what's this going to do?" I ask.

His voice comes a ways down the hallway. "I'm almost sure it will disarm the trap."

"And if it doesn't?"

"It will trigger the trap."

"And that's going to turn my blood to pus?"

"That was more a colorful example than a prediction," he calls. "It's fine. I'm sure you'll be—no, Calamity, don't come any closer!"

"Why do I have to do this? It's your spell!"

"Suck it up, Dreadnought," shouts Calamity from far down the hall.

"Go ahead and blow on it—gently, now!" says Codex.

I do. There's a flash, a bang, and I slam twenty feet across the room, go spanging off a metal guardrail and spin hard into a bookcase. As a half-ton of paper and ink rains down on me, I can't stop giggling. My face is numb yet somehow burning, and even behind closed eyes the explosion was so bright it hurt to see.

All right, status check:

Eyes? Check.

Pat my face for wounds—shit, that stings!

No blood on my glove though.

Lattice is good. Body is good. I'm good.

Try again, Graywytch.

"Dreadnought, talk to me!" shouts Calamity.

"I'm up! I'm up," I say as I climb to my feet. The ground wobbles out from beneath me, and I collapse across the aisle, catching myself on a guardrail. "Uh, gimme a moment."

Clutching at the lattice should steady me, but instead gives me the most bizarre frisson of vertigo as the world seems to spin.

The others are coming into the library now. Calamity jogs around two sides of a square to get to me as I peel myself off the rail.

"You all right, partner?"

"Hold on, something's wrong with my balance."

"You need to evac?"

"I'll be fine once I find something expensive to vomit on."

Walking is an adventure, and flying is out of the question. With an arm under my shoulder, Calamity helps me make my way to the others. I was really hoping I'd stop being the one who needed to be carried through an op, but on the other hand, this does mean I get to lean up against Calamity as much as I want, so really we're coming out even here.

Calamity and I manage to three-legged walk ourselves across the bridge to the center reading area where Codex is poring over the books on the reading table. Kinetiq is standing guard, posture loose, eyes everywhere. They glance behind us and suck in a breath.

Calamity and I turn around, and Graywytch is there, resplendent in robes that seem to bounce and sway like smoke. One moment it was just the four of us, and then the next she's standing on the bridge we just walked across like she's been there all along.

Calamity points a .357 magnum at Graywytch's forehead and thumbs back the hammer. "Hands. Now."

Kinetiq provides all necessary bravado: "You're out of the Legion, and we're jacking your shit!"

Graywytch says something, but I don't hear it through the discomfort that shoots through my head upon seeing her. Luckily, the uncomfortable feelings are smothered by the low rumbling thunder of rising anger.

Anger's good. I can *do* anger.

I bite down hard on the lattice, ignore the vertigo, and go at her, full power. Graywytch slides apart like a puff of fog, nothing but vapor left behind as I wobble through her and just barely pull back before crashing face-first into a wall of books.

Calamity's guns are barking at a shadow, there and gone. Wide sweeps of blue light erupt from Kinetiq's hands as they hose the whole place down with refracted light. For an instant, Graywytch is spotlighted, surprised and exposed, but then she shakes her billowing sleeve and wraps it about her face, sinks down, down and out of sight just as Calamity's bullets start cracking into the furniture beyond her.

"Rotate your spectrum!" snaps Calamity as she falls back to the center.

"On it," says Kinetiq, and the light erupting from their hands starts to pulsate through the entire rainbow.

Graywytch steps from nowhere and shoves a knife into Calamity's back. A lifetime of movies has me primed to expect the world to slow down and go quiet, but it doesn't. Everything is happening so damn fast. Kinetiq whirls to blast Graywytch with a short-range beam even as Calamity twists away from the knife and throws a sharp elbow at her head.

"No!" I'm still not flying worth a damn, but I manage to put thirty relatively straight feet behind me in a heartbeat, and my outstretched fingers snag on Graywytch's robes, jerk her away and over the edge of the walkway. She tumbles down into a shadow and disappears.

I whirl back to my friends, and the world keeps going, and I almost fall to the floor before I catch the guardrail. "Calamity!"

"I'm still here, keep fighting!"

"I've got the book, we should leave," says Codex as he slings his backpack into position.

"You ain't even had time to read it!" says Calamity. "It might be the wrong one."

"We're fighting a world-class practitioner on her home turf," he says, voice tight, "which is the most colorful suicide I can imagine. We. Need. To. Leave."

"He's right, of course," says Graywytch, from everywhere and nowhere at once. "You don't stand a chance." There's one exit from this room; a set of steel bars slams down across it. "But you're not leaving. You're surrendering."

"Get out here, coward!" I shout. "You're fucking dead!"

"How typically male," she says. The air reeks of ozone, and fingers of groaning electricity reach out for us.

Codex is throwing a rough and dirty circle of salt down on the ground and shouting at us to all turn widdershins, whatever that means. She must have a way of jumping a charge past the insulation of my suit, because a bolt of electricity sparks me good, jolting my chest and making my wrist snap with pain where the charge exits me to pass into the railing. Calamity cries out, and as much as it makes me feel like I'm getting turned inside out, I focus on the lattice and try to spot some fragment of Graywytch behind whatever illusions she uses to hide from us. Kinetiq calls the lightning to their arms and wraps it into a twisting braid of crackling, buzzing electricity that they throw up at the skylight.

The skylight cracks and goes dark, plain ceiling tiles behind the glass, the illusion shattered. The room is plunged into darkness for a moment, and then emergency lights kick on and throw everything into harsh glare, dark shadows. Smoke wafts heavy in the air from the burnt ceiling.

I've got to keep my hands locked to the rail—and hope there's no more electricity to come—to make it back across the bridge, but I manage it. Codex has finished throwing a broad circle of salt on the ground and Calamity is reloading her guns and snapping the cylinders shut.

"How bad am I bleeding?" she asks.

"Not much," says Kinetiq after a quick glance.

"Dreadnought, get in the circle," says Codex as I cover the last few yards in a stumbling lurch.

"Oh child, you don't honestly expect something like that to be of any use, do you?" says Graywytch. There's a hiss and a pop in the air, and Codex grunts, claps his hands to his mouth. "My patience is not unlimited, children. I have stayed my hand thus far out of concern for my collection; that will not last forever. Surrender now, and some of you may even get to leave."

A few books from the upper shelves slide themselves out of their spots in little trails of dust. She must not care about them that much, or maybe they were decoys, but whatever the case, they open up and fall apart. Every sheet of paper neatly pulls away from the binding. A fluttering swarm of loose leafs circle the room above us. The flock stops and hangs in the air for a moment, the papers all go flat and hard.

"Oh shit," says Codex, voice thick.

The sheets dive at us like spinning razors. Calamity tumbles away as they *tha-thu-thunk* inches deep into the hard floor. Kinetiq's got a field of superheated air above them that incinerates a few, and Codex, well, Codex's got me laying across him, shoulders hunched against the razor gale.

They cut against my back, my legs, my shoulders. They barely break the outer seal on my suit and cape, but Codex gets one in the leg where his calf stuck out between my own. A spurt of crimson, and he hisses in pain. The razor hail stops, and as soon as I'm sure there's nothing else coming down I let him scoot out from under me to clamp his hands on the wound.

"Graywytch!" shouts Calamity. "You listen here! That door is coming open and we are walking out with whatever we care to take, and that's my final offer!"

Real, genuine laughter is coming from all around us. My eyes are screwed shut as I throw everything I have into scanning for some sign of where she's hiding. My stomach roils and my head feels like it's about to slip off my neck. Forget about finding subtle hints; I can barely make sense of the lattice at all in this condition. The rumbling thunder of my rage cracks open, hot and piercing.

"That's your offer?" says Graywytch through peals of laughter. "Your *offer*? I thought you, at least, knew what you were about, Calamity."

"Kinetiq?" says Calamity, loud enough for all to hear.

"Yeah?"

"Starting from the top shelf, incinerate every bit of paper in this room."

"No!" shrieks Graywytch, all humor lost as Kinetiq claps their hands together and makes a thermal cannon. Hungry, rushing currents of heat swirl away from the beam of superheated energy bursting from their palms. They sweep it across the top shelf of one side of the room, books that look decades, maybe centuries old going up in ecstatic bursts of yellow cinders.

While that's happening, I've gone stumbling over the rail, ass-over-skull, into a heap in the slate floor below. Just for a moment, when the horror of how Calamity's ruthlessness was sweeping across her, Graywytch's illusion faltered, fell. I saw her.

As I pull myself to my feet, hand over hand against a bookcase, Calamity calls down another ultimatum.

"You have no idea what you've done!" shouts Graywytch. "No idea!" A barely audible whine begins to rise, and the air smells of thunder, but I'm going to stop this before she launches another attack.

I take a moment to exhale, gather my strength, and heave aside the vertigo as I bite down on the lattice as hard as I can. Zero to crash in the blink of an eye.

There it is. That perfect still moment. Me, bursting through the wall of books, paper falling from me in shredded waves. Graywytch, her eyes locking on me in sudden fear. This is something I've dreamed of for months. Maybe not this way, and not this fight, but this moment, this moment when she realizes that there are some people she shouldn't push, some fights she shouldn't have picked, has danced in front of me, a golden hypothetical begging to be made real.

The frozen moment ends, and I crash upon her, bone-to-bone, flesh-to-flesh, and we keep going, through the next bookcase, shattered wood and a blizzard of destroyed manuscripts. There are four distinct snaps, wet and satisfying.

We tumble apart against the floor. She skids one way, and I end up spilling the other. The world is jumping, spinning away from me. This time, I really do vomit. But I've *hurt* her.

One hand over the other, I crawl to where Graywytch is still gawping at the sheer amount of pain a human body can experience. My stomach roils, and the world spins about me; I don't think I could call on the lattice right now even if I wanted to.

But I don't have to, not for this. She makes a puppy-like effort to shove me off her and away, but I bat her arms aside and fasten my hands around her neck.

And squeeze, squeeze, squeeze.

We make eye contact, and right at that moment there's an instant of quailing, a mote of hesitation in my fingers. Is this right—yes! Yes goddamnit! She deserves this! *I* deserve this!

So I squeeze, squeeze, squeeze.

No. I deserved so much more than this. I deserved so much more from *you*. But you treat me like shit, you tell me I'm worthless. Make me hate myself, make me a coward. Make me weak.

Squeeze, squeeze, squeeze.

You hold me down and torture me. For years! And nobody stops you. Nobody cares. And all I can do is run, run, run, until I'm small in everyone's eyes. In my eyes.

(Someone's calling my other name; I don't pay attention.)

Squeeze, squeeze, squeeze.

Well, not anymore! Not today! Today you get what you

deserve. I'm not running anymore. Never again. You made me weak! YOU MADE ME WEAK—

Something tugging at my cape, hauling me back. "Dreadnought, that's enough!" Calamity is shouting.

"No!" The lattice squishes away from me when I try to grab it, a new cloud of nausea slipping in from the edges. Graywytch's face is crimson shading to purple, and with a shaking hand, she twists a ring and disappears—air rushing in with a thump to fill the vacated space.

"I had him!" I shout twisting away from Calamity. "I fucking had him!"

She looks confused. "Who?"

"Graywytch! I almost—Goddamnit, Calamity! I was this close to ending it!"

"I'll run 'er down for you," she says in an even voice. "Get on upstairs and start working on those bars across the door. We need an exit in case she gets a second wind."

"I can do this," I say, shaking with frustrated rage.

"Dreadnought!" Calamity snaps the moderation out of her tone. "Upstairs. Now."

Calamity isn't my commanding officer or anything so grandiose. But she does call the shots; we all agreed on that. Capes listen to their shot-caller. It's how things work, no matter how much I wish I could ignore her right now.

Goddamnit, Sarah.

I thought you understood.

One hand over the other, I start climbing the bookcase. It's hard, with the world swaying and dipping at every random moment, and my fingers get tight and trembly before I'm able to slip one arm over the edge of the walkway and start levering myself up. The floor twists and bobs below me, and when I tip over the guardrail to collapse on top of the bridge, I have to take a moment to let the world stop spinning before I can even think about making it to my feet again.

Below me, gunfire. Two shots. Some scuffling. Kinetiq dives

into the maze in a burning corona of power, flashes of their power lighting up a thick fog that appeared sometime during my (very slow) climb.

Lying there, panting, I listen to the rest of my team harry Graywytch, press her, push in for the capture. I clench a fist and slam it into the floor in frustration—the tile shatters magnificently, but the wobbly spins aren't worth it.

What I miss while I'm lying on the ground: Codex finds the book he needs. The bars come down. Graywytch gets away. We don't talk much on the flight home.

CHAPTER TWENTY-TWO

So now I'm in one of the medical beds in the safehouse. Again. I'm really starting to hate the feel of these kinds of pads—they're not even really mattresses.

The world continues to spin around me, though it's bearable as long as I don't provoke it. Doc can't figure out what's wrong with me. She wants Charlie to take a crack at it, but Calamity and I agree that he needs to get to work on hacking Graywytch's magic. That's all we seem to agree on right now.

After—I can't speak to Sarah. Not right now. And she seems to feel the same way. Why is this so difficult? Why can't she understand?

Doc finishes her last scan and sets the devices aside on a crash cart before pulling up a chair. Curled up on my side, I watch her, trying to make my face convey just how skeptical I am about the idea of hashing this out right now.

"Is there anything you want to talk to me about?" she says.

"No."

"Is there anyone you do want to talk to?"

"No," I say, with a slight edge to my voice.

"Calamity says you went a little apeshit back there."

"Graywytch was trying to murder my friends."

"So you took her through a bookcase." Doc frowns thoughtfully and nods. "Fair enough. What about the part that came after that?"

"What part?"

Doc doesn't roll her eyes. That, more than anything, is what finally gets through to me that she's really not kidding about this.

"You know the part I mean, Danielle," she says. I've got nothing to say to that. "It's okay to be angry," she says. "You've got more right than most people to be mad at the world. Especially this week. But you can't let it change you."

It hurts to hear her say this. It hurts in ways I can't feel properly because I don't really understand them. A sort of twisting, inward feeling, deep in my chest, and a clench high in my gut. So I do what I'm always doing these days: I try to hit back.

"What if it's not changing me, Doctor? What if this is who I really am and you all need to get over it? She deserves to die."

Doc looks down at her folded hands for a moment. "Look, kiddo—we're superheroes. Violence is part of the job. But that doesn't mean we execute people without a trial. We take them alive, every time. And if we can't, we'd better have a damn good reason for why not. Better than anything you've had today."

"The other Dreadnoughts killed people."

"That's true." She nods. "But I guarantee you they never did it because they thought it'd make them feel better."

"That's not—!" I sit up to spit indignant denials at her and regret my decision immediately.

"It *is*, Danny. And I think we both know it. There might come a day when you need to kill someone; I think we can both admit that. But when that happens, it's forever. The other guy is dead, so he doesn't care anymore—but you'll have to carry that for the rest of your life. When you kill, it had better be in battle. It had better be someone who is still a threat. It had better be when you don't have a choice, when seconds count and lives are on the line. Because I know you, Danielle, and you're too good a person to be happy with a murder on your conscience."

There's that word I've been avoiding. My voice comes out quieter than I'd like when I reply. "You said I had to take them down. That we couldn't tolerate what they did."

"That's right, I did. But I was thinking more along the lines of putting her in prison and then making funny faces at her from across the glass. You've been through hell; I get it, and if I had anyone else who could do your job, I'd use them instead and get you into therapy pronto. Not because I think you can't hack it, by the way, but because even you have limits, and I don't like seeing you get hurt. It's clear to me now that you're in way more trouble than I thought you were. If I had known you were in this kind of pain, I would have never sent you on that mission. But we don't have a deep bench here, so I need you to be strong enough to keep a grip on yourself, at least until we're out of this fight. Can you do that for me?"

With great effort, I roll over to put my back to her. "Just leave me alone."

Her answer is immediate: "I kind of can't. Not about this."

"Do you have any idea what it's like being Dreadnought?" I snap at her. "You don't even *want* to be a cape—but this is the only thing I've ever been any good at, and she tried to take it away from me!"

"So be good at it. Take some time to think about this. We'll talk before you go out again." Doc gets up, leaving the sound of her stool gently spinning as she walks away across the hangar.

Before I go out again. What is that, a sick joke? I can't go out, not like this. Not until the spell wears off. Or until Charlie finishes his research and has time to fix me. God, I spend so much time waiting for other people to come along and save me. I hate this. I hate myself.

And there I sulk for an embarrassingly long period of time before it occurs to me that I can try to fix this on my own. Looking into the lattice is hard right now, but that doesn't mean I can't do it. And I was able to undo a little bit of what was going wrong in Karen's head. Maybe the magic screwing me up is weaker than that, and I can actually fix this.

Carefully, very carefully, I slide my mind back into the lattice. The world shivers under me, and a new wave of nausea sweeps through me. But I'm in. It doesn't take long to find the magic.

There, in my inner ears, in the fluid chambers that tell me which way is down, there are flitting little yarn tangles of nothingness. Every shift of the fluid is magically enhanced to a great big sloshing, and even when I'm still, the fluids tremble and bounce randomly, teased into motion by the nonsense inputs of the spell.

Very, very slowly, I reach out to the lattice and gently pick at the strands of the charm.

There's a lot of things I can do with the lattice besides fly and punch things. (Though those *are* two of my favorite things.) But magic is still more or less an unknown frontier for me. Tweaking the lattice beyond my basic powerset is a dangerous hobby in the best of times, with sprains and broken bones as a constant risk for failure, but this will be worse because I don't even know how magic actually works. Working on Karen was the first time I tried to counteract magic with my powers, and it nearly gave her an aneurysm. Doing this inside my own head has the feel of digging up an armed landmine with only a bayonet. While drunk. I don't see that I have much choice, though. I need to be able to fight. Hell, I need to be able to *walk*.

Someone pushes aside the privacy screen and sits down on the stool. I crack an eye open. It's Calamity—no, she's not wearing her hat and her bandanna is down, so this is Sarah.

"Hi," she says.

"Hi."

Sarah shifts nervously. "Um, I think we might consider keeping Dreadnought and Calamity separate from Danielle and Sarah. At least when I have to be a hardass. Deal?"

I reach out a hand, and when she takes it I give her a gentle squeeze. "Deal."

Her whole posture relaxes, and a woozy smile of relief blooms on her face. I think she thought I would honestly dump her for telling Doc what happened back there. Not even I'm that stupid. But then again, maybe she doesn't understand how amazing she is. Maybe being a chokingly beautiful, untouchable badass is normal to her.

"I'm trying to fix my head," I tell her. "I'll need to concentrate for a while. Can you stay with me?"

Sarah scoots the chair closer, takes my hand, clasped between her own, into her lap. "What are you doing?"

"I can see the magic from Graywytch's trap. I'm going to see if I can pick it apart in the lattice."

Sarah's forehead crinkles. "Oh. Um, what?"

She doesn't really like it when I giggle at that, but I smooth it over quickly. "I'm sorry, I forgot I've been vague about my powers. You remember how I can see the backside of reality? I can sort of see magic too."

"If you say so."

"There are these strings that make up everything. Like," and here I go quiet for a moment while I shove down the nausea long enough to look at her arm, I mean really look at it. "Oh. Uh, damn. I didn't know your prosthetic goes all the way into the spine."

"You can see inside me?" she asks quietly.

"Yeah. You're beautiful."

Sarah blushes and smiles. I like making her blush like that. I need to think of more ways to do it.

With that pleasant image in my head, I close my eyes and focus on dissolving this magic, one hesitant pull at a time. A little bit, a little bit more. It's slow going, and I need to stop to take plenty of breaks. A grinding ice-pick feeling has started in one of my sinuses, but the pressure abruptly disappears.

"Danny, your nose is bleeding," says Sarah. Still in the lattice, I switch my gaze "down" and check it out. Just a burst vessel in my nose, nothing to worry about.

"It's fine," I say, keeping my eyes closed. Just a few more, I'm almost there. And then, all at once, I pull on one last strand, and the whole thing springs in on itself and evaporates.

The fluid in my ears begins to settle and the world finally wobbles to a stop. With a sigh of relief I sit up. "Good as new, I think."

"Are you sure?"

"One way to find out," I say, swinging my legs off the exam bed. I hop off—and stay hanging in the air. "Yeah, I think I'm good."

Sarah takes my hand again and pulls me through the air to her. Our lips meet, and then she rests her forehead against mine. "When this is over, do you want to go see a movie with me?" she asks quietly.

"Uh, sure. You don't want to go caping instead? You know, just hang out on the roofs like we used to?"

Sarah considers for a moment. "I like caping. But I've never been on a real date."

"I'd like that."

Her smile makes my heart flip over, and it would be so easy to stay here, floating, forehead to forehead. But there's work to do, so far too soon, Sarah pulls her bandanna up, drops my hand, and becomes Calamity again.

Time to get back to work.

CHAPTER TWENTY-THREE

While I've been fiddling around inside my head and making out with Sarah, Charlie has been hard at work. Graywytch's grimoire is splayed out across the workbench, and he's cross-referencing with two of his own books.

"What's the word, Codex?" asks Calamity as we walk up. Well, I'm walking. She moseys.

Charlie puts his finger on one passage and flips through a few more pages in another book. "Aaaahhh…hold on…yeah, yeah, it's safe to start knocking his satellites out of the sky."

"Are you sure?" asks Doc.

He taps one of the books he's been flipping through, a leather-bound volume with handwritten pages. "Yes. We snagged her current project book—that's the notebook she uses to keep her project's details straight—and none of these incantations leave room for booby traps, which would have to be baked into the main spell to avoid having them interfere with each other. If the satellites do have defenses, they won't be magical, I can say that much."

"Cool!" I say. "Let's do it!"

Doc and I put our heads together and calculate a flight plan. By the time everything's settled, it's on toward dusk. Like I mentioned earlier, orbital flight is really complicated, so I need to wait for a launch window before I take off. Stars start to prick out of the gauzy purple sky, and the countdown timer displaying on my wrist just passed two minutes and dropping.

The door opens and out comes Doc Impossible. With effort,

I keep my face neutral. I don't need another lecture about how terrible I am right before I risk my life to save the world.

Doc holds out a pair of goggles. They're low-profile, like swimmer's goggles, rounded at the edges with a hefty strap that looks like it would hug a skull quite nicely. "I just finished these up. They're a telemetry HUD so you can spot your flight track without your glove holograms. It should let you push a satellite and watch where you're going at the same time. Keep the holograms ready for backups, though."

"Thanks," I say, and a tension in my chest releases. I'm even smiling. When I slip the goggles on, they blink to life and hook up with my suit's computer. Above me, a line of golden nav-gates float in the air, tracing a line up, up into space and towards my first rendezvous.

"This is a solo mission," says Doc. "Defend yourself if you have to, but remember—"

"I got it, Doc." Shit, she's really stuck on this, isn't she? I search for something to say to reassure her. "It's going to be fine. There's lots of room to run in space."

Doc smiles, relieved. "Good. Good."

Not that I intend to run from a fight, of course. Dreadnought doesn't run. She wins. And I need to get back to winning.

The launch window timer hits zero, and with a last wave goodbye, I push off from the ground. The industrial lot falls away, the city falls away, the state falls away. When I'm high enough, my suit vibrates in my ankles to tell me I'm above the noise ordinance ceiling, and I really kick into it hard. Sonic booms string out behind me, wisps of condensation slithering across my shoulders, down my back, until I'm dragging long, white contrails in the sky with my boots. Time to take a deep breath. I won't get another for the next five hours if this mission goes right.

The wind's roar dwindles and dies with the atmosphere. The horizon is a fuzzy blue curve that gradually falls away until entire continents and oceans spread out beneath me.

Doc is feeding me real-time navigational data to steer me to the closest of Garrison's satellites. I follow the holographic nav-gates projected against the lenses of my goggles into a twisting climb that brings me onto a new orbit. The nearest satellite is only nine hundred miles away—I'm practically scraping paint off of it already in astronautical terms.

I'm coming up on it from the retrograde position—essentially, I'm chasing it down from behind—which is the safe way to approach something else in orbit. Otherwise you get closing speeds in the dozens of thousands of miles per hour, and my reaction times are only *barely* superhuman, certainly not enough to avoid disaster at those kinds of speeds. It's not just satellites, either, but bits of space debris that travel along with them, old bolts and splinters of metal and even things like cans of paint and lost blankets. They all hit like cannon shells and the last time I ran into one of those on an orbital jump it snapped my arm like a dry branch.

There's the satellite, up ahead of me now. Only fifty miles out, a pale gray dot slightly more defined than the other pale dots up here. My goggles automatically wrap it in glowing brackets and zoom in a picture-in-picture window to verify that it's the one I'm going after.

It's pretty big—think slightly smaller than a city bus, with the usual solar arrays unfolded and pointed at the sun, a cylinder for the main body, some antennas hanging off it, all very normal.

Well, except that at one end is a huge crystal dome, sort of like the giant golf ball building at Disney World, and inside sits what appears to be a miniature Stonehenge. There's even what looks like real grass turf along the bottom of the dome. The stones are all deeply carved with geometric patterns and they seem to catch the light reflecting off Earth, channeling it into gleaming lines of blue power swirling from pattern to pattern, stone to stone.

Right, that's the one. With a last burst of acceleration I bring myself up close and set up to push this thing out of orbit. The eastern US is passing below me now, a yellow field of stars blanketing the ground, right up to where it stops in a hard line at the Atlantic Ocean. The plan is to push the satellite down with a short, sharp deceleration that will burn most of it up in the atmosphere and drop the rest in the ocean. Then I'll hopscotch all over low orbit doing the same thing again and again until Garrison's entire fleet is knocked out.

The skin of the satellite is cold, so cold I can feel it through my gloves, so cold it's uncomfortable even for me to touch it. The way orbital mechanics work means that best place to do this from is the "front" of the satellite, where I can kill its speed while pushing it down at the same time. Unfortunately, this is also the hardest place to push it from. This thing is so heavy and it's moving so fast that it's going to take every pound of thrust I've got to drop its speed fast enough to hit the mark I need to hit to get it on a steep enough path to burn up properly. That's without directly channeling its momentum through my own pattern in the lattice, of course. I've gotten a lot better at that sort of thing since I shattered my ribs trying to catch an airliner, but the amount of momentum that satellite carries is a step or five above something as minor as a falling jet. I think I'll skip the broken ribs today and stick to shoving for now.

For the first few moments, it's like pressing up against a granite cliff. This thing is *moving* and I can't feel any change in velocity whatsoever. Crap, this plan might need to go in stages if they're all going to be this hard.

As if sensing my thoughts, my HUD turns green and a chibi illustration of Doc pops up in my field of view; she's got a huge anime smile and a word bubble floating above her head that says, "Atta girl! You can do it! Fuck that shit up!"

Okay, maybe I need to cut Doc some slack.

Now the momentum is dropping enough that I can sense the difference in the lattice and then a few moments later, with my hands. The whole satellite begins to twist under my palms and sink away from me as Earth's gravity brings it down for a big, burning hug. I stay with it long enough to give it a nice hard boost into the atmosphere, and then squirt back up to a stable orbit of my own.

Garrison's satellite is dropping more and more vertically

now, twirling away like I dropped it down a well. In a matter of moments I've skimmed far past it, my own orbit carrying me thousands of yards further along. I turn away and start the flight to my next waypoint. Multibillion-dollar acts of vandalism are not how I thought I'd save the world this month, but being a superhero is a weird gig sometimes.

It's a tough threading-of-the-needle involving a change of altitude and a course correction that has to happen within a thirty-second window, but I manage to put the satellite down in the North Sea before turning and climbing hard to where another satellite will be passing south over Europe at about the time that I am scheduled to arrive. The plan is to keep hopping from orbit to orbit this way, and knock out Garrison's entire network before he's got time to launch a counterattack. Fighting in space is stupidly dangerous for a list of reasons that would take all day to explain.

I get as far as Germany before I have to start fighting in space.

• • •

An instant before impact, I get a bare flash, a fuzzy outline behind and above me. I'm so focused on hitting my next waypoint that I don't even have time to get curious before he blindsides me with a kick to the back of the head that jams my chin into my chest and throws me spinning off course. For the first few moments of the fight, I'm more confused than anything else. How the hell am I getting hit? Who is hitting me?

Then I bite down and arrest my spin, turning with my hands up just in time to block another scything kick, and there's Red Steel, his rust-colored silk Cossack shirt rippling oddly with his momentum in the vacuum of space.

We catch eyes with each other, and I break out in a huge grin. Red has made his way as a mercenary since the Soviet Union fell apart. Garrison must have hired him to defend his satellites. Which means that I get to fight Red Steel, the greatest hero the Russians ever came up with.

Excellent.

And that instant of recognition is over, and now we're in a faster, harder fight than I've ever been in before. If he's got any doubts whatsoever about accepting a contract on a kid, he left them back on Earth. Punch meets counter-punch, kick meets pivot and riposte. It's a complicated, nasty little fight, a hectic, dizzying swirl of dodges and counters as we each jockey for a superior position.

We've both got an extra weak spot in this fight—the solar plexus. One good hit there will evacuate all the air from our lungs, and whoever loses their breath first will have to disengage and get back into the atmosphere as fast as they can. So we're both hoping to protect ourselves, while at the same time trying to get in close enough to do unto others before it's done unto us. And because we're in space, there's nothing to inhibit our movement in any direction. No ground, no buildings, hell, not even any clouds to hide in. Without the air to slow us down we accelerate faster and turn harder. And all of this is happening in perfect silence. You don't think of fights as quiet, but they're often just a bunch of grunts and slaps and thuds. This is even less than that.

As I pivot up over him to get behind him for a sort of weapon-ized Heimlich maneuver, he sinks down and away, twisting to keep his front to me. When he loops wide, I come in tight on his flank. Earth and night dance around us, and I've completely lost track of my course. Altitude, heading, it's all gone, there's only this punch and the next one after it.

Twice he goes to get his arms around me in a squeeze to clear my lungs, and twice I make him pay for it with headbutts and knee strikes. When I throw a hard, spinning kick at his head, he catches me by the ankle and snaps me like a whip. Tendons and ligaments all over my body scream. I curl up on myself, use my own trapped leg as a lever to slingshot in close and plant my kneecap in his nose with a crunch I can feel, but not hear. We go tumbling end-over-end, and somehow he's gotten hold of my cape and whips me about in a tight circle. My cape tears away from my shoulders, and I go zipping away at the better part of a thousand miles an hour.

This isn't working. He's got a reach advantage on me. Well, they almost always have a reach advantage on me, but usually I can mitigate it with speed or durability or pure, unfiltered aggression. Not here. Not with him. Everything I can do, he can match. Everything he can do, I scramble to keep up with. It doesn't even seem like he's getting worn down; he's just got this focused look on his face like I'm a puzzle and he only needs to figure out how to unlock me. Time to change things up. Instead of turning to head back into the fight, I use the momentum he's given me to boost hard away from him. Red Steel tosses my torn cape aside (Dude, not cool! That thing cost more than most people's cars! You could at least tuck it in your belt so I can get it back after I'm done kicking your ass.) and powers after me.

Crap. Without my cape I can't escape this fight quickly. If I descend fast enough to escape him, I'll burn up. If I descend slow enough not to burn, he'll catch up and keep whipping my ass. *Maybe* he'd let me slow down enough to reenter the atmosphere without getting torched, but you know what? Screw that. I'm going to win.

My suit buzzes with an incoming text from Doc. You're off course. What's going on? is printed in big yellow letters across my goggles. With a flick of my thumb I bring up the keypad pattern on my forearm and tap out a quick reply.

Fighting RS. Talk later.

Don't fight, she texts back. Run.

Can't, I reply. Lost my cape.

Even now that I know he's here, Red Steel is barely a presence in the lattice. He's more like an absence than anything else. I have to actually twist and look down between my legs, and yeah, he's still with me, about a hundred yards back and crawling to close the distance. With these few seconds of peace in the middle of the fight, my body is starting to report on how much pain it's in. My lips are stiff with frozen blood. My left leg is hanging limp, basically useless. A deep, formless ache sings about how hard he punched my kidney. And I'm tired too. This whole fight has been maybe two minutes long so far, and I'm already exhausted. Every time we get close, it's like I'm holding on with my fingernails. One good punch. That's all either of us need, and I'm getting less and less able to hold off his attacks.

It's hard to tell from this far away, but I don't see him bleeding the way I am. My knuckles all ache already, and I've got no idea if anything I've done has even hurt him.

No. Stop. Think positive, and get angry. He brought the fight to me, so I get to bring it back twice as hard. We're evenly matched. Well, except for a few things, like how he's faster and stronger and tougher and more experienced and all but invisible to my sixth sense. I mean other than that, it's a total coin flip.

Shit, no wonder the other Dreadnoughts always took this guy seriously.

Fighting harder than him isn't a great option. I need to fight smarter. I can beat him. I know I can. Garrison's satellites are in a pretty low orbit, well below most other spacecraft. My plan, such as it is, is to drag Red Steel higher, into the zone where satellites are more common.

More satellites mean more space debris. And I'm betting my life on the hope that he can't see those little flying chunks of death as well as I can. I've turned west. We're flying anterograde, directly into the oncoming swarm of satellites and debris.

Bring him over New Port, texts Doc. I'll shoot him down with an anti-orbital cannon.

You have one of those?

Not yet. Gimme ten minutes, she replies.

In the lattice, I see a burning corona of momentum behind what looks like an astronaut's hand tool. It's coming right—

—it snaps by me as I desperately pivot out of the way.

By the time I think to look and see if it hit Red Steel, maybe a half-second later, it's already miles behind us. Then a bolt slips by me so close it musses my hair, and I go icy with belated fear. My suit buzzes at my shoulder blades, and big red letters scroll across my goggle lenses: NAVIGATIONAL HAZARD—YOU HAVE ENTERED A KNOWN DEBRIS FIELD—DESCEND IMMEDIATELY—NAVIGATIONAL HAZARD—

I squeeze my eyes shut and blot out everything but the lattice. There's no room for fear; I've got to focus on pushing my perceptions as far out ahead of me as I can. Swirling currents of radiation skitter and dance off the Van Allen belt high above us. The night sky is alive with trailing, twisting lines of momentum. There, a screw—

And as it's passing, I grab its momentum and pull it through my pattern. A hot buzzing behind my navel, like some cosmic string is being tugged through my guts, the heated crunch of my left ring finger breaking, and I've dragged it off its course and shot it right at that haunting void behind me. A half-second later I open my eyes to glance behind me, and Red Steel is twisting in the night, one hand clamped onto his shoulder where the screw hit him.

Okay, yeah, so this is a game plan.

Then he shoots me with his friggin' eye lasers, and *why the hell does he have eye lasers, that wasn't in his file!*

Scalding emerald beams rake my chest and arm, my suit instantly going black and crinkled wherever they land. The pain is hot and instant, and I have to bite down on a scream that would have lost me all my air. His eyes glitter with emerald energy again, and I bank left before rolling right. Beams cut the sky where I was, and now the fight has reversed again. Glancing hits are bad enough, but if he manages to put those things on me for more than a moment, I have no doubt they'll reduce my chest into cinders. Maybe these beams cost him too much to use casually, or maybe he just likes to keep them secret, but I get the feeling that his decision to use them signals he's decided not to screw around anymore. An instant later I realize the fact that I didn't know he had these might suggest that everyone else who's ever seen him use them is dead.

Now there's a comforting thought.

Flying backwards with my eyes locked on Steel as I weave and bob means I've got to split my attention between him and the lattice. Another hunk of debris is coming, but I notice it too late to grab its momentum and tweak it onto a collision course.

Red Steel does not have that problem and stabs lasers at me again and again. There's no real dodging a laser beam. So the only real way for me to not get toasted here is to beat Red's reflexes, to be somewhere else at the moment he fires his shot.

It's a lot of fancy flying, with rolls, loops, twists, and hard turns thrown out one after another. Again and again, twin beams sear through the night to the left or right of me. Twice I get tagged again, and twice more I clench against the pain.

My own counterattacks are not going as well as I hoped. He's started his own evasive flying, so I don't land another hit. Not every screw or nut I throw at him comes at the cost of a broken bone, but enough of them do that I'm seriously concerned about how I'd stand up against him if it came to a close fight again. I send a dropped screwdriver spinning at him end-over-end, and miss by dozens of feet—but the strain of altering its course breaks two of my toes. The adrenaline has finally arrived, and that helps with the pain to an extent, but every time I check myself in the lattice I can't help but notice how efficiently he's killing me with a thousand little injuries. Burn wounds here, strained ligaments there…

Ready to fire, texts Doc. I look down, and we're passing over the Northwest, the lights of New Port halfway between me and the curve of the horizon.

He's the one behind me, I tap back.

Doc's reply is a glittering cobalt beam that geysers up from the outskirts of New Port and turns the night pale with the intensity of its power. Half the metropolitan area gutters and goes dark by sections as rolling brownouts claim most of Washington state.

Supercharged ions splash a glancing blow off of Red Steel before streaking up and away into the night. He's knocked into a rough spin, and he's hurt. His shirt has been burned away, his shoulder mottled red and black. But even as I start pushing toward him to finish this, he straightens out and cuts the sky with a broad sweeping attack. I barely twist away from the beams in time, and I'm forced to put more distance between us.

How the hell do I beat this guy? He took a hit like *that* and kept going? My own attacks hurt me as much as they hurt him. There's no advantage I can find, no strategy or cheat that's going to steal a win for me.

Hit him again, I tell her. If nothing else, Dreadnought must go down fighting. That, at least, I know I can do. One way or the other, this ends soon. Flying backward, face-to-face across a hundred yards, I square my shoulders for this one last effort. He sees that. Body language is hard at this distance. I think he nods.

Recalibrating to a wide angle spread. I've got power for one more shot. Can you make it count?

My fingers dance across the keyboard. I'm not sure how to tell her that I'm out of ideas, that the rage I rely on hasn't shown up, that maybe I'm scared and I shouldn't even be—

Wait. There, ahead of my flight path, just at the very edge of my lattice perception and coming up fast. It's huge, dark, and entirely cold. It's been dead since a Nemesis fragment killed it two years ago. The largest single piece of space debris in history, a navigational hazard so massive NASA considered a mission just to pull it safely out of orbit.

The Hubble Space Telescope.

All at once, I understand how I'm going to win, and the thought of it fills me with dread. This is really, *really* going to hurt.

Yes, I can make it count, I reply. Then I close my eyes and put all my attention into the lattice. Red Steel scores another hit up the side of my thigh, and I grit my teeth. The Hubble is big, and it's tearing along at an almost unimaginable speed. With confidence I only half-believe in, I reach out and start to run the fingers of my mind over the shape of its momentum. The trick to this is to be gentle but decisive. Hesitation kills.

There. That's the main string, the blazing white weave in the pattern that holds its course together. The Hubble is coming up fast now, terrifyingly fast.

Doc fires again. The lattice is lit up with a swirling corona of electrons pouring off the front of the cannon shot as it blazes up from the surface. This shot is more shotgun than rifle, a dozen smaller beams rising in loose, random formation. Most fly harmlessly into the void, but some of them slash hard against Red Steel and batter him around. By themselves, not enough to do much but drag this out.

Another half-second to double-check my feel of the telescope before I grab its momentum and *heave*—

It's like no sensation I've felt before. The hot, buzzing thrum of power is more energy than I've ever channeled, and at these speeds, it's not simply a difference of scale, it feels like a phase change between ice and water, between water and steam, between steam and plasma, but all of that compressed into a single still moment. For a moment, just a moment, I'm back where I was on that day I changed. I can see everywhere. I understand everything. Life is beautiful. We are all beautiful, all one, all linked in a joyous harmony. Even as I'm realizing it, the epiphany is fading.

—the Hubble off its course, and I haul it down and to the side by a few crucial degrees. By reflex I'm squirting up, up, out of line with Red, and the Hubble is already here, from a dot to a colossus in the time to blink an eye.

Red Steel encounters the Hubble Space Telescope the way a baseball encounters a home run derby. The telescope disintegrates into flayed sheets of aluminum and a huge constellation of shattered glass. Red goes spinning away, completely out of control and shooting towards Earth.

My back screams, every muscle between the bottom of my skull and the top of my pelvis howling in outrage. Smothering clouds of fatigue try to blot out my mind. For a moment, I think I've lost consciousness.

Almost over. I can do this.

With one last hard push I blast after him, crash through the spiraling debris, and get ready to finish this.

When I catch up with Red Steel he's still whirling in all three directions, and still he somehow feels me coming and greets me with an emerald blast. My chest, neck, face light up with pain and then impact. I punch him like an angry god, the kind of punch that would shatter windows for a dozen yards in every direction if we were down on Earth. Again, and again. He gives me one on the chin, and I knock aside the follow up. My left leg is stiff with pain, but I wrap it around his neck and use my other ankle to lock it down so I've got him pinned. His eyes start glowing, and I clap my hands over his face just as he fires. My palms light up with scalding agony, but what hurts for me is torture for him, his whole body convulsing as the energy is reflected back into his skull.

We're falling now, our orbital momentum almost completely wasted. This is it, no turning back now, so I shove aside my fatigue, shake off the pain, and burn away our altitude as fast as I can. His hands come up to claw at me, to punch my wounded thigh, to try and peel me off him. The initiative is mine now, and if I lose it I die, so I ignore my broken fingers, switch to open palm strikes, and rain punishment down on him.

But it's not until the first wisps of the atmosphere start to flame off his back that he realizes how much danger he's really in. My smile is tight and savage, my protective anger finally here at last.

You took my cape. You took my heat shield.

That's okay.

I have *you*.

With one hand I hold his head in place, and with the other I throw a punch that comes all the way up from the root of my spine. His eyes, now milky with cataracts, roll up in his head, and for just an instant, Red Steel goes limp. An instant is all I need to unhook my ankles, roll him between my thighs, and get his arms twisted up behind him in a lock. He squirms and bucks, tries to turn this against me. Too late. Far too late. Clawing for every ounce of speed I can, we head down, down into the atmosphere.

Orange and red whispers grow to flickers. Flickers grow to torches. The silence of space gives way to the roar of reentry. We enter a tunnel of fire that drags behind us for miles. With one last spasm he tries to get away from me, and I can feel his flight pushing against mine, trying to shove him in any direction, anywhere that will get him away from the pain, but I've got momentum and gravity to add to my own strength, and it's no use. His resistance shudders, collapses. He goes limp in my arms, his legs kicking and jerking against the howling plasma.

The flames pull away from us and we're down in the atmosphere, hurtling toward the ocean. When I poke my head over Red Steel's shoulder, I spot a small island, mostly rock and sand in dark, chopping water. I bank us toward it. He's starting to stir, and the last bits of his charred hair are flaking off in the blasting wind. I redouble my grip on his arms and push on as hard as I can.

Just a hundred yards off the deck I let go, curl my legs up, and give him a kick with everything I've got, right in the small of the back. Red Steel hits the island at Mach 5 and is instantly hidden by a huge explosion of dust and gravel that pings off me like shrapnel.

After the howling winds of reentry, the sudden quiet is almost disorienting. There is only the lapping of the waves and pattering of falling pebbles.

My leg sends shooting pain up my pelvis when I gently touch down, and I let it curl gently. My back is screaming, pulled muscles and torn ligaments stabbing at me no matter which way I turn or hold my weight. My face and chest sting where his eye lasers gouged me again and again. Two of my fingers are broken quite badly, a throbbing pinch at the end of my hand, but the six hairline fractures I've got elsewhere sort of balance them out. The goggles Doc made for me are gone, probably blown off in that last, desperate charge. And I'm *weary*. Oh God, I'm so tired. Everything is heavy; even my arms hang like weights at my side.

I should get in there and finish this. Standing around is foolish, but I can barely keep myself vertical, much less muster up the gall to go look for more trouble.

The sky is the deep purple of late evening, the western horizon still pale with the sun. Above us and far to the east, a new constellation of shooting stars marks the Hubble's final passing. The moon is out, and is nearly full. It really is a beautiful night. I'm glad I got to live long enough to see it.

The ocean breeze tugs the cloud of rock dust away, and at the center of a shallow crater, Red Steel is stirring, struggling to shove himself to his feet.

"Stay down, old man!" I shout at him. "Stay down, or I will do things to you that you will not come back from!"

He doesn't listen. Too stubborn, or too professional, it's hard to say. When Red Steel gets to his feet, I give him a few moments to come to his senses and surrender. He doesn't. Damnit. We close for the last time, and in the instant before impact, I think I see him smile through his burned and twisted lips. But then my fist snaps his head back in an uppercut that takes him twelve feet straight up. He hits the ground like a bag of wet dirt, and when I'm literally standing over him with my boot pressed down on his windpipe, he finally, finally passes out.

My own will gives out a few moments later, and I collapse to my knees with a squeak of pain. For a moment I feel a clammy chill under my supersuit, and I'm sure I'm going to barf. Taking slow lungfuls of cool, salty air helps the feeling pass, but now I'm trembling with fatigue. Of course I never expected fighting Red Steel to be easy, but holy shit. This guy has no quit in him.

The giggles start low in my chest, and there's an absurdity to them, some sense of inappropriateness that makes me clap my hands across my mouth to stifle them. Oh my God, I just beat up Red Steel! Calamity is going to freak out when I tell her. I collapse laughing, aching, riven with burns and tender spots. The shaking of my laughter hurts, and that only makes it funnier. Every little stab of pain is another reminder of the pure, simple joy of being alive.

As the laughter fades, my mind refocuses on the more pressing issues. I've still got to take those satellites out. I don't think Garrison has more than one orbital-capable mercenary on staff, or he'd have sent both of them to be sure of the job. If I can rest up for a few minutes, I might be able to get back up there and take out the rest of the satellites, or at least some of them. I activate my sat-phone and dial Doc. A few moments later, the interface section on my forearm turns red and says NO SIGNAL—CHECK ANTENNA. A quick diagnostic tells me that my satellite phone has been knocked out, and with it my ability to get orbital telemetry from Doc. Without telemetry, there's no way I can finish the job before my body gives out. To be honest, it's mostly a relief to have a solid excuse to abandon the mission. Time to get my ass back to New Port.

Which raises an interesting question: just where the hell am I, anyhow? We were passing over New Port when Doc started firing, but our momentum would have carried us considerably further west. The sun has just barely set. We're in the middle of the ocean, but I think I saw a few other low, gravely islands around here when we were coming down. Um, the Aleutians? Man, I hope the Aleutians. The alternative is some islands way, way down near Hawaii, and that's a much longer suborbital flight.

"All right, sleepyhead, I'm getting you to a hospital," I tell Red Steel. His breath whistles through his charred nostrils, which is the only way I know he's not dead. Man, he's ugly right now. Do not ever reenter the atmosphere face-first. It's super bad for you.

Hoisting him over my shoulder is far harder than it should be. I've carried an airliner, and this man, who can't be more than three hundred pounds, feels heavier than that. Through pain and fatigue that leaves me shaking on the ground and wobbling in the air, I somehow manage to get us airborne.

Red Steel doesn't have a healing factor, not really. It's a well-known strategic weakness of his that if he gets injured he'll heal perfectly, but only as quickly as a regular metabolism can work. After the battle against Mistress Malice in 1961, he was out of action for three years while he regrew his legs. With him in the hospital for the next few weeks, I can probably operate freely in orbit. And if Garrison finds someone else to send up against me, I'll knock them down too. Bring it, dickhole. I can beat you.

But, you know, maybe give me a few days to rest up. It's only fair.

A few dozen miles out to sea I spot the running lights of a fishing trawler. Definitely the Aleutians in that case. They shout with alarm as I come down on the main deck and drop Steel on top of the fish-gutting table.

"Do you guys speak English?" I ask them. Oh, sure, they're *probably* Anglophone Canadians or Americans, but I've learned not to make assumptions when I'm in the middle of an ocean.

"What's going on?" shouts a man who I take to be the captain.

"I'm Dreadnought," I say. "This man needs medical attention, and I need a look at your charts. Get the Coast Guard on the radio for a medevac, and then show me to your maps."

And they hop to it. It's amazing how much the sight of the supersuit gets people to cooperate. Even after months of working with the public, it's still a little weird to me that I can just tell people what to do, and nine times in ten they won't even question me. Being Dreadnought is more than wearing the cape, more than having my powers. I've got a heritage now. There's something about the blue and the white that makes people see me as something more than an oddly strong girl who is barely old enough to drive. At first it was cool, but now it's almost kind of scary. Every time I talk to a member of the public in uniform, the size of my responsibilities comes home to me.

I limp up to the bridge with the captain. He lets me look at his maps, points out where we are, and I do a rough calculation in my head. Plotting great circle paths is not exactly an intuitive operation, but spend enough time in the air and you can at least start to rough them out. The trick, of course, will be holding to the course without a GPS to guide me—my nav computer used the same antenna as my satellite phone.

"Okay, this will work," I say to myself. The captain has been hovering around while I study his maps. I give him my best interview smile. "Do you have any aspirin? I am in an incredible amount of pain."

CHAPTER TWENTY-FOUR

I'm a few miles out from New Port when the cell phone antenna—a different system than my satellite antenna—sniffs a signal and tells my suit to rumble with a blizzard of incoming texts. Five from Doc, three from Cecilia, three from Detective Phạm, and one from Calamity.

The text from Calamity is the newest one, and when I pop it open, all it says is Take care, partner. They're gunning for us now.

Which is not the most comforting thing I've ever read. The next in line is from Cecilia: Danny, do not meet with the police. Come to my office immediately.

You ever feel your sphincter tighten up all on its own? Yeah.

One from Detective Phạm is up next: Dreadnought, we need to talk. Meet me on the roof.

At the edge of panic, I flick through my texts until I slam into one from Cecilia that says plainly what's going on: When you get this, come to my office immediately. The NPPD has a warrant for your arrest for the murder of Vincent Trauth, your parents' lawyer.

I hang in the air over Puget Sound, stunned into silence. There are things you never expect to deal with, that you never expect to happen to you. Even after getting superpowers and becoming a celebrity and all the other stuff, there's some foothold on normalcy you try to keep. Nobody ever expects to get framed for murder.

With a shaking finger, I flick through the rest of the texts. Here's one from Doc: Dreadnought, if you're not dead, get back to the safehouse. They're counterattacking.

I nose over and head downtown at a couple hundred miles an

hour, calling Doc Impossible as I go. Her phone goes directly to voicemail. The black waters of Puget Sound give way to the glass towers of downtown. I call Calamity next, and she picks up on the second ring.

"Glad to hear you're still with us, partner," says Calamity. Her voice is oddly muffled, and there's a lot of background noise. But through the noise, I can hear the grin in her voice. "You and the commie have a nice playdate? Things have gotten busy since you were gone."

"He's down. Have you heard anything from Doc? I can't get through to her."

"Not since I left to—" She cuts off abruptly, and one note of the background noise rises above the rest: the high, hard whine of her roadbike, the monster-engined crotch rocket she uses when she's in costume. After an audible grunt and a sharp reduction of engine noise, Calamity continues "—run an errand for her. But I'm a mite bit distracted at the moment, haven't been keeping up with the niceties."

"What's going on?" I've slowed way, way down as I enter the gleaming canyons of the city core.

"You know all those warrants the cops had out for my arrest?" asks Calamity. Far below me, on one of the main traffic arteries, I spot her riding her bike flat out up the wrong side of a six-lane boulevard. What appears to be every police car in the city streams after her, sirens wailing. "It seems they've decided to make an issue of them."

My guts turn to water. "I'm coming to get you," I say as I throw myself into a dive.

"No!" she says sharply, and I stop myself. "Danny, I was wrong. Dreadnought can't fight cops. People need to believe in you. I'll be fine, you hear?"

With a screeching of tires I can hear from thirty stories up, Calamity swings her bike into a hard, curving stop in the middle of an intersection. The cops have sprung an ambush on her and are penning her in on all sides, cruisers strewn across traffic, doors open, guns out.

They're pointing guns.

At *my* Calamity.

"I will *not* let them take you," I say. One of cops shouts at her to surrender over a bullhorn.

"That's real sweet, sailor," she says, her voice touched with affection. "But I can't let you do that. Run along now, and I'll catch up when I can." She reaches behind her to pour something across her back tire.

"Calamity—"

"Gotta go, partner. See you at the watering hole."

Calamity cranks her engine and cuts a burning doughnut on the asphalt. Billowing white clouds of smoke erupt from where her tire licks the road, far more than any normal friction would cause. A cotton-thick cloud smothers the intersection in a matter of moments. Cops begin firing into the cloud, cracking pistols and booming shotguns. The urge to dive in and protect her writhes and bites in my chest. A moment later her bike bursts free of the smoke, tipped up on her back wheel and streaming fingers of white behind her. She slams it through the just-too-narrow gap between two cruisers, then bolts across the street and down the concrete stairs of a subway tunnel.

My suit tells me the call has been dropped. The smoke drifts and clears from the intersection. At least three cops are laid out on the ground, writhing and clutching at brand new bullet holes.

Good.

I hope it hurts.

Before any of them look up and see me, I flit away into the night. We very carefully kept the location of our new safehouse secret from the cops. They knew there was a big explosion out there earlier in the year, but it was only after they finished the paperwork that Doc moved in and took over. At the time I thought Doc was being paranoid, but she was right. We can't trust them. Not really.

My suit isn't so damaged it can't still color shift, so I set it to a nighttime camo pattern. I haven't used it much since I stopped wearing throwaways, but right now, the last thing I need is to be spotted by a police helicopter. A few button presses later, I'm a black-on-black smudge headed quickly out of town.

Several miles from the safehouse, I pass a pair of trucks from the utility company parked on the shoulder of the road and a half-dozen men standing around a blown-out transformer. A big flat-bed truck with a crane on the front is rumbling up the road with a new transformer strapped to its back. If they figure out where the huge load spike came from, our secret lair might not be secret for very long. I purse my lips and press on. There's nothing we can do about that right now.

Nobody is waiting for me when I get back to the safehouse. I touch down and immediately regret it as every broken bone and torn muscle I'd forgotten about in the initial shock and excitement remind me of their complaints. A strangled scream leaks through my lips before I can fight it down. The entrance stairwell is dark except for the night lighting as I wobble-float myself down the stairs and into the underground hangar.

"Doc," I call out as I cross the vast space. The particle cannon she was mounting to the front of the tilt-engine has been pulled off the aircraft, gutted, thrown back together, and pointed up at where the sky would be when the bay doors are open. At her bank of screens and computers, all three of Doc's bodies are typing inhumanly fast on various keyboards.

"Are you okay?" one of them asks without looking up.

"Give me some morphix and a couple of days to rest up and I'll be good as new," I reply. Morphix is a pretty common hyper-tech painkiller. All the fun of opioids without the addiction risk. With today's fight pushing me over the big Five-Zero in the How Many Bones Has Danny Broken This Year tally, I have become *very* fond of the stuff. "What's going on?"

"About two minutes after I finished with the supporting fire, I got hit from all sides by some pretty badass hackers," says one of the Docs. "I'm holding them off for now, but it's only a matter of time until they've got my physical location, so we're abandoning the safehouse. There's an improvised landing area out near Mount Rainier we'll use for the time being."

Charlie and Kinetiq emerge from the server rack area with carts loaded full of computer equipment and are wheeling them over to a staging area near the tilt-engine. "Dreadnought, you wanna give us a hand with this stuff?" says Kinetiq.

"Can't," I say and have the presence of mind to avoid shaking my head. "Gotta shoot up with pain killers and then go get arrested for murder."

"Wait, *what?*" says Charlie.

"I'm being framed, and I'm almost certain Cecilia is going to insist I surrender so we can get it cleared up in court." The medical bay has yet to be packed up, so I float over to the supply cabinets and start gingerly digging around for a hypospray.

"So you're just going to give up?" asks Kinetiq. They sound almost offended.

"Of course not," I say as I push aside some cartons of broad-spectrum antibiotics in search of a bottle of don't-call-it-morphine. "But I'm not going to clear my name by running."

"You're not going to clear your name in front of a crooked court, either."

"We don't know they're crooked."

"Yes you do. First of all, *every* American court is crooked, and second of all, this one must be especially crooked if you're going up for murder just coincidentally at the same time you pick a fight with a supervillain."

The little blue bottle I've been looking for finally comes into view, and I snap it into a hypospray with a grunt of triumph. A little bit of cold on my neck as I pull the trigger, and the morphix is pushed through my skin as an aerosol spray. The trick now is to keep from injuring myself even worse until my healing factor can take over.

"I don't run from fights, Kinetiq," I say as the pain gives way to a cool, soothing release. "Not ever."

"It's not a fight, it's a scam," says Kinetiq with vehemence, and oh wow, they're *worried* for me. Even with everything that's going wrong, even with the nagging fear that Calamity will get killed or captured, I find myself smiling.

One of the Docs pushes away from her computer and walks over. "We can talk for a moment. What happened up there? Are you okay?"

I slip behind a privacy screen to swap my damaged supersuit for a replacement, and while I'm doing that I tell them briefly about what happened in orbit. Even through the morphix, the kind of contortions necessary to change out of a skin-tight body-glove are energetically unpleasant, but with Doc's help I eventually get there. Doc sets about with the bandages, splints, and so on, and the new suit gets a surface tension adjustment to fit over all the medicinal crust I tend to pick up after a big fight.

"Did you know that Red Steel has eye lasers?" I ask Doc.

Doc shakes her head. "No, he doesn't."

"He does now," I say. "They might have gotten Phase Two off the ground after all. Or maybe Phase One works on people who already have powers."

Doc frowns. "So what you're saying is we face a potentially unlimited number of superpowered mercenaries."

"Not unlimited," says Charlie. Doc looks at him hopefully, but he continues, "I mean, there's only seven billion people on the planet, and probably not even 1% of them would be willing to be mercenaries so…"

"That's less helpful than you might hope, Codex," says Kinetiq. They and Charlie start arguing about the merits of specificity in doomsday scenarios while one of the Docs walks me back upstairs.

"So Red Steel. Is he still alive?" she asks, her tone deliberately light.

"Yeah, but he might wish he wasn't. I dropped him with some fishermen and had them call for a medical evacuation chopper."

Ever so slightly, Doc's shoulders relax. "Good. Good. Hey, Danny, before you go, I just want to say I'm proud of you."

"I win fights, Doc. That's what I'm for."

She shakes her head, and I get the feeling that I've misunderstood her. "Look, if you go into court, people are going to say terrible things about you. I want you remember that the people who know you don't believe them for a second. Okay?"

I nod. "Okay."

Doc steps back so I can take off. "Go find Cecilia before she has an aneurysm."

With a wave I push off into the air and go find my lawyer. She's got a balcony in her office—she represents superheroes, so of course she's got a balcony for comings and goings—and the glass door is wide open when I arrive.

One of her assistants sees me and calls out as I nudge my way through the curtains. Cecilia cuts a phone conversation short and comes over to me. There's another round of what's-going-on to work through, and when everyone's up to speed, we drive to the police station. Cops are everywhere downtown. We pass through two checkpoints on our way into the government district, and they shine lights into the backseat. Some of them have blurry photos of Calamity clenched in their hands, and I fight to keep my face neutral and pleasant. We're not going to give them any reason to call me uncooperative.

When we arrive at police headquarters, there is already a crowd of reporters milling around waiting for something to happen. They descend upon us like a swarm of piranhas, and Cecilia does an amazing job of cutting a path for me. A constant strobe of camera flashes follows us up the steps. Cecilia's called ahead, and they're waiting for us. Detective Phạm and a few senior officers I know by face, but not by name. They usher us inside, and the moment we're out of view of the cameras, Detective Phạm turns to me with a studiously blank look on her face.

"Danielle Tozer," she says as she pulls handcuffs from her belt, "I am placing you under arrest for the murder of Vincent Trauth. You have the right to remain silent. Anything you say can and will be used against you in a court of law…"

CHAPTER TWENTY-FIVE

Smile for the mugshot! We combed my hair so that the shaved strip with its row of bloody stitches is obvious to the casual viewer. That, plus the snarling line of laser burns on my face, makes it pretty clear I've been in a fight. Cecilia says it never hurts to remind people I put my life on the line for them. It's not enough to keep me out of prison; we've got to keep my reputation intact as well or I could lose my contract. We haven't even spoken about what this might do to my still-pending federal license. I'm beginning to think it will be years before I'm allowed to fight for Northern Union.

After I get fingerprinted, some officers lead me to an interview room. One of them handcuffs me to the table, and I look up at him with what I hope is withering skepticism. "Really?"

He blushes. "It's policy."

"Uh-huh."

The cop scuttles out of the room, and then it's just me with four gray walls and the linoleum. Cecilia was with me when I got arrested, but they split us up for the booking part, and now we've got to wait for them to decide to let my lawyer talk to me. All that noise you hear about having a right to an attorney? It doesn't mean having an attorney at whatever time is most convenient for you.

So I sit, and I stew, and I try to hold still so I don't aggravate my injuries. They're healing well. Already my hairline fractures have begun to fuse. In a few hours I get more healing done than most people do in a few days. My healing factor isn't much compared with some capes, like Deathwish or Infinity, but it's plucky, and it's mine, and it gets the job done. The breaks all look clean, so in another day or two I'll be combat-ready again, and Red Steel will still be laid up in traction.

A vicious thought occurs to me. If Garrison really did give Red Steel eye lasers he didn't have before, he might have boosted his regeneration powers in the bargain. I might have to face him again before this is over.

I open up the phone program on my suit and tap out an email to Red Steel's public address.

> Hi!
>
> This is Danny. We kicked each other's asses earlier today. No hard feelings, I hope, but if I see you fighting for Garrison again, I will put you down for good. It's not worth your life. Walk away.
>
> Hugs and Kisses,
> Dreadnought ^_^

A few minutes later, my suit buzzes with an incoming message. It's from Red Steel and my heart flips over. Already? I was kind of hoping that after the ass-whooping I handed out, he'd still be asleep.

> I am a professional, and my contract has been fulfilled. Do not resume your attack on the satellites, and we will have no further quarrel. As an aside, if you threaten me again, I will kill you.
>
> -RS

So of course I have to write back.

> Okey dokey! When this is over can we get a selfie together?
>
> -D

> I do not believe you will survive the next seventy-two hours.
>
> -RS

> Okay, but what if I do?
>
> -D

Then, yes.

-RS

Cool beans. How are you feeling, by the way?

-D

Perhaps you should threaten me, and we shall see how I am feeling.

-RS

I know from that last scuffle on the beach that he can sense his surroundings even when blind with cataracts. Maybe it lets him send emails as well, or he's dictating them to someone. Or maybe he's already back in action and simply wishes to sit the rest of this out. I decide that I need more practice at the better part of valor and close my email program.

A few minutes later the door creaks open and an officer shows in Cecilia. She slams down a fat sheaf of folders on the table and sits heavily in the chair across from me.

"So?" I ask her. Little flickers of trepidation swirl around my ribs. I know I'm innocent, but being handcuffed in a police station for a few hours has a way of bringing home all sorts of unpleasant possibilities.

"Something's rotten," says Cecilia as she opens the first folder. Her voice is clipped. "They found his body a little under six hours ago. The coroner says he died early this morning."

The trepidation explodes into full on anxiety. "That…doesn't sound right. I mean, that sounds a little fast, doesn't it?" I say this, but of course I know the answer, I'm just scared to say it out loud. The government can't even decide whether or not to wipe its ass in six hours.

She nods. "No kidding. To go from body to warrant in less than a day is impossible. Someone has their thumb on the scale. I've got little birdies and they tell me pressure is coming from way up high."

I lean forward anxiously. "But we can beat this, right?"

"I think we need to look beyond the legal case. It's no coincidence this is happening now. This looks like a backup plan to me. Garrison wanted to recruit you, but since that's fallen through he wants you off the field and tied up in court. We need to focus on getting you out of custody as quickly as possible so you're free to counter whatever he's following this up with." Cecilia starts flipping through folders and arranging papers on the table. "In the longer term, their case doesn't look too solid. At the very least, we can account for your whereabouts with GPS data for most of the past week, including the time you were supposedly—" Cecilia's voice halts. Her fingers go white around her pen. After a moment, she continues, voice steady. "Supposedly murdering Vincent."

"Cecilia, are you okay?"

Her lips twist into a sour smile. "Superhero law is a very small community. He wasn't…we weren't friends. But he was one of us."

"Garrison is going down for what he did. I promise."

She meets my eyes. "Good."

Night court is not normally a big deal, but this isn't any old session of night court, this is the arraignment of Dreadnought, which means?

Reporters. So many goddamn reporters. The police walk me down the hall from the holding cells to the courtroom, and when we turn the last corner and run into the crowd gathered outside the courtroom door, there's a grunt of excitement, as if the press is a single organism sighting its prey.

Nearly solid camera strobes blind us, and a thousand pictures of me being escorted in handcuffs into the courtroom hit the Internet in a matter of minutes. Given how frequently I'm in the public eye, I've developed some love-hate feelings about the press over the past few months, but I shove all my frustration with them aside and make sure I'm all smiles and confidence as we run the gauntlet. A few of the reporters smile back, ask questions that I try to answer as the bailiff chivvies me along. We even manage to laugh, and I have a moment where I think this isn't going to be so bad. People know this is ridiculous. I'll be out on bail in an hour, maybe two.

This isn't some musty basement hearing room like the one where my emancipation hearing was held. (Was that only, what, four days ago?) This room is designed to communicate the full weight and majesty of the law. Tall, with plenty of seating in the audience and a raised jury box.

The prosecutor is a man I know by face, but not name. I've testified in cases he was working on before, but usually I was on his side as his star witness.

"ADA Hawser, you're moving up in the world," says Cecilia with crystals of ice hanging off her words. "I would have expected the DA himself to take this one."

"It's a team sport, Cecilia," says the prosecutor, a shade defensively. He seems like he can't tell if he should be excited or nervous. Well, he's trying to put a superhero away for murder. Maybe he's both.

The judge enters from his chamber. Judge Wickles is an older man, hair like slicked-back steel and wrinkles that stand up like oak bark.

"All rise," says the bailiff, and there's a general scraping and shifting as we all get to our feet. The morphix is starting to wear off, and I try not to visibly flinch when my weight settles onto my cracked femur.

"We're here today for the arraignment in the matter of The People of the State of Washington v. Danielle Tozer," says Judge Wickles. "Before we get started, I want to say right now that the defendant's contract with the City of New Port is completely immaterial to these proceedings as I understand them so far. This court will not tolerate any argument, from the defense or the prosecution, that hinges upon her activities under the name of Dreadnought. Should her work with the city become relevant to the facts of the case, we will determine the extent of that relevance during the evidence hearing. Is that understood?" He points a hard eyeball and an arched brow at both our tables. Cecilia and ADA

Hawser both mumble their understanding. "Good. Let's begin," says the Judge, and away we go.

No sooner has everyone found their seats than the judge asks me to rise again. With a twinge in my hip I get to my feet and lock my fear behind the same bulletproof mask I use to stare down supervillains.

"Danielle Tozer, you stand accused of murder in the second degree," says Judge Wickles. "The District Attorney's office alleges that you did seek out your parents' lawyer, Vincent Trauth, that you found him at his home at approximately five in the morning earlier today, that you had an argument with him, and that in the heat of the moment, you broke his neck and killed him. As a licensed superhero, you are automatically required to be tried as an adult, and so the penalty for this crime is ten to eighteen years in prison. Do you understand the charges laid against you as I have described them?"

All that brief, buoyed confidence I was feeling has melted, puddled in my boots. "I do, Your Honor."

"Very well. You may enter a plea of guilty, not guilty, or no contest. How do you plead?"

With a heroic demonstration of self-restraint, I avoid pointing out that if I were going to murder someone, it would be stupid to leave their body lying around to incriminate me when I could very easily dispose of it by burning it up in the atmosphere. Instead, I settle for "Not guilty, Your Honor."

"Very well. I see you have retained counsel, so we will move on to the matter of setting bail. You may sit," says Judge Wickles. "Does the prosecution have anything to enter into consideration for this decision?"

Hawser rises from his seat. "Your Honor, the prosecution moves that the defendant be held without bail until her trial. The unfortunate truth is that, other than by keeping the defendant in a special containment cell, the New Port Police cannot ensure the public's safety. They simply don't have the capability to confront her, to say nothing of the obvious flight risk of a suspect who can actually fly." With a glance at me that's one part nerves and two parts excitement, ADA Hawser sits back down. I guess he thinks this is going to be good for his career. Dick.

"I see." Judge Wickles shifts his gaze to Cecilia. "And you, counselor?"

Cecilia rises and smoothes her skirt. "Your Honor, the defense moves that the defendant be released immediately upon her own recognizance pending trial. Aside from her sterling record of heroism and self-sacrifice, she is flatly innocent and wasn't even in the city at the time the murder occurred."

Judge Wickles takes the bait and asks, "Where was she?"

"She was being held prisoner by a supervillain who had contrived a way to temporarily nullify her powers."

Hawser jackknifes out of his chair. "Objection! Your Honor, this is a conversation for the trial."

"She was rescued earlier today by Doctor Impossible and a freelancer from California called Kinetiq," says Cecilia, like Hawser hadn't even spoken. She gestures at the railroad track of staples running through my scalp. "As you can see, my client was wounded in the ensuing gunfight. How could she sustain a *bullet wound* if she'd had her powers?"

That's as far as she'll go in suggesting how corrupt we think this whole process is. It wouldn't do me much good to have my lawyer get held in contempt of court before the trial even begins.

Judge Wickles looks at me curiously. "Who was holding her captive?"

Cecilia takes a deep breath and accuses the eighth richest man in the world of kidnapping and attempted murder: "Richard Garrison."

Her words are almost immediately drowned in a swell of noise as dozens of reporters take that in and begin the slow, deliberate process of losing their goddamn minds with how juicy this story is going to be. The judge has to bang his gavel and shout for order for a solid minute or so. "Do you have evidence to support this claim?"

"We have GPS logs of her suit, and both Kinteq and Doctor Impossible are willing to testify."

"Objection, Your Honor!" ADA Hawser is practically shouting. "These are topics for a trial, not an arraignment."

Judge Wickles purses his lips and nods. "We won't be considering exculpatory claims at this time. I do, however, find the prosecution's argument that the defendant is dangerously uncontrollable to be implausible—at the very least, she has submitted to an arrest that, by your own admission Mr. Hawser, the police have no power to physically compel. I see no reason to deny her bail."

"She is a danger to the city and everyone in it," says Hawser, gesturing at me. "This is not the first time her temper has gotten out of control, and in fact, she has a history of threatening people she has disagreements with. If her temper has gotten the best of her in the past, it can in the future as well."

"You have evidence of this?" asks the judge.

Hawser nods at his assistant who stands and approaches a video deck that's set up at the side of the courtroom. He puts a thumb drive in and clicks open a file. With a sinking feeling, I know what it's going to be even before it starts playing. A projector throws a large image on a blank spot of wall, big enough the whole room can watch. The image is grainy, but clear enough to see.

The inside of a condo. The camera is somewhere up high, on top of a bookcase, maybe, hidden among the leaves of a potted plant. Graywytch is sitting down to breakfast. The door explodes inward on a cloud of splinters. There's no sound, but there doesn't need to be. I stalk in, every line in my body heaving with rage. White-faced, clenched fists. Shouting at her.

The image cuts to another camera. I'm tearing the stone off the wall, crumpling it in my hands. My face is twisted, sour with hate. And Graywytch is scared. Now that I'm watching it through the distance of a screen, it's obvious she's terrified. Her smug voice, her sneering smile, it was all bluster. Her body is pulled in tight and high, she's cleared her line of retreat. Her eyes are darting around.

One last shot of me kicking out her window and leaving. After I'm gone, Graywytch sits down heavily and puts her head in her hands.

The video finishes playing. I'm cold.

Cecilia sags in her chair. After a moment, she turns to me, trembling with barely suppressed fury, and forces her words through clenched teeth, "Don't you think I might have wanted to know about this?"

I bunch my fists in my lap. "This doesn't have anything to do with *anything*. She had that coming." She's got to believe me. Graywytch was acting, making it look worse than it is. And anyhow, it turns out I was right about her—she had already been working with the bad guys for months by the time this happened.

Cecilia thrusts a trembling finger back behind us, at the packed audience section. "Look. *Look* at them, Danny."

I turn.

The entire room is staring at me in undisguised horror. As I watch, two get up from the front row and start making their way to the back of the room, throwing harried looks over their shoulder. Everywhere my gaze lands, people flinch and shy away. A reporter from Channel 2 who I did my first interview with, who I've always liked, is wet-eyed with fear at being within arm's reach of me.

Every good thought I ever had about myself shrivels up and dies. I think I'm going to vomit.

They're not just upset with me, they're terrified. Of me. Of what they think I've done.

Of what you tried to do, whispers a little voice in my head. *Of what you wanted to do. If Calamity hadn't stopped you...*

The wind goes out of me with a whoosh. I find myself rising, and the Channel 2 reporter lets out a little squeak of terror.

"No, I...I didn't—I would never hurt any of you," I say, and become dimly aware that Cecilia is hauling on my cape, trying to force me back into my chair. The hearing dissolves into noise and chaos. A *lot* of people leave, whey-faced and throwing nervous looks at me.

When order is restored, the arraignment barrels on to its inevitable conclusion. The judge makes his decision, and it's not as bad as it could be, but it's still pretty bad. Bailiffs come to take me away.

Bail is set at ten million dollars.

CHAPTER TWENTY-SIX

The Metahuman Containment Cell is deep in the subbasement of the New Port Police Headquarters building. Down a long, mildew-and-moisture-chic hallway, there's a vault like you'd find in a large bank.

Cecilia fought tooth and nail to keep me out of this cell. She said it was a deathtrap, said the last person they put in there was murdered, said I had enemies who would come after me and put the lives of officers and civilians at risk. None of those arguments worked.

They've taken my suit and cape. I've got to wear jailbird orange until the trial. Or, I suppose, until someone raises ten million dollars for me. Which will happen approximately never. As well paid as I am, Doc and I don't have even close to that much money between us, and virtually all the money we do have has been sunk into real estate and hypertech supplies. Being an A-level superhero is expensive, so we've never had more than a few thousand dollars ready cash between us.

With my hands hanging together in front of me in clinking steel bracelets, I am escorted by a phalanx of MRU officers down the hall. They're going to throw me in another hole, and it takes everything I've got not to snap my cuffs and bolt. I've got to play along. If I freak out now I'll play right into Graywytch's hands. Nobody will ever trust me again if I don't cooperate.

Detective Phạm is waiting for me near the vault door. She looks haggard, drawn. The phalanx halts while one of their members begins the elaborate unlocking procedure to start opening the door.

"Danielle, I'm sorry it went this way," she says.

"Me too."

She pulls a silver cross on a delicate chain out of her pocket and holds it out for me. "Prisoners in solitary are allowed to have a religious token. Here."

I don't know how to react politely to that. It's almost like she's stuck her foot in the door and asked me if I've accepted Jesus Christ as my personal lord and savior. Detective Phạm doesn't seem any more comfortable about this either, the barest hint of blush forming at the edge of her cheeks.

"Um, thanks, Detective, but I'm an atheist."

"Really?" she asks. "Your friend Sarah was really insistent that you'd want it. She said she and Charlie worked hard on finding the right one for you."

That sure has hell catches my attention, and I freeze my face before I give anything away. How much does she know? And then coming directly on the heels of that, the blissful, glorious realization that Sarah escaped from the police. I hold out my cuffed hands and Phạm drops the necklace into my cupped palms. A little bit of work gets the cross settled around my neck, and I get the barest sense of a static charge as it comes to rest under my shirt. When I look at it in the lattice, I see the cross is squirming and alive with magic, and that the spell extends around my whole body, like a plastic bubble shell. It makes me feel a little bit better. At the very least, I'll be able to keep my powers if Graywytch and Garrison decide to teleport in and try and slit my throat.

The vault door lets out a huffing blurt of steam and begins to crank open. "That's enough, Detective," says one of the MRU goons.

Phạm nods and turns to leave. "Hang tight, Danny," she says as she leaves.

"Don't worry, I'm not going anywhere," I say, and that startles a laugh out of her.

The MRU is all looming black gasmasks and high-powered riot prods. A few have heavy shotguns that are probably loaded with some ungodly expensive discarding sabot depleted uranium slug rounds or something. One of them nudges me into the vault with the butt of his prod, and I think of all the times I showed them up, and start to wonder if rumors about cops tormenting inmates are true. I guess I'll find out.

The centerpiece of the cell is a firm pad like a medical bed attached to a big metal X-rack with magnetic-clamp shackles for the ankles and wrists. They push me onto the cross and lock my ankles down with heavy thuds. A metal ring clamps down across my neck. They twist the adjustment knobs to make the thing small enough for me to fit in properly. When they undo my handcuffs, everyone's ready to jump in and tase, gas, and shoot me. Once, I'd have found that funny, but now everything feels like lead sheets pushing down on me. My chest feels funny and light. I can breathe, but it doesn't feel like it's doing any good. The magnetic shackles thunk closed around my wrists, and I screw my eyes shut and try to keep it together.

"Are you gassing the room already?" I ask them between deep breaths.

Two of the cops look at each other. "You'll know it if we gas you," one of them says.

"Are these shackles really necessary? I've been cooperative." My lips are beginning to buzz faintly. My skin feels cold.

The MRU cops don't reply. One of them pulls a cord down from the ceiling and strips the sterile wrapping off an IV needle that he attaches to the thin tube. The needle bends against my skin, and the cop pulls it off and tosses it to the floor. "You're going to be fed intravenously, or not at all," she says. "We know you can take blood tests, so let this needle through your skin or starve."

Once they've got the feeding line hooked up, there's a really embarrassing moment involving a catheter that was inserted earlier by the jail medics upstairs. As it was explained to me, once a prisoner goes in the stocks, she doesn't come out again for any reason except a court date, a transfer to Yucca Mountain, or a judge's order.

The officers file out of the vault and the door grinds shut behind them. Then it's just me, alone, in the big, steel room. The florescent light flickers irregularly.

I can't breathe. Like, at all. My lungs pump and air moves, but I can't get any use out of it. I yank at the shackles in desperation, and they hum and groan as the magnetic field fights back. My still-fragile bones groan in complaint, and I can't go at it as hard as I'd like. In the shape I'm in, I don't think I can break this steel, not spread-eagled without any leverage.

The X begins to click and hum. It tilts with a clanking rattle until I'm lying on my back. Then the lights go out and are replaced by a dim red night-light that's probably just bright enough for the low-light level cameras to get a clean picture.

"I can't breathe," I tell them. "Please let me out."

I move on to less polite requests. It does nothing. They can't hear, or don't care. My heart is going like a rabbit. My head is swimming. Eventually, a little voice in the back of my head tells me to remember that first aid merit badge I got, the only one I earned before dropping out of Boy Scouts. I'm hyperventilating. With an effort of will I take a big, deep breath and hold it. Hold it. Let it go slowly.

That helps, so I do it again. Again. By the tenth breath, my heart has slowed and my lips aren't numb anymore.

But I'm still in a hole.

• • •

I turn around.

And they recoil.

I turn around…

…and they *recoil*.

They're scared of me. Over and over in my head, I relive the moment when I realize that they're all scared of me. The people I fight for. New Port is my home. These are my people, and I'd die for any one of them. Only now do I realize they might not let me. I might lose their trust forever.

I don't understand. It's not fair.

But it's completely fair. Idiot. You let them see too much. What did you think was going to happen? Of course they were always going to hate you. You can't do anything right.

The morphix has faded. Aside from slow, even breaths, I hold very still. As long as I don't move, the tears in the muscles and the cracks in my bones won't hurt. Not too much, anyway. With only dim light to see by, I focus entirely on the lattice and examine my own injuries in sick fascination. It's kind of amazing I could even stand upright long enough to get in this cell.

But of course, I deserve it. Dreadnought gave me his powers, said the world needed me, and I became this. I became something that scares people. How did that happen? It seemed like that's what I was supposed to do. Like it was right. Like it was necessary.

But it wasn't, was it?

• • •

Is there something in the IV? My head feels thick, drowsy. I ask if I'm being sedated, and I get no reply. Sleep comes with strange, twisting dreams that evaporate when I'm awake. Dreams where I'm alone, on the outside. Where people are scared of me and want me to leave. Where everything hurts, and everything is cold.

• • •

Someone is in the room with me. They stand behind me where I can't get a good look at them. In the lattice, they're only a shimmery smear that sets a glass pendant on my chest and runs a knife across my throat. Graywytch hisses with frustration and steps back into the portal she entered through and disappears.

• • •

With the intravenous drip in my arm, I don't get hungry. It's hard to tell when I'm awake. When the door hisses steam and begins to open I am startled out of a stupor. The X-rack cranks back to a vertical position as some MRU cops troop in. It's hard to tell if they're the same ones, since they're all wearing bulky tactical gear and gas masks.

Two of the cops begin unhooking the tubes and unlatching my shackles.

"You made bail. You'll need to reclaim your belongings before you leave," one of them says. For a dizzy moment I wonder if this is a dream. It's only been a couple hours. There's no way we could get ten million dollars that fast.

Once again flanked by a squad of police who don't seem to acknowledge that their guns would be little more than expensive comfort blankets if I was uncooperative, we head upstairs. The moment we get above ground I realize it's been more than just a few hours. Outside the window it looks like high noon. After another uncomfortable moment with the jail medic, they take back their jumpsuit and sign my stuff back out to me—it goes quickly since that really only means my suit and underwear.

With my suit back on, I check the clock and see it's only been about fourteen hours since I was arraigned. Then I see a calendar and realize, no, it's been *two days*, which explains why I can walk without limping. I'm probably not up to full strength yet, but I'm battle ready, and that's what really matters.

Another tedious police escort brings me to the front of the station, the publicly accessible area. As we're coming around a corner I hear raised voices.

"That's your plan?" It's Magma. He sounds at the edge of shouting. "You're taking children into combat now?"

"They're capes." That's Doc, with a hard defiance in her voice I haven't heard before. "They know the risks."

"They know the—this isn't going up against some two-bit

diamond heist crew, Doc! What happened to your impassioned opposition to minors in the field, huh?"

"You think I *like* stealing her childhood? She's who we have, that's all there is to it."

Magma lets go of a full-throated roar: "*Whose fault is that?*"

The cops and I come around the corner and see Magma and all three Docs squaring off in the waiting room. A bunch of uniforms stand around wide-eyed and mute, unsure about what they can do to stop the developing superhero screaming match. But Magma's reformed supervillain girlfriend, Aloe, is on the ball and puts a hand on his arm as soon as I step into view.

He bites down on a further explosion, but Doc is already rolling with her counter-attack: "I am done letting you use my rape against me, you oversized hunk of shit!"

Magma snaps his attention back to Doc, reels back like he's been physically slapped. "Doc...I didn't..."

"*Fuck* you, Magma," spits Doc, red and wet in the face. "It's not always about your—" One of her bodies sees me, and they all shut up and go stiff. That's about the time everyone else notices me walking in on the loud family fight as well. Magma, Doc, Aloe, and a few dozen cops all stare at me, and it's quickly apparent Doc and Magma are both charting new maps for previously unexplored realms of mortification.

"Do you guys wanna finish this up? I can go back to my cell," I say, hooking a thumb over my shoulder.

"Danny, are you okay?" asks the Doc who has kept herself together the best. The other two are hastily wiping their eyes and trying not to melt through the floor with embarrassment.

"No." Whoops, that wasn't what I meant to say. "I mean, it's been a bad week."

"I'm sorry to hear it," says Magma, turning away from Doc. "I want you to know that the community is behind you, 100%."

"Or at least the parts of it that matter," says Aloe with a smile. "We didn't have much trouble raising your bail money." And there's a twinkle in her eye that makes me think that most of the money they 'raised' was simply cash that the Federal prosecutors hadn't managed to recover when they convicted her. Not that I'm in any position to be picky right now.

By mutual, unspoken accord we've been slowly drifting together, our voices dropping to a quieter level. If the conversation is not private, at least it is something approaching discreet. Doc and Magma are stiff and uncomfortable standing so close to each other, but I'll take that over more shouting anytime. The uniforms in the lobby go back about their business with a mingled air of relief and disappointment. A few, though, are still watching me the way a deer might watch a wolf.

"Thanks," I say to Aloe. "But, uh, I think maybe you're looking at the wrong girl right now. I'm not really sure I should be a superhero anymore."

"What?" yelps Magma. I swear to God. He yelps. "Why? You're a natural. How about you just take some time off, let us figure this one out? You don't need to be hasty. About anything."

The feel of Graywytch's neck under my hands comes back to me, how soft it was, how I could make out her sliding muscles and tendons beneath the skin. (Did she try to kill me last night, or was that a dream? My guilty conscience trying to make it better?) Sharp on its heels, the image of the courtroom, and how scared they were of me. "I'm not sure I'm doing it for the right reasons anymore. Kinetiq is who you should talk to. Or hell, call in Northern Union."

"Danny, if you want to retire I will respect that," says Doc softly. "But we should get out of this fight before you make those kinds of decisions. I tried calling the Union, but Graywytch got to them and they're refusing to budge without more evidence. It'll be too late before they move on this. And if you back down now, blackcapes will be gunning for you for the rest of your life."

"There are ways to hide her, Doc," says Magma. "And she's right, even if the Union won't budge, there are other capes."

"Who are you kidding?" says Doc. "Short-notice ad hocs are almost impossible these days, and you know it. Especially with Graywytch poisoning the well."

"We failed Danielle before," Magma says to Doc, and he even manages not to snarl. "Don't let that happen again."

"Danielle is right here, and she can make her own decisions," I say. "My record is fourteen and one. If a blackcape is stupid enough come after me, I'll put as many of them in hospital beds as I need to make my point. But I don't think—maybe looking for trouble isn't something I should do anymore."

Doc and Magma both look unhappy. Aloe seems quietly impressed. Then, a moment later, she seems like she's uncomfortable. It starts slowly at first, a confused crinkle in her brow, and then widening eyes and labored breathing. She's suffocating.

"Honey, wh—what's..." Then Magma is feeling it too. His hand goes to his collar, tears off the top button, and the huge man begins to sway.

Doc and I trade looks. We're both reaching the same conclusions, and we're both horrified. One of her bodies begins twitching, seems to spasm and reboot.

"What?" grunts Aloe as she collapses.

Magma is on hands and knees barfing. The vomit splatters the linoleum, bubbles and melts it, the sudden fog smelling of sulfur. Cops shout out in alarm, and Doc goes into crowd control, pushing as many baseline humans back, *back* as she can.

Before it can get any worse, I undo the neck fastenings of my suit and pull out the cross that Charlie made. The moment I force Aloe's fingers closed around it, she sits back on her haunches and takes a heaving, convulsive breath.

"The hell is going on?" she says between heaves of fresh air.

Prickles of ice are running up and down my spine. This is why Garrison wanted me out of the picture for a few days. He's already activated what remains of his satellite network and started the takeover. When I try to look into the lattice, it's gone again. I hope Charlie can make more of those counter-spell amulets, or we're all extra screwed.

As quick as I can, I explain to Aloe what the cross is and why it works. She passes it to Magma, and he stops vomiting long to draw breath and uncross his eyes. When he's steadied himself, he passes it back to her, and arm in arm they begin shuffling out of the police station. They'll have to share until I put a stop to this. And it's going to have to be me. Me and Doc and the rest of our little baby Legion. People who rely on their powers to survive are going to start dying now. Suddenly there is no more time for arguments.

The endgame is calling: ready or not, here it comes.

CHAPTER TWENTY-SEVEN

Engines screaming, the jet pushes off in a cloud of dust and heaves itself into the sky. Inside, Codex is handing out more antisuppression field amulets. It looks like he got a deal on cheapo trinkets at a discount store, because they're all pewter crescent moons or unicorns or stars. There's some long explanation about the Laws of Similarity and Contagion that I don't really follow, the important part being that they are duplicates of the sympathetic charm he made for me to wear when I was in jail. With these charms on, Sovereign can't shut our superpowers down. Doc stopped glitching out when she put one on, and now there are three or four of them glued to the computers that run the tilt-engine. The best part is Charlie figured out a way to reverse the protective effect with a simple act of symbolism—when worn under our clothes, they protect us from the power suppression field, but when the chain the charms are hung on is used to tie someone up, they can nullify powers just like Garrison, even if they would otherwise be immune to it. We all take three or four and stash them away.

"Legion One to ground, we have taken off," says one of the Docs from the pilot's seat. She, like her duplicates, is decked out for battle. "Our altitude will be nape-of-the-earth until we are over the Pacific, how copy?"

"Negative, pilot! That call sign has been deactivated pending review," snaps an audibly shaken ground controller. "Return to ground immediately! I don't know who you are, but you need to file a flight plan like everyone else."

"Sure thing, buddy," grumbles Doc. Her hand flies over the

console, creates with a few tapping motions a crisp manga-styled drawing of herself giving the viewer the finger before attaching it to an email and sending it to the New Port International air traffic controllers. Then the Doc sitting in the copilot's seat switches the radio off. No way we're wasting any time on paperwork. No way. People are dying.

• • •

Other than a brief snap of relief and a tight hug, Sarah and I didn't have much time to check in with each other before Calamity took charge and ordered everyone into the jet for an immediate takeoff. Doc had barely finished debugging the more advanced hypertech components inside before we were pushing out of the hangar and into the sky. Garrison's moving fast, so we need to move faster. Even now, Calamity's head-down with a tablet, trying to work out a plan of attack alongside the third Doc with a few muttered remarks, some poking at the screen.

The tilt-engine jumps and bumps with the micromaneuvers necessary to keep us close to the ground and out of the way of civilian air traffic. The guns strapped to the ceiling in crash webbing rock back and forth with the motion, sort of a dull, clicking wind chime. The cabin feels like part military gunship, part business jet. Somewhere in the back, in the open-plan cargo section behind the seating area, Kinetiq is doing something with a can of spray-paint. Charging off to save the world never quite looks the way you expect it to.

Curled up in a leather seat, watching the world snap by at four hundred miles an hour just a few dozen feet below us, I struggle to get back into the mindset of Dreadnought. All I can think about is that courtroom. The shock on their faces. How terrified they were of me. And how much I had enjoyed doing the thing that scared them so much.

I'm a horrible person. The world shouldn't have to rely on someone like me. They deserve better.

SOVEREIGN

"Look, I'm not really comfortable getting that close to MANPAD Island again," says Doc, pointing at something on the tablet she's sharing with Calamity.

Calamity rubs her nose with frustration. "Well if the EMP doesn't work, we're going to need to insert somehow, so..."

They quietly go round and round, proposing and rejecting a half-dozen different plans. That's what does it, that's what fixes me. During the handful of seconds we had together before we piled into the tilt-engine, Sarah told me that her mother was walking across the house when the power suppression field slammed down; she's currently stuck halfway through a wall, still alive, but in agony. Even as worried about her mom as she is, Calamity is still doing her job. If she can suck it up and keep going, then so can I. People are dying. This isn't the time to mope.

I am Dreadnought. I am undefeatable. They came after me because I'm the one who scares them. Because they knew I was the most dangerous. Well, they were right, and I'm going to prove it to them. A smile grows on my face. Tomorrow...tomorrow I might retire. Take my savings and buy a little cabin out somewhere, hide away from the world so I can't hurt anybody. But today?

Today I'm going to beat some motherfuckers 'til they cry.

We reach the coast, a strip of rocky beach flashing beneath us, there and gone. Pilot-Doc pulls back on the yoke and kicks on the afterburners. A thundering climb brings us up to altitude and speed before she pulls us into a sharp left turn to head south toward the waters off of California.

"Do you guys have a plan so far?" I ask.

"Circling in on one," says Calamity, not looking up.

Doc nods. "With the intel we have, I think this is as good as it's going to get."

"All right. Gather 'round partners, we gotta have a chat." Calamity sets the tablet down in the center of the floor, and we all lean in to look. Codex looks up from the grimoire he was studying, and Kinetiq climbs back up from the cargo section, refastening their ballistic armor as they go. Their vest has a thin, cardboard stencil taped to the front now, covered over in yellow spray paint.

"You will not be getting any of that paint on the leather," says Doc with narrow eyes. Kinetiq smiles and makes a big show of their clean hands.

"Knock it off, we've got business to discuss," says Calamity. "With Doc's help I bugged Cynosure last time I was down there." I have a flash of memory of her tossing handfuls of mechanical roaches as we ran from Garrison's goons. "Good news is, we've got a notion about where the ritual room is."

She taps an icon and brings up a grainy black-and-white image of a miniature indoor Stonehenge that looks like it was taken from inside a ventilation duct. In a separate window, aerial photographs of Cynosure have a red circle highlighting where the spell room is—deep in the heart of the big mansion suspended between the three towers, it seems.

"Bad news is they've stepped up security since our last visit." Calamity taps another icon and more windows pop open, showing heavily armed and armored figures patrolling walkways, guarding doors. "By our count they've got at least sixty goons in full gear."

"We've IDed them as heavy response teams from a private military contractor called Silver Mountain," says Doc. "*All* of Silver Mountain's heavy response teams, in fact. These guys are bad news. Lots of ex-Delta Force operators, former SAS, French GIGN, so on and yada yada. They do a lot of work in Mexico and parts south; really anywhere people are shooting but the media isn't covering. They're not going to do much against our heavyweights, but myself, Calamity, and Codex really need to take them seriously."

"So what do they have that could be a problem for Dreadnought and me?" asks Kinetiq.

"Tough to say," replies Calamity. "Princess Panzer has been pretty aggressive about setting up defenses. She's installing and reconfiguring new automated weapons systems by the hour. 'Course she's got the attention span of a goldfish, so most of them don't stick around for much *longer* than an hour, but that only means we don't know what to expect. It's hard to tell what her gear does, but we had best be wary.

"As for the rest of his metahuman staff," she continues, "Thunderbolt's still in the penalty box from last time we paid these fellas a visit—" Another grainy photo, this one of Thunderbolt on a bed in Cynosure's infirmary. Kinetiq grunts with satisfaction. "—or at least he was until about fourteen hours ago when they wheeled him out to parts unknown. Graywytch was pretty messed up last time we danced, but we haven't had eyes on her since we rustled her grimoire. Codex says she could do her part of the game from a long way away if she had to, but isn't in any shape to fight right now. And Red Steel should still be in the hospital."

"If he's not, he promised not to interfere as long as I didn't go after the satellites again," I say.

Calamity looks up, surprised. "You've been talking to him?"

I nod. "As far as killers-for-hire go, he seems pretty nice."

"The shit you get up to," says Calamity with a chuckle. "Anyhow, we know for sure we're going up against Panzer, and if Garrison hired Red Steel, he might have hired more free agents to bolster his Silver Mountain troops."

Codex speaks up. "Are we sure about that?"

"We haven't seen any," says Doc, "But Cynosure has some powerful counter-surveillance equipment, and my roachcams are programmed to self-destruct to avoid detection so we've only got three or four left. And we can't discount the possibility that they've brought in more metahuman mercenaries."

"Let them. It won't help," says Kinetiq. They touch a finger to the painted stencil on their armor's chest piece and find it dry enough to peel off. Big yellow block letters read EAT THE RICH.

"The worst part is they've got about thirty civilians on hand, who look to be Garrison's mundane employees," says Doc. "Cooks, mechanics, maids, that sort of thing. They're not tied up and wired with bombs or anything, but it does mean we can't just pull back and shell the whole island with plasma bursts if things get too hot. We're going to need to get in close and check our targets.

Indications are they'll go to ground in panic rooms, but watch your fire all the same."

"So we're fighting an unknown number supervillains, and we've got to pull our punches because they've got human shields, that about the size of it?" asks Kinetiq.

Doc nods. "That's why we get paid the big bucks."

"Speak for yourself," says Kinetiq. "I'm a stringer."

Codex speaks up. "And my allowance is crap."

"Hell, I do it for free," says Calamity.

Doc and I trade a look. "Man, you guys are getting screwed," I say. There are a few chuckles, a little bleeding of tension.

"All right, the plan is simple enough," says Calamity. "Step one, we hit them with an electromagnetic pulse. It probably won't work but it's worth a try. Step two, Dreadnought goes in first and draws as much fire as she can. Kinetiq, you're up high behind her, doing that mirage trick you showed me. Drop the hammer on Panzer's gun emplacements as they reveal themselves. Doc can provide long-range fire with this here particle cannon as needed. Wreck up their heavyweights as good as you can, brush off their tactical goons, and signal us when you've got control of the mansion. We'll drop in once it's clear; I'll pull security for Codex while he does his thing and kills the spells. Then we rig the ritual room with C4 and blow it all to hell. Doc'll be ransacking their hard drives at the same time, and we leave with enough evidence to put them all in Yucca Mountain for the rest of their lives." She looks at each one of us. "Anyone got a better notion, now's the time to say it."

"I notice that plan only really talks about Panzer," says Codex.

"Dreadnought and Kinetiq will improvise if she's got serious backup," says Doc. "Without more intel that's all we can do."

Codex doesn't look happy, but he nods his assent.

"Listen," says Calamity, "I know it's cheesy to go on about freedom and democracy and all that noise. God knows I'm an ornery, cynical cuss when it comes to that sort of talk. But that is what we stand to lose here today. Garrison said it straight out—he wants to end equality. He wants to kill democracy. His world is a world of blackcape dictatorships. If he gets a monopoly on superpowers, nobody will be able to stand up to him. Nobody. We don't win today, our grandkids won't even know what voting was." Her eyes get hard. "We win this fight, end of story. Dying's fine, but we ain't losing. Anyone got a problem with that?"

Nobody does.

CHAPTER TWENTY-EIGHT

Our first inkling that this fight isn't going to go as planned is when Princess Panzer shoots us out of the sky. The Doc in the pilot's seat shouts in alarm a half-second before her upper body gets mulched into gloopy, white android gore by an antiaircraft cannon. A hypersonic slug punches through the glass canopy, tears out the back of her seat, and blasts right through the cabin and out the back of the tilt engine. The exit hole in the rear of the cabin is about nine inches to the left of Calamity's head. The blast pressure of the round combines with an explosive decompression to suck every lungful of oxygen out of the jet as the whole thing wobbles and noses over toward the ocean. An instant cacophony of alarms and sirens is all but drowned under the roaring of the wind, but I can still hear the two surviving Docs shouting at me to get out of the jet and into the fight. Everyone else is stunned unconscious or headed that way. We're still twenty minutes out with the counter-radar running at full power—we weren't expecting to make contact yet.

Even now, I sometimes freeze up at the start of a fight, and this one has begun so abruptly I have to force myself to get out of my chair and start heading back to the sliding doors. From a long way away I note that Calamity is pale, slouched in her seat, blinking slowly as I step across her to the cargo area. She's bleeding freely from one ear. Codex is flexing his fingers like they're new to him, like they're the most important thing he can think of. We're all a little shell-shocked, and so for some reason I fixate on Kinetiq's spray paint bottle rolling across the floor as the jet's dive grows steeper. When I haul open the door and that icy wind hits me like a punch in the mouth, I snap out of it quick. The tilt-engine is trailing a thick line of black smoke and beginning to roll onto its back. I slam the door behind me.

Just as I'm about to grab the wing and set it right, a flare in the lattice warns me of another incoming round. With a burst of speed, I get out in front of the jet and guard my face with my arms. The sabot round clips off my shoulder like a chisel from God, a radiating burst of pain that makes me gasp in surprise. It continues past me and blows the wingtip clean off—better than another round in the cabin, at least.

"Get the jet back in the air!" I shout through my comm link as I power down hard to where the shots are coming from. The ocean is miles below, a glimmering steel floor waiting to greet us at terminal velocity.

"Flameouts in both engines! Avionics are gone!" says Doc. "Hydraulics are gone!"

Between shepherding the tilt-engine to a safe water landing and taking out Panzer, I've got to leave something important undone. Without time to think, I choose to take the fight to the enemy and leave the rest of my team on their own for now. At this altitude, Doc should have enough time to figure something out before they smash into the ocean. That's what I tell myself as I'm passing through the sound barrier, twisting up and out of the way of another round aimed right at my nose. It tears a clean hole through my cape and continues on into empty sky.

As I close the distance, Princess Panzer comes into view. She's standing on some kind of gleaming, silver platform that hangs in midair. Next to her is a long-barreled cannon chased with gold filigree and cranked way up on a gimbal to trace my flight path. Sensor bulbs glitter like gems as they fix and refix my position. It fires, and though the range is shorter now almost by half, I still have enough time to twist away before impact. Panzer really is just a little kid, I guess. She should be shooting at the jet so I'd have to let myself get hit, but I guess she's not that thoughtful in her tactics yet. Lucky me.

What she lacks in strategy, Princess Panzer tries to make up for with pure aggression. She throws out her arm in a dramatic gesture of command, and her cannon glows with an eerie inner light before refolding itself into a triple-barreled chain gun that immediately begins vomiting tracers at me. Panzer sprays the sky, puts up far too much lead for me to dodge away from all of them, and the ones that connect hit like stinging hammers. Already the tender spots from a week of bad fighting are waking up, registering complaints.

With a wrenching twist, I throw my course down toward the deck as hard as I can and put every ounce of focus into clearing Panzer's line of fire. A blizzard of yellow tracers follows me down. Arms pressed tight to my sides, I overshoot the platform before porpoise-twisting back up to come at her from below. She's just reconfiguring her platform to let the gimbal track down that low when I smash into it from underneath and upend the whole damn thing in a shower of broken silver and smashed components.

Up close like this, I can sense her personal force field generator going into overdrive as shrapnel spangs and bounces off her as she falls, arms windmilling with some desperate, useless reflex. That's why I have no hesitation whatsoever about kicking her in the head as hard as I can. Princess Panzer rockets away from me and down to the waves, cartwheeling into a series of tall white splashes across the surface of the ocean.

I should go down and finish it. Get to grips with Panzer and smash whatever hypertech gizmo is giving her all this artillery, or if it's something innate, try out Codex's magic handcuffs. That's the smart play. But when I look up, the tilt-engine is still nose-diving back to Earth, a noxious ribbon of smoke behind it.

Sarah is on that plane.

"Legion One, I'm coming to get you," I say into the radio and hope I'm making the right call. Taking a deep breath for focus, I reverse course and blast into the sky.

"The jet's toast, we've got to bail," says Doc.

"Nothin' doin'!" snaps Calamity, and my heart nearly pops with relief. "We ain't dead yet!"

"Give it about forty seconds and check again," says Doc. "In the meantime, stow the lip and put your goddamn parachute on."

"Uh, hello, can you hear me?" says Codex over the radio. "Kinetiq has a concussion. I don't think I can get them into a chute in time."

"Dreadnought, can you catch the jet?" says Calamity, cool as September rain.

"On my way!" Wind pulls hard at my hair and squeezes my shoulders as I leave the sound barrier far behind me.

"Doc, fix Kinetiq. Other Doc, get those avionics back."

"Calamity—" Doc's voice is strained. Calamity might be the shot caller, but Doc is the oldest and most experienced. If there's going to be a mutiny, now's the time.

"Dreadnought, how close are you?" Calamity asks.

"I'm almost there!"

"Doc, do it," says Calamity. And then, "Danny, you'd better catch us or I'm gonna look like an asshole."

Simple interception isn't the problem. I've got to catch them in such a way that their momentum doesn't smear them all against the walls.

"Backup power links are severed—rerouting," says Doc. "Damnit! There's some kind of mechanocite infection in the flight computers."

I snap hard over to match the tilt-engine's course and speed. It's all but vertical, nose-down, racing to the ocean at terminal velocity. My fingers brush the fuselage, find a handhold, and then slip away. The damn thing is covered in low-friction hard gel to help boost its speed during flight. It's almost impossible to get a firm grip.

"Avionics are back," says Doc. "Hey lookit that, we just passed five hundred feet and falling. *Any fuckin' time now, Danny!*"

"Dreadnought, sooner is better," says Calamity.

"I'm working on it," I mutter. Aw, screw it; Doc can chew me out later. I punch a hole in the bottom of the fuselage. A few more shrieking impacts and I'm wrist-deep and groping around for something solid to grab onto. We're low enough that I can see the waves below.

The weight of the tilt-engine settles on my shoulders, and I start pushing it into a gentle curve back to horizontal. We've still got a few hundred feet of altitude to burn and I don't want to hurt anyone inside with a hard-G turn. "Tell me if I'm going too fast."

"Faster, turn us faster," says Codex as the jet continues hurtling to Earth.

"How's Kinetiq doing?" asks Calamity.

"It's not fair that I have a hangover," says Kinetiq. "I didn't even get drunk first."

We pass horizontal and the weight of the jet begins to pull up away from me as the wings bite air and generate lift.

"Altitude is going back up," says Doc with considerable relief in her voice. "Dreadnought, bring us ten degrees to starboard and we'll be back on course."

"What's going on?" says Kinetiq.

"Panzer started things early," says Codex. "Calamity, what does this do to our plan?"

"Blows it to hell, mainly," she says. "Dreadnought, get us to Cynosure as fast as you can. We're going to have to force a landing and fight through the hard way."

"What does that do to our ROE?" asks Kinetiq. ROE stands for Rules of Engagement, another one of those little things that bleeds into cape culture from the military. Where a cape stands on what's become known as the Killing Question has a bunch of really big implications about where they stand on a lot of other political issues within the superhero community.

Calamity is silent on the radio for a long moment. "Listen up. We're not lookin' to kill nobody, but these are hard men, and they ain't gonna roll over only because we ask nicely. If it's them or us, we pick us. Don't hesitate. We clear?"

"We're clear," says Kinetiq, sounding more and more alert with every moment. Whatever Doc did to push aside their concussion seems to be working, but I wouldn't want to bet on them getting out of bed for at least a few days after this is all over. Hypertech medicine is cool, but it's not *that* cool. "Where's Panzer?"

"Radar shows a contact on our six, fast and closing," says Doc. "I'm trying to get the engines lit back up to give us a push." The engines whine and cough and flame back out. "Uh...let's try that again."

A huge bloom of thermal energy pulses through the lattice, and I throw my shoulders hard into the tilt-engine. We're only a yard or two out of the way when a scalding purple beam lances past us.

"She's gaining," says Doc.

"I can't fight her and carry you at the same time, guys," I say. "What do you want me to do?"

"Number one, do not drop us," says Calamity. "Kinetiq, can you fight?"

"Try and stop me."

"Sit the hell down," says Doc. "You're not good to go for at least another ten minutes."

"You want to fight Panzer, be my guest," says Kinetiq. "Otherwise, I'm going."

There's a lot of cursing and grumbling as I heave the aircraft hard over again, another powerful lance of energy zipping past and leaving floating green ghosts in my vision. Apparently Doc has no more objections after that, because a moment later the hatch opens, and Kinetiq tips out into the sky.

They give me a thumbs-up and then rocket back towards Panzer on twin pink funnels of light. A few moments later, distant flashes of light, green to blue to red to yellow and back again.

"Doc, get those engines back online," says Calamity. A few moments later, they come wheezing to life, and with the extra boost we make good time to Cynosure. The battle between Kinetiq and Panzer falls further and further behind us, until it's finally just an occasional flicker beyond the horizon.

A few miles out from the seastead, a dozen white smoke trails leap towards us from the roofs of all three towers. "Hoo boy, here it comes," says Doc. Small hatches on each side of the tilt-engine's fuselage pop open and eject a fizzing blizzard of flares and chaff to either side of me. I don't need to be told to lean hard over and yank us onto a different course. Anti-air missiles hiss past us to the left and right. Nearby airbursts slap me with blast pressure and scour the hull with shrapnel. The armored blister mounted on the chin of the tilt-engine pops open, and Doc's particle cannon swivels out.

"I choose me," she says a moment before it starts hurling cobalt fire at Cynosure. The top floor of the nearest tower is obliterated in a cascading series of explosions. A huge black and red cloud rises into the sky while plumes of shattered glass fall from the tower like pollen. Please tell me there were no civilian staff members on those floors.

"Hope they got the message," says Doc, "because the gun's overheated."

Men on top of the other two towers throw down their weapons and sprint for the roof access doors. "Yeah, I think they heard you," I say.

Doc cuts the engines as we soar between the towers of Cynosure. There's one of those strange moments of quiet that you get between bouts of violence during a battle as I bring us down onto the lawn surrounding the mansion suspended between the towers. The ocean breeze tugs gently at my cape and hair, the air salty, damp, and clean. The grass is a deep, healthy green, clipped to a tight, even height. As the side hatch hauls open and everyone jumps out of the stricken jet, I can't stop wondering what it would feel like to lie out here on the ground with Sarah.

Then the bad guys open up with the machine guns, and that idyllic moment evaporates. Muzzle flashes wink and spit from the upper windows of the mansion. Codex and Calamity hit the ground as bullets tear into the sod around us, spang and crack against the hull of the jet. The two surviving Docs bring weapons that look like oversized shotguns to their shoulders and fire. An instant smokescreen explodes between us and the house, muddy brown clouds that sit heavy in the air, strangely resistant to the stiff ocean breeze.

"The smoke won't slow the bullets for very long, come on!" one of her shouts as the other begins bounding forward to find cover behind a stone planter.

"Smoke don't stop bullets!" shouts Calamity as she hauls herself to her feet and draws a revolver.

"Mine does," says Doc before firing another smoke round. "Let's go!"

I take to the air as the ground team disappears into the cloud. I'm angling forward to go ruin the machine-gunners' day when a bolt of yellow lightning thunders out of the clear blue sky right in front of me. The flash clears, and Garrison floats in front of me. He's wearing the most blunt, obvious, I'm-here-to-rule-you-peasant supervillain getup I've ever seen: a black bodyglove with a white cape that's got the huge flared collar and is edged with gold—he's even wearing a circlet, an actual literal crown.

"Dreadnought. Why aren't you falling to your death?"

"Because you're not *actually* the smartest person in the world, Garrison," I reply.

"You may call me Sovereign."

"I'm gonna call you Dingus."

Here's the thing: supervillains have a greatly exaggerated reputation for monologuing when they should be fighting. In the real world, this doesn't happen too often. But it does happen. It happens just enough to keep the myth alive, and I've got a feeling that Dingus here is going to be one of those special capes who simply cannot escape the lure of tradition.

So even as he's wrinkling his nose at my disrespect (Can I not see that he's wearing a crown? Where's the genuflection, the subtle terror? Kids today, honestly!) I continue: "You stole Thunderbolt's powers."

Not a question. Not even an accusation. Bait.

Beneath us, Calamity's grapnel fires out of the smoke. It finds purchase just above the window where a machine gun is spitting fire, and she comes zipping out of the cloud. A moment later she's kicked her way into the window, and the gun falls silent. Doc is taking turns with herself to lay down covering fire for Codex as he takes advantage of the lull in the fighting to sprint up the grass. His leg wound from the other day still forces him into a hopping limp, but adrenaline is a powerful fuel. I see all this in the lattice without turning my head, and my chest unclenches fractionally.

Garrison shrugs extravagantly. "When he came into my employ, he should have read the fine print. In a way, it's your fault. If you'd simply agreed to be my spokeswoman, a lot of unpleasantness might have been spared. But no, you rushed the timetable, so now we're doing things the ugly way."

He's not really into it enough yet. His eyes are still darting around, still expecting a shift in bodyweight to clue him in to an attack. But he should be throwing punches by now, and he's not. I only need to wiggle the lure a little bit more: "I like the ugly way. The ugly way works for me. It's about to suck for you though, I'm not gonna lie."

Sovereign chomps down hard on it: "You're too late, you know. We've broadcast the press package already. People will be dancing in the streets for me now that I've gotten rid of all the supervillains. Order is preferable to chaos, even the peasants understand this—" And then Sovereign makes a truly adorable noise, a sort of grunt and a squeak at the same time, when my fist smashes into his solar plexus hard enough to crumple steel. As he rockets backward from my first hit, I stay with him, and my second fist cracks a nasty hook through his jaw, snapping his head over, spinning him 'round just in time to meet my first fist again as it comes the other way.

The first rule of combat is to get in the first shot.

The second rule is that cheap shots are the best shots.

I really like the second rule.

Rich boys can't fight. This isn't going to take long. There's no way he—

—except that I am now soaring end-over-end, the sky and the world tumbling about me, and there's an incredible pain in my throat, and all I've got to explain it is this ephemeral flashing image of a wicked punch snaking in through my guard. When I catch myself in the air, Garrison is right in my face, and the world shrinks down to a frantic defense against punches, kicks, head-butts, and more. My rhythm has gone right out of my mind, and now I'm running on equal parts improvisation and desperation. Powder kegs of pain explode against my forearms, my thighs, my outer ribs as I do everything I can to protect my vitals and claw back some initiative.

This doesn't make sense. After a scything kick that folds me around his foot and slingshots me most of the way through one of the towers before I come to an abrupt stop against a steel girder, I start to think that maybe this is going to be harder than I expected. I peel myself out of the Danny-sized crater and peer through the tunnel of shattered glass and torn drywall. Sovereign isn't following me in. He's floating out there, arms crossed, a punchably smug grin on his face.

Another segment of drywall I was using to haul myself to my feet cracks and crumbles under my grip as that rage I need so much finally arrives. I'm gonna feed you your *teeth*, old man. Maybe I haven't figure out how yet, but you're going to a hospital one way or the other.

"Kinetiq, how's it going?" I ask through the radio link.

The roar of wind is heavy on the other end. "Little busy right now."

"Bring the fight over to Cynosure."

"What?"

"Get over here."

"Not a—shit!" A high-pitched keening sound, and then several detonations. "Panzer's not surrendering; I can't get close without going full power."

"Don't bother with surrender. Bring her over here, and then put her down hard."

There's a long silence. Or maybe not that long. Time gets funny when people want to kill you. "Danny, she's twelve."

"If she's old enough to fight, she's old enough to lose." Sovereign shouts something down the tunnel at me, and part of me dimly logs it as boastful blackcape nonsense, but another part worries maybe he's about to come in here after me. "Garrison stole Thunderbolt's powers and he's kicking my ass; we need to psych him out."

Calamity cuts in over a background of gunfire and Doc Impossible's screaming profanity. "Gotta agree with Dreadnought here. You don't have to kill her, but this ain't the time for kid gloves."

"Shit. Fine. Shit," says Kinetiq.

I leave the tunnel with as much dignity as I can. How the hell is this guy punching so far above his weight?

"Oh, I forgot to mention," Sovereign says with a sneer I'm sure everyone loved in high school, "I've got three black belts."

Oh.

Well, poop.

CHAPTER TWENTY-NINE

All right, screw it. Round two, shithead, let's go.

You can have your kung fu and your Krav Maga or whatever else you got, I don't care. Utopia had an antireality cannon and look what happened to her. I blast in close and start laying out the hammer blows. Dollars to dog shit says he doesn't know how to deal with attacks that come from directly above or below. I bet his expensive senseis didn't have much to say about chicks who can fly.

This twists the fight into a swirling, looping thing, each of us diving, climbing, swooping for position. Sky, tower, and ocean are an almost interchangeable blur around us. The snap-flap-cracking of capes in the wind. The grunt and wheeze of bodies pushed far, far beyond human limits. Crashing glass, crumpling concrete. The slap of fists to meat that comes off like gunshots.

And hey, did I mention he's got lightning powers? Because he's got freaking lightning powers, and it's really pissing me off. My suit is a powerful insulator, which is the only reason I'm not dead yet, but even so, his lightning burns and stings and makes every punch land harder.

Sovereign pivots backwards as I loop above him and snaps a pair of neck-breaker kicks at me. With my arms up to take the blow, I get close and ram him ten floors straight down into the brickwork of the promenade. He catches my arm and tries to break it, so I ride with the torque and whip him through a concrete column. Searing electric bolts leap at me from the dust, and I'm tearing up brickwork from the ground to fire back.

We close in on each other for another blistering round of

271

attacks and counters. It's too many hits—I need to break contact—but he grabs my ankle as I'm taking off and whips me into the ground. Dust and shattered brick explodes beneath my cheek, a boot like doomsday stomps on my spine. I bend backwards to lock my ankles behind his knee, yank on the lattice to spin him into the ground, and pivot back to my feet. As I'm gripping his leg for the ol' stomp-and-twist that's supposed to shatter his pelvis and end the fight, he blasts me with a white bolt that sends me flying backwards in buzzing pain.

And it just keeps going like that. This isn't outer space—there's not unlimited room to run and endless options for maneuvering. We get stuck in and we stay stuck in, an endless back-and-forth that's grinding us both down to a nub.

Time dissolves. No space for thought, no room for plans, only instinct and rage. I love it. I am alive down to my toenails, and I can't stop smiling.

Detonating an uppercut into his chin and taking a diamond-hard knee to my ribs in exchange. An explosion of dry splinters as I tumble end for end through an unused sauna. Cascades of shattered glass as I run him face-first across a tower's windows, machine-gunning punches into his kidney as we go. Scalding bolts heating the air as they tear past me, blowing a marble fountain's statue to gravel—

—tumbling through a wall together, jewels of shattered glass spinning from our bodies, and for a still moment noticing that beneath us Calamity is taking apart a tactical team with her bare hands. Doc has dropped her guns, is firing energy blasts from her palms—

—and then through the mansion and tumbling across the sod, great ribbons of grassy turf thrown into the sky as Sovereign and I savage each other again and again.

Kinetiq and Panzer streak past us, a flying lightshow of lasers and muzzle flash. Kinetiq gives Sovereign a burst of crimson energy right to his face as they pass, but Panzer's got the same idea, and I catch a rocket with my gut.

"Kinetiq, that psych-out would come in handy any time," I call over the radio.

"Working on it!" they reply, voice labored, breathing heavy. "The brat got a second wind!"

Great strategy, Danny. Really, you should go pro.

"If one of you'd finish your side of the dance and come give us some air support, I wouldn't tell you not to," says Calamity. The sound of gunfire is evermore hectic over her comms. "Codex, how we doin', partner?"

Gunfire is a bit muffled, but still an obvious baseline under his reply. "It's one of those good news, bad news things."

"Bad news," says Calamity.

"Graywytch set up some more magical booby traps. I need to untangle them."

"And the good news?"

"They're not very *good* booby traps. I think I can do this without getting my head blown off."

"Wait, that doesn't make sense," says Doc. "Are you sure?"

"Pretty sure," says Codex.

"Gift horses, Doctor," grumbles Calamity. "Keep going, Codex. Tell us when—SHIT! DOC, THE LEFT! WATCH THE LEFT!"

Meanwhile, Sovereign and I are trapped in a tight, spiraling dive of punches, kicks, locks, and counter-locks. He's better at the lock stuff than I am. A lot better. But arm and leg locks usually assume that the target isn't in midair, and so far I'm able to keep finding ways to escape. Being as flexible as an entire gymnastics team helps a lot too.

Kinetiq and Panzer are throwing more fireworks at each other than the Fourth of July. Everywhere they go, windows shatter and pavement explodes. Force fields sparkle against fusillades of tracer fire. Gleaming ablative armor appears an instant before concentrated heat beams evaporate it in a shower of yellow droplets.

Every so often our duels cross paths, and I manage to take a swipe at Panzer or Kinetiq lands a sucker shot into the back of

Sovereign's head. And the reverse happens about as often. It's hard to track Calamity and Doctor Impossible's fight over the radio, but we seem to be holding our own.

The problem is that *holding our own* is only a polite way of saying *not quite losing yet.*

We're grinding each other down to a bloody pulp, and the first side to break will get chopped to pieces in a matter of seconds. It's a fair fight, the worst sort of fight, and the first side to figure out how to cheat absolutely—

Sovereign's boot catches me in the gut and sends me through two walls. While I peel myself out of a bent and twisted commercial-sized refrigerator in the kitchen I smashed through, he darts through a door and disappears. I lift my leg high to step through the hole I plowed on the way in, scanning the lattice, alert for an ambush.

What the hell are you—oh shit. There he is again, with two men who look like they were cooks hiding in a walk-in cooler. Holding them by the back of their jackets, Sovereign floats out over the promenade and beckons me to the fight with his head.

It's too risky to throw more bricks at him; I've got to close and engage. But when I drive a hard punch at his face, suddenly an innocent cook is in the way to block me. I manage to pull the attack just in time to catch the back of Sovereign's boot with the side of my head. The cooks are screaming, pleading, and he doesn't care. Another kick erupts from between the two of them, and I barely turn the blow with my shoulder—the wounded one where Panzer shot me. Crimson spikes of agony stab up and down my arm and I cry out.

Back up, back up *fast* to get distance and reconsider.

"So that's it? Stalemate?" I call to him across the chasm between the towers. "That's your big play?"

Princess Panzer tears between us on jets of pink flame, Kinetiq right behind her, cobalt beams lashing from their eyes.

"I don't see a stalemate, little girl," Sovereign says, an instant before he charges. My heart clenches—baseline humans can't take acceleration like that! That moment of horror is all Sovereign needs. He lets one of his hostages go—

—the poor man keeps flying—

—and Sovereign clenches a fist that explodes a galaxy behind my eyes. Cool ocean air on my cheeks, and my eyes snap open while I'm still falling. My eyes ransack the sky until I find the hostage, still falling. Not for much longer. I'm dimly aware that Sovereign is closing with me, but I set that aside and focus on the lattice.

The man's momentum is terminal; he'll never survive impact with the bricks of the promenade below. I can use that. In the lattice, I wrap the strings of momentum around me, focus and redirect them.

Sovereign has seized my arm, is pulling me.

A few feet above the ground, the screaming hostage seems to bounce in the air. His momentum killed, I release my hold on him and let him tumble safely to the promenade.

The other hostage is falling now. There's no time to be confused or sense any other danger. This is all happening on a timescale of eyeblinks. It's instinct and reaction speed, not planning, not thinking.

I'm grabbing the second hostage, arresting his fall—

The bones in my arm twist and shatter into red, grinding ruins. I am stunned breathless by the pain. Sovereign has locked my arm against itself and given me a new joint. His elbow catches me in the throat and fastballs me through a window and two walls of sheetrock. Clouds of white dust kick up around me as I come to rest, crumbly bits of wall skittering away. I push myself to my feet and then he's in here with me.

It is a very different fight now. This isn't fighting with one hand behind my back. This is worse. This is fighting with one arm as a weak spot, a place that beckons for more punishment, which I can't even hold and protect without jiggling up little explosions of pain to distract me.

Block and twist, counter and spin, I do everything I can to

keep distance between us, to keep more blows from falling. It's not working. I check the lattice—the walls behind me are thin. When I hunch my shoulders and fly backwards into them, I'm able to punch out the other side of the building without hitting any structural girders. Once in open sky, I flip around and push for speed.

"I'm in trouble," I say over the radio. "Kinetiq, can you help me?"

"Tied up," is all they say, voice clipped and tight.

"Get out to her," says Calamity.

"Not hap—" Their transmission cuts off in a grunt of pain. "Panzer's pushing me too hard. I don't feel so good; hard to focus. Sorry, D."

Shit. I glance behind me, and Sovereign is right there, coming hard after me as I bend my course around the outside of the towers and come back through the center space of Cynosure. Crackling forks of lightning chase me, strike glancing blows that make my legs and back sting. Think. I need to think.

What can I do that he can't? He's not as strong or fast, but that's not holding him back. He's as tough, but I'm wounded. We both fly, and his ranged attack is better than mine. If I press him too hard, he can just take more hostages. (Press him too hard? With this arm? Who am I kidding?)

Well, let's see how good his acrobatics are. With a hard bite on the lattice, I slam myself into reverse, catch him in the nose with the heel of my boot as I flick past. It's a good hit. A solid hit. It tells me he still doesn't grasp the full range of superhuman flight.

And it's not even close to enough. He snorts blood and comes at me again, only now he's wary, he's watching, and that trick won't work twice.

A bolt of lightning tags me right in the chest and my back arches tight with pain. It shakes me enough that Sovereign slams into me, catches me around the waist. We angle down to the grassy field in the center of Cynosure, far beneath the suspended mansion. A pillar of grass and sod geysers up from where we land, my arm screaming, fear wringing my heart tight. The blows come like hammers, on my face, my arm, my neck, my shoulders.

A plan arrives.

He's about to push my nose in flat and I jerk my head to the side—he goes wrist-deep in the ground, and I whip my head back to pin him there while my legs slither out from under him, wrap and lock tight around his middle. With my good arm I gouge my thumb two knuckles deep into his eye socket and use the distraction of the pain to get us airborne again.

If this doesn't work, I'll probably die here in the next few minutes. Either way, this son of a bitch is going to know he was in a fight.

My shoulders smash through the broad stairs leading to the field like a ship's prow, tossing up a spray of stone and dust. My thumb squelches in his eye, and I've hooked it around to get a grip on his skull from the inside.

His punches are frantic, wild. My nose crunches, my molars are loose. My broken arm is one glowing brick of pain. It doesn't matter. Because I've remembered something important.

There was a group photo taken after the Northern Union superteam stopped that asteroid from hitting us three years ago. I remember I bought a glossy copy because I was hoping to get it signed someday. In that photo, Thunderbolt was wearing a pressure suit, unlike the old Dreadnought. That's because Dreadnought could hold his breath for hours on end. So can I. Thunderbolt couldn't. And Sovereign is using Thunderbolt's powers.

We hit the water at nearly the speed of sound. Half-delirious with pain, struggling to keep my hold on the lattice, I didn't fly well. It feels like I hit every wall and piece of furniture I could on the way off the island. But it doesn't matter, because my legs are still locked around his waist, and my hand is still locked into his head, and we are headed as far down as I can drag us.

The water is cold. It's heavy. The salt stings my wounds. In a matter of moments we're in darkness, and the pressure is a vice grip. The water slows his punches—they hurt, but not so much.

My thumb comes out of his eye with a blooming black cloud, and I make a steel band of my arm around the back of his head, lock him in tight to my chest and throat.

Down, down, deeper we go. The anchor cables for Cynosure slide past, a dark bamboo forest reaching down to infinity. High above us, daylight winks dimly through the rippling scales of the surface.

I can tell the moment he figures out what's going to happen. There is a horrified stillness, and then he begins to thrash. Electricity floods out from him, as much as he can make, but in his panic he can't focus it to make it behave unnaturally like he normally can. It flows over my suit's insulation and heads to the sea floor, harmlessly. My broken arm is as far out of the way as I can get it, and I clench tight to him with every other muscle I have. You're down here with me, Sovereign. You're down here until I decide to let you go. You don't get to hurt anybody else. It's over.

Flickering bolts of power squirm up and down his arms as he tries to shock me loose. The first bubbles escape his mouth, and just for a second I loosen my thighs so that I can slam them back down and turn the trickle into a geyser. A lungful of air bloops out of his mouth and races to daylight. He's clawing at me now, fingers digging for purchase against my screwed-shut eyes. I turn my head to deny him leverage and hold on.

I watch his heart slam in his chest. I watch his legs thrash and twist. Not much longer now. He's still hurting me. His attacks still land. But I'm tougher than he imagined I was, and more deliberately cruel. They never see it coming. They never expect that someone who looks like me could have so much calm, considered malice at her disposal. By the time they figure it out, it tends to be too late.

The last handfuls of breath escape his chest. He spasms, seawater rushing into his lungs, plumping them out tight. He thrashes again, harder than ever, and then goes still. Cautiously, I loosen my legs. He stays limp in the water and begins to sink.

I am not undefeated.

I am undefeatable.

• • •

Up, up into the air, water streaming off my shoulders, pouring off my cape, Sovereign's ankle clenched in my good hand. His face is pale, his eyes half-lidded. It takes some effort to shake the water out of his lungs, and when I drop him onto the promenade he lands with a wet smack. First things first, I pull one of Codex's trinkets out of the low-profile cargo blister on my thigh and use it to tie his wrists. It's tricky with only one hand, but I've still got most of my teeth, and I manage. The magic makes the necklace chain as strong as titanium wire, and it should dampen all his powers—including his power-dampening field. Magic is weird. When I roll him onto his back he's still not breathing. A roll of nausea twists up my throat, and I move straight into CPR.

The chorus of "Staying Alive" by the Bee Gees happens to be the perfect rhythm for the chest-pumping part of CPR. With a cold, urgent fear driving me, I push his ribs in to the beat of the song I'm whispering under my breath. (I've heard that paramedics hate this song. Now I know why.) Please. Wake up. Doc was right. Please, wake up. I blow into his mouth. With my ear down at his lips to listen for breath and watch his chest, a little voice in my head screams, *the lattice, you idiot!*

Right. Duh. Most of the water is out of his chest, but his heart is spasming, and spasms don't pump blood. Uh, crap, what the hell am I supposed to do about that?

Before I've got time to come up with an answer, Princess Panzer comes screaming out of the sky. She lands in a flurry of vernier thrusters and unfolding weapons platforms that gleam in the sun. In a half-second I'm staring down a tank platoon's worth of firepower.

"GET AWAY FROM MY DADDY!" she shouts, rigid with terror. At least three railguns are pointed at my head, their capacitors crackling with stored charge.

"He's inhaled a lot of water. I'm trying to save him—"

"MURDERER!" Two of the laser pods floating behind her

paint me with targeting beams. In the shape I'm in, if all that fire-power hits me at once—well, at least it wouldn't hurt for too long.

As calmly as I can, I raise a placating hand. "The CPR isn't working. He needs a defibrillator. Is there one of those on the island? Do you know where to find it?"

Tears are rolling down her cheeks. Panzer looks from me to her father and begins to shake. "I don't—I don't know," her voice is tiny. "Please, Dreadnought, you can't let him die."

"Can you make one?" I ask.

She nods, more a spasmodic jerk than anything else. The rail-guns fold up and disappear into the nowhere they came out of.

"You need to have the right amps and volts or else—"

"The magic does all that," she says distractedly. Panzer's eyes are unfocused as a pair of silver paddles edged in gold appear from folds of light. With a quick yank I tear the front of Garrison's suit open and then sit out of the way as the paddles float down to rest on his chest. A thump of electric charge, and his body jumps. Another. Another, and he's taking a breath before vomiting. He groans as all of his ribs that I broke while trying to resuscitate him make themselves known. The defibrillator paddles evaporate along with the rest of the ordinance as Panzer throws herself at her father.

"Daddy!"

Garrison grunts back a cry of pain as she fastens her arms around him. With his arms tied behind his back, the best he can do is lean his head into her. "Lilly…"

"Fire in the hole," says Calamity over the radio link. A moment later, a muffled bang echoes against the sky.

Panzer looks up sharply. "What was that?"

"The fight's over. Calamity just blew up the ritual room," I say.

"You—you what?" shrieks Panzer. She bolts upright and begins summoning more guns.

"The fight's *over*, Panzer," I say in my best hardass voice. "Look around, kid. You lost."

And it's true. Cynosure has seen five different kinds of hell in the past—crap, two hours? How'd we lose two hours? Broken glass and shattered concrete are everywhere. Fire sprinklers have popped all over all three towers. Emergency lights swirl amber, and only now with the absence of fighting can the alarm sirens be heard.

Panzer takes a step forward, murder on her face.

"Princess," rasps Garrison. She stops dead, and looks down at him, her face stricken. "No. I can't lose you. Not after everything else."

Panzer collapses into sobbing. Garrison sits up as best he can, leans against the lip of a long, low planter box. She crawls to her father and curls up in his lap. Garrison whispers to her, says that it's going to be okay.

For a moment, I don't understand why I am stabbed with envy.

CHAPTER THIRTY

A clean salt breeze blows in through the shattered windows. Calamity leaps up on a chair and sticks two fingers between her lips to bless us with an ear-cracking whistle. Everyone is congregated in the triage ward next to the infirmary. Dozens of prisoners look up at the sound, and the (very) few muttered conversations in progress wither and die. Helmets are off, weapons thrown overboard. Those who gave us trouble got their hands tied, but most are cooperative. The mood in the room is defeated, low.

"Doc says she needs nurses," shouts Calamity. "Who here is a combat medic?"

A few of the prisoners raise their hands, including one whose wrists are zip-tied together. Most of the prisoners and walking wounded were escorted over by Calamity and a bemused Codex, who looked incredibly uncomfortable to be holding a submachine gun. A few of the more serious injuries were strapped to stretchers so I could airlift them directly into the surgical bay.

One of these was Kinetiq. We found them collapsed on the steps of the mansion, bleeding heavily from the gut where one of Panzer's bullets had gotten in under their armor. Letting Kinetiq's stretcher dangle from my good hand while one Doc rode me piggyback and the other clamped onto my legs, we got Kinetiq across the gap and into the surgical bay in one of the towers in a matter of moments.

Just before they went under the anesthesia, they turned to me and said, "I can't believe I got smoked by The Littlest Princess."

And then Doc was stripping off their armor without bothering to cut it, just tearing the fasteners apart with inhuman strength. Her other body tied my cape into a sling for my arm before it shooed me out of the surgical bay and told me to set up a triage point in the lounge outside.

That's how we came to organize an olly-olly-oxen-free for every Silver Mountain goon who hadn't been taken out in the fighting. Calamity got on the PA and told them what was up and that they had ten minutes, and then she was going to personally shoot every goon she could find who hadn't surrendered or fled. Further, she informed them that she'd run out of everything except plain old lead bullets. It turned out to be a powerful motivator.

A few made a break for the marina and escaped on a pair of speedboats, but we don't really care. The Coast Guard is on the way, and they're not likely to make it to land without getting arrested. Most of the ones who stayed behind did so because they had broken bones or worse, and Calamity bribed them with morphine. Once Kinetiq was stabilized, Doc started taking the more seriously wounded prisoners into surgery as well.

The mercenaries who volunteered to be nurses file past us. Calamity snicks open a utility blade and cuts the zip ties off of one, then deftly slips the tip of the blade a little ways up his nostril, just far enough to get his attention.

"I want to remind you that both the Doctors Impossible shoot lasers out of their hands and that the fine young lady in blue over yonder is literally Dreadnought. Of course you know what *I* can do. So are we going to have any more trouble out of you?"

He doesn't meet her eyes. "No, ma'am."

"Get goin', partner," says Calamity as she straightens up and snaps the blade closed. The nurse-prisoners file into surgery and begin washing their hands. Calamity hops down from the chair and walks over to me with a bounce in her step. Her prosthetic hangs limply from her shoulder.

"Can you believe it?" she says, "I got shot in the same goddamn arm."

But now that we've got a quiet moment after the initial rush of activity, I can see the strain in her eye. "I think things will hold here," I tell her. "Do you want to take a walk?"

She hesitates for a moment, so I put my hand on her good shoulder and gently maneuver her toward the door. Without further prompting she falls into step with me, ends up leaning on me by the time we're out in the hallway. Curtains torn to ribbons flutter in shattered windows, and the thin carpet crunches with broken glass under our boots. My arm is bound up in a sling, but Doc gave me a dose of the good stuff so the pain is sort of a non-issue.

"We did it," I say, wrapping my good arm around her shoulder. Dart in for a kiss on her cheek. "You did it."

Without preamble, Sarah drops the Calamity voice and says, "We killed thirteen men today, Danny."

My smile curdles. "Oh."

"I'm not naive. I know with how rough I play…" Sarah pulls away from me, leans up against a wall. "It's different when I can't pretend the ambulance will show up in time."

"We didn't have a choice. They forced this."

"I know that!" she says, not angry, but urgent. Helpless. "But, I close my eyes and I see the bodies, and—I didn't know it would feel this way."

I step in close, slowly, and her posture opens, lets me in. "You're a good person, Sarah," I whisper. "I trust you. I love you."

Forehead to forehead, we stand for a moment, my fingers tracing through the hair behind her ear. The excitement of battle has faded, leaving us low. I'm glad that she lets me comfort her. It means I don't have to think about myself.

Calamity pulls her bandanna mask down and kisses me, hard. My arm wraps around her neck and I return every ounce of it, low moans rising from the base of my throat. After hours, or seconds, she breaks away and searches my eyes.

"Did that help?" I ask.

"I don't know." She pulls the bandanna back up over her nose. "Let's go check on Codex."

We set off down the hall, to the room where we separated out the metahuman prisoners. I lace my fingers through Calamity's. Her blush climbs up over the edge of her bandanna, but so does her smile. She squeezes back.

We head into the lounge a little way down the hall. Garrison and Panzer are sitting together up against one wall, wrists tied down by Codex's magic necklaces, ankles bound with zip ties. Codex guards them. He's dragged one of the coffee tables over so he can face them while he fiddles with a bag of magical paraphernalia he's spread out in front of him. Everyone reacts to the stress crash at the end of a battle differently—I make out with Calamity, and Codex gets his nerd on. Off to one side, almost as an awkward afterthought, a stolen submachine gun sits as a silent threat to anyone who gets stupid ideas.

"What's the word, Codex?" asks Calamity as we enter.

He shakes his head. "My parents are going to kill me when we get home."

"Are you kidding?" I ask. "You saved the world."

"You don't know my parents too well." Codex looks up from a mirror with a high rim set flat on the table. There are a bunch of colored marbles on it, and he's pushing them around, seeing how they knock off each other. "The spells are stable, their powers are muted. They're not going anywhere."

"If the spell works by mimicking Garrison's powers, then shouldn't binding him make the other amulets not work?" I ask.

He shakes his head and returns his focus to his work. "No, that would violate recursive causality," he says, as if that should mean something.

"None of this will stick, you know," says Garrison. With his hands and legs bound and his suit all ripped up, nah, I'm not calling him by his supranym anymore.

"Yeah, whatever, Dingus."

"You stupid child, you still don't understand—everything you've done today, I can undo with the stroke of a pen." His smile is thin and cruel. "My attorneys will gut you and have your skull for an ash tray."

"Pay him no mind, Dreadnought," says Calamity with a warning in her tone. It hurts that she feels like she needs to keep a leash on me, but maybe I earned that.

Still, I can't resist twisting the knife. With a reassuring squeeze of Calamity's hand, I smile at Garrison. "And how are they going to do that when they're deciding if it's even worth keeping you out of prison? Whoever you had spying on me should have done a better job of reading my mail—my federal hero license finally came through."

It was a close call. The license arrived while I was in jail, and Cecilia had to make some big promises—desperate promises, really—to keep it from getting instantly suspended until my trial was complete.

Garrison's face goes blank. I think he knows what's coming, but it's so fun spelling it out: "You're about to get acquainted with my three favorite words in the world—*civil asset forfeiture*. When I was in the holding cell, Cecilia did an analysis of your public earning statements compared with the sort of costs that would be necessary to fund this operation, and it looks like your entire fortune is bound up in this scheme, isn't it? That makes everything you own an accessory to kidnapping, murder, and terrorism. So we're seizing it all. Every company you own, every account you hold, every last penny. I bet it'll be hard to pay for lawyers when your money is all tied up in court. When you said you could make me a rich woman, you weren't thinking you would do it this way, were you?"

"Nothing you can prove I've done is illegal," he says, but with the way his skin has gone the color of sour milk, I don't think anyone believes him. "Spectral evidence is inadmissible. You can't prove a thing."

"Once she's done sewing up your men, the best hacker in the world is going to go have her way with your hard drives. There's no security you can buy that will keep her out of a drive she has physical access to, and I will bet that she'll find things you were trying to keep secret. When you get out of prison, you're going to be a poor old man nobody remembers or cares about."

Garrison doesn't shout or freak out or threaten vengeance unto the third generation or whatever. He breaks out into a cold sweat and his eyes bug. Words jam up in his throat, trip over each other as he chokes on them.

"Why don't you just leave us alone!" shouts Panzer. She's at the edge of tears, and for a moment I feel bad about saying all that to her dad in front of her. "Because of you, the world's going to keep drowning in poor people and losers!"

Welp. Never mind.

"Codex, you good?" asks Calamity.

"I'm good," he says.

"If you're done antagonizing the prisoners…" she says, gently pulling me toward the door.

"Call if you need anything," I say over my shoulder, and he waves without looking up.

We're at the door when it happens. A deep thrum of power running right through my chest, shooting down to the soles of my boot and up to the top of my skull. The world seems to go pale and blue, and then I'm falling. My guts are a greasy knot pulled tight, painfully tight, spasms in my legs, my hands, flaring every injury to a fizzing scarlet beacon. Someone is moaning in agony, and as Calamity flips me over on my back I realize it's me.

On the heels of that, I realize it's Codex and Garrison too. A great wail of voices raised in misery drifts down the hallway from the triage point. The pain passes, and leaves in its wake a sense of profound disquiet. All my injuries seem worse, and I am so tired I can barely lift my head from the carpet.

Doc's voice crackles in my earpiece. "What the fuck? Two of my patients just coded."

A second later, her other body radios, "Everyone in the waiting room is down—team, talk to me!"

"I'm up," says Calamity. One hand is on my chest, possessive and protective, the other up at her earbud. "Dreadnought and Codex are down. Garrison too."

"Daddy? Daddy!" Panzer is kneeling over her father, patting his cheek with her bound hands. "What's wrong with everyone?"

"It's new magic," says Codex, hauling himself back up. He reaches into his robe vest and pulls out a slip of paper and a lighter. The paper burns with a bright green flame. "Graywytch. It's Graywytch."

The worst of it seems to be passing, though my body still aches. It seems like the painkillers have been flushed right out of my system. I try to sit up, and Calamity pushes me back down. "Stay down 'til we know what we're dealing with. Codex, I need details!"

"The satellite system is active again," he says after consulting his mirror for a moment. He pulls a crystal from one of his pockets and lets it dangle from a leather thong. It hangs for a moment and then rises up to point northwest. "It's broadcasting a new spell that's being bounced up from the surface. It's probably coming from New Port."

"But what's she doing?" asks Calamity, voice tight with urgency.

Codex ignores her. "Doc, is everyone in the triage center down?"

"No, I've got two who didn't feel it."

"Do they happen to be women?" Codex and I make eye contact.

"...yes."

No.

Oh God, please no.

CHAPTER THIRTY-ONE

Wind tears at me. At Mach 3, the friction is so high I can feel my sweat evaporate the moment it rises to the surface of my skin. The Pacific Ocean flashes beneath me in the afternoon sun. My cape snaps and thumps against my chest, and I've got to hold my bad arm in tight to keep the sling in place.

"Getting the first casualty reports on the news," says Doc in my ear. "It's bad. She's hitting everywhere."

I don't have the energy to answer. Everything is going into speed. I tear up the West Coast as fast as I've ever flown, but anxiety clutches at me until I feel like I'm standing still.

Another swell of the killing spell hits, another nauseous twist of my insides. My vision blurs and goes double. I lose my grip on the lattice and begin to tumble through the air. My skin is clammy and wet inside my bodyglove. My nerves are buzzing, my chest feels empty and packed tight at the same time. When I hit the water at two thousand miles an hour, it slams into me like concrete. My arm goes white hot with pain.

When I come to, I'm floating facedown in the ocean.

Coughing, gagging, spitting, I haul myself into the air and push for speed again. Please don't let that have been longer than a second or two. There's no time.

Passing up the coast, my suit's nav computer vibrates, and the screen on my good wrist tells me to come right by five degrees. My course takes me over land. The line of the coast flashes by, horizon to horizon, and is gone in a matter of moments.

Graywytch's revenge spreads out beneath me. A highway snaps

APRIL DANIELS

past—a pillar of smoke, a sheet of flame, then I'm over it. There's a dozen-car pileup frozen in time—and I'm already beyond it. The blooming cloud of an airliner's final resting place rises from somewhere near the horizon. I pass over a small town and see people in the streets. Almost every intersection has a collision.

At my top speed, I can cover the distance from Cynosure to New Port in a little over twenty minutes. I never thought that would feel slow. Another pulse of the spell sweeps over me, and I grit my teeth and put myself on an upward trajectory before it becomes too much. Once again the spell makes me lose my grip, but I'm on a ballistic trajectory now and keep going up. I peak and begin the long, uncontrolled descent into a forest. At the last instant, I'm able to catch myself and get back in the air before I go smashing through the trees.

A small cabin in the woods is on fire as I pass. A woman is pulling a limp man out of the burning building. That's all I have time to see before I'm thousands of feet beyond her.

She did it. She really did it. Graywytch told me this was coming, and I didn't realize what she meant. When she had me strapped down to that table in the dungeon below Cynosure, she said women can only be pushed so far before they push back. And of course, her definitions of *man*, *woman*, and *push* are all so fucked up it could have meant anything. It could have meant anything, but it meant this:

The flat-out murder of half the human population.

All the signs were there, and I missed it. Her neglect of her superhero duties. Her strained alliance with Garrison. The shoddy magic she performed for him—almost as if her real concern was somewhere else, on a different project. Now that it's happening, I can see how they all fit together: if her definition of what makes a man and what makes a woman isn't respected anymore, she'll simply remove men from the discussion. "Men" like me. Like anyone with a Y chromosome, I bet. More than three-and-a-half billion people, all dead, and then a mad scramble to figure out how to keep the species going.

The moment we realized that, Calamity didn't even have to tell me to go before I was blasting off to head north as fast as I could. With the tilt-engine out of commission and Kinetiq still in serious condition, I'm flying solo for this one. My body hurts. Every part of it. My gorge rises and I don't have time to stop, so I vomit in midair, just point my head down and spew on whatever happens to be beneath me. I'm so tired I'm shaking in the air. My arm is one loud screaming pain that tugs at my mind incessantly.

They've radioed ahead to tell the NPPD to arrest Graywytch, but if the highways and towns I've been flying over are any indication, downtown New Port will be such a mess it will be amazing if the cops can even get to Legion Tower on foot, much less with enough firepower to do anything about this.

I reach the southern outskirts of the New Port metro area, and it's worse than I expected. Columns of smoke sprout like black toadstools after the rain. Crashed cars, crashed planes, crashed helicopters. Damn near every machine in the sky has come smashing down. Most of the big trucks have run off the road too. A gas station goes up in a flare of yellow and heat as I pass; the gasoline pouring from an unattended nozzle next lying next to a dead man's car found an ignition point.

Ahead of me, the towers of downtown are wreathed in smoke. Another wave of the spell hits, this one faster and harder than the others. It takes me by surprise, and so I am helpless to stop myself from plowing through an office tower. Cubicle walls shatter and monitors are tossed like pillows as I tumble end over end across the length of the building and smash out a window on the other side.

I didn't hit anyone. Did I? I remember making an instant of eye contact with a terrified woman as I flopped past her, and coming so close to a woozy looking man that his sleeve brushed my cheek. But I don't think I hit anyone. I hope I didn't.

I get myself back in the air, and there's Legion Tower. This close into town I should be slowing down, but I keep the speed on until the last instant, smashing through the windows into the main conference room. I skid to a stop, my boots digging a pair of floor-destroying gouges as I grind to a stop.

"Codex, are you still with us?"

His voice is weak and raspy over the radio. "Yeah. I'm here."

I have to fight down another surge of nausea to get my next sentence out. "What do I do?"

"Find her. Stop her."

I screw my eyes shut to focus entirely on the lattice, peer through the floor and into the level above me. Nothing. The magic should be plainly visible, but there's nothing here. In the back of my head, I was toying with the idea of undoing the spell directly, the same way I cured my vertigo, but right now I can't even locate the ritual room, much less begin to puzzle out how to unweave the spell. My strength gives out, and I collapse to my knees. My joints are screaming, and my insides feel disconnected, floaty and poisoned.

"I don't see her. What do I look for?" And now I do vomit, a half-mouthful of acid and bile. There's nothing left in me, but I still can't get right. My ears are ringing, my lips are numb.

"Can't even begin to guess," says Codex.

"Dreadnought, she'll be in her library if she's anywhere," says Doctor Impossible. "That's where she always disappeared to when she needed to work something big."

With an effort that makes my head swim I push myself back to my feet and try to get over to the elevator. Between one step and the next I forget how to walk and end up sprawled cheek-down on the floor.

The floor that I now realize is shaking with ponderous foot-steps. I roll to look back over my shoulder. A twelve-foot-tall golem of concrete and rebar looks down at me, eyes like two burning points of green fire. The monster stares down at me, cocks its head. Knives edged in green-white fire begin to push themselves up out of the concrete. I can feel the heat radiating off the blades even from down on the floor.

"Oh, come on!" I shout. "That's not even *close* to fair!"

Even as I'm trying to scramble away, the golem reaches down with a blade-fingered paw and grabs me by the calf. The hot knives slice through my suit and into my flesh. Graywytch's little helper whips me through the air along the whole length of the conference room and into a pillar, smashing off the stone cladding in a shower of marble gravel. I cough, salt and copper on my lips. My leg screams with pain from deep, urgent burns that feel like they go all the way down to the bone. At least it's not numb—numb is even worse. When I fight up to my feet, I find it can't support my weight anymore. Taking to the air is barely any better; my mind is so frayed by pain and poison that I can barely keep off the ground.

The golem begins trudging across the room towards me.

"Codex."

"Yeah?"

"She's got some kind of cement monster. I…do you know how to kill this thing?"

"Try punching it."

"Not really…shit." Every word is a battle now. "Not really an option, to be honest." And then I have to take a deep breath. "I think I'm in trouble."

"Seawater," says Doc.

"What?"

"Seawater always blocked her. Abort the mission, get out of there." Doctor Impossible sounds like she hates herself right now. "Once you're under the ocean, her magic should have trouble reaching you. You'll be safe."

"No."

"You just need to hold your breath for twelve hours, I can get to you!" She's at the edge of pleading.

"Can't do that, Doc. All those people will die."

"We can clone more sperm, and the species will go on. There's no reason to throw your life away!"

Does it make me a bad person that I like hearing her say these things? I don't know. I don't care. If I'm going to die, I'm happy to die listening to someone trying to trade half of humanity for me. But quitting isn't an option, and she knows it.

My body hurts. My organs squirm. The golem is just a few yards away now, and I can't beat it in a fight. Not like this. But I've got to try. With that knowledge, all my pain seems to evaporate. It's just information now. Information that's barely relevant.

"Sarah, are you there?" I ask.

"I am," she says.

I close my eyes and savor the sound of her voice. "I'm sorry I waited so long."

"It's okay. I should have said something." Her voice is wavering, but she's holding it together. It makes me happy to know she'll be okay. "I love you. Die proud."

"I love you too."

"Danny, I'm so sorry," says Doc. "I should have—I'm so sorry."

My fist tightens. One way or the other, this will be quick. Take a deep breath—

The tip of a sword bursts from the creature's forehead with a screech of steel on stone. With a screaming shower of sparks, the sword forces its way through the golem from forehead to groin. The golem crashes to the ground in two twitching halves.

Karen stands behind it, dressed in steel armor, her wings unfurled. No, wait. That's not Karen. She's wearing Valkyrja's armor, holding Valkyrja's sword. She carries herself with Valkyrja's posture, and when I look into her eyes there is no mistaking the ancient intelligence gazing back at me.

But Karen?

Karen is gone.

"You killed her." I'm dimly surprised at myself. Karen betrayed me, abandoned me to be tortured to death, and still, I am outraged. Nobody deserves to be eaten from the inside out like that. Nobody.

Valkyrja shakes Karen's head. "No. I embraced my nature. It is the way of things."

"You going to kill me too, now?"

A troubled look passes over her stolen face. "I have much to atone for. Please, let me begin."

"This is another trick."

"You are too weak to fight me. Graywytch has nearly won, and I could kill you without effort. Were I working with her, there would be no possible motive for deception," says Valkyrja. She steps to a clear place on the floor and begins cutting a pattern in the carpet with the tip of her sword. "She has secreted her ritual away in another realm. It is a strategy I have seen her use before. I must open the way for you."

"Why?"

"You don't have the skill—"

"Why did you kill her?"

Valkyrja looks up, eyes flashing. "I'm not dead, Danielle! This was my choice! Now is not the time to speak of it." She steps back from the design, and with a hard thrust she stabs her sword through the barrier between worlds—the blade disappears into thin air, a silver mist billowing from the wound. Gripping her sword with both hands, she pulls the blade up and around until she has cut a rough oval in midair. Beyond it lies grass and trees and a night sky that is lit by a brilliant purple nebula.

"Win your battle," says Valkyrja. "We will speak later."

"I'm in no shape to fight. You want to atone? Go do it yourself."

"I cannot open the way from the other side, nor keep the door clear once I leave it. I must stay here."

"You could seal me in there."

She nods. "I could. I won't."

I don't trust her. I don't trust this. But what choice do I have? Half-limping, half-floating, I cross into another world, and hope I'm not too late.

The wind on the other side is cool, crisp. The stars spill across a dark sky, and a luminous purple ribbon of nebular gases reaches from horizon to horizon. A glowing fog hugs the landscape in the distance. Flecks of light like campfire embers rise in swirling funnel clouds from the center of the fog bank. That had better be Graywytch's ritual. The silver-edged portal dwindles rapidly behind me.

A strange, dark forest where the trees are clad in glowing blue moss passes beneath me. Foreign animal sounds—and until now I had not realized an animal could ever sound *foreign*, but believe me, it is possible—ripple through the night as I pass. A flock of four-winged night-sparrows snaps out of the trees, surrounds me, and disappears into the night. There's no road to follow, no path to track. I can only hope that she didn't think I'd follow her here, that the beacon I'm closing on isn't a decoy.

The forest rises and dips in gentle hills. There's a crashing stream that jumps with fish, their scales winking ruby in the moonlight. Bent down at the edge, a creature that's not quite a deer, not quite a wolf.

I'm nearly at the end of my endurance, and another swell hits. This close, the magic is like a physical slap in the face. I go down in the forest amid an explosion of twigs and splinters. It's not pain—it's worse than pain. It's something foul and invasive that saturates every tissue. I choke on bile and begin to shiver with a sudden chill. The wave passes, and I'm back into the air again as quick as I can manage.

There, the ritual site is just ahead, in a clearing under a full, red moon. There's no time for subtlety, no time to check for traps or defenses. No time to find Graywytch and take her out first. I put everything I've got left into one headlong dive. It's another Stonehenge wannabe. I aim myself at the biggest arch of stones in the center and get my good arm up to shield myself. In the instant before I hit, I see Graywytch lying in the grass, her robes stained with drying vomit.

Impact. I hit the standing granite as hard as I can. With a grinding twist it begins to tip and fall, and I stay with it to help it go down. The crosspiece of the arch slips and comes to ground with a thud that shakes trees hundreds of yards away. The eerie glow centered on the stone circle fades away. Red moonlight from an alien sky shines down in its place; dimmer than day, brighter than night. Soothing relief rushes through my veins. The very last reserves of my strength fold, and I collapse in a heap onto the grass. My chest pumps in cool air, and with every breath I feel myself come back. A tremor I'm powerless to stop passes from my head to my boots and fades away. When I push myself to my feet, I feel that shaky weakness you get after a bad flu sometimes, but not worse than that. The grass is soft beneath my boots as I walk over to where Graywytch still lies crumpled on the ground.

When I come to stand over her, she gets a look on her face. A look I'll never forget. I can tell the exact moment she comes to the same realization that I have. That we're alone. Truly alone in a way most people never experience.

It's just her.

And me.

And no witnesses.

CHAPTER THIRTY-TWO

So we come back to that tired old cliché: who you are in the dark is who you really are. If I go home, they will believe anything I tell them. I could say it was self-defense. I could say there was no other way. Nobody would know.

Nobody except me.

My boots creak as I kneel down near her head.

Graywytch stares up at me, eyes wide and white. She doesn't move. She barely breathes.

"I don't remember when my father started screaming at me," I tell her, and I'm as surprised as she is that this is coming out now. "But I know that by the time I was in kindergarten I was already afraid of him."

Graywytch licks her lips. "What are—"

"Shut up, or I will kill you." She closes her mouth, and I keep going. "He used to sit me on the couch and scream himself hoarse at me. Over any little thing. Not always the same things. Sometimes, forgetting to clean my room wasn't a big deal. Sometimes it was a huge deal. It hurt. A lot. But nobody would help me. My mom abandoned me every time it happened. Grandma and Grandpa refused to get involved before they died. I think Mom was telling them I was exaggerating. I told a cop once, and he said to buzz off. So I grew up scared. I didn't talk to people at school, more or less, because I didn't know if I'd say something that would make them angry at me. And it got worse when I realized I wasn't like the other boys. It got so much worse because this was something that I *knew* I couldn't show. And I was terrified, all the time, every day, that I'd be found out. So I hid myself. All the time, on reflex. I would disappear, and when I couldn't disappear I would try to be forgotten.

"Dreadnought died. He gave me his powers. The Legion came to collect me. And for a few minutes there, you know, I thought I'd finally be safe. But then I met you."

My jaw clenches. I have to force the words out, wet and raw. "And you *took* that from me. You did everything you could to make sure I wouldn't have any place to be safe. For no reason. *Why?*"

She's silent for a long moment. "Because—"

"I never cared that you don't think I'm a girl, Myra!" I shout, and she flinches. If possible, she goes even paler than she normally is. "And I never wanted to be in your club. I just wanted there to be one place in the world where I wasn't scared anymore. Where I didn't have to hide myself. Would it have killed you to just keep your mouth shut?"

Graywytch stays silent. She's petrified, and maybe I should feel bad or good or *something* about that, but I don't. I rock back on my heels and land heavily on my butt, my knees drawn up protectively in front of me. All those years of pain, all those memories of tight fear and blaring terror, they're all coming back. It's like he's here again, screaming at me until I want to die just so it can be over. Other kids' dads teach them to fish or to play catch. Mine taught me I was too weak to defend myself. That it was always my fault. That nobody would ever love me.

I tremble and my throat clenches up. I'll never be free of it. What he did will haunt me for the rest of my life.

And I hated Graywytch for letting me know that so soon.

But I don't cry. Not because I'm ashamed or anything—with Graywytch half-dead from her own magic, I finally realize I have no reason whatsoever to give a shit what she thinks about me. I don't cry because I realize I don't need to. Because they gave me their worst, and I'm still here. Dad doesn't get to choose if I'm happy, and neither does Graywytch. I sniff and wipe my eyes. The pain seems to slide off me and melt into the ground.

Graywytch lies there, statue-still. Eyes locked to me. We stare at each other for a long time. She's got dried vomit all over her chest. I make a sweeping gesture toward the mess. "Let me guess: your spell was targeted to the Y chromosome, but you've never had a karyotype test."

It's such a left-field question that it startles an answer from her. "What?"

"Your chromosomes. You never had them tested, did you?"

Her brow furrows, and the first emotion that isn't fear works its way onto her face. Disgust. "Don't lump me in with you. I'm a woman. I menstruate."

"So? Sex is just as fuzzy as gender is. You might not be trans, but you could be intersex. If you'd just looked it up you'd see there are women with Y chromosomes who can give birth. It's not common, but it happens."

She huffs. Graywytch seems so much less impressive now. "No. Magic is dangerous. I miscalculated, is all. Standing this close to the center, it could have gotten anyone."

I get to my feet. "Maybe. I'm sure you'll have plenty of time to think about it in prison. I bet they'd even run a blood test for you, if you asked." I hold out my hand for her. "Get up. I don't think I'm strong enough to carry you safely yet, so we've got to hike out of here."

She looks at my hand, wary for a trick.

"For fuck's sake, Graywytch, I'd just kill you if I was going to."

She takes my hand and lets me pull her to her feet. With her arm still in a sling, and her ribs bandaged, she grunts with genuine pain on the way up and even leans on me for a moment before pushing away and standing with as much dignity as she can muster. From somewhere out of the darkness, her raven flaps down to alight on her shoulder.

"If you're looking to prolong the pain, I can tell you I won't give you the satisfaction. I'll die fighting first."

"We're going to hike back to New Port so you can get arrested. That's all that's going to happen, I promise."

She still doesn't believe me; it's etched in her face. "Why? Why spare me?"

I smile. "Isn't it obvious? I'm better than you."

CHAPTER THIRTY-THREE

I don't end up retiring after all. Things can't keep going on this way, but if I'm honest with myself, I don't have it in me to quit. I like the power. I like the action. I love the look on people's faces when they realize I'm there to save them. But I've got anger issues, and those are going to get somebody killed if I can't figure out how to control them. That moment under the water with Sovereign, when he stopped fighting—I was so proud. Now it makes me feel uneasy to think about it. It's just luck that Panzer was there to save him. So I'm taking a break. I'll keep patrolling long enough for Kinetiq to get out of the hospital and take over my contract, and then I'm putting away the cape for at least six months.

Doc knows a therapist who specializes in the treatment of superheroes. We're going to have appointments twice a week at first. Hopefully I'll get better.

The break isn't only for my health. Cecilia says I need to get out of the public eye for a while until the dust settles. My arrest and arraignment did a lot of damage to my reputation, and that will take time to fix. And, to be honest, she just doesn't have enough hours in the day to be my publicist *and* my lawyer right now. Whatever remaining anger she had at me for breaking into Graywytch's apartment evaporated when she got a look at just *how much* money we seized from Garrison. Uncle Sam took the lion's share of it, of course, but Cecilia managed to snag ownership of Cynosure and what looks like enough money to cover the repairs as well. The rest of Sovereign Industries will be parceled out in court to Garrison's business partners, and likely will be subject to ongoing legal disputes for years, if not decades. Cecilia says we can't take it all for ourselves, but we can be damn sure that Garrison won't get any of it back, either.

Speaking of lawyers, when Doc cracked Garrison's hard drive (his password was *password2*), she unleashed a legal apocalypse. It turns out he had more than fifty judges and prosecutors on his payroll in one of the largest law enforcement corruption scandals in American history. That's how he arranged to have me arrested for murder, among other things. He figured that Cynosure was safely under his control, and so he kept meticulous records of a whole range of illegal financial maneuvers, political bribery, and the occasional murder for hire. There's so much here that it's impossible to believe his lawyers didn't know he was a criminal, and so they've dropped him as a client and are in full damage control mode to save themselves. His new lawyers are very much the B-team, and Cecilia thinks they're out of their depth.

He's going to die in prison, it looks like. I think I'm going to visit him, and show him some of the money I took from him. You know, in case he misses it and wants to say hi.

• • •

Graywytch is dead. I didn't kill her, but she's dead. They found her in her cell the morning after her arrest, without even a mark on her body. People are outraged. They wanted justice, and it's been stolen from them. I'm frustrated too. I wanted her to see the world turn its back on her. I wanted my choice to spare her to mean something.

For more than fifty years, Mistress Malice was the heavyweight champion of supervillains, with over a quarter-million confirmed deaths during a six-month rampage. Graywytch made Malice's crimes look like a liquor store robbery. They're still counting the dead, but it's easily the worst supervillain attack in history. The global death toll might top three million, mostly men, but hundreds of thousands of women died as well. Not just trans women and intersex women, but cisgender women too; nearly ten thousand airliners crashed when their (overwhelmingly male) flight crews were disabled by her spell. Not to mention women who were on the operating table with male surgeons who collapsed, who were killed in traffic accidents and building fires, or any number of collisions caused by half the human species falling over all at once. Graywytch killed some of every kind of person that exists.

There were cries for justice, for punishment. Since people died in every country on the planet, there was going to be a huge fight over who got to put her on trial for mass murder, but all of that's been stumped by the simple fact that she's dead.

Except that I'm not sure that she is.

• • •

"Where does this one go?" I ask, holding up another textbook.

"They'll have copies there; I'm leaving that behind," says Charlie. We're in his room, and the first snowstorm of the new year is caking up against the window. Sarah and I are helping him pack, because our little bookworm Charlie is now a bone fide high school dropout. He's going straight on to the Invisible College, an institution we've never heard about, but which electrifies Charlie. His performance during the crisis has impressed the Council of Avalon, and they've taken an interest in his professional development.

His room is a disaster area as we pull it apart and find everything he'll want to take with him. Charlie's parents were not happy with me for dragging him into combat. Then they almost tripped over themselves to agree to let the Council of Avalon come take him to a private university where he'd be given a full-ride scholarship and an apprenticeship that would keep him out of trouble. Congress has already passed a sweeping new anti-magic law in the wake of Graywytch's attack, and they're hoping he'll be safer out of the country until the paranoia about magic users dies down. If it ever does.

APRIL DANIELS

A question that has been running around in my mind pops out of my mouth: "So do you know what happened to Graywytch?"

Charlie freezes, and Sarah looks up from the pile of books she's sorting.

"Not for sure," he says.

"But you've got a suspicion."

"Yeah."

"Are you going to tell us?" asks Sarah.

Charlie crosses his room and shuts the door. "Look, you cannot repeat this, okay?"

Sarah and I trade a look. "Go on," I say.

"I think the Council of Avalon added her to their Library," says Charlie quietly.

"What does that mean?"

"It means they tore her soul from her body and bound it to service for all eternity. She's as good as dead, except when somebody wakes her up to ask a question. That's all anyone outside the Council knows about the Library, and I shouldn't even be saying that much."

Sarah sums up my feelings: "Holy shit."

Suddenly, I'm not so frustrated that she never stood trial. I'm not sure how I feel about it, but at least it can't be said she escaped punishment anymore. With that fog of horror hanging over us, we go back to inventorying Charlie's baffling array of magical doodads and gewgaws.

"What's this?" asks Sarah, holding up a brass and crystal device that looks sort of like a sextant on an acid trip.

"Expensive and delicate, please put it down," says Charlie.

"Okay, but what *is* it?"

"I don't think you'd understand," he says, which is the wrong decision.

Sarah's eyes narrow. "Oh really?"

Seeming to realize his mistake, Charlie gingerly reaches out for the device. "Uh, I'll show you how it works."

Sarah keeps it out of reach and plants her prosthetic hand on his chest. Yeah, he's not getting that back for anything less than his best groveling. I kiss Sarah on the cheek.

"Stop teasing the prodigy," I murmur in her ear, and then head downstairs. I've got to check on someone. Out in the front yard, snow scrunches under my feet.

"You know, you can come inside with us," I say to the sky as I leave Charlie's house. Valkyrja is up in the tree in the front yard, sitting easily on a branch that is thinner than her wrist. In deference to Charlie's parents' new (and strictly enforced) no capes around their house rule, she at least left her armor back in Legion Tower.

"What use is a sentry who stays indoors?" says Valkyrja. She scans the horizon again.

"Would you at least come down so I can talk to you?"

She nods and scoots off the branch, falling to earth in a slow, gentle descent.

"If you're going to be following me around all the time, you could at least try to blend in when we're doing civilian stuff," I say.

"I gave you the terms of my atonement and you accepted them." Valkyrja chews on her lip for a moment. "Must we continue reliving this discussion?"

She told me she had an honor debt to me, an old Norse tradition that is suddenly very important to her, and asked that she be given a chance to redeem herself. Calamity and I talked it over and offered her a spot in the Legion. She promptly declared that she would remain a member until the day she died, though her wording was on the interesting side of gory. "Yeah, until your guts are steaming on the ground, I remember. Do you have to act like you're Secret Service, though?"

"I shouldn't inflict myself upon them any further."

"You're weird. You're not *that* weird." I reach out to take her shoulder and shuffle her inside, but Valkyrja shrinks away.

"I like him." It still throws me for a loop when those little bits of the old Karen break through. She says she was wrong, that her mother wasn't obliterating her, but simply adding to her. Changing her. The life she thought she could have is gone forever, but there are other ways to live.

"And I think he'd forgive you if you asked."

She shakes her head. "I cannot. Not now."

"Why not? He's right there," I say, pointing up at his room, "And believe me, this stuff doesn't get better just because you ignore it."

Valkyrja is quiet for a moment, and then takes a breath as if she has come to a decision. "Now is not the time to broach a relationship. There is…a kindness I must ask from you. I have a task I must complete, and I have put it off too long. It will take time, and then I will return to you."

"What kind of task?"

"A…ritual. A family tradition. I must secure my mother's legacy. Until then, I cannot indulge distractions."

"How long will it take?"

Valkyrja's wings curl protectively around her. "About nine months."

Oh.

"Are you sure you want to do that?" I ask. The other part of the question is left unspoken: do you want to do that *to your daughter?*

"It is the way of things. It will bring me solace."

I won't even pretend to understand that. "Okay. Do you need to get going?"

She nods. "Sooner is better than later."

"Well, I'm not going anywhere. I'll see you when you get back."

She smiles with relief and clasps my hand in an old-old-in-credibly-old school wristlock shake. "I shall return."

Valkyrja spreads her wings and takes off. I watch her until she disappears behind the skeletal trees and is lost to sight.

• • •

The one thing that everybody agrees on is that those damn satellites need to go. Nobody should have the power to cast a spell over the entire planet ever again. I boost up into orbit again and start knocking them down. Red Steel sends me another email, congratulating me on my victory, and stating that because his employer turned out to be a criminal and the satellites were weapons of mass destruction, that he has generously decided he will not be seeking vengeance upon me for defying his warning. I send him a fluffy cat picture in reply.

• • •

Kinetiq is up and walking around. Slowly, and with a cane, but Doc expects them to make a full recovery. They're settling into Legion Tower nicely. At the brief press conference I held after the fighting was over, I made sure to mention how important they were to victory, and how I'd be turning over protection of New Port to them while I recovered from what I'd been through. They couldn't stop blushing when the cameras turned to them.

We're up on the main lounge floor, just across the hall from the cavernous briefing room where Valkyrja killed the golem. The city spreads out beneath us, a canyon of steel and glass.

"So have you thought about who you're going to give the money to?" Kinetiq asks me. It's a topic that's been hanging over our heads. They're clearly unhappy with the sudden influx of wealth. We nearly died taking down the guy I took this money off of. We'd be well within our rights to keep it. Kinetiq hasn't been shy about how much they disagree, and I guess now is as good a time as any for us to decide not to avoid the issue any longer.

I shrug, and regurgitate a line I heard from Cecilia: "Until the asset forfeiture case is settled, it would be premature to spend any of it."

"Don't dodge the question, Dreadnought." Kinetiq leans on their cane and pivots to face me. "Who are you giving the money to?"

Getting angry isn't going to help. More and more I'm trying to rein in my temper. "I'm thinking that we'll keep it." Technically, it's going to be a group decision, but everyone has been looking to me to make a proposal. I tried to pawn the responsibility off on Calamity, and she literally laughed in my face.

"You don't want to do that," says Kinetiq. "Money changes people, and never for the better. Besides that, no fortune that large can exist without the exploitation of the working class—it's stolen money, Dreadnought. Blood money. You have a moral duty to return it to the people. How you do that, what charity you choose, that's your choice, but you can't keep it."

"It's not go-crazy money, okay? Most of the cash got hoovered up by the Feds. We've only got enough to repair Cynosure, and maybe a couple million left over after that."

"Why repair it? Bust that damn thing up for scrap."

"What good would that do anyone?"

"What good would it do anyone to keep it?" they reply, almost before I'm done speaking.

"I was thinking we'd put up a free clinic that provides the full range of transition services to anyone who asks. Or a halfway house for queer runaways who need to start a new life away from their family." I very carefully do not look at them when I say that last part.

"Oh," says Kinetiq quietly.

"It's easier to do that if we own the buildings. We could put it in Legion Tower, but I've had to have a fight here twice already. I think it might be safer to keep our charity work separate from our capework."

"Yeah. Yeah, I could see how that would be," says Kinetiq. I glance over and they're blinking rapidly.

"I was thinking, though. It might be good to have one of us stay on the island to make sure all the kids are okay. You could see to it that it's just not another way of throwing them into the system."

They snort. "Lay off. You made your point."

"So you're okay with this?"

"Yeah. I think so. I think I'd like that."

• • •

Professor Gothic lands in New Port after almost a month spent in hiding—it's the first flight into town since the biggest disaster the airline industry ever suffered. The Nemesis is not quite public knowledge yet, but we think it's only a matter of time until word leaks. Most of the world's governments already know, and are scrambling to decide what—if anything—to do about it. The Nemesis sits on the other side of the moon, watched by Garrison's remote cameras. Cameras Doc Impossible has taken full control over, along with every other piece of his surviving outer space infrastructure.

As Cynosure makes the final turn to pass the mouth of Puget Sound and sail to the patch of water we've leased as a berthing point, Professor Gothic turns back from the window of one of the handful of untouched conference rooms aboard the seastead. Doc and I are sitting at one of the conference tables, watching the coastline slowly pass by.

"The status quo is untenable," he says.

"The status is *not* quo, man," says Doc. She's slouched deep in her chair, exhausted from a seventy-three-hour death march of programming as she integrated Cynosure's systems into her own infrastructure.

He turns from the window, brow furrowed over crimson goggles. "I'm not sure I know what you mean by that."

Doc shrugs. "That's okay, sometimes I just like hearing myself talk. Anyhow, you were saying?"

Gothic purses his lips, clasps his hands behind his back, very solemn. "The current state of affairs cannot continue. The Nemesis' proximity to Earth will continue to create quantum instabilities and promote the development of alternative physics models. That it exists as a singular object and obeys the laws of gravity suggests that the fundamental skein of reality will remain intact, but beyond that, it is difficult to predict where this will take us. So we come to find we are faced with two choices. We can return the

Nemesis to its three-thousand-year orbit and see the slow leeching of superpowers, magic, and hypertech from the world until it returns again. Or, we can keep it behind the moon and inevitably create a world where everyone has access to this kind of power."

The immensity of the decision settles down on us. Doc controls the surveillance and defense platforms that oversee the Nemesis' stable orbit on the other side of the moon. Nobody can so much as get near it without her say-so. In a very real way, the next era of human history relies on what we decide here.

"Let's keep it," I say.

"Oh yeah, obviously," says Doc.

Professor Gothic looks like he swallowed a bug. "So that's it? Just like that, we decide to upend the fabric of human civilization?"

"What, would you rather us debate in circles for a year or two?" asks Doc. "If sending that asteroid away will eventually cause hypertech to break down, then you might as well ask me to kill myself."

"And after what happened last month," I say, "I don't think the world would be better if the only kind of power was money. Right now, most people just have to go along with whatever the rich and their pet governments tell them. Maybe if *everyone* could do the things that I could do, things would be better."

"Or they could become catastrophically worse," says Gothic thinly.

"We *already* have supervillains," says Doc. "And even without them, we'd still have existential threats that we'd have to confront—only we'd be doing so with vastly reduced capabilities. Climate change doesn't get easier just because we all go back down to the baseline. If things get too hot, we can move the rock to the L-point on the other side of the sun."

"I see," says Professor Gothic. "And you're both quite certain?"

"Yes," I say. Doc nods.

"Very well," says Gothic. "Then I should like to put together an institute to study these questions as we go forward. A think tank, but one with empirical testing models and field experience. Frau Doktor Impossible, would you like to join me in this endeavor?"

"Sure," says Doc. "Whatever floats your boat."

"Is this how you make all of your decisions?"

"No," she says. "Just the big ones."

• • •

On my last day of patrol before handing the city over to Kinetiq, I come back to Doc's condo to find most of our things in boxes, and the maidbots getting ready for the move into Legion Tower. Guts the pug senses something is up and trots up to me, whining for comfort, so I scratch him behind the ears. Doc's in the kitchen, pouring her liquor down the sink. Empty bottles line the counter next to her.

"Hey kiddo, how'd your sendoff go?" she asks as she cracks a bottle of rum.

"It went well," I say, though I was barely paying attention. My fingers are pinched white against a manila folder I'm holding against my chest. "Lots of people waving."

"Cool," says Doc. *Glug glug glug* goes the rum down the drain. "Hey, uh, I finally got the guts to write a software patch for my little happy juice problem. Would you...um, would you feel weird if I asked you to hold my hand while I uploaded it to myself?"

"What? No, of course I will," I say, my heart leaping. She's talked about this, but I haven't dared hope that the rough times were over so soon. If she's serious, then this means—my eyes drop down to the papers I'm holding. Now's the time, I know it is. If I chicken out now, I'll be putting this off for months. But holy crap, this is scary. "Yeah, I'd be happy to help you through that. So, uh, I've got some good news of my own today."

"Yeah?" Doc smiles. "Keep me in suspense, really, that's what I need today."

"My parents dropped their objection to my emancipation papers. So I've signed them and I'm free."

Doc's jaw drops with open delight. "Kickass! What do you want to do to celebrate?"

Oh man, I hadn't even thought about that. My tongue fumbles for something to say as I focus on not tripping while I cross the room. "Oh, uh, I wasn't—probably not much, it's just a formality. But um. I did have Cecilia draw up some other papers; I was wondering if maybe you'd take a look at them? I mean, if you want to." I set the folder down on the counter next to her.

Doc wipes her hands on a paper napkin while she regards me with curiosity. "Sure, okay." She opens the folder and starts to read, and I try to keep my heart beating. Every twitch and flick on her face seems to shout. Curiosity. Surprise. Understanding.

"These are adoption papers," she says quietly.

"Yeah, well. I mean, if you don't—look, it's not that big a deal and, I was just thinking, so, you know—"

Doc's face falls, and so does my stomach. "Danny, I'd…I'm honored, really. But I'm not human. I don't have a birth certificate or a social security number or anything. I've got incorporation papers, and that's it. Corporations can't adopt people. I'm sorry."

"Oh." My face feels numb. My chest is filled with lead. In between the space between hearing and understanding, between understanding and despair, I make one last grasp at it: "Can you hire me?"

Doc's composure stumbles, quickly covered by a tremulous smile. "Yeah," she says weakly. "I can hire you." She sets the papers aside and opens her arms. "Hey, bring it in, kiddo, come here."

And then I'm hugging my mother and she's hugging me back, tight and protective, and finally, finally I'm home. After a while something occurs to me.

"Hey, Doc. What's your first name?"

She looks at me blankly. "You didn't know? It's—"

• • •

The waters of Puget Sound lap at the pebbly shore. Sarah kisses me on my bullet scar as we stand and watch the sun disappear behind the Olympic Peninsula. Her organic arm is snug around my waist, and her helmet hangs from her gloved prosthetic fingers.

"So have you thought about where you'd like to come down?" I ask her, voice quiet, almost afraid to break the mood.

"How long is this going to take?" she says.

"Depends on how long we decide to stay. No more than two hours travel time, round trip. More if we go the long way, but not much more."

"I've never seen Hawaii," says Sarah. "It'll still be light there, won't it?"

"Yeah." My fingers trace her flank. I will never get tired of the feeling of her body in my arms. "For another few hours, at least."

Sarah leans down to kiss me. Her teeth gently pluck at my lip as we part. "Then let's go."

"And you're sure about this?"

"Quit stalling, Danny." She steps away from me and settles the helmet onto the steel collar of her spacesuit. It locks into place with an equalizing hiss, and the close fit of the material grows downright snug as hypertech fibers work to prepare the suit for orbit. Technically, we're not supposed to use the spacesuit except on superhero business, but how can we use it if we haven't trained with it, right? This is totally business. We checked our flight plan to be sure it was free of orbital debris and everything.

We double-check the harness that connects her suit to mine by a yard or so of titanium-strong tether, and then come back together for the flight position. Face-to-face, my arms tight around the small of her back, hers tight around my shoulders.

"And you remember the signal if you need to go down?"

"We're going up?" says Sarah, her voice coming to me through my earbud radio. "I'd assumed we were going to stand here until we rot."

"Smartass."

She smiles, and I take great pleasure in the way her eyes bug when I bite down hard on the lattice and blast us into the sky at three Gs. Her hands clamp down on my shoulders as the ground drops away beneath us, and by the time we're pushing through the wispy clouds, the color has mostly returned to her cheeks. From the look in her eye and the twist in her smile, I can tell I'm going to pay for this when we're on the ground. I will probably enjoy paying for it.

Sarah shifts her hold to look back down over my shoulder at the world as it falls further and further away from us. Even through two suits, I can feel the shiver of excitement run through her. The horizon curves away from us in a gauzy blue line. To the west of us, the last rays of the afternoon light the Pacific. To the east of us, the grid of city lights spreads in drips and drabs across North America. I want to show her everything so we travel east, and head deeper into the night until the blanket of amber stars beneath us becomes an almost solid pattern.

I let off the acceleration and let us coast into a low orbit. In the perfect silence of the night, there is nothing but us, the Earth, and the stars. Sarah looks everywhere at once, her face open with wonder. Below us, a panorama greater than any other. And above us, numberless stars, more vivid than seem possible. We float above the world, hand-in-hand, more alone and more together than anyone else. When I tug her close with a twitch of my wrist, she gently clasps her arm around me.

She speaks, and my earbud vibrates silently. Her helmet automatically projects a transcription on her faceplate in illuminated turquoise letters: "I love you, Danielle."

There's more than enough air in my lungs for a little bit of extravagance. I exhale on the front of her helmet, fog it with a thin rime of ice. In that ice, I trace characters with my finger:

I ♥ U

What feels like a few minutes later, the sun comes up over the horizon. A new day is born in gleaming fire, rippling pools of light racing in from the horizon. It is one of the most breathtaking sights you can see. And we miss every second of it.

We only have eyes for each other.

ACKNOWLEDGMENTS

In all the hectic stress of getting my first novel out the door, I forgot to ask at what point I should write the acknowledgments. Consequently, *Dreadnought* went to press without any such page, and that's an error I hope to rectify now. Consider the following as the acknowledgments for both books.

Thank you to my agent, Saritza Hernandez, who fought for these books and helped me get my feet wet as a professional writer.

Publishing is a team effort. To everyone at Diversion Books, thank you.

Many friends listened to me spitball ideas or answer gut-check questions. They listened to me whine and moan when I was stuck, and also to my wildly optimistic bragging when things were going well. Many friends also read early versions of my manuscripts and gave me their honest and valuable feedback. Special thanks to Erica, Autumn, Clarissa, Tor, Devin, Sara, and Cal.

Thank you those special teachers who, from kindergarten on up, kindly tolerated my habit of ignoring them to read instead.

Thank you to my mother, who raised me, among other feats of endurance.